The Princess Behind Thorns

Also by the Author

The Guardian of the Opera

Nocturne

Accompaniment

Dawn Melody

Collected Pieces:

Overture, The Confessions of Christine Daaé, and *Entr'acte*

The Beyond the Tales Quartet

The Wanderers

The Storyteller and Her Sisters

The People the Fairies Forget

The Lioness and the Spellspinners

Contributing Author

Plot Twist

The Servants and the Beast

After the Sparkles Settled

The Princess Behind Thorns

The Thorns Saga, Book One

Cheryl Mahoney

Stonehenge Circle Press

ISBN-13: 978-1-68012-649-5

ISBN-10: 1-68012-649-0

First Edition

Cover images courtesy of Ironika/Shutterstock (Rose) and
Salenta/Shutterstock (thorns). Cover design by Cheryl Mahoney.

The Princess Behind Thorns

Part One

Late Winter, Year 512

Chapter One: Rose

The garden was shrinking at night. By day it was still as big as the whole world. It *was* her whole world. Once, long, long ago, she had not lived in the garden. There had been a castle. A city. A mother, a father. But it had all gone blurry with time. She vaguely recalled that once it had alarmed her, the forgetting. Now, the Before Time seemed rather unimportant. Now she had the garden. And her cats. And by day, they were all she needed.

She spent the sunlit hours tending to the plants and flowers, walking along the curving paths. She had explored everywhere so long ago that she could no longer remember when any of it had been new or unexpected—the lavender walk, the three ponds, the grove of birch trees, always rustling as though sharing tree secrets.

She never wandered too close to the brambles, even when the sunlight was brightest. Curving walls of thorn branches surrounded her garden, high, high walls with sharp, sharp thorns. They protected her. They guarded her. And she never went too close to them.

When she wanted something active to do, she climbed trees or used the swing hanging from the biggest oak tree or chased kittens across the sweeping lawns. She always had a fine flock of kittens, though most wandered mysteriously away as they grew.

When she wanted something quieter, she read. Sometimes she read in her bower, her circular, sunken home at the center of the garden, where she kept her books and her dresses and her statue of the god Mariqwe. She spread her blankets on the moss there, living tree branches woven together to form walls around her, overarching branches and the sky above her only ceiling. Sometimes she carried a book elsewhere in the garden.

Day flowed serenely into day, each one nearly identical to the last, and so it had been for almost as long as she could remember, for much more time than she could define. She had stopped counting time long ago. Years ago.

Only the cats changed. Her favorite kittens, the ones who stayed, eventually grew into cats, grew old, gave place to new cats. Her only sad duty in the garden was when another cat had to be laid to rest. She used one corner especially for that purpose, marking each little resting place with a stone. Sometimes, when she visited that corner, it troubled her that more than a score of stones had spread across the grass.

She herself never changed. Not in any way that she could tell, at least. She had one small looking glass in her bower, a hand mirror backed with silver roses, and her face was always the same. No lines appeared at the corners of her mouth or her blue eyes. Her hands were still unwrinkled, as unchanging as the small gold ring on the smallest finger of her right hand, a ring she couldn't remember putting on for the first time. Her pale hair still reached to her waist when unbound, and it never became harder to chase kittens or climb trees.

But lately—just lately, and she couldn't say how long it had been—*something* was changing in the garden. At night.

She used to walk the paths by moonlight too, looking up at the stars above. But just lately, she hurried home to her bower when the shadows of the thorn branches began to stretch across the lawns and overtake the paths. Lately, she had begun to feel that the shadows were somehow wrong—too dark, reaching too far, not merely hiding the garden in their blackness but actually stealing away the edges of her world. Shrinking the garden in the night. And it was getting worse.

Tonight was worse than it had ever been. She had been sitting out on the long lawn with her cats, so big a lawn that by day she didn't even mind the thorny wall bordering the far edge. Her latest two favorite kittens, Silvertips and Emerald Eyes, were especially adorable today. She had been teasing them with a long grass stem, laughing at their antics, and she hadn't noticed the descending sun until the shadows had nearly reached them.

She looked up at a sudden chill on the back of her neck, scrambled instinctively backwards on hands and knees, away from the reaching shadow of the thorn walls. It was long, so, so long, deep, deep black, and mere feet away from her. For a moment she tried to look through the shadows, to see the grass that *had* to be there, that had been there minutes before.

Nothing but blackness.

In another moment she jumped to her feet, caught up a squirming kitten in each hand, and ran. She ran through her garden, heart pounding in her chest, ran through the paths she knew by heart, and shied away from even normal shadows.

It wasn't only the shadows. It was the noise. The sound of creaking, rustling, scraping branches. The thorn branches were moving, swaying and shaking and writhing. There was often a gentle, tricksy breeze in her garden, but tonight the thorns thrashed as if they were caught in a storm, a malevolent, howling storm. Except that she could feel no wind at all.

She ran all the way to her bower, dropped the kittens and fell onto her mossy bed, onto her soft spread of blankets. She hadn't been a child for many, many years, but some buried instinct told her that she was safe with the blanket over her head. She lay huddled, shaking, listening to the thorns scrape and groan, for a long, long time. She breathed a prayer to Mariqwe, God of Passion, and her wish for everything to stop, to go back to normal, seemed passionate enough to deserve a response. But nothing changed. Her kittens scrambled in beside her, and only their warm furry comfort let her finally fall asleep.

In the morning the sun rose and all seemed well. She walked the edges of her garden, exploring. Half-afraid of what she would find, eyeing any shadows suspiciously. But all seemed well.

Until night, when the shadows reached out and the thorns moved again.

For five days and five nights this went on. She couldn't concentrate on her books, couldn't find amusement in her kittens. She was afraid all the time, exhausted by each night's heightened terror. By the sixth day she was avoiding every shadow, jumping at every rustle, staring obsessively at the interlaced branches bounding her world.

And then halfway through the morning, she heard it. The scraping, scratching, groaning of the thorn branches moving.

"No," she whispered desperately, "no, it's *day*. It's day!"

She was in the long lavender walk, took a step towards her bower. Then she stopped, inhaled a slow, deep breath, and fought all of her instincts as she turned and walked towards the sound of the moving branches. Maybe if she could see what was happening by daylight—maybe she could learn something. Maybe she could find out what the thorns wanted, find out how to stop all this.

She walked through the roses, past the smallest pond, up a hill and out to the long lawn. At the far end, shadows pooled under the thrashing brambles. She forced herself forward, step by step, searching for any hint, any clue, any reason behind this new behavior.

And then the thorn branches parted.

They *parted.*

In all the time she had been here, in all the long, long days, the thorny wall surrounding her world had never, never opened. But now a narrow archway formed within the branches, a tunnel barely wide enough to walk through, faint glimmers of light banishing the shadows just at the edges. As though angry at the incursion, the shadows on either side pooled all the deeper, all the blacker.

She was still staring at this impossible tunnel when a greater impossibility appeared. Moving shadows within resolved themselves into a silhouette. A man, pushing through between the thorns. He staggered and stumbled out from between the brambles, advancing a few paces onto the lawn.

She froze where she was, hands clenched in fists at her sides, breath tight and heart so loud in her ears that she could barely hear the shifting branches.

He wasn't looking at her. He was looking at the ground, one arm raised to shield his face against the thorns. He took another step, another, turned around to look at the wall of brambles behind him, then very quietly collapsed. He sank to his knees, threw his head back, fell onto his back on the grass, and lay still.

The archway closed as though it had never existed, the wall of spiked branches solid and impenetrable again, and everything went quiet. Everything was as still as the man lying on her lawn.

She slowly, so slowly, let out her breath. She crept forward one step, then another, until she was standing over him.

He was covered in scratches. His clothes, fine silks and velvets, were rent by at least a dozen tears, and she counted three bleeding scratches on his face alone. She studied that face. He seemed young, with only the faintest shadow of a beard on his cheeks, a small scar by his left eyebrow. His eyes were deep brown.

His eyes. His eyes had opened.

She yelped and took several hurried steps backwards.

He sat up, staring at her, those dark eyes wide in shocked wonder. "You're awake," he said.

This seemed so much like what she ought to be saying that it only muddled her further, any words of her own flying from her mind.

He got to his feet and she backed up farther. She was used to only cats and he was so *tall*. "Please, don't be afraid," he said, holding out one hand. "I'm here to rescue you."

"I don't need rescuing," she spat, catching her pale blue skirts up in her hands, heart hammering even harder. "I'm fine—I was fine. It was *you* upsetting the thorn branches. That's what was wrong with them. I was *fine*. Go away and leave me alone. Go *away*!"

"But wait," he protested, "I—"

She was already turning, lifting her long skirts free of her feet to run. He didn't belong here, he wasn't supposed to be here, she didn't want or need anyone. She fled through the garden, through the paths she knew so well, barely even seeing where she was until at last she could dive into her bower.

She hid there, curled on her bed, listening to Silvertips' purr. It felt like a long time before her breath slowed, before her heart grew quieter. The tension in her body, the zinging, terrifying energy shooting through her, didn't go away. She lay there, and tried to remember.

A rescuer. They had told her, long, long ago, that there would be a rescuer. She hadn't thought of it in years. She must have decided that no one was coming.

A rescuer. She tried to remember how she had felt about the idea, back at the beginning, back when this all began. Was that where her nameless, formless fear was coming from? Had she had a reason for the fear, a reason she had forgotten? Why was she supposed to need a rescuer? Why was she afraid to be rescued?

Perhaps an hour passed. Perhaps more. She didn't think it was much past midday though, judging by the sun, when she cautiously got to her feet, cautiously ventured out. Maybe he was gone. Maybe he had made the wall of thorns open up and let him out again.

She crept through her garden, carrying Silvertips against her chest for comfort, looking for him.

She wasn't truly surprised when she found him. He was sitting by the smallest pond. She watched him through the trees, watched as he wet a handkerchief in the pond and dabbed at his chest. He had taken off his cloak and his shirt hung as though it was open, though from here she could only see his back.

"Do you know if those thorns are poisonous?" he asked without turning around, and she froze. "I suppose," he continued conversationally, "I'd be feeling sick by now if they are."

He turned towards her, fastening up his shirt as he did. The buttons reached nearly to his chin, and he tucked a gold ring on a chain beneath the shirt before he fastened the final two. "Have you decided to talk to me, Princess Rose?"

Her name. She hadn't used her name since—why did he know her name? Curiosity warred with fear but she still might have run again. While she hesitated, Silvertips squirmed and leapt free from her hold, to scamper over to the strange man, her gray tail waving.

Reluctantly, Rose stepped out from between the trees, still keeping a good distance between them. "Why are you here?"

"I'm here to rescue you," he said again, said it with a smile.

The words sent a renewed stab of fear through her and she swallowed, fighting to hold her ground. "Why?" she forced out. "Why are you here to rescue me?"

Now he hesitated. "Well. That's a longer story." He shrugged, rubbed the back of his neck with one hand. "Do you know, I never expected to have to explain it to you." His gaze drifted around him, looking at the garden, returned to her. "But I never expected any of this."

"What did you expect?"

"Oh, you know. A tower. A sleeping princess."

Sleeping. Asleep. The words stirred something inside her, echoed with a long ago terror.

"Have you been awake all this time?" he asked.

"No," she said automatically, trying to chase down the root of this newest fear. "I sleep at night."

She was surprised when he laughed. The sound was—pleasant. Light and free and entirely new in this garden. She'd never heard anyone's laughter here but her own. Her fright, and any explanations behind it, retreated before that laugh.

She took a cautious step forward, then another, noticed that he was petting Silvertips' head and the kitten seemed to approve, then in a sudden decision sat down on the grass, drawing her knees up and tucking her skirts around her ankles. "Who are you?"

He grinned and it looked like his laugh. "I'm doing this all wrong, aren't I? I swear I was taught all the courtly manners." He executed a half-bow while sitting down and said, "I'm Prince Terrence Philip Elliott, fourth son of the king of Avala."

Words came automatically to her lips, ghosts from long ago. "I am Princess Rose Amelia, crown princess and heir to the throne of…" She stopped, because what he had said made no sense. "Of Avala," she finished. "But you…?"

"As I understand it," he said, "my great-grandfather was your fourth cousin."

"Your great-grandfather," she echoed numbly, mind working to grasp the implication.

His voice was soft. "You've been in here a long time."

They sat in silence after that. She was staring at the pond, fingers locked tightly around her ankles, mind raking back over her time in the garden, searching for memories of the Before Time, veering just as quickly away from them when a memory started to surface. So many years. So *many* years. It didn't feel as though she had been here that long. So many days that had been so similar…it all had blended together, had seemed like much less time. And yet…the Before Time seemed so long ago, so hazy in the past.

At last, rather suddenly, she rose to her feet, too agitated to keep sitting, too full of questions she didn't want to ask, answers she didn't want to explore.

"Please don't run away again," Prince Terrence said, rising too. He took a step towards her, stopped when she backed away. "Please. I won't hurt you. I'm actually not at all frightening, I promise. But I have so many questions—and I'll answer any you have."

"I don't know," she said. "I don't know if I want answers."

He seemed to seriously consider this, head cocking slightly to one side, gaze on her face. "I always thought it was better to know. If you don't know, you have to deal with every possibility. If you know, you only have to deal with the one that's real."

This sounded so much like something from one of her books that it reassured her to a surprising degree. "You are a philosopher."

He shrugged, shoving his hands in his pockets, smile on his face again. "I'm the studious one who's only decent with a sword and was routinely beat up by three older brothers. I found out I'd better accept that too, instead of pretending it was different."

She turned this over in her head too. She couldn't remember any men who so cheerfully admitted their failings. Her mind did a sudden sheer away. She couldn't remember any men. Not clearly. So.

"One question," she said at last. "I will ask one, and I will answer one. How long have I been here?"

"The records are a little uncertain," he said, and seemed to be watching her face closely. Perhaps waiting to see if she would panic again. "There's some dispute, some records saying a year or two different from others. But, give or take maybe five years at the most, it's been a hundred years since you were cursed."

"Cursed?" she repeated, and watched his eyes narrow. She had thought it a safe question to ask. His great-grandfather. A hundred years. It was self-evident. But—cursed?

"My turn," he said. "Were you cursed by a wicked enchantress?"

For just an instant, the memories flashed back into her mind. The Before Time, the beginning, how this had started. She shoved it all away, locked it back behind the haze of many—of one hundred years. "No," she said curtly, coldly. Then she bent down and picked up the gray kitten nosing among her skirts, held Silvertips to her chest. “I am going to walk in the rose garden,” she announced. “Don’t follow me.”

She walked away, spent the afternoon pacing amongst the flowers, tickling Silvertips and trying very, very hard to think of nothing at all. The prince didn’t follow her, and she was relieved.

Chapter Two: Terrence

Terrence had not expected anything like this. He had not expected anyone like her.

She left him standing by the small pond with the lilies drifting on its blue water, nearly the same shade as her dress disappearing between the trees as she fled from him. She wasn't quite running this time, so maybe he wasn't making an entirely terrible impression.

Even so, as soon as she was out of sight he sat down again, let himself drop onto his back on the grass. He stared up at the arching sky above the tree branches and wondered what he had got himself into.

Somewhere deep down, he had never truly expected to find the Princess Behind Thorns. He had heard stories about her all his life, about the sleeping princess under a curse, waiting for a champion to set her free. Some people said it was only a story, something invented over the decades. The thorns were real enough, but no one knew what was actually behind them. The woman had been real too, but no one knew for certain what had happened to her; she had disappeared from sight when she was eighteen years old, supposedly vanishing under a spell. His father had a portrait of Princess Rose Amelia in his throne room, an elegant woman with golden hair piled up on her head, wearing a dress cut in the fashion of a century ago.

At least, Elena said it was the fashion of a century ago. He couldn't judge that himself.

He wished Elena was here. She could help him figure out what to do, now that he was faced with, not a portrait, but an actual, living woman. She looked enough like the princess in the portrait, even in her plain dress with her shining hair pulled into a simple braid, that he could assume she was the right one—and at that thought, he laughed at himself. Because what was the alternative? That someone *else* was living behind a wall of thorns, pretending to be a princess?

Thinking of the thorns, he pushed himself up to his feet. He didn't know what to do about Princess Rose, who wasn't asleep and didn't want anything to do with him, but the next logical step in a rescue was still obvious.

He retraced the path he had taken to the pond, following his own footprints on the dust of the garden paths. The sharp edges of his boots stood out in marked contrast to the soft hollows of her footprints. Her steps were everywhere, an endless layering of clearer prints atop nearly worn away ones, criss-crossed by the outlines of tiny paws.

Terrence hadn't expected cats either.

He came out between the trees to face the long lawn where he had entered the garden. Another mystery. He knew meadows, and he knew lawns, and this was indisputably a lawn, as neatly clipped and cared for as any around his father's castle. Somehow he couldn't imagine Princess Rose going out with a scythe on a regular basis, so—magical grass? Magical servants? Invisible goats who cropped the grass?

He shook his head, and stepped onto the lawn with only a slight hesitation. Nothing happened. Of course not; he'd already crossed it once, coming in. She'd been standing on it too.

He was undecided if it made things more comfortable or not that the lawn was pretending to be normal grass. The wall of brambles wasn't hiding its magic, which at least was honest and aboveboard. He walked across the lawn until he was within a dozen feet of the thorny branches, then stopped and looked up.

And up and up. The hedge had to rise at least thirty feet high, an endless array of interlocking branches; it looked, if possible, even more formidable from this side than it had from the other. Sickly leaves, so dark green they were almost black, did nothing to hide the thick, barbed thorns covering the branches. Not a single flower softened the picture.

He had arrived at the wall of thorns this morning. Barley, his horse, had started fighting him a mile out, fretting and anxious and suddenly trying very hard to go any direction but the one Terrence wanted. Barley was a trained warhorse with a naturally calm disposition, and Terrence had never seen him behave that way. The strange behavior had started happening at about the same point when he realized the birds had disappeared from the trees. The forest itself looked normal enough, no strange shadows or dead trees as the stories liked to say about cursed areas, except that it was too quiet.

It had also been a forest that looked the part for the time of year, trees mostly bare, only the first hints of springtime buds appearing, the air cool and crisp. It was very unlike the lush green landscape on the inside of the thorns.

He had finally left Barley behind in a small clearing with long grass growing, hoping that would be enough to keep him calm and in one place, and walked the final distance. He felt a twinge of worry now for his horse. He hadn't expected to be gone this long.

It had seemed most likely that he'd end up turning around and coming directly back. Even when he'd found the wall of thorns, he hadn't at first seen any way through.

He had circled the entire enclosure without seeing the slightest break in the woven branches with their inch-long spikes. It hadn't been a long walk, and he had the uncomfortable feeling now that what he'd already seen inside the wall was bigger than the distance he'd walked around it.

But magic was uncanny by definition, so he tried to shrug the feeling off. He'd grown up seeing his father's enchanters do strange things.

After he had made a full circuit of the enclosure, he'd tried the direct approach. Stepping closer to the wall, he had only half-drawn his sword before the branches started rustling. The sound had been ominous, and not only because no wind was blowing.

"All right then," he had said, sliding his sword back into its sheath. "So you don't like swords. Or do you not like me?"

He had tested it. Approaching with his sword undrawn produced agitation among the branches, but less. Taking his sword belt off, setting it on the ground and approaching again caused no disturbance.

"So we won't cut any branches," he'd said, not sure if it was to himself or the thorns. "Maybe we could just—move a few aside? Rearrange a few?"

He hadn't really thought this made sense, the way the branches were so thickly entwined. But he'd reached out, carefully wrapping his hand around a segment of branch in a space between two thick, hooked thorns. Gently, he'd eased the bough a little to the side, trying to maneuver so that he wouldn't break any branches. The smooth wood tingled against his hand in a way that no plant ever had before. He was going to overlook it—until a sudden vibration within the hedge made him snatch his hand back.

"Maybe we won't—" he'd begun, then stopped as the thorn branches went on rustling, more violently now.

He'd backed away as the branches directly in front of him twisted and writhed. After a moment, he could see they weren't lashing out towards him. They were rearranging themselves, moving aside, re-entwining to form a narrow tunnel.

"All right then," he'd said under his breath.

He could have walked away. Now, now that he was on the inside, he wasn't sure yet whether he wished he had. But he had been reading about adventures his entire life, and he had come here to rescue the princess. How could he have walked away from that?

Besides, if he didn't go forward, the only alternative was to go home. He'd have to face his father and his brothers and admit he hadn't rescued the princess. His father would see it as one more example of how his youngest son failed to impress anyone, Gregory would remind him about it any time they argued, and nothing in his life would change.

So he'd taken a deep breath, put his right hand on the lioness tattoo on his left forearm, and prayed for whatever divine help Mariqwe, God of Passion, was willing to give him. Then he'd gone into the tunnel.

Once into its shadowy depths, all his self-control had been needed to keep walking forward. The branches never stopped shifting around him. Periodically one would reach out and mark him, thorns biting straight through his clothes to slice at his skin. He'd stopped short at the first one—but it wasn't deep, so he'd kept going. None of the cuts were deep, as though they were only meant to be a reminder that he was at the thorns' mercy. He'd done his best to shield his face and kept walking. He counted steps, the longest 22 steps he had ever walked.

The relief was overwhelming when he emerged from the tunnel into the light and air again—warmer and brighter than the world had been at the other end of the tunnel. Though however relieved he was, he wouldn't have let himself collapse on the grass if he'd realized Princess Rose was watching.

All the stories said she was asleep. *Every* story said she was asleep. Though most also said she had been cursed by a wicked enchantress. He had never given much weight to the ones with the alternative explanation, because surely no father—well, maybe she'd be able to explain it all. If she ever decided to talk to him.

Right now, he had a wall of thorns to deal with, from the inside this time.

"How about opening up another tunnel?" he suggested, definitely talking to the brambles this time.

No response came back.

Bracing himself, he reached out to see if moving a branch would work from this side.

He hadn't even touched the hedge before he saw another branch moving out of the corner of his eye. He stepped back, a second too late, and the rope of thorns slashed across his upper arm.

He stifled an exclamation, clasping his arm with his opposite hand. That was worse than any of the cuts he'd gotten on the way in. Not anything too serious, he'd been hurt worse sparring with his brothers, but apparently the thorns wanted to make it clear that their earlier restraint didn't have to continue applying.

He tried to imagine if even a few of those branches wrapped around him, stabbing in a dozen places with those vicious thorns, again and again…a person could die that way. Not quickly, but it would come.

According to legend, it had, for a lot of past champions.

He let out a slow breath. "I guess I'm not leaving right now."

He hadn't exactly wanted to, not yet. He hadn't rescued the princess yet.

The princess who didn't want to talk to him, but who might have some answers.

He tied a handkerchief around his bleeding arm as he moved further from the brambly wall. He kept one eye on it as he looked out over the lawn, trying to think what his next step should be.

A dozen feet away, a small black cat was sitting on the grass, studying him with its head tipped to one side.

"Hello there," Terrence said, instinctively crouching down and reaching out a hand. The kitten scampered forward to sniff his fingers and blink up at him with brilliant green eyes. "At least someone is friendly in here," he said with a smile.

He could go look for Princess Rose, try to get some answers. But she had told him not to follow her.

If he thought she was only angry, he would have done it anyway. But the way she kept a distance between them, the way she held herself with her shoulders tight, her gaze locked on him as though she needed to watch for any sudden movements…she was afraid of him. Making her angrier by approaching her would be one thing, but making her more frightened was something else.

Even though part of him wanted to do something, *anything* immediately, to get to work assessing all the possibilities for getting out of here, it wasn't going to help to move too quickly with the princess. She'd only be more likely to keep on avoiding him, to refuse to answer questions, to run away from him again. Better to give her a chance to approach him. He couldn't wait forever, but he could wait longer than this brief span. She had come back once already; surely she'd do it again.

He scratched the kitten's head. "Too bad *you* can't give me a tour of this place. Point out any secret exit, for example."

The kitten flopped onto its back, paws waving in the air, batting at his hand.

"Or where to find something to eat," Terrence continued, recognizing a possibly more pressing need. "Your princess must be eating, right?" Princesses who were asleep for a hundred years wouldn't need food, but one that was awake under an enchantment would. He thought. At least, he was hungry, so he hoped there was something to eat in here somewhere.

"I guess we'll go exploring," he told the kitten, who seemed happy to scamper along with him as he set off back towards the trees.

Chapter Three: Rose

The prince found his own way to the orchard. Rose discovered him there in the late afternoon, when hunger from her missed midday meal drove her to seek out food.

"Oh, hello," he said, lifting an apple in one hand like a salute. He had rolled up his shirt sleeves, revealing a lioness tattoo on one forearm.

Rose wondered about that but didn't ask, merely nodding in response to his greeting.

"I found the pantry," he continued. "Have you been living on fruit all these years?"

This was another question, contrary to her earlier limit, but she let it pass. "Not just fruit."

She moved to one of the special trees, pulling a giant nut free from its branch. Cracked, it revealed an assortment of cheese and bread. She never knew what one of these would open to reveal: pot pies, roast pheasant, baked potatoes, jam tarts.

"That's amazing," Prince Terrence said in what sounded like genuine delight, reaching for one of his own.

"Is it?" she said, nibbling on a piece of cheese. She had been mostly sure that such food hadn't grown on trees in the Before Time, but the orchard's offerings had long since ceased to appear strange.

Were other parts of her garden strange? Were there other things the prince was going to find unusual and exciting? She tried to think back to before the garden, tried to compare the two. The Before Time was still hazy, but she was surprised to find more memories than she had expected. She had so rarely tried to think of her life outside the garden. She remembered there had been a castle, a bedroom, a room with an actual bed, all very different from her bower now. She remembered there had been far more people about, though she thought, possibly, she had been lonelier then than she had ever been here.

She wasn't sure how much she wanted to remember.

She wasn't sure, with a prince here and her world changing, if she had much choice anymore about remembering.

When she had eaten, she turned again to leave.

"Are we just going to go on like this?" Prince Terrence asked. "Mostly ignoring each other?"

"I expect so," she said, despite knowing that likely wasn't possible. The garden wasn't *that* large. But she had no better solution; she hadn't any idea what to do about him. "I'm going to bed," she said, and a sudden renewed stab of fear made her tone harsher as she said, "*Don't* follow me."

He must have heard the change in her tone, because he held up his hands in a gesture of innocence, and his voice was softer when he said, "I wouldn't think of it."

She stared at him for a moment, wondering if she could believe that, then nodded. She had walked several paces towards the edge of the orchard when she paused and, with some reluctance, advised, "Don't sleep too near the thorns."

She didn't wait for him to respond or to ask more questions. She retreated to her bower, curled up in her bed, and watched the last rays of sunlight fade from the sky overhead.

In the dark, the thorn branches groaned again. At the first sound, she squeezed her eyes shut, body tensing, disappointment washing through her. She hadn't admitted to herself how much she had hoped it was over now, that it was only a prince outside disrupting the magic. But that had never truly made sense as an explanation. Something in the garden had been going wrong for weeks, and surely Prince Terrence hadn't been trying to get in all that time.

Maybe it had nothing to do with him. Maybe, after a hundred years, the spell had simply gone on for too long.

The sound of the twisting, scraping branches grew louder, and she shrank down among her blankets, holding Silvertips and Emerald Eyes within the circle of her arm, curling inward and trying to still her body's shaking.

With the shadows, with the thrashing thorns, memories were coming back. The memories she had shoved away earlier in the day forced themselves on her now in the darkness.

The prince had asked about a wicked enchantress. There had been no wicked enchantress. There had been her father, and his court enchanters. There had been heated talk about ensuring a strong succession. A powerful king. Because they were cursed with only a girl in line for the throne. Not considered an acceptable heir, her primary role was as a marriageable chess piece in the political game. They wanted a strong king, but more than that, a king all the other countries would *know* was strong. They wanted a good story.

And someone had an idea. A challenge. A magical challenge that would capture the imagination, that would require courage and strength to overcome. They would create a magical obstacle for one brave champion to conquer, and they would place her at the center. A prize to be seized.

"No," she whispered. "No, *no*." She would not remember any more, she would not, she would *not*.

In desperation she reached for quotes memorized from her favorite books, for a litany of all the flowers in her garden, a naming of each of her cats over the years, anything she could use to fill her mind and keep the memories away. She buried her face against Emerald Eyes' softly purring side, forced herself to inhale, exhale, trying to breathe evenly and failing more often than not.

She couldn't banish the memories entirely, but she held them back, kept them far enough away that she didn't have to look at them, held them in the distance until she finally fell into an exhausted sleep.

In the morning, she nearly tripped over Prince Terrence as she went to the nearest pond to wash her face, leaving the kittens still asleep in her bower. She was tired and agitated and she stopped short a step away when she suddenly saw him asleep, stretched out full-length with his green cloak pulled over him, beside the smallest pond.

He had good ears or her steps were louder than she'd imagined because his eyes blinked open almost at once. They focused on her, and he sat up immediately. "Last night, after it got dark," he said, words tumbling out, "the thorns—the shadows—"

"Yes, I know," she said, skirted around him and knelt beside the pond. She reached one hand out to the water, hesitated, and then drew a handkerchief from her pocket. Usually she simply splashed her face, but she had never had a guest before. She dampened the handkerchief, patted it over her cheeks and eyes.

"But what was it?" he asked. "The shadows started stretching out from the wall of thorns, and they just—they looked *wrong*. And the noise from the branches—what's going on?"

"Is that your question for today?" she asked, realizing only as she did that evidently she meant to permit a question again today. Every day. Which meant more days. But that was nonsense. Of course he had to leave. Somehow. She wiped her face with the dry corner of her handkerchief, and her hand only trembled a little.

He blinked at her. "I—yes. I guess that's my question."

She sat back on her heels, spread the damp handkerchief over her lap and ran her fingertips across the embroidered roses in one corner. "I don't know what's going on," she said without looking up. "It's only been happening for…maybe a few weeks, at most a few months. It's hard to track time in here. It's been much worse the last several nights. It's like the shadows from the thorn walls eat away the garden during the night, then daylight restores it." For now. A terrifying thought, one she pushed hurriedly away.

"That's why you warned me," he said. She could feel his gaze resting on her face, though she didn't lift her eyes. "About not sleeping near the thorns. Thank you."

"You're welcome," she said automatically, a habit she hadn't had any occasion to use for many, many years.

"What's your question today?"

She wasn't certain she wanted to ask any more questions. She didn't want any more memories stirring. But maybe answers would help. Maybe the known would stop the fear that the unknown allowed. She looked at him through her eyelashes. Dark hair, dark eyes, thin scar by his eyebrow, a firm jaw with a little stubble beginning on it today. Nothing about his face sparked recognition in her, no memory of someone else from the Before Time. She didn't think she'd known her fourth cousin, the one whose descendant had somehow ended up with her father's throne. "How did your family become rulers?"

If the question surprised him, it didn't show on his face. He just leaned back on his hands and answered. "After you were—here, there wasn't any clear heir to the throne. Your father…" His eyes tightened a little, voice going softer again. "I'm sorry, your father died."

She only nodded. "After a hundred years, he must have." Everyone must have. She felt no regret over that, and wondered if she should.

"Um, yes. Well, he died pretty soon after you—disappeared, so they hadn't passed any law or decree yet about who would inherit if you hadn't been rescued. The council tried to work out who was next in line, but there was a lot of disagreement and chaos. That's why some of the records are confusing; people wrote different things, and some records were lost.

"Everyone with any claim to the throne tried to seize it, along with plenty who didn't have any real claim at all. The country went through a whole series of assassinations and minor skirmishes and people trying to build up loyalty in key factions. The throne changed hands at least five or six times in just a few years, and most people who seized it tried to wipe out the records of the ones who came before, so—well, that contributes to the historical record being murky.

"My great-grandfather was the one who finally managed to hold onto the throne long enough for the dust to settle on all the fighting." Prince Terrence shrugged. "The official records say he was a great hero and everyone else were cruel pretenders, but my great-grandfather got to write the official records, so…it's hard to say exactly how it all happened. He told the story that worked for him."

She could imagine it all. A lot of powerful men, wanting the throne that would give them more power. A lot of strong, powerful… She shut the thought down, the memories whispering behind it. No.

"Very well," she said crisply, folded up her handkerchief and tucked it into her pocket. "Now. Breakfast."

She walked to the edge of the clearing before he spoke, not having moved from where he sat. "Am I allowed to follow you this time?"

She hesitated. The orchard was the only place for food. It seemed unkind to bar him. "If you must." And it was—nice of him, to ask.

Chapter Four: Terrence

Princess Rose didn't order him away after they ate breakfast, or run away herself, so Terrence cautiously asked about a tour. He had scouted the garden the day before with the small black cat, but he hadn't uncovered anything particularly useful. Both cats had wandered into the orchard while they were still eating, but he didn't expect he'd do any better if he got the gray kitten to give him a tour today. His best chance at finding a way out was with the princess as a guide—and getting out seemed significantly more urgent this morning, after seeing the shadows advance in the night. He had never seen anything so unnatural; nothing his father's enchanters had done could compare.

So it was all very practical, the idea of exploring the garden with Princess Rose.

And also, he just wanted to.

She was—interesting, this woman who could be frightened of him and still give orders.

He was surprised by how pleased he was, though, when after a considering moment she waved a hand and said, "This is the orchard. In case you weren't sure."

He made himself nod gravely. "Important first stop on a tour."

She smiled, a small, almost hidden smile, that made him feel he had given the right answer. Then she glanced around, and turned towards a side path lined with birches. "We can go this way."

He let her walk ahead of him, and didn't try to take the lead or even to walk next to her. It wasn't a wide path, and it would have been hard to walk side-by-side without brushing against her skirt, without their hands bumping into each other. He still felt as though she might shy away at any moment, run off and go back to avoiding him if he made the wrong movement.

Not to mention there was the possibility of tripping over the two kittens, who were trotting along beside the princess.

Walking behind her let him study her unobserved too. She held her shoulders in the perfect posture of the court ladies, but walked lighter on her feet. Maybe it was being barefoot. When she lifted her right hand to brush a stray bit of hair back, he got a better look than he had before at the gold ring on her smallest finger. It looked very like a signet ring, a more feminine version of the silver one his oldest brother wore. The one the heir to the throne would have.

He needed to get back to his family, back to his world. He and Rose needed to get away from whatever magic was going wrong with the thorns and the shadows at night. He should probably be asking her more questions, trying more directly to find a way out of here. But he still didn't want to push her too hard, and the garden was so peaceful that it felt strangely easy to relax, to let problems wait until later. Part of him wondered why he was doing that, but most of him ignored that one objecting part.

The path twisted here and there, apparently content to meander, white birches standing like pillars to either side, leaves and branches casting dappled shade below. "I like a twisting path," he remarked after they'd been quiet for a while. "It's more interesting."

"So do I," Rose said, sounding surprised. "That's strange."

Liking a twisting path, or the fact that they both liked it? He settled for the neutral, "Why?"

"Straight paths are safer. You can see what's coming."

She quickened her pace then, more wisps of golden hair escaping from her braid, floating as they caught the breeze. A few moments later the last turn in the path revealed another pond, much bigger than the one he'd slept near.

"This is the Round Pond," Rose said, as the two kittens frisked past her skirts and over to the pond's edge. "It's not the only round pond, but it's the biggest, so it's *the* Round Pond, instead of just *a*...I probably should have named it." Her hands smoothed her skirts, he suspected in a nervous gesture. "I haven't had to describe things to anyone before."

What would it be like to be alone for a hundred years? He got lonely in less than a day, the rare times he'd been alone for that long. "No one else has ever come through—?"

"I said one question per day," Rose interrupted, and though she didn't sound angry, the words were *too* bright, too forcefully cheerful, and completely absolute. He wouldn't have pushed the question after hearing that response, but she also didn't give him a chance, immediately saying, "The best flowers are over there, the far side of the pond."

It would take more than a few minutes to circle this pond, and he didn't like the tension that had come into the air. He shouldn't have tried to ask that question; he should have known better.

If he was trying to build a rapport with a nervous horse, he'd keep talking to her, tell her that everything was going to be all right. He didn't think that comparison, or that reassurance, would go over well—but he could keep talking.

"I wound up dumped in a pond like this the first time I tried to ride a horse," he remarked, pitching his voice conversationally, as though he didn't feel the unease radiating off of Rose. And as if he wasn't wondering again what had happened to his horse Barley, left somewhere on the other side of the thorn wall yesterday. "It was this old mare I wasn't supposed to be riding, of course."

The story lasted them all the way to the flowers she had pointed out, and if she didn't relax enough to laugh, she at least smiled again.

A small stretch of grass—neatly cropped like the long lawn, Terrence noted—bordered the pond, before giving way to a section vibrant with color. Narrow paths wound between bushes and rows of flowers, every color of the rainbow represented. The castle gardens had not been nearly this full of blooms when he left two days ago, and he noted again how unseasonably warm it was within the thorn walls, how strangely green for the end of winter. If there was anything uncanny about the flower garden, it didn't bother the kittens, who promptly scampered off to chase each other between the plants.

"This is where I do the most pruning," Rose said, bending down to pick up a woven basket sitting almost hidden beneath a flowering shrub. She brought out a pair of garden shears. "It's the best place for bouquets."

So the princess did some gardening after all. He still rather doubted she was trimming the lawn.

He studied those garden shears as Rose clipped a few blossoms and pointed out her favorite flowers. They looked like very capable shears for cutting a bouquet, but not large enough to make any meaningful dent in the wall of thorns. Were there other gardening tools around, tucked under other bushes? Would it matter if there were? The brambles hadn't stood still when he'd approached with a sword; they weren't likely to quietly let him hack through them now. His arm stung as he remembered the violent response merely touching the branches had prompted the day before. The scratches he'd picked up coming through the wall were minor enough, already scabbing and easy to ignore. The ones on his arm, the ones he'd gotten inside the walls, were deeper and still hurt. When he paid attention to them, at least.

He tried to put that aside, refocus on the princess and her garden. If he wanted her to like him, to trust him and not, say, decide she needed the garden shears as a defense, he should say something nice about her flowers. He had no real idea what any of the flowers he was looking at might be—but now that he was paying attention, he did think he recognized a scent on the air. He sniffed, trying to be sure. "Are there gardenias somewhere near here?"

"Yes, over by the violets. You can tell by the smell?" She sounded surprised, but pleasantly.

He supposed she hadn't known any men who could recognize flowers by scent. He didn't know any who could, and he couldn't really do it either—only this one. "Gardenias were my mother's favorite perfume."

"Oh." She kept her gaze on the roses she was cutting, her voice soft as she said with careful emphasis, "They *were*?"

"She died six years ago." It wasn't as hard to talk about now as it had once been.

"Oh. I'm sorry."

He just nodded, because he still didn't know exactly what to say to that frequently-expressed sentiment, though he appreciated the intention. He lifted his hand, touched the ring he could feel through his shirt, where it was hanging on a chain around his neck. The ring had been his mother's; she'd given it to him not long before she died. He'd been wearing it ever since, so familiar now that he wouldn't feel right without it.

"What was your mother like?"

How could he sum her up? "She was…the most wonderful person I've ever known."

Rose paused with red blooms in her hand, head tipping slightly to the side in a thoughtful gesture that reminded him of her cat. "Then you were very lucky to have her. It must have been hard to lose her."

The statements were obvious, and yet she said them with a kind of sincerity that made them seem meaningful—and as though she was genuinely thinking the ideas out. He remembered her lack of emotion at the news of her father's death, and wondered how she would describe her own mother. He had no expectation she would answer that question if he asked it. So finally he just said, "Yes. Yes, it was hard to lose her."

It was a day he didn't like thinking about. He'd rather watch Rose drop her flowers into her basket, walk a few steps down the path and reach out to a bush dotted with white flowers. "The gardenias are here." She fingered a petal. "Does it make you sad to smell them?"

This was a less obvious idea; in fact, it was a question no one had ever asked before. "No. I like to remember my mother." He strolled down the path to join her by the gardenias, inhaling the stronger scent. He didn't like remembering the end, but he liked remembering earlier times. The best times of his life had been with his mother. His mother, and Elena. "I think the scent makes Elena sad, but I like it."

"Who is Elena?" Rose asked, adding a pair of gardenias to the flowers in her basket.

Someone he had simpler emotions about, and Terrence grinned. "Elena is the other most wonderful person I've ever known."

"Oh?" Rose said, turning away from the gardenias and walking farther down the path.

Terrence's eyes narrowed as he looked at her back. He hadn't thought about the possible implications in what he'd said before he said it, might still not have if Rose hadn't turned away just then…but what was she imagining his relationship was with this woman he said was wonderful? And did she not like what she was imagining?

He was being ridiculous. Why should Rose care what Elena was to him? Why should *he* care if Rose cared…well. That was less ridiculous.

"Elena is my cousin," he volunteered, because letting any misconception go on was even more ridiculous than anything else. Elena would tell him he was being an idiot if he did that. "My mother's niece. She lived with us, so we pretty well grew up together. I spent whole years of my childhood pretending Elena was my sister." Just in case the cousin clarification wasn't enough.

"Oh," Rose said again, apparently intent on collecting some bright yellow blossoms to add to her basket. He couldn't tell if there was any change in her tone, any hint that this was welcome news.

Would it be better if it was? Maybe, if he still had any hope of carrying out his original plan in coming here. Or maybe everything was already far too muddled for the straight-forward, naïve ideas he'd originally had to ever work out.

Chapter Five: Rose

They spent the rest of the day together. Rose showed the prince her garden, introduced him to the other cats prowling around, listened to stories about his life. Of the questions that were asked, none were the important kind, the charged kind, the kind that counted for her one question a day rule. The closest was when Prince Terrence asked why there were cats in here, but she didn't mind talking about that.

Rose shrugged. "I always liked cats. Cats always liked me. And cats go wherever they want to." They had always been here. Maybe she had wondered about it at first, but she had accepted it long ago.

All in all, she realized with some surprise as she lay down to go to sleep, it had been a nice day.

She was nearly asleep when the thorn branches shifted again. The sounds carried on the night air, louder than before, groans and creaks filling the garden, branches grinding and crunching and shrieking.

Wide awake again, heart beating hard in her chest, she curled herself into a ball of frightened misery. She should have expected it, and it felt worse because the pleasant day had so lulled her, so distracted her from the larger problems. And in her fear, the memories she had been ignoring slipped in. The memories that had tried to stir when the prince told her about the fight for the throne, the memories she had been able to push back in daylight. Now they saw their opening in the darkness, in her fear. They rushed back to her, and no amount of reciting flower names was going to keep them away.

Powerful men who wanted to be king. The champions who came to try the challenge and win the princess. They had filled the castle in the final days, in the last of the Before Time. She had looked at them all with wide eyes and trembling hands. The warriors, so large and loud, heavy and coarse. The political schemers, with cold eyes and cruel jaws, haughty and proud. All of them had stared at her. Openly, hungrily. They had leered at her and laughed at her and made remarks about her that they didn't care if she overheard. They called her pretty, and tasty, and a nice little bonus, and a delicious treat. They critiqued every part of her body, and the compliments were as terrifying as the criticisms. They said she looked pliable, obedient, easy to manage and easy to control.

And she was to be given to one of them.

Her father had looked over the lot of them with approval, seeing only the strength that he wanted to someday hold his throne. Her mother never looked at them, and would not look at her either.

Had all of them been that bad? She couldn't remember anymore, couldn't remember if any in the crowds had been different, if she was only remembering the worst or if it really had been that terrible.

None of them had ever talked *to* her. Only about her.

She had not wanted any of them to rescue her. Not one.

"The shadows were worse last night," Prince Terrence said the next morning.

"Yes," she agreed, because why deny it? They had met in the orchard today, were picking fruit for breakfast. She was tired from too many memories and not enough sleep. "It's been getting worse for days. I don't know how to stop it."

He cut right past that idea, asked instead, "Do you know how to leave this place?"

They both knew that was today's question. It had too much weight not to be.

"No," she said, studying the peach in her hand. "I don't know how to leave. I haven't thought about leaving in a long time." Truthfully, she couldn't remember if she had wanted to leave at the beginning. It was possible she never had. But things were changing now. The garden, or at least the thorn walls around it, were turning against her. And a prince had come. "What do the stories say? You came to—to rescue me. What was your plan for doing it?"

If he noticed the momentary stumble in her voice, he didn't comment on it. He tossed an apple up in the air, caught it again. "I expected you to be asleep. The stories all said that, and it was getting past the thorns that was meant to be the hard part. Waking you up was supposed to break the curse. But I guess it isn't a curse exactly, and you're already awake."

He expected her to be *asleep*. Another memory reared up with a sudden snap of fear and anger. She tried to push it away but it was there, battering at her attention, refusing to be ignored any longer. Clinging to her self-control, she said curtly, "I'm going to the birches. Don't follow me." She had to leave, to get away, to escape from him because she couldn't escape from this memory.

She told herself she didn't notice the hurt on his face as she left the orchard, kittens trotting agreeably in her wake.

She ran once she was far enough down the birch path to be out of sight around a curve. If she ran fast enough, far enough, could she flee from this memory? Could she leave it behind back there in the orchard with this man who kept stirring things up after so many peaceful years?

She couldn't. Even as she fled, the memory was forcing itself into her mind, images and sounds and ideas growing clearer and clearer. She collapsed finally in a grassy place beneath a tree, curling into herself as the past filled her mind, obscuring the sunlight of the present.

She wasn't supposed to be in a garden, wasn't supposed to be in a position to remember anything—or to have forgotten anything to begin with. Because she was supposed to be asleep. That was part of the magic, part of the decisions made by her father and his council. As if it wasn't obvious enough that she was a pawn in this game—less than a pawn, who could at least move one square—she was to be sent to sleep as part of the spell. She was to lie asleep at the center of the challenge, waiting.

The idea had terrified her. All those men in the castle, all those men panting and eager to brave death to seize the kingdom and her, one of them was going to come for her and she was going to be asleep. Helpless. Unable to move or speak or do anything, anything at all.

Would she be aware? Would she know what was happening to her? She had asked herself that question, in the final days, with no answer to allay her gnawing fears. And what *would* happen? What would one of these men, these hard, hungry men, do to her, when they had braved the danger and reached her sleeping body? She would be defenseless and alone with one of them.

And that one would own her ever after. He was winning the right to claim her, to marry her, to possess her for the rest of her life. She would be asleep and powerless when he came to take his prize, but she would be just as powerless ever after.

She put her hands over her face as she curled beneath the birches, pressed her palms against her temples as though she could hold the memories in, back and away.

She remembered the terror she had felt as the day for the spell had approached. She remembered standing before them all, the champions gathered in her father's throne room. She had scanned their faces, looking for any hint of kindness.

She didn't recall finding it.

Her father had made her walk through the crowd, the men parting but not very far, to let her pass through. Every man had stared at her with devouring eyes.

Her parents and the eight court enchanters had attended her up the stairs to her bedroom, where they planned to enact the spell. She had stayed silent until now, but halfway up the spiral stone stairs she had begun murmuring.

"Please. Please don't do this. Please, not like this, there has to be something else, please."

"Hush, girl," her father had said. "I'm getting you a fine strong husband."

They reached the bedroom and she had resisted, refusing to lie down on her bed. "No—*please*, no. Mother! Mother, please tell them not to do this!"

It was an absurd request. Her mother sat on a throne like her father, wore a crown like her father, but she had no power. Maybe Rose had only wanted the comfort of her mother trying to save her.

But her mother had only said, "Lie down, Rose, and stop making all this fuss."

She lay down then. She closed her eyes, tears trickling past her eyelashes and slipping down her cheeks. She didn't bother to pray. What was the use? No people ever listened to her; why should any god? She lay still and quiet like everyone wanted, as the enchanters intoned the words of their spell, until the world faded away.

She had opened her eyes in her bower. She still didn't know why. Maybe one of the enchanters had been kinder than the others, made a change to the spell. Maybe the magic itself read something of her wishes, tried to accommodate them. But awake she was, in a garden that seemed designed to keep her happy. Even many of the things from her bedroom had found their way here—her statue of Mariqwe, her books, her small silver mirror. She couldn't explain that; magic items were rare, and these had never shown any sign of enchantment before the spell. But here they were, and the cats had somehow found their way in too.

And so she had been here, for all these years, the fear and the memories drifting away together. Until recently. Until the shadows had started growing, the thorns moving, and Terrence arrived.

She wiped tears from her cheeks. She must have cried often, early on, but hadn't for a long time now. She had forgotten that tears could be a relief.

Rose drew in a deep breath, sat up straighter, found that the fear had lessened now that the memory was in front of her. She was far more disgusted. And angry. And the people she was angry with had been dead for decades, so what was the use of it? She needed to deal with now.

Terrence. Prince Terrence, rather. What was she going to do about him?

He had come to rescue her. He must have expected to marry her, just like all the others had. But he hadn't said anything about that, and he didn't match her memories of the champions. He didn't look at her like they had. He talked to her, instead of about her. But was he different, really?

She thought of that scar by his eyebrow. He had said he was the studious one, but people didn't get scars reading books. Perhaps he had other scars too, less visible ones. She didn't know if anything he said was true. She didn't know it *wasn't*—but she didn't know it was either.

It occurred to her suddenly that he hadn't followed her to the birches when she told him not to.

That was a comfort. And somehow, disappointing too.

Nonsense. Absurd.

What had his plans been, really? He had expected to wake her up, but that was barely the beginning of an answer. Maybe it would be better to know than not. She scooped up her two kittens, who had curled beside her, and went to find out.

Terrence wasn't in the orchard anymore. She found him in the rose garden, surprised him smelling a big pink blossom. She thought of telling him that the white ones smelled sweeter, then pushed the thought away for more important business.

"How were you going to wake me up?" she asked abruptly, not giving herself time to back out. She let her squirming kittens down to run off through the flowers.

She startled him, and he nearly stepped in the rose bushes as he turned suddenly to face her. "How I—waking you up?" he fumbled.

"How were you going to do it?" she repeated, heart hammering in her chest. She was committed now, and if she didn't want to know the answer after all—when had it ever mattered what she wanted? "You didn't really answer the question, about how you planned to rescue me. You must have had a plan to break the curse you expected. Can you do magic, or did you learn how to lift the curse?"

The royal family had had no magic in her own time, not even the more common, low-level magical affinities, but maybe something had changed in the past century. Maybe magic was how Terrence had got through the thorns, and would be the answer now. Or had he intended something as prosaic as shaking her by the shoulder until she awoke? Were there secret words he planned to say to break the spell? How was this all supposed to work? She didn't remember those details, or she had never been told them. Either seemed possible.

His cheeks were turning red—so at least she wasn't the only one uncomfortable in this situation. "I…no, I can't do any magic, but the stories said…it shouldn't require magic, because the way to break the curse was supposed to be…to kiss you." He cleared his throat, straightened his shoulders. "I was going to kiss you. To wake you up."

Well. That could have been worse. A kiss was much more personal, much more intimate, than saying a few magical words over her. But it could have been worse. "The stories all say that would end the curse?"

"That's…what they say."

She nodded, because she had no choice then. She tried to push down the awkwardness and fear uncurling in her stomach. "I suppose we had better try it."

He blinked at her. "What?"

He was going to make her say it again? "I suppose—you had better kiss me." The shadows were getting worse. She couldn't stay here anymore even if she wanted to, the way the spell was breaking down, so this had to end. She had had no choice all those years ago. Why should she imagine she had any choice now?

She lifted her chin and closed her eyes, fists tight at her sides, body braced and tense, and waited.

Nothing happened.

She cracked open her eyes to see that Terrence hadn't moved. "What is it?" Had he changed his mind about kissing her, now that he'd met her?

He rubbed the back of his neck. "You don't seem to want to do this."

Why did he think that mattered? What she wanted had never mattered to anyone before. And there wasn't any choice; surely he could see that. "I told you to do it. We have to break the spell." She closed her eyes again.

A moment later, she felt the barest pressure against her lips for a second or two.

A few more seconds and she opened her eyes again. Nothing appeared to have changed, except that Terrence had turned even redder.

"Well," she said, slowly letting her breath out, slowly letting her fists uncurl. "It was an idea."

Chapter Six: Terrence

Terrence expected Rose to run away again, or to order him away. Or that they would have to talk about what had just happened, what they had just done, and what they had failed to do.

But Rose wouldn't meet his gaze immediately after he kissed her, and he didn't quite have the courage to name any important topics—kisses or curses or betrothals.

They just stood there for what felt like ages, as he tried to think of something to say, something to do. He could feel how hot his cheeks were, an extra humiliation for this awkward, painful moment. He ought to be charming or clever—wasn't he supposed to be the clever one, among his brothers, the one who always knew how to talk to people? Probably any of them would have handled this better. Edward, who always knew the diplomatic thing to say, or Tyler, who was never awkward around women, or Gregory—

"I suppose I'll take the kittens out to the long lawn," Rose said, still without looking at him, looking down at her hands smoothing the unwrinkled folds of her skirt. "I suppose you—may as well come. If you want to."

It felt like a lifeline, and he took it. "That sounds nice."

They *should* talk about the important things. But he had no idea where to begin. And maybe he would be asking too much of her if he tried to force her to talk about things she so obviously wanted to avoid.

That sounded good. Considerate. Not cowardly at all.

It felt easy, somehow, to let the important topics slip away. There was something about this place that made it hard to concentrate on any problems, hard to feel the proper urgency he knew he ought to feel. In a circular kind of way, he knew it should worry him that it was so hard to keep up a reasonable amount of worry, but he couldn't seem to get decently worked up about that either.

Maybe it was just that the princess was distracting. That was possible.

So he went with her out to the lawn, both trying to pretend that nothing was wrong as they sat down on the grass in the sunshine.

"There's a lawn out back of my father's castle a lot like this," Terrence said, seizing on the first possible non-controversial topic he could think of. Grass, he was going to talk to her about grass? But no, it didn't have to be that bad… "The servants run races out there. The stableboys and footmen, you know. I joined sometimes, when I was younger." Eventually he had got older and passed some invisible line, the line that meant he was a prince and they were servants, and after that they couldn't cross over anymore, couldn't play together. But it had been fun when he was younger.

The lawn had never been this green though, or the grass this soft.

"I think I remember that lawn," Rose said, gaze on her kittens, but her voice was beginning to sound more natural. "The court ladies used to sit and do embroidery."

Very slowly conversation grew easier, at least as long as they kept to comparatively insignificant subjects.

He sat leaning on his hands, watching her wave a long strand of grass for the batting paws of Silvertips, and told stories, some about his life, some he had read.

While he talked, and in the silences between conversation, he thought that he liked this, sitting in the sun with Rose. And though he could mostly stop thinking about the curse for now, it was harder to stop thinking about kissing her.

Maybe he should have really kissed her. Not that fleeting, impersonal peck, but actually taken her into his arms and drawn her close and really kissed her. Maybe it would have worked on the magic. Maybe he should have done it even if it didn't.

Most of him hadn't wanted to. Part of him had. Maybe if he hadn't wanted to at all, he would have.

She was intriguing and beautiful and kind and sad and even though she told him so little of herself, so little of her life, he still somehow felt she wasn't ever hiding who she was, wasn't lying or pretending. She was open and vulnerable and he wanted to protect her and to apologize for intruding on her and to ask for permission to go on intruding, for a long, long time.

He had wanted to kiss her the day before, when she was standing in the sunshine with her hands full of flowers, head tipped to the side as she listened to him talk about his mother. He wanted to kiss her *now*, as she laughed unself-consciously at the kitten she was teasing.

But that moment earlier, when he might have done it—she had stood there, with her eyes closed and her jaw tight, everything saying so clearly that she didn't want to be kissed, that she didn't want him to kiss her, even if she said something different out loud.

When he'd imagined coming here, rescuing the Princess Behind Thorns, he hadn't minded the idea of pressing his lips to the unresponsive ones of a sleeping stranger. But Rose wasn't asleep and she wasn't a stranger, she was a living, complicated, captivating woman, and he didn't want to kiss her like that. He'd be trying to take something she didn't want to give him, and that would make it worse than meaningless.

He'd be like whatever man in the past had caused her to be so afraid. Someone must have, or she wouldn't have reacted the way she did when he first came into the garden.

And even if it could somehow be a strictly neutral, strictly business-like transaction—he didn't want that either. If he kissed her, he wanted her to kiss him back. He wanted to touch her hair and find out if it was as soft as it looked, to feel the warmth of her lips against his, to feel her press against him and want to be there with him…

He had to stop thinking like this; he could feel his cheeks warming already and she'd notice if he turned red again—he flopped backwards onto the grass, looked up at the sky instead of at her, and hoped she wasn't looking at his face.

He had come here with every intention of rescuing and marrying the Princess Behind Thorns. If she existed, if he had even believed she was here.

So far, he was failing abysmally to rescue Rose, and he doubted very much that she had any desire to marry him.

It only seemed to make it worse, that he didn't at all dislike the idea of marrying her.

Chapter Seven: Rose

They didn't mention the curse again that day. Instead, unspoken, they pretended together that everything was fine. Rose liked it better that way. It had been good here in the garden for so many years. It was easy to pretend that it still was. That maybe they could just stay here, like this.

Which was a strange thought too. Did she want Terrence to stay here?

He was lying on his back on the grass, looking up at the sky while she teased the kittens and covertly watched him. He had been telling her stories, but had grown quiet now. Was he thinking that he wanted to get away from here? To go back to his proper life in his father's castle, with his brothers and his horse and his cousin Elena. Such a world seemed impossibly distant, impossibly different from her own world in the garden.

Maybe the kittens sensed her distraction, because they swiftly went in search of new entertainment. Both bounded over to Terrence, Emerald Eyes leading, and leapt onto his chest.

"Sorry!" Rose said hurriedly, reaching out even though they were too far away to easily snatch up. "They shouldn't…"

But Terrence was laughing, rubbing tiny heads. "It's all right." He lifted first one kitten down and then the other, but both scrambled back again, delighted by the game. Rose giggled and Terrence laughed harder as he tried to fend off the little cats aiming to clamber onto his face.

Then Emerald Eyes slipped, flailed out a paw, and drew a line with one claw across the back of Terrence's hand. Rose looked at the blood and felt a sudden stab of fear—which made her realize how entirely she had stopped being afraid of Terrence—and dived forward to grab up her kittens.

"I'm sorry—he didn't mean to—"

"No, of course not," Terrence said easily, sitting up and inspecting his hand. He reached out with the other and rumpled up Emerald Eyes' fur. "I expect you haven't learned yet that your human friends' skin isn't as tough as your sister's fur." Then he looked up at Rose again, eyes crinkled a little, and said with a smile, "It's fine. Just a scratch."

Emerald Eyes mewed, squirmed, and wriggled away, while Rose held the purring Silvertips against her chest and felt her heartbeat calm again. She should have guessed it would be all right. He had been nothing but courteous and pleasant so far.

The kittens liked Terrence, had liked him right from the start. And, she realized with distinct surprise, she liked Terrence too. A man who would roll on the grass with a pair of kittens, and not be angry when one of them got a claw in his hand by mistake, was hard not to like. And very different from the people she had known before.

Not that she had ever really known many people. The Before Time was still many years ago, most memories still vague. But it was becoming clearer than it had been for a long time, and no memory was emerging of a friend or companion. She had been the princess, the daughter who should have been a son, the chess piece few people thought of as a person. She had been lonely then, lonelier than she had ever been while alone in her garden with her cats.

And now, for the first time, she wasn't alone. Someone had finally come to rescue her, and he wasn't at all what she had expected, when she had trembled in fear at the thought of a rescuer so long ago. Maybe not all of them had really been as bad as she had thought. Maybe her own fear had distorted them.

Or maybe, because her father had chosen and approved them, maybe they *had* been that bad.

It didn't matter now. None of them had come.

Why had none of them—no, it didn't matter. What mattered was here and now.

She watched Terrence as he sat up, straightened his rumpled shirt. The chain around his neck had become twisted, and he reached to adjust it.

Impulsively, she began to ask, "Can I see…" and then she remembered that they weren't asking questions. "I'm sorry, it's probably private."

"No, not really," Terrence said, drawing the chain over his head, gold ring swinging on the end. "Personal, not especially private."

He held it out, and she let go of Silvertips to cup the ring in her palm as he released the chain. It was a narrow ring, a metal braid of slender strands. It was too small and delicate for a man, plainly a woman's ring, and she wondered about that. What woman was important enough to him to wear her ring around his neck? His cousin? Someone else?

She wasn't sure if she was going to ask, but he volunteered the information before she could anyway. "It was my mother's ring," he said, gaze on the gold band in her hand. "She always wore it, so when she gave it to me…I should have realized what it meant, but I didn't want to believe she was that sick."

"Was it a gift from your father?"

"No, my uncle—my mother's brother gave it to her before she was married."

Rose offered the ring back to him, feeling queerly honored that he'd let her see it, even if he said it wasn't private. Personal though, that was clearly true. "Tell me a story about your mother."

He smiled, with the light in his eyes she had already noted came when he talked about his mother. "She always wanted our family to be closer. She loved it when she could do something together with me and all my brothers. I remember this one time, when we had a picnic in the walled garden outside her rooms…"

Rose pushed back memories of her own past, focused on Terrence's past instead.

Her past was long, long ago. She was here now, in this moment. And in the sunlight, as Terrence told his story, this moment was a nice one.

They pretended that nothing was wrong all day, but it grew impossible to keep up the pretense as the sun sank lower. The conversation trailed away, until they were both staring at the darkness pooling under the thorns, reaching out for them.

"These shadows are wrong," Terrence said at last, staring at the blackness stretching across the lawn. "They're too long, too dark. And they're moving too fast."

"I don't know what to do," Rose said shortly, sure that he expected her to have an answer.

Terrence ran a hand over his hair, still staring at the shadows. "We should have been talking about this earlier—we should try to do something, try to think how we can—"

"I don't know how to fix it." Rose's breath was tight in her chest. She had never been enough, and she wasn't enough to fix this. "Neither of us have any magic and the thing you said would break the curse didn't work and there's no way out through the thorns! There's nothing to talk about, nothing to try."

"So you're just going to keep hiding from this?" he said, with the first trace of irritation she'd heard in his voice.

"That's what I *do*," she snapped. "No one has ever let me do anything else!"

"You don't need someone to let you…"

But she was already stalking away, away from the shadows and away from him and away from her own inadequacies. It had been a nice day. She should have left sooner, while it was still nice.

At least she didn't expect any more memories tonight. Surely, she had remembered the worst of it now, and that particular torture, the resurfacing of old horrors, was over.

She fell asleep almost as soon as she curled up among her blankets, exhausted from the many bad nights, the very strange days, with the two kittens purring beside her. But she woke up again, somewhere deep in the night.

The thorns were screaming.

They were thrashing and scraping and it was so loud and so violent that the branches crashing together screamed on the night air.

She curled into a ball, hands over her ears, tears flooding her eyes.

Another memory was forcing its way out. Because there used to be screaming. In her first days in the garden. The screams as the champions tried the thorns and died. She had huddled in her bower with her hands over her ears then too, guilty because she had wanted them to fail, guilty because now they were dying, guilty because she still hadn't wanted any of those hard, cruel warriors to come through and claim her. Surely she hadn't wanted this, didn't want them to die—but she still hadn't wanted them to succeed.

She didn't know why it had happened the way it did, why they had all died in the thorns. She huddled up tighter now, not wanting to examine it, not wanting answers, but her mind kept ticking relentlessly on. The spell was supposed to stop most, but someone, someone strong enough and powerful enough, was supposed to get through to rescue her. No one had. Not until Terrence. But why him? Why was the one who wasn't frightening the one who had got in?

If the spell had changed itself because of her wishes, had it changed this part too? Had it changed itself to keep out all the men who scared her?

And didn't that make it her fault, that they had died?

She moaned as it all came back to her, as the thorns screamed and the remembered screams echoed in her mind. It had gone on and on in those early days. So many men, and none of them died quickly in the thorns. Sometimes shrieks and cries filled the air for days at a time. Sometimes a lull came, and she began to hope it was finally over, and then it would begin again.

And now the thorns were shrieking, like the champions, like the dying men, like the ones who had screamed and pleaded and cursed her name as they died.

She didn't know she was screaming herself until there was a stumbling of footsteps, a thrashing of nearby branches that sent a new, sharper stab of fear through her, and then Terrence's voice saying from close by, "Rose? What is it? What's wrong?"

She had reached out for her cats in the dark before and now it was the same instinct that made her reach out for him, to bury her face against his chest and sob out her terror and guilt. "I killed them! It's my fault, I killed them!"

"Who?" he said gently, arms enfolding her. "Who could you possibly have killed?"

"The champions," she gasped. "The rescuers. They all died in the thorns, all of them."

"That wasn't your fault. The thorns killed them. The magic killed them."

"But I didn't want to be rescued!" She sobbed out the story, the horrible champions, her terror, how the spell had changed from what her father and the enchanters had intended. He stroked her hair and listened and let her cry on his shirt.

And when she was finished, his voice was tight, with an anger that was obscurely comforting, as he said, "The people who put you in here are to blame. They never should have done it. They never should have done that to you."

"Thank you," she whispered, exhausted now that her story was told, now that she'd run out of tears and emotions. "No one ever said that before."

Rose woke up first in the morning. She was curled next to Terrence, who was asleep on his back with Emerald Eyes purring on his chest. She considered being embarrassed. But she seemed to be past that now. She'd told him everything, the awful stories of her past, and it had been all right. Waking up next to each other shouldn't be more embarrassing than that.

She propped herself on one elbow, studied his face as he slept. He looked younger, even with the darkening stubble on his jaw. But his expression was peaceful, black lashes lying against his cheeks. The scratches from the wall of thorns were healing. Her gaze drifted up to the scar by his eyebrow; maybe some time she'd ask how he had got it. Or would that be too personal? Her gaze drifted down again, down to his mouth, and she remembered asking him to kiss her. It had been so—awkward, so ridiculous, and so useless.

And it was useless to lie here staring at him. She got up, slipped out to the orchard. She brought back breakfast and found him awake, sitting up petting Silvertips and Emerald Eyes.

"Good morning," he said as she entered, and she watched the red appear on his face again. She liked his blush.

"Good morning," she said, sitting cross-legged, skirt tucked around her legs, and spread out the fruit she'd brought for breakfast on a cloth. She could see him hesitating, could see on his face as he weighed whether they should talk about her confessions of the previous night. She didn't want to revisit the subject, and so with determined cheerfulness she remarked, "The kittens like you."

"I'm honored," he said with a half-smile, and glanced around the bower. "So this is where you live?"

She nodded, though really she lived in all the garden. But she saw what he meant.

"What do you do when it rains?" he asked, looking up at the sky through the branches overhead.

"It doesn't rain," she said, and tried to remember if that had seemed strange to her, in the beginning. The idea of water falling out of the sky seemed rather strange now. Even in the Before Time, she hadn't been outside much, to experience rain.

"The shadows were even worse last night," he said quietly. When she didn't answer, kept her gaze on her apples and peaches, he continued, "They covered most of the garden. And not the shadows from the trees or—any normal thing. It was the dark shadows from the brambles, but they reached in farther and farther. This place, this is right at the center. But the shadows were almost everywhere else. They were halfway across the pond outside when—well, in the first part of the night."

What was the good of talking about it? Neither of them had any answers, not to these questions. She had no magic, and if what she wanted had changed the spell when it was first cast, it wasn't making any difference now.

"Why did you want to rescue me?" she asked abruptly. "I asked you that, at the beginning. You never told me. Not really."

She watched his face, watched him shift his attention from the enchantment to this question, watched his gaze drift to something only he could see, something in his past, and then down to the kitten next to him. "I wanted to be king," he said at last.

It didn't frighten her, but it did—disappoint her. She felt as though she had lost something she hadn't known she had, couldn't quite define even now what it had been. But apparently he wasn't so different from everyone else after all. "I see," she said, voice brittle.

He looked up quickly, must have heard something in her voice or seen it on her face, because he said, "Wait, let me explain it—tell you the longer version of the story."

"I understand all about men who want to be king."

"But I don't want to be king," he said, a direct contradiction of his own words. "I mean—it's not that simple. My father, King Elgin…he's a hard king. A strong one. But not a kind one. I don't think he knows how to be a king like that. He thinks it's more important that we be a powerful country, that we have armies to conquer or defend against our neighbors. He thinks the good of the country is more important than the good of any particular people, that it doesn't matter very much if some people don't send their children to school, or can't build a house with a decent roof. Or don't have enough to eat during a hard winter."

Rose found herself nodding. She knew about that kind of king. She knew about kings who didn't care at all if their people had enough to eat, never mind whether they thought something else was more important.

"I don't think he realizes all the need there is in the country. He only listens to the nobility, not the ordinary people. He hasn't held an open court in two years, so he doesn't even hear the problems. It doesn't bother most people at court, but—it doesn't seem right to me.

"My older brothers, Gregory, Tyler and Edward, it doesn't bother them either. He did his best, you know, as a father. He tried to teach us to be strong. My brothers are." Terrence was looking down at Emerald Eyes, scratching the kitten's head in an idle way, a little hint of red creeping across his face again though his voice was steady enough. "I've always been the different one; I don't know why. Maybe it's being the youngest. I spent more time with our mother. I never—fit in as well, with my brothers."

Rose wondered what he wasn't saying. What was being left unspoken in the pauses. Hadn't he said something, back when he first arrived, about being beat up by older brothers? She didn't ask, let him keep talking.

"I can use a sword well enough, but I never have beaten my oldest brother in a fight. And I'd rather read in the library than go out hunting. I'm the studious one." His slight smile was a little twisted. "I read philosophy and history, and I know that countries don't have to be the way mine is. Kings can be strong *and* kind. It can be better for the people in a country, all of the people, with the right king, making and enforcing the right kind of laws. I want that, for my country."

She hadn't known there were other ways to rule. She hadn't known anyone thought about that. She looked down at her hands, at the gold ring on her right hand, with its small oval printed with a stylized letter *A* backed by a crown. It was a symbol of rulership, of a power that had only ever been a theory for her.

Terrence sighed, rubbed the back of his neck. "The trouble is, my father and my brothers, none of them will ever be that kind of king. They have their own ways of thinking. And just recently—well, there were some promises made to our soldiers, about giving them land, setting up schools for their children. Gregory is crown prince, so the council put him in charge of that. And it's not going to happen. He's good at fighting, not administration, and he just—doesn't think it's very important. We're going to end up breaking those promises, and that's wrong. So I got to thinking, if *I* was crown prince, I could do something. People would listen to me more. And if I was king someday, I could really change things.

"I think, if I had the chance, I could be a different kind of king, and I'm the only one in the family who would be. So it has to be me, even though I'd rather stay in the library with the books. Only, I also knew it wouldn't ever *be* me. I'm the fourth son, too far from the throne. My two oldest brothers are already married, Gregory a couple years ago, Tyler last year. No children yet, but they'll have them soon enough. The succession line is never going to reach all the way to me.

"But there was you. The Legend of the Princess Behind Thorns. There are a lot of stories told, ballads sung. And you're still officially the heir to the throne. Every year on Coronation Day, part of the ceremony is to read out the line of succession, and you're still in it, next to inherit from my father. It's you, then Gregory, Tyler, Edward, me. A lot of people say you don't even exist, that it was all a story and the ceremony is only symbolic, but I looked into it. Officially, legally, you're still heir, and whoever rescues you…" He trailed off, and she was unsurprised to see the blush creep across his face again.

"Whoever rescues me becomes the next king," she finished, passing over unspoken the linking step. Her rescuer was supposed to marry her.

He nodded. "It seemed simpler, in the abstract. I mean, I wasn't even sure that you were really here. It was just this wild idea I had. I didn't know—what it would be like."

"You didn't expect me to be a person," she said quietly. She never had been, not really, to any of them.

"I'm sorry," he said, eyes crinkling as he finally looked into her face. "I'm sorry that I wasn't coming for purely altruistic reasons, just to rescue the princess under the curse. I'm sorry I didn't know who you were." His gaze shifted away, back down to the black kitten, who had rolled onto his back to have his chin scratched. Terrence's voice was very low as he said, "If I had it to do again, I would come just to rescue you. Even if there was no kingdom attached."

She had the strangest feeling that she was going to cry. She had become so emotional, these past few days. She looked away, blinked a few times. “Do you have a question today?” she asked at last, when she trusted her voice again.

It was a long while before he answered, long enough that she thought maybe he wasn’t going to ask a question at all. Finally, he said, “Do you want to be rescued? If the shadows weren’t encroaching and the thorn branches weren’t behaving strangely, would you want to leave?”

She hadn’t thought about it. She must have thought about it often, early on, but she was so used to the garden now. The garden was her world. Anything beyond it seemed—as mythical as she no doubt was to everyone out there. If she could go back to how it had been before the magic turned dark, before things went wrong, before Terrence stumbled out of the hedge… “I don’t know. That’s not much of an answer, but—I don’t know.”

Chapter Eight: Terrence

They had to do something about the thorns, about the spell on the garden. Terrence told himself that, very firmly and repeatedly, because the idea kept trying to slip away. There was something about this garden. He hadn't noticed anything definite at first, but by the fourth day—*was* it the fourth day? He made himself stop and count off. There was the day he arrived, explored with the cat, slept by the pond; the second day when he explored with Rose; the third day, when he kissed her and she screamed during the night; and today, the fourth day. Yes. By the fourth day he was convinced that part of the spell was to keep people inside from thinking about the spell. Or from paying attention to time passing.

Rose had changed the subject when Terrence initially tried to bring up the encroaching shadows, and it had been all too easy to shift into another topic, even a topic that was uncomfortable in its own way. But he managed to drag his attention back to the larger question afterwards—they had to do *something.* It wasn't even a question of gaining the throne, or his personal pride about rescuing a princess. It was about survival.

If someone had told him he'd someday be afraid of shadows killing him, he would have laughed. His brothers would laugh at him now, if they knew. But they hadn't seen those shadows. Seen the way they weren't really shadows, but the absence of anything. As though whatever they touched was consumed and disappeared.

So far the garden had been restored, unharmed, every daybreak, but how could they know it would keep happening, or that it was the same for people? They weren't part of the spell the way the garden was.

"We should explore again today," he said after they had finished eating breakfast. "Just, you know, see what we find."

It wouldn't help to directly say that they should look for a way to escape, or a solution to the threat of the thorns. Every time he'd tried that, it had only upset her.

She had been in here far longer than he had. How much had the spell worked on her, stopping her from thinking about it or how to leave?

It wasn't like being indirect fooled her anyway. "There isn't a way out," she said, but at least she said it with a slight smile, instead of growing angry.

"We can still look," he said with a shrug, trying to keep it casual. If she refused, he could search on his own. But he'd rather she came too. Because it would give them a better chance of finding an answer, obviously.

And of course that fully explained his pleased feeling when she picked up her kittens and agreed to explore with him.

As much as they could, they circled the outer edge, following the wall of thorns from inside. Terrence couldn't explain what he hoped to find, but it had to be better to do something than nothing. At least when he was doing something, it was easier to hang onto the idea that he *should* be doing something.

"There's no secret tunnel," Rose said, carrying Silvertips and lagging a few steps behind him as they walked. Emerald Eyes darted ahead of them. "I would have noticed it."

"I know," Terrence said, because he recognized it couldn't be that simple. "But maybe there's something…"

He tried reaching out, touching the nearest branch. It had worked from the outside. It hadn't worked when he tried it from the inside before, but maybe this time would be different and he could open a passage, or inspire the branches to do it for him.

He narrowly snatched his hand back in time to avoid a slashing branch striking towards him. No, apparently the thorns still didn't want to cooperate with him.

"Maybe you shouldn't touch them," Rose said dryly.

"The branches opened into a passage when I touched them before. From the outside, I mean." He didn't want her to think he was completely mad. Or an idiot.

"Did they?" She had her head tipped in that thoughtful way again.

Maybe he was an idiot after all, because he didn't realize what she was going to do until she set Silvertips down and stretched her hand towards a branch.

"Maybe you shouldn't—" he started, stepping towards her.

A branch lashed out, stabbing the back of her arm with three wickedly sharp thorns. Terrence flinched, reached out to haul her away even as she was already retreating. She backed into him, stumbling, and he caught her arms to steady her. The rustling wall of brambles subsided into silence again.

"I think that's the first time that's ever happened," Rose said, sounding more curious than concerned, looking down at her arm. Blood was welling up from three small scratches on her forearm, a few inches below where his fingers were wrapped around her upper arms. Her skin was warm and soft and she was leaning back against him…

Terrence hurriedly let go, moving a step away. He dug into a pocket in his jacket, produced a clean handkerchief, and offered it to her.

"Thank you," she said absently, and wound it around her arm.

He was a *terrible* rescuer. He knew the stories, and this was emphatically not how it was supposed to go. He wasn't supposed to let the princess be injured, he was supposed to find a way to get her out of here—but he didn't know enough about magic, he didn't know how this was supposed to work, and the best he could offer was a *handkerchief.*

Why hadn't there been more information in the royal library about this spell? It was such an unusual working—an enormous undertaking, on a scale beyond ordinary magic. A good number of people had affinities, a magical connection to a craft or an animal or a special skill. A few people had enchanter-level magic, capable of casting spells and reshaping the ordinary world. But this was on a level beyond that, the kind of enchantment that required either multiple enchanters or one very, very powerful one. Even when magic had approached this level in other cases, it was usually something far more standard, like battle magic or healing a plague.

Maybe the information was out there, somewhere, but he'd been so enthusiastic about his own absurd idea that he hadn't searched long enough to find it.

He glanced at his forearm. Though it was hidden by his sleeve, he could picture the lioness tattoo beneath. Did Mariqwe want him to be here? And if she did, what was he supposed to be *doing*?

Terrence sighed, staring at the wall of thorns looming above them. "I wish Gregory was here. Maybe he'd know what to do."

"That's your oldest brother, right?" Rose asked, tying off the ends of the handkerchief.

That felt strange. He'd never met someone before who didn't know the answer too well to ask that question. "Right. The crown prince." The one whose inheritance he was here to take. He didn't like to think about it that way though. He began walking again, following the curve of the thorn hedge without getting too close.

Rose fell into step beside him, Silvertips chasing around by her feet. "Is Prince Gregory good at puzzles? Or does he have magical ability?"

Terrence's brow furrowed. "Actually…no, not really." No one in the family had magical talent, not enchanter level or even any sort of affinity. In an academic way, Gregory probably knew no more than Terrence did about enchantments, and he definitely knew less about puzzles or old legends.

"Then why would he know what to do?" Rose pursued.

"I don't know—he's always been the one who was best at everything. When we were growing up, you know. I guess I tend to assume…" Gregory was the best at military things. The things that mattered to their father.

"How much older is he?"

"Ten years."

"*Ten—*" Rose looked at him with eyes suddenly wide. "Then *of course* he was better at things while you were growing up!"

He knew that. Of course he knew that. But it wasn't as simple as Rose was making it sound. "Yes, but—I mean, that doesn't really account for—Gregory's just naturally better at…" He gave up, because he didn't know how to explain this. "You probably would have had to be there."

"Hmm." Rose was studying the clouds overhead as they walked, her voice entirely too light as she asked, "Does your cousin Elena think Gregory is better than you at everything?"

If he said yes, he'd likely win this—was it an argument? But it would also be lying. "Elena…is probably somewhat biased."

"I think I'd like Elena," Rose remarked, bending down to scoop up her black kitten again.

Terrence let her walk ahead of him, so he could watch her while he tried to decide what that was supposed to mean. Did Rose think he was better than Gregory at some things? But she couldn't know; she'd never met Gregory.

And he didn't see that he'd done anything since he got here to impress her. After all, they were still here.

Chapter Nine: Rose

Terrence kept looking for an escape from the garden long after Rose felt it was pointless. Though really, she had mostly thought it was pointless from the beginning. She understood why he wanted to get out, understood perhaps even better than he did the threat of those encroaching shadows every night. But she saw no solution in reach, had no faith that one existed, and somehow, it was very hard to keep believing that it was worth searching for an answer that probably wasn't there.

After all, why would anyone cast a spell and give *her* the power to break it?

She had never had power, and she had never had magic. A distant memory from the Before Time told her that, some time, when she was very small, she had thought that having the latter might give her the former. That things would be different, if she ever showed herself to have the elusive talent needed to become an enchantress. Maybe because she saw her father's court enchanters, and knew they had power inside of them.

But she'd never shown any magical ability, not even an affinity. Perhaps she had some small talent at gardening, but in an enchanted garden, any magic in her plants was probably nothing to do with her. And any talent certainly didn't extend to controlling magical walls of thorns.

Eventually, even Terrence gave it up for the time. They had wandered all morning, and Rose wanted to curl up with one of her books. She surprised herself a little, when she told Terrence he might come with her.

They spent the rest of the day reading in the bower, kittens alternately napping and tumbling about. Terrence recognized some of her favorite books, and she offered up others. They read passages aloud, talked about them or laughed over them or argued about different ideas. She liked his laugh, and she liked how he looked when he laughed.

When they glanced over a book about the gods, Rose remarked on Terrence's lioness tattoo. Perhaps she wouldn't have if his sleeve had been down, but he had rolled it up again and the black and gold ink was clear in the dappled sunlight. She recognized the design, the traditional depiction of the god's symbol animal.

He glanced down at the tattoo, reached out with his opposite hand to lightly touch the lioness' forehead with two fingers, a gesture that seemed both habitual and reverent. "It's the custom for princes to swear to a god when they turn sixteen. Not swear in the priestly sense, just in the follower way. Did they do that back in your day?"

"Maybe." She couldn't really remember. It hadn't made much impression, if that had been the custom, and it wasn't hard to guess why not. "We didn't have any princes." That was how she had ended up in here to begin with.

"Oh," Terrence said, cheeks faintly pink. "Right. Of course."

She hadn't meant to embarrass him, and tried to brush past it. "Do you follow Mariqwe in their love or warrior aspect?" The God of Passion, Mariqwe was strongly associated with both, though most depictions emphasized one or the other. Her own statue, tucked into a niche, was a female warrior.

Terrence shrugged. "Not exactly either. I mean, not either one exclusively. It never seemed to me that the two should be separated completely. It would be nice if love was easy with no aspect of battle, but it isn't always that way—and a warrior shouldn't be completely without love either."

"More philosophy," she said with a half-smile.

"The studious one, remember?" he said, raising the book he was holding in salute.

The conversation drifted on, and she didn't ask about the choice he *had* made. He might not want to divide the two sides of the god's nature, but he had chosen a tattoo that was clearly a female lioness, choosing the god in feminine form. She wondered about that decision. She was almost sure that the men she had known before had preferred their gods to look like themselves.

The day gradually passed away, and as the world around them darkened, Rose could see the shadows even from the bower. She could see the way they were stretching closer and closer. Surrounding them.

"I suppose," she said, "you had better sleep in here tonight. It may not be safe, out by the pond."

He cast her a long look she didn't know how to read, and then merely nodded agreement. They lay down on opposite sides of the small space, to listen to the thorns shriek and scream again. No new memories came to her this time. Maybe she had finally remembered it all. Or the worst, at least. Or maybe it made a difference not being alone.

Somewhere, deep in the night, she heard Terrence say her name. "What?" she asked, lifting her head.

"I just wondered if you were asleep."

She shivered. "No."

"We could talk."

"I'd like that."

They talked through the long hours of the night, sometimes dozing but never for very long. And somehow, gradually, they moved closer together, until they were side by side in the middle of the bower. Finally the sky overhead began to lighten, to turn gray and then blue.

The shadows didn't retreat. The thorns went on scraping and shuddering.

Rose sat up, looking out through the gaps in the bower's woven walls. Blackness crouched all about them. She shivered, wrapping her arms around herself.

"The spell must be breaking down," Terrence said, sitting up too, staring at the shadows. "It wasn't meant to last this long, and now the magic is coming apart."

"But we don't know how to end the spell," she said, voice shaking. "And we're trapped here." Maybe they should have kept trying the day before. Or maybe it was better, that they'd enjoyed their one final afternoon.

"You're certain there was nothing, when they cast the spell—you didn't know *anything* about how it was supposed to end?" Terrence demanded.

They had been over this all before! "Someone strong enough to get through the challenge was supposed to wake me up," she recited, gaze fixed on the shadows. Were they moving? "That was what they kept saying. But it twisted, it changed. The spell was never supposed to look this way, and it didn't lift when you came through the thorns."

Terrence shook his head, dragged one hand through his hair. "It has to be something to do with you. You're at the center of this. The spell changed for you, the way to end it must—"

"I don't *know*! No one told me anything. They *never* told me anything, they never believed I could think or feel or care about anything. I never mattered except for my bloodline, I never had any choices, I was never allowed to want anything, in my entire life!"

She was shouting over the noise of the thorns now, and they were still getting louder. Louder and louder and she didn't think she could shout loud enough now to be heard. And the shadows were coming. They were spilling through the branches around her bower, swallowing up the walls, swallowing up her bookcase, her bed, her goddess statue.

She bumped into Terrence as they both scrambled backwards, to the very center of the space. She turned towards him, reached out—and this time, the instinct wasn't like reaching for one of her cats. She clung to him and he wrapped his arms tightly around her. She buried her face against his shoulder as they pressed close enough that she could feel the hard circle of the ring beneath his shirt, couldn't tell if she was hearing his heart pounding or her own. He was warm and alive and real, the realest thing she had ever known, the last thing left in her world. Even the kittens had disappeared.

It would all be over in another moment. The shadows were still coming, were closing in around them. And she felt—not afraid.

She felt angry.

She had never had a chance. She had never had any chance to want anything, to make any choice. To live.

And now it was all going to be over. She had only minutes, seconds left.

She wanted something, she realized. She didn't know when she had started wanting it, but now, in this moment, she wanted just one thing. She had one chance to make one choice.

Rose lifted her head from Terrence's shoulder, twisted in his embrace so they faced each other, so close his features were blurry in her vision. Then she kissed him.

She pressed her lips against his and clenched her fingers in his shirt and kissed him, and after a heartbeat he was kissing her back.

It wasn't like before. His lips moved against hers and she could feel him and she could taste him and she thought dying while kissing Terrence might be the best way her world could end after all.

So she didn't actually see the spell end.

Her eyes were closed and every part of her was focused on Terrence's mouth on hers, his body against hers, and when she finally noticed that the world had stopped howling it was with a surprised jolt. She pulled away, opened her eyes, and looked around at an empty, commonplace, sunlit meadow.

"What happened?" she whispered, gazing at this ordinary, extraordinary sight. The world had been ending, and suddenly…

"You kissed me," Terrence answered, a smile in his voice.

"I know *that* part," she said, and she was disentangling herself from his arms as she spoke, rising up to her feet to stare around her. An empty meadow of gray-green grass, stretching into the distance but still smaller than her garden had been, bordered by nearly-leafless trees. It was almost more disconcerting than the walls of shadows. "Where are we?"

"I think this is where the thorns and your garden were," Terrence said, slowly standing up. "That looks like the right forest. Not that most bits of a forests look all that different from each other. But I think this is the same place I came to. Just…with no magic anymore."

"Because the spell ended," she said softly, taking a deep breath, trying to find her balance again. The air felt colder, an unfamiliar chill against her skin. "Just at the last moment. The spell ended."

"Did you guess that would happen?" he asked, still looking at the far-off trees. "Is that why you kissed me?"

Before she could answer, two small furry shapes popped up out of the long grass, bounding over to twine between her ankles. "My kittens," she cried, scooping them up and holding them to her chest. "I knew it! Cats go where they want to."

The kittens squirmed against the bodice of her dress—a different dress, she realized, not the blue one she had been wearing only moments before. This one was white, with silver accents, and her feet, bare before, were in silver slippers. She remembered these clothes; she had been enchanted in them. Apparently this was another aspect of the spell ending. Terrence's handkerchief, tied over the scratches on her arm, had also disappeared, but the scratches had already begun to heal anyway.

Between the clothing and the kittens, it was a moment or two before she realized Terrence was watching her, face intent.

"What is it?" she asked, looking back at him over her armful of purring kittens.

The moment their gazes met, he looked away. "You don't have to marry me. Just because I got through the thorns and now the spell is broken—you don't have to. We both know that's how it was supposed to work, but that's—I didn't even rescue you, not really, but that doesn't matter, it wasn't right to begin with and I wouldn't—presume, and you don't—you don't have to."

Slowly she let the kittens drop, studying him, wondering with a little shiver of fear what this meant. Was he trying to be kind? Or had an abstract princess been easier to imagine marrying? Did he not want to deal with her after all, and if not, what was she possibly going to do? And yet, when they had kissed, it had felt like…

"I know it wasn't exactly the kind of rescue you were expecting," she said carefully, watching his face. "I mean, *I* kissed *you* and broke the spell. But it was like I—it was like I woke up," she realized, "in that last moment. In a way. So maybe you did wake me up. And maybe I still need…"

"A friend?" he cut in dryly, and something in his voice, something in his face, suggested he really hated that answer.

And that started a warm glow in her chest, made a smile form on her face. "No. Not a—friend." They stared at each other, a slow smile beginning on his face to answer the one on hers. "If I don't *have* to marry you, does that mean I can't?"

"No," he said, smile broadening. "It doesn't mean that."

Her degree of relief frightened her. She took a breath, then waved one hand at the meadow around them. "You know, there's no spell to end now. But you could still kiss me. If you want to."

No more hesitating and pausing now, he crossed the space between them in two steps, swept her up and kissed her. She wrapped her arms around him, held on tightly and kissed him back. It didn't have the same desperation of that kiss as the shadows had surrounded them, but there was still the echo of that urgency, that hunger to come together, to feel and touch and explore.

"You ought to know," she said at length, breathless, "I didn't know kissing you would lift the spell. I just did it because I wanted to."

Part Two

Late Winter, Year 512

Chapter Ten: Rose

The world was different outside the thorns. Rose couldn't stop looking at the horizons, at the meadow stretching on and on around her, to the distant trees and sky. The meadow was smaller than her garden, but she hadn't been able to see across the garden like this. For a hundred years her world had been surrounded by high hedges of thorns, cut up by stands of trees. It had been so familiar that she knew every path and every shrub. Now the spell had lifted, her garden was gone, and she had the entire world before her.

What was out there? *Who* was out there? How was she going to face…whatever there was?

But there was Terrence. She had Terrence. She gripped his hand, and it was warm and reassuring while the air was cool and everything else was uncertain.

"It's only a day's ride, but a long walk back home," he said, glancing around. "My horse Barley must be long gone by now. I hope he headed home, or was caught by someone who'll take care of him…" He frowned, looking troubled. "I didn't expect to be behind the thorns for five days."

"I didn't expect to be there for a hundred years," Rose murmured. Would it be any easier, if she had been asleep as planned, if it felt as though only a single night had passed? She remembered the last, terrible day of the Before Time, the day the spell was cast, and her fingers tightened instinctively on Terrence's.

No, it probably wouldn't be better if that was more recent in her mind.

She hadn't missed Terrence's casual reference to going *home* either. Home to Lavernon, the capital city. Home to the king's castle. His home. It had been her home, once, but would it all be different now, or still mostly the same? She wasn't sure which prospect was more alarming.

He was smiling at her, a smile that helped to force back the ghosts of long ago, her fears for the future. "I didn't expect a lot of things when I came here."

"You expected a princess," she reminded him.

"But I didn't expect *you*," he said, drawing in closer to her and she knew he was going to kiss her again. But just before he would have, he jumped instead, and looked down at the kitten who had pounced on his leg. "I didn't expect kittens either."

Her other cats seemed to have wandered away as mysteriously as they had arrived back at the beginning of the spell, but her two kittens were still frolicking around them. She smiled, letting go of Terrence's hand to pry Silvertips away from his boot, to scoop up the gray kitten and cuddle her beneath her chin.

"Can we find a horse somewhere?" Rose asked, tickling the purring Silvertips.

Terrence was watching her with an expression that made her blush and look away. After a few seconds, he said, "I expect we could get a horse at the nearest village. It's a couple of miles. If you'd rather rest here, I could go—"

"I'd rather come with you," she said instantly. She wasn't ready to be alone in this big new world. "I've been chasing cats for decades. I can walk a couple of miles." Perhaps it was a good thing that her clothes had transformed back to the ones she had worn when she was enchanted, including her shoes.

"All right. It should be this way." He gestured toward the tree line, but didn't move immediately. He was looking around, and after a moment shook his head. "My sword's gone too. Not that we should need it—this is a safe enough area. Maybe someone from the village picked it up."

She hadn't pictured Terrence having a sword. He was the scholar—but hadn't he said that he knew how to use a sword? Still, it felt like a new piece of the puzzle, of the idea of him she had in her head. There would probably be a lot of new pieces. That was disquieting. But it would be all right—he was *Terrence*. She knew him. She didn't know all of him, but she did know him.

Holding hands and wrangling kittens, they walked away through the meadow and under the trees, following a faint path. Someone had been coming here, in all the years she had been hidden away, but not many people. What had it been like, the first few months and years? When the champions she remembered had still been alive to come and try their lives among the thorns.

She had never traveled this path to come here. She had gone to sleep in her bedroom at the castle and awoken behind the thorns. So she had no memory of the village, couldn't compare it from the past to the present. Whatever it had been before, now it was barely big enough to be dignified with the name. Just a tiny cluster of a half-dozen ramshackle buildings, with no one in sight except the owner of the establishment that appeared to serve as blacksmith, hostelry and tavern all rolled together. As befitting a blacksmith, he was a huge man with muscles bulging beneath his sleeves as he tossed hay at one end of his building.

Terrence called a cheerful and apparently unself-conscious, "Good morning, Blake!"

The man—Blake—stopped work to lean on his pitchfork, staring at Terrence with a broad smile breaking across his face. "Your Highness, you're all right! We wondered what had become of you after you rode out of here." And then his gaze shifted to Rose, and stayed there.

It had been so long since she had seen anyone, and this man was—well, not Terrence, though she wouldn't be able to classify the entire world's population as *Terrence or not* for long. For the moment, she fought her instinct to step behind Terrence, to instead stay where she was and not look away.

His attention also shifted to Rose. "Ah, Blake, this is—"

"Rose," she interrupted. She wasn't—quite ready, to greet anyone as the cursed princess, object of song and legend. Although if she really was a legend, giving even her name was probably too much for anonymity. "Just…Rose."

"Milady," Blake said with a deep nod, gaze growing no less curious. Perhaps the title meant he guessed something, or perhaps he was just responding to the obviously fine clothes she was wearing and the company she was keeping. This was probably foolish of her—the man had to know a princess was enchanted near his village, and now a woman in an elegant gown appeared…

Terrence cleared his throat. "So I got into a bit of a spot a few days ago, and now I'm wondering if my horse came back this way."

Blake jerked a thumb over his shoulder towards a low building, presumably a stable. "Yeah, I've got him in the stall at the end there. He wandered in not long after you left. We thought you might have—well, we looked around in the woods for you, and sent a message to the capital. No one's come yet."

A prince's horse came back riderless, and in five days no one from the palace had come to investigate the matter? It didn't ring right to Rose, but she wasn't sure what to conclude from it. Only that it was information, and any information about the world she was returning to was worth having.

Terrence seemed far more pleased than bothered. "I didn't mean to worry all of you. And that's a relief about my horse; I was worried about *him*. Come on, Rose, come and meet Barley."

Rose had never been taught to ride—princes got to ride, while princesses were neatly shut away in carriages—and mostly knew horses as large, strange creatures at the front of those carriages. She summoned up a smile though, and followed Terrence to the stable, the kittens trotting along after her.

"You'll like him," Terrence said, leading her between the rows of stalls. "He's very friendly. Well, as long as I'm friendly to someone. He's trained for battle too, all princes' horses are."

A whicker cut in on the conversation, and a horse's face thrust out from the last stall, clearly looking around for whoever was talking. Or maybe the horse knew who was talking, and that's why he was looking. She didn't know enough about horses. Terrence laughed and quickened his pace. She didn't want to look cowardly so she let him draw her on.

"Barley, this is Rose. We like her," Terrence said, apparently seriously. He turned to her again. "Let him sniff your hand."

She cautiously extended one hand, felt a warm horse's nose against her palm. It tickled, which made it easier to not think about that casual remark about battle training. Barley was brown and huge, and she had no idea how to judge him beyond that—though presumably he was a very fine horse if he was a prince's particular mount.

It made her smile, when Terrence rubbed Barley between the ears and the horse responded by nosing all over his shirt with apparently equal delight. She might have guessed Terrence was the type to view his horse as a friend.

They left Barley in the stall, the kittens staying behind to make friends with the big horse, and stepped out of the stable. Blake had disappeared, and Terrence frowned. "I wanted to make sure I paid him for taking care of Barley. Let's check the tavern. We should get something to eat anyway before we leave—oh, are you hungry?"

She was, and there was no orchard to go to for breakfast. Food was suddenly a whole new complication in this big new world, and did she want to go into a tavern to look for it? Could she suggest staying in the stable with Barley, who now seemed like the less alarming prospect?

No, because that would be cowardly too. She was going to have to get used to people again—though she had a bad feeling she'd never been all that comfortable with them, even in the Before Time. "Breakfast sounds good," she said, managing a smile.

The tavern was small and dim, but not too dim to show three people, one of them Blake, in huddled conference at a table.

"Good morning," Terrence said without apparent awkwardness. Though he did put an arm around Rose's waist, a support she was grateful for.

The group at the table all but sprang apart. A young woman darted off towards the back room, then stayed in the doorway peering at Terrence and Rose, while Blake and an older woman approached.

There was no possible way they didn't realize who Rose was.

"Your Highness, it *is* good to see you back again," the woman said to Terrence, bobbing a curtsy, glance sliding over to Rose. "When your horse came back alone, and we knew you'd ridden off towards the thorns—well, we imagined the worst might have happened. My man here went to check the thorns and didn't find you among them, but of course we couldn't be sure of anything."

Rose blanched. She had somehow never quite put the thoughts together to picture what would have happened, if Terrence *hadn't* got through the wall of thorns. If he had been caught like the other champions instead—she would have had to listen to him dying, though of course she wouldn't have known he was *Terrence*, and then—

"Are you her?" the woman asked eagerly, giving Rose very little time to cope with the grisly thoughts she was having. "Are you really—I mean, anyone can see at a glance you're a fine lady, and as beautiful as the stories say, but are you really—"

"Now, now," Blake rumbled, "it's none of our business—"

"Yes," Rose said, because what was the point of denying it? "I'm her. I'm the one from the story."

A kind of sigh went through Blake, his wife, and the girl in the doorway—their daughter, maybe? "The Princess Behind Thorns," Blake's wife said in reverent tones. "I've been hearing ballads all my life but I never thought I'd see you awaken and—"

"We were just hoping for some breakfast, Margery," Terrence cut in, tightening his arm around Rose's waist, "if you don't mind? And I'm sorry for any trouble you were all put to, looking for me, or sending a message to the capital. I'll pay you for your time, of course."

"Oh no, no," Blake said, "we weren't expecting anything like that. Only did what seemed right—"

"And might keep the capital from blaming us, if anything—that is—" Margery turned hurriedly away. "I'll get that breakfast for you, won't be a moment."

"I'm sure no one could blame you," Terrence said, but Rose could see what they were thinking. A prince rides into a small village and isn't seen again. That's the sort of situation that can bring a lot of trouble down onto that village. "And at least let me pay you for Barley's keep. I know he's a big eater."

The conversation moved into a discussion of horses and the going rate of hay. Rose sat down at the nearest table, and Margery mercifully delivered bowls of very decent porridge without resuming her ruminations on the legendary Princess Behind Thorns.

Rose hadn't known that was what they were calling her. Terrence had mentioned it, but she hadn't given it too much thought at the time. Apparently she was going to be hearing it a lot from now on.

They were almost finished with breakfast when Blake and Margery's daughter approached, gaze shyly lowered, and offered a sheathed sword, belt wrapped around it, to Terrence. "My father found this near the thorns," she said softly. "We thought it must be yours."

"Thank you," Terrence said, taking it from her, and smiled at her. "You've saved me an awkward explanation with the castle armorers. They don't like it when we lose swords."

The young woman blushed and fled without another word.

Rose wondered if *she* looked like that, that awkward and uncomfortable with people. It must be nice, if you had to be that way, to live the kind of life where you could flee if you wanted to.

Done with his meal, Terrence stood up to strap his sword back on, and Rose looked down into her nearly empty bowl. It didn't change anything, just because Terrence had a sword and was comfortable wearing it.

They got on their way soon enough after that, after Terrence paid a handful of coins for breakfast, the care of his horse, a basket for Rose's kittens, and a bundle of food for the road. She hadn't thought about money in years, couldn't recall that she'd ever had much opportunity to use it in the Before Time either.

Terrence boosted Rose onto Barley's back, and she pretended that she didn't feel precariously high from the ground. It was a little better after he swung into the saddle behind her, with the ease of obviously long experience. She held onto the basket with the kittens on her lap, and appreciated Terrence's solid presence behind her.

She could remember imagining something like this, in the first days of the spell. Carried home triumphantly on some champion's horse. She had expected to be a prize, the property of whatever man came to claim her. She had never been able to imagine the man in the pictures as more than a vague outline, had shied away from whatever dark images her mind began to conjure.

Now she looked back at Terrence and smiled. She had not imagined the reality could be this good.

They talked and laughed and the sun shone warmly and even the kittens behaved well, eventually falling asleep in their basket, and though it was more tiring to sit on a horse than she would have guessed, she still would not have minded a long, long journey like this. But the shadows were only just starting to stretch, the sun still well above the horizon, when Terrence said they were reaching the end of the forest, coming close to their destination.

They came out through the trees and Terrence pulled Barley up to a halt on the brow of the hill, looking down at the first sight of the castle on another hill in the distance, the capital city spread out beneath it.

It was the same castle, and the sight of it brought more of the Before Time back into much sharper clarity. She wondered if this would be any easier if it was a different place, but castles survived so much longer than people. She looked down at it, at the gray stones that looked forbidding even in the sunlight, and shivered.

Terrence's voice was soft in her ear, his breath whispering across her neck. "Should we stop here for a few minutes? Before we go on to the capital?"

It was only delaying the inevitable, but she didn't feel ready yet for that next step. "That would be nice."

They got down from the horse, sat on a large rock alongside the road. Even if she had been sitting all day, sitting on a horse was very different and it felt good to take a seat on something more stable. Terrence wrapped his hand around hers, and she knew she was probably holding on too tightly as she looked down at the castle again.

Terrence squeezed her fingers. "Are you all right?"

"Yes," she said, because it seemed like the only thing to say. She wanted to be all right. Probably she would be all right. Nothing was actually *wrong*, just because the castle he lived in reminded her of her own life so long ago, a life that was so different from what she'd known these past years in the garden. If there was anywhere else to go—but there wasn't, was there? She knew nothing about this world, knew no one else in it.

His voice was even softer when he asked, "Are you afraid?"

She sighed, leaned against him. She could lie and pretend, but—he'd probably see through it anyway. And she didn't want to lie to Terrence. "Yes."

"Anyone who frightened you before has been gone a long time."

"I know." She wasn't afraid of anyone specific. It was more the idea of people, curious crowds of people like the villagers this morning. And more frightening –

powerful people who would look at her and see a chess piece in a complicated game. She hadn't forgotten that Terrence had said his father was not a kind king. Or what else he had said, very early on, before she knew him well enough to care—that he was the youngest one who was beat up by three older brothers. She wasn't certain she wanted to meet those brothers. "There will be other people, though. People who won't be—kind." More people who wouldn't be Terrence.

She felt Terrence's sigh across her hair. "True. But you're not alone. I won't let anything happen to you. And there are good people here too. I have friends here."

"Friends," she said, trying the word out. "I never had those." Maybe something was still hiding in the holes in her memory, but she didn't think so. Surely she would have remembered by now. All that came to mind when she tried to connect the idea of friends to her past were images of the castle cats.

It must be nice, to have friends. Maybe there would be people here who weren't Terrence, but were—a little bit like him.

He wrapped his arm around her, a comfort. "It's going to be different now." He lifted his free hand, lightly touched her hair, fingers gentle. "Look at me?"

She turned towards him, lifting her face to look into his a few inches away, at his dark eyes and the little scar by his left eyebrow.

He touched her face, drew a tingling line down the curve of her cheek. "What frightened you the most?" he asked. "Before?"

She had been afraid so often. But mostly it had come down to one thing. "Not having choices. Not having any say in my life."

"It won't be that way now," he said, gaze steady. "I'll never take your choices away, and I'll help you against anyone who tries."

His words warmed her, gave her courage to say the other thing that had frightened her most, the one choice that had been most important and least her own. Her gaze dropped, her voice with it. “And I was afraid…of being forced to marry a cruel man. One who would hurt me.”

“Never,” he whispered, arms drawing her closer to him. “Never, never, never.” He pressed a kiss against her forehead and it felt different than their earlier kisses; it felt like a promise, like something solemn and deliberate, his lips lingering against her skin.

She wrapped her fingers in the folds of his shirt and lifted her face again to his. “Kiss me,” she whispered.

He did and it was different too, not the hungry ardor of before but soft, sweet. His lips were gentle against hers, just barely parting to run the tip of his tongue along her lower lip. The kiss deepened slowly, not overwhelming her but drawing her in, filling her with gladness to be here, now, with *this* man. A man who could kiss her like that, who would think to kiss her like that when she spoke of being frightened—that was who she wanted to be with.

Chapter Eleven: Terrence

It felt strange, riding down to the capital city with Rose sitting so straight and still in front of him. Terrence could see the castle, up at the top of the hill with all the other buildings of Lavernon covering the slopes around it. His father's castle.

He was going to have to face his father, and his brothers, and all the rest of the council and the court, and it was not going to be easy.

It was probably going to be terrible, actually.

The whole idea, coming back with the Princess Behind Thorns, claiming the right of inheritance through a betrothal, had seemed much more abstract when he set out. As abstract as the princess herself. With no real assurance that she was even there, he hadn't needed to think too hard about this part.

It had all been a wild, improbable, fantastical quest. Would he even have done it, if Gregory hadn't beaten him in a sword fight the day before he left, in front of his father and brothers and the entire rest of the court? And if that hadn't happened directly after the council had dismissed his carefully-prepared plan for how they could keep their promises to the soldiers, distribute land and improve education?

But now he was about to ask for the succession to change, and half the court, most especially Gregory, were never going to forgive him for it.

His mother would have been sad about that, about conflict between her sons. But maybe, Terrence hoped, she would have been proud of him too. She would have understood what he was trying to do, why he *had* to do this. That it wasn't because he wanted to hurt Gregory or anyone else, but that he wanted to be a different sort of king, a better one, who could make things in the country better.

What really counted was how his father reacted. His father valued strength and ambition and boldness, qualities he had never thought Terrence had in sufficient quantities. Maybe this would finally prove something. Or maybe his father was going to hate the idea of his youngest, never very satisfactory son becoming his heir.

He'd have to see too what Elena thought of all this. She was more likely to approve; she was always more likely to approve, whatever he did. Unless she told him he was an idiot for setting off on a fool quest and upsetting everything. But no, hopefully she'd understand. Hopefully she'd like Rose. And she would certainly have a flood of questions about everything.

He drew in a deep breath as Barley approached the main road. He'd have to face whatever came, from Elena's questions to his father's probable disapproval, and he'd better stay composed in the meantime if he didn't want to spook Barley or Rose. He knew how to calm Barley, but he really, really didn't want to make Rose any more afraid than she already was, whatever he had to do to prevent it.

Terrence looked down at her, at her blond hair and the curve of her cheek just visible from this angle, and found himself smiling in spite of his fears. After all, whatever reason had set him off on this quest, he was glad he had gone. Whatever happened next, he was glad about Rose. And he'd be glad in the long-term, if he could make the country better as a result.

They picked up the main road a short way out of the forest, joining a stream of other travelers. Most were on foot, and at this time of day most were going the opposite direction, home after a day of selling goods or buying supplies in the capital.

They didn't talk to anyone on the road. Between his horse and his clothes—and probably Rose's dress—people recognized they were at least aristocracy. Some may have been able to identify him, though most people who would be able to do that lived in the capital and wouldn't be leaving now. The travelers on the road gave them a wide berth, staring but not speaking. This usually happened when he went riding, even when he didn't use the saddlebags with the royal insignia; he disliked it as a rule, that people thought avoidance the best way to respond to nobility. Today though, he was relieved for Rose's sake. There would be enough people to talk to in the city. So he just smiled and nodded to the people staring—which generally made them stare more—and kept riding.

They arrived before the main city gate was closed, the usual four guards on duty, brown uniforms against the gray stone. There were other ways through the wall that circled Lavernon proper, but this was the easiest one, and the one he had left from.

The commander of the guard hailed them as they approached, and Terrence searched his memory for the man's name. Simond, that was it.

"Welcome back, Your Highness," Commander Simond said, a wide grin splitting his face. "We started to think you weren't returning." And then his gaze moved very definitely to Rose. He nodded respectfully. "My lady…?"

The question was unspoken, but evident. He and Rose had agreed on the road that there was no reason to be secretive at this point. He felt the people ought to know that the Princess Behind Thorns had returned, and Rose had agreed it was better that way—though with the thoughtful tilt to her head that made him suspect she was thinking more than she was saying. He wanted to know what she was thinking, about everything, but he still wasn't certain how many questions she was going to be comfortable answering. They had to be past the one question a day rule, but he wasn't sure that meant they were in a place where all questions were welcome.

Now that they were up to it, Rose only inclined her head in acknowledgement but stayed silent. His line, then.

Pride warmed Terrence's voice as he said, "This is Princess Rose Amelia. The Princess Behind Thorns."

Commander Simond's eyes went round. "The princess…you awoke the princess…? Your Highness!" This time the title seemed directed at Rose, a bare second before the commander dropped to one knee, head bowed.

His men followed his lead, knees bending and heads dropping in respectful acknowledgement, then bobbing up again almost at once to look at Rose. Many of the people approaching the gate or passing through stopped as well; more were drawing closer, driven by the curiosity that always gathered a crowd for any spectacle in the city.

Murmurs and whispers rippled out through the growing throng, and more heads bowed, more knees bent.

Terrence felt Rose tense, and he tightened his arm where it wrapped around her waist. What must this be like, after a hundred years alone in a garden?

She surprised him when she lifted her head, took a deep breath, and sent her voice out over the crowd, carrying easily above the footsteps and whispers. "Thank you for your support, my friends, and for your kind welcome. I am so pleased to be among you once more." Then she leaned back and murmured for Terrence alone, "Start riding, or we'll never get out of here."

Had her father had the same rule his did, about traveling through the city? Never stop moving. Usually he disliked that rule, but today she had a point. He started Barley slowly forward and the crowd gave way, still gazing up at them. "You did that well," he said into her ear.

"I remember some things about being a princess," she said, and sounded more grim than pleased.

It made him want to stop and kiss her and reassure her again—but this was emphatically not the time or place. They'd never get through the crowd that way, plus his father had another, even more unbending rule—the family could never display personal feelings in front of anyone, certainly not crowds of the curious. If he was seen kissing the Princess Behind Thorns on the main avenue, the entire city would know about it within hours, the entire country within days. He didn't want something that felt new and special and private flying around the country as gossip about the royalty.

They kept moving, and the crowd at the gate proved only the beginning. Word had to be spreading through town faster than they were riding. No doubt someone was running for the castle this minute. As they rode up the high street, more and more people flocked to line the way, to catch a glimpse of them. He'd been up and down this road all his life, and he'd never seen this many people gather, outside of a planned parade.

He kept one eye on the crowd and one on Rose and didn't worry about Barley, who was used to people. Rose kept her head up, and though he couldn't see her face well, when she turned far enough he could glimpse that she was smiling. He wasn't sure if it was the same smile she'd worn in the garden. Her shoulders seemed tense, though her posture remained perfect.

The crowd waved and cheered as they passed. A few called his name, as always when any royalty rode through, but many more were calling, "Princess Rose," or "the Princess Behind Thorns."

Now and then he recognized someone—the butcher who sold meat to the castle kitchens, the woman who sold Elena's favorite yarn, the baker who made the best cookies in the city, though he'd never wanted to tell the castle baker that. He waved an acknowledgement to the people he knew, appreciating familiar faces in this enormous crowd.

"They like you," Rose said softly.

"Me? It's you they're excited about."

"Not only me."

He shifted. Just because he knew a few people, that hardly signified. "I'm just friendly, that's all. Even when I was small, I used to wave back when I was supposed to look, I don't know, regal. My father always hated it."

Had a messenger got to the castle by now? Did his father know what was coming up the hill?

He looked back at the crowd, searching for more familiar faces, and swiftly spotted one right at the front, slightly ahead on the road. Camden, a shopkeeper from the main market, was standing there with his small daughter Abigail on his shoulders, both looking wide-eyed at Rose.

"That little girl there, with her father," Terrence said, nudging Rose to direct her attention to the right. "I know him, he sells roasted nuts in the market. If we pause there…"

Abigail was holding out a flower, the bloom waving in her small fist. "Of course," Rose said. "The crowd will love it."

He had mostly thought the little girl would, but Rose was right too. They stopped just long enough for her to accept the small red flower and tuck it into her hair. A renewed surge of cheers accompanied them on the last stretch up to the castle.

These gates were open too, though normally they'd be closed at this time. They rode in through the wide doors, under the stone arch, and Rose shivered as the archway's shadow fell over her.

He brushed a kiss on the top of her hair, whispered, "All right?"

"Yes," she said, but the word was faint and he didn't believe her. She was still tense, as though she was holding herself tightly together.

Most of the population of the castle seemed to be out in the courtyard. At least, all the cooks and maids and stableboys and castle guard. Terrence knew all but the newest by face and name, could identify most of their roles. And it didn't even require that kind of knowledge to recognize that no one here was aristocracy. That meant they had probably already gathered somewhere else, most likely the throne room.

For a fleeting moment, he wished they'd found a way to slip in unnoticed. But that would likely have been impossible.

He drew up Barley in the center of the courtyard, and all those gathered people dropped to their knees. He wished they wouldn't. It felt different than the guards at the gate, and unlike the crowds outside, these people were silent. They stared less openly too, though most couldn't resist peeking.

Terrence swung down from his horse, and lifted Rose down as well. For a moment they stood together, her hands on his shoulders, not immediately stepping out of position.

"Would it be inappropriate to say welcome home?" Terrence asked, trying to catch her eye, forcing himself to smile despite the strangeness of this moment.

Rose smiled back at him, but it definitely wasn't the smile he'd come to know in the garden. Maybe hers was forced too. And was it for him, or for all those staring eyes? "I think," she said carefully, "you had best introduce me to your father."

Chapter Twelve: Rose

Rose carried Silvertips in one arm as they walked through the halls of the castle, her other hand clasped in Terrence's. Emerald Eyes seemed content to frisk along beside them, staying close by in this new landscape.

Everywhere was familiar and strange, the outlines wakening memories, the details jarring with the pictures in her mind. The same halls, but different curtains, different portraits. Different people. Rose looked at the faces, feeling a disconcerting sense of echoes. None sparked recognition exactly, yet many set off a tickle of familiarity. Family lines and shared features, perhaps many were the descendants of the people she had once seen, in the Before Time.

Every person they passed stared, and though their eyes were wider, more intrigued than the people staring in her memory, that was familiar too. She remembered that she hadn't liked that feeling in the past, of being constantly on display. It didn't bother her so much now. Perhaps that was because they wanted to see what she was going to do, and she had a queer sympathy for the feeling. She wanted to see what she was going to do too.

She had spent so many years alone, and now there were people everywhere. It set off a thrum of anxiety in the pit of her stomach—but she thought possibly some excitement was mixed in there too. Everything had always stayed the same in the garden. The world beyond it had so many different things to see and explore. It wouldn't be all good things—but it would be *new* things.

She and Terrence walked silently behind an elegantly-attired servant who had appeared in the courtyard and undertaken to lead them to the throne room. To the king.

Rose had been there often in the Before Time, and when the tall doors were flung open she saw that this room had changed less than most. It was a long room with a raised dais for the thrones at the end, arched windows letting in light from high on the walls. The space was filled with people, a confusing impression of silks and furs; she took in only enough to tell her that here were gathered the aristocracy, the highest society of the castle.

She didn't look at them closely because her gaze was drawn to the far end. To the dais, with its three steps up to the thrones. They were the same thrones, dark wood with high backs, covered in intricate carvings, a crown just at the top where the back reached a peak. The one where her mother had once sat was empty, a long black cloth draped over it for Terrence's mother, the queen who had died.

That had never been the throne that mattered though, and her gaze went on to the other. The king's throne. All her life she had seen her father sit there, as cold and remote as the stars. When she remembered him, she remembered him there, sitting above her, looking down as though everyone was so small beneath him. Even her. Especially her, the girl who should have been a boy, the girl who was so very useless and always had been.

But that was a hundred years ago. There was a new king now. King Elgin. Terrence's father. Her stomach tightened, nerves making her hands want to shake. So much depended on this man, on what he thought and did, on who he was.

Rose and Terrence began a slow walk up the long center of the room, the crowds of people parting to let them through. She had walked out this way too, all those years ago, past the mob of champions.

She had walked out alone. She looked up at Terrence next to her, walking back in with her, and pushed away the past's ghosts. The present was at least better than that. She lifted her head higher, held Silvertips tightly and vowed that even if she was afraid, she wouldn't let all these people see it.

They were coming closer to King Elgin now, and though Terrence had told her his father was a hard man, she found herself searching for something, some hope in his face. Some hint of Terrence's kindness. This king was older than her father had been. His hair was given mostly to gray but his back was still straight, his hands strong as they grasped the arms of the throne. She could see something of his son in his eyebrows, in the shape of his jaw. But the eyes, though dark like Terrence's, held a very different expression, coldly assessing her as she approached. She fought to keep her own face impassive, her gaze lifted.

She and Terrence stopped a dozen feet from the dais and he let go of her hand, stepping off a pace, leaving her with only Silvertips to hold, Emerald Eyes sitting by her feet. "Your Majesty," Terrence said into the silent room, inclining his head to his father. "I present the Princess Rose Amelia of Avala." The faintest of whispers ran through the crowd. "I have rescued the Princess Behind Thorns." His voice still rang with pride, but she could hear a small shiver of worry beneath it, worry that hadn't been there when he'd announced her at the gates.

Very carefully, Rose curtsied, the precisely correct curtsy for the crown princess to the king, and not one inch lower. She had been drilled in that, in the Before Time. She could do it now even with every muscle taut with tension.

And King Elgin smiled. A broad smile as he rose to his feet, descended the steps, calling, "Our dear cousin. How glad we are to have you restored to us."

He extended his hand, so she had no choice but to offer her own for him to bend and kiss. It was a perfect, appropriate, courtly gesture. But his lips were dry and cold against her skin. When the king released her hand she drew it back to her side, resisted the urge to wipe the place he had kissed against her skirts because he would see it. Everyone would see it.

King Elgin turned to Terrence. "And so, our youngest son has proved himself capable of heroic deeds. How pleased we all are." He left no time for a response, barely enough time for Rose to start teasing apart the hidden layers of the words, but immediately turned back to her. "You must be exhausted from the journey here and wish to rest. I am certain we can find you suitable guest chambers."

She felt an unexpected rush of relief that he wasn't suggesting a return to her long ago bedroom, a possibility she hadn't previously thought of. Did they even know which one it was? But to return to her old rooms—the bedroom where the spell had been enacted—no, a guest chamber was preferable.

"I had thought," Terrence said suddenly, "that she might stay in the Queen's Rooms. They're empty, after all, and it seems suitable for the heir to the throne."

King Elgin cast Terrence a look Rose didn't entirely know how to read—but it was not friendly—then smiled again and said, "Of course. What a clever solution. I'll have a servant show the princess there at once. You and I must join the council to discuss these new…developments."

Instinctively, automatically, she reached for Terrence's hand again. She had known they'd be separated eventually, but she wasn't ready for that yet. Only after their fingers were entwined did it occur to her that the entire court, and the king, had seen that gesture, had seen her reach for Terrence. What would they read in it?

Without looking at her, Terrence's fingers tightened around hers and he said evenly, "I'll show Princess Rose to her new rooms first."

A longer look from the king this time, and did she hear a faint murmur in the crowd? But finally King Elgin said, "My youngest son has grown suddenly bold. How…remarkable." He turned away, to return to his throne. "Very well then. I expect you to join the meeting directly after. We have much to consider."

For an instant, this felt like a solution. And then some part of Rose rebelled, maybe the same part that had been so angry when she first remembered her enchantment, or when she thought she was going to die in the shadows. Because this was a solution, but it was a dismissal too.

She didn't want to be that woman anymore, the one she had been in the Before Time. The mere girl who was sent off into another room while the men discussed important things. While they discussed *her*. And if she had just showed the king and all his court that she couldn't stand without Terrence next to her—it felt as though, if she didn't make some gesture right now, right at the beginning, she would never be anything more than she had always been.

Every instinct said to get away from this cold-eyed king, from the staring crowd, but that instinct wasn't going to help her be who she wanted to become.

Squeezing Terrence's hand, wanting him to know she wasn't trying to reject his effort to help, she carefully, clearly said, "I appreciate Prince Terrence's very kind offer, but I would like to attend that meeting. To discuss my return to court."

This prompted a louder murmur among the crowd, and the king stopped a step away from his throne. He turned very slowly back around to look at her, eyes narrowing. It was a searching look, an assessing look, and Rose kept her back straight, her chin high, while her stomach clenched and her legs shook beneath her skirts. She focused deliberately on the warmth of Terrence's hand locked around hers, on Silvertips purring in the crook of her arm.

She had been stared at before, often, by powerful men. They had rarely looked beyond her outward shape, staring openly enough at her face, at her body. King Elgin was looking past that, or trying to, intent and calculating.

He smiled, that same broad smile he had greeted her with, and she knew she couldn't trust that smile. "Of course. How pleasant to have you join us. We should adjourn to the council room, then. Terrence, I'm certain you can escort Princess Rose there; it's only across the hall."

This time Rose was sure she heard the subtext, that Terrence could handle this simple task, if nothing else.

She gritted her teeth, indignant on his behalf—but Terrence merely nodded, so Rose curtsied again and they turned to go. As they turned, she caught a glimpse through the crowd of one of the statues against the side wall—Mariqwe as a male warrior with a roaring lion beside him. She unthinkingly squeezed Silvertips tighter, the kitten emitting a squeak of protest. It was so different from the statue in her garden, the female warrior who had made her believe in her own strength too. This statue had been her father's. She had never liked it.

She could feel Terrence looking at her, and she made herself look away from the statue, look up at him and smile.

After a second or two, he smiled back. They started the walk down the long room, and Terrence leaned in closer to remark, "I always liked that portrait." He nodded towards the far end of the hall.

Rose's gaze followed where he indicated, to the back wall of the throne room, to the painting directly above the doors.

She remembered that portrait. She remembered standing stiffly in place for hours while it was painted. The artist had been a master at his craft, which had not made her like him any better when he snapped at her to stop moving if she so much as shifted her weight. But there she was, in the same long white dress she was wearing now, hair piled atop her head, gazing into the distance with a contemplative look. She appeared so much more serene than she remembered feeling. They had painted miniatures from this painting, to circulate around and encourage champions to come and try the challenge—as if the throne wasn't enough incentive.

Sometimes she had regretted the painting ever existed. Now, though, that portrait was probably one reason everyone accepted that she was who she claimed to be. It was an excellent likeness.

"I used to look at it," Terrence murmured as they walked, "and wonder what you were thinking when it was painted."

The thought of that younger Terrence, wondering about her, made her smile. "Probably that the hairstyle was hurting my head. It took hours to do my hair that way."

Chapter Thirteen: Terrence

Terrence loved knowing that Rose's hairstyle had taken hours for her portrait. He loved knowing such a human detail about a figure in a painting who had always seemed almost mythical. It linked the portrait he'd seen his entire life with the woman walking next to him. Also, it helped to have something to smile about as they went into what was undoubtedly going to be a difficult council meeting.

He'd never liked the council room, and he didn't like it any better today as they stepped inside. It was too dark. Dark wood furniture, dark red curtains blocking the last of the afternoon's light, dark stones on the walls and floor, lamps casting an inadequate light over the company as they gathered, entering from the throne room.

He instinctively stepped closer to Rose as the room filled with the dozen members of the council. He thought he understood why she had come, that she wanted to hear any decisions made, but he worried about her too. Only a few days ago she had been frightened just by him; now they were surrounded by all the men of the council. It was a far smaller crowd than had been in the throne room, but still an intimidating group, looming up taller and sterner as he tried to look at them through Rose's eyes.

It was only a minute, not long enough for much to happen good or bad, before the king entered with Terrence's brothers in step behind him. Terrence had seen them in the crowd in the throne room, but it hadn't seemed the moment for making introductions. Apparently neither was this, as his father sat down at the head of the table in the largest chair, followed by the rumble of footsteps and scraping of chairs as everyone else found their seats too.

The council's twelve members were mostly hereditary positions, the most powerful lords from each of Avala's eight provinces. The eight lords were supplemented by a few appointed positions, like the head of the court enchanters, the High Priest of Mariqwe and General Graybourne, who led the army. The king, of course, always sat at the head of the table, and Gregory had the position to his right as crown prince. Terrence and his other brothers were admitted to the meetings but had little official role. Terrence and Edward attended every meeting, Tyler less often.

It felt suddenly like a lot of people, and they filled even the long council table. Everyone had a regular seat—except Rose, of course, and Terrence hesitated, standing next to her.

"We have no room for a girl at this table," Gregory said, already seated beside their father, his voice cold.

"She can have my seat," Terrence said, regretting that he hadn't thought a little faster and managed that arrangement before anything was said. He looked at Gregory's face, at the hard set of his mouth, and looked away again. It would be easier if he believed Gregory was only talking about the arrangement of chairs and nothing else, but he knew that wasn't true.

Things were going to be very unpleasant with Gregory, possibly for a very long time. It was Gregory's inheritance Rose's arrival threatened, and Terrence couldn't blame him for being angry about that, for resenting this upending of the expected order. He hoped they could find some way past it. Their mother would have hated to see them on opposite sides, a possibly impassable rift between them.

For the moment, he led Rose to his own seat, halfway down the table, and drew it back for her. She sat down in a rustle of skirts, while Terrence nodded to Rupin, Lord Quintrell, sitting in the next chair over to the right. Rupin had always been his favorite council member. He was the only one who smiled at Rose now—at least, the only one Terrence saw.

"So you really claim to be the Princess Behind Thorns?" Gregory said, while Rose was still smoothing her skirts.

Terrence put his hands on the back of her chair as he stood behind her. He would have liked to put them on her shoulders, to reassure her and…because he liked touching her. But it seemed too intimate a gesture for a council meeting, for this audience. He looked down but couldn't see her face—only her hands, tightly clasped in her lap where they wouldn't be visible to anyone sitting at the table. And the small shapes of Silvertips and Emerald Eyes, sitting quietly by her feet.

"I *am* Princess Rose Amelia," she said, voice steady, "heir to the throne, and I have spent the last hundred years behind thorns."

"How do we know you're not an imposter?" Gregory persisted. Terrence recognized the edge in his brother's voice; he'd heard it often growing up, usually just before a fight. "Princess Rose Amelia could have died decades ago. Probably did, after a hundred years."

"You can see she's the living image of the portrait in the throne room," Terrence said, wishing Rose had agreed to be taken to her bedroom. He hadn't meant to bring her here to go through this.

"I still have my signet ring," Rose said, lifting her right hand, small gold ring catching the light. "And if anyone checks on the thorns, they're gone."

Gregory shifted in his chair. "That could still be—"

He broke off when their father held up one hand. "We can investigate the thorns," King Elgin said. "More importantly, our entire country knows the legend of the Princess Behind Thorns, and our capital is already in an uproar at the return of the princess. In a few days the whole region will know." He looked over Rose's head to Terrence. His eyes were cold, the hard lines visible around his mouth that meant he disapproved of something. "You really felt it necessary to announce it at the city gates?"

What else could he have done? And why *should* he have done anything else? "The people deserved to know," Terrence said, fighting his instinct to drop his gaze. He usually won that battle these days though the instinct never quite went away.

"Let us accept, for the moment, that the princess is who she says she is." The king kept his attention on Terrence. "I expect you intend to make the ancient claim recorded in the legend and marry her?"

"I do," Terrence said, because while the politics might be complicated, at least he knew *this*. He had wanted to marry the Princess Behind Thorns when he set out to find her, and he felt incredibly lucky that he wanted to marry Rose even more.

The next question really should have been to ask Rose if she agreed to the betrothal. But his father didn't do that. He went on looking at Terrence, and asked, "And she intends to assert her claim as heir to the throne?"

"I do," Rose cut in, voice just as firm as Terrence's had been. Though, of course, they had been speaking on two different matters, and the lack of any remark on the first subject suddenly seemed like a problematic thing.

He *thought* they had understood each other this morning, after the spell had lifted, talking about the possibility of marrying. And just before that, when she had reached out for him, kissed him with so much urgency, so much passion—that had felt like some kind of declaration, more eloquent than words. But it felt different, official in a new way, discussing it in front of his father and the entire council.

They had been in a different world before, and now they were back in his world, the world of the court, and it all seemed more real, more complicated.

The king, meanwhile, was looking hard at Rose. After a long moment, he said, "There are many stories about you, Princess Rose. It will be interesting to see which ones are true." Then he leaned back in his chair, surveyed the length of the table. "So. We have always regarded the lost Princess Behind Thorns as official heir to my throne, as the laws state and as the ceremony on Coronation Day every year makes plain. But it never signified anything until today. Now our long-time heir is among us, and as a result we have a change in the succession among my sons. Thoughts?"

Terrence felt a curl of unease in the pit of his stomach. *Thoughts* was what his father always said when he wanted the council's opinion on a decision he was making. And of course he'd known there would be many decisions to be made in this situation, but wasn't his father framing the discussion…sort of too broadly? Rose *was* the heir, they *were* betrothed—surely that much shouldn't be under discussion.

Not everyone had that impression. Lord Bellham spoke up first from his spot near Gregory, twisting his many rings in the way that meant he was agitated. "This whole business is ridiculous. A character from a ballad shows up and we're to change the line of succession? Such an idea is preposterous."

"It's not only ballads though," Rupin cut in. "The legend of the princess comes from a legal and historical reality." He was the acknowledged scholar at the table, and people tended to listen when he spoke about the law. "I'd have to look up the relevant decrees to quote them in detail, but the broad strokes of the legend are accurate and known to everyone. The Princess Rose Amelia was heir to the throne when she was enchanted, and she has been legally regarded as heir ever since. Your Majesty's grandfather's claim to the throne was based on his relationship to the princess' family. We don't have a change of dynasty here, just a—unusual leap between family branches. The laws and decrees made prior to your grandfather's ascension have always been considered still legally valid. The legend and the law also validate Prince Terrence's right to marry the princess as her rescuer, and the right of inheritance of anyone marrying a crown princess is, of course, too obvious to dispute."

Relief washed through Terrence at hearing it all put so clearly and absolutely. None of it was new exactly, but it reassured him that he hadn't been wrong. Murmurs went around the table, but it was difficult to tell their tone.

"The situation seems clear then," General Graybourne said in his deep rumble, cutting across the murmurs. His position was at the foot of the table, looking directly at the king at the head. "If the law is clear, the situation is clear. We must abide by the law. We have a change in succession, and the only question is how we're going to handle that."

"So it would seem," King Elgin said, words clipped. But then as he let his gaze sweep around the room, his broad smile returned. It was good when Terrence's father smiled, though he knew from difficult experience that it didn't always mean everything was all right again. "All of this will, of course, take time. Preparing a royal wedding, arranging a proper ceremony to acknowledge a new heir to the throne—we will need to make appropriate plans. Let us begin to discuss those plans."

Terrence let out a breath, leaned harder on Rose's chair, and hoped no one in the room had seen either of those things. Because that was an agreement, wasn't it? This mad idea he'd had about rescuing the Princess Behind Thorns, marrying her, becoming crown prince and someday king—it was all going to happen. It was dizzying and thrilling and terrifying. It was what he had wanted—and now he had to live up to it.

The rest of the council meeting descended into long discussions around the minutiae of ceremonies, the etiquette of betrothals, the legalities of hereditary thrones, and so on. Terrence didn't mind standing—he had been through military training much worse than this—but he couldn't help remembering that he hadn't slept much last night, and had ridden most of the day. And, more importantly, that the same was true for Rose. He tried to keep his attention on the discussion while sparing enough to watch Rose for…he wasn't sure what. Somehow, he didn't think she'd let herself slump at the table even if she wanted to.

All in all, it was a relief when his father finally adjourned the meeting, and the councilmembers made their way out.

Rose didn't rise to her feet, so Terrence dropped into the seat on her left as soon as it was vacant.

Rupin, on Rose's right, remained seated as well, turning to her. "May I introduce myself?" he said, over the footsteps of the retreating council. "I'm Rupin Quintrell, Royal Librarian."

"The Royal Librarian sits on the council?" Rose said, then dropped her gaze. "That is, I'm glad to hear it, I just…"

"The council position is hereditary," Rupin said smoothly. "I chose the library. My family has been in council serving the king for many generations, and so here I am. My grandfather served your father. He used to tell stories about you."

"Did he?" Rose said with no great enthusiasm in her voice.

Terrence tried to remember those stories, to put them in the context of the woman he had met.

Quiet. Mostly he remembered she was supposed to be quiet. Most of the stories, actually, had been about the enchantment, and they'd been so contradictory and confused that he hadn't put much stock in them anyway. He hadn't gone to rescue her based on who the stories said she was. He had gone because she was the heir to the throne, and because he'd been looking at her portrait in the throne room for as long as he could remember. That she'd turned out to be Rose was far more than he'd ever hoped for.

A pause in the conversation was starting to linger, so he swiftly said, "Rose is very fond of reading. And Rupin here likes nothing better than talking about books."

"Very true," Rupin said, eyes gleaming. "Terrence and I have had many long conversations on favorite volumes. Did you visit the library often, when you lived here?"

"No," Rose said, with a half-smile that looked regretful. "But I always wanted to visit, more than I could."

Terrence wondered what story was behind that. He wanted to know all the stories that hadn't been told about her, the true ones.

"You must come to visit me soon," Rupin said with enthusiasm. "I'll introduce you to all my nicest books."

"I'd like that," Rose said, and Terrence thought she meant it, though her smile faded after the words. "Today…has been a very long, very strange day…"

He caught the point without further hints, and welcomed the opening. "I'll escort you to your rooms, and I could have someone bring up supper. Enough public appearances for one day, maybe?"

She offered a smile of agreement, and rose to her feet without speaking. The kittens had fallen asleep in a heap under her chair long ago, and now they stretched and sleepily rolled out to follow as they left the room.

He walked her to the Queen's Rooms, and they spoke little on the way. He snuck glances at her, but whatever she was thinking, she wasn't letting it show on her face. Only an expression of remote serenity was there, making her look more like her portrait than ever.

He didn't like that. He wanted to know what she was thinking and feeling, especially after that council meeting, after the decisions that had been made there.

Terrence pushed open the door for her when they arrived at his mother's old suite of rooms. "I thought this would be good. The rooms haven't been redecorated, but they're not full of my mother's clothes or anything ghostly like that."

The rooms were a little ghostly anyway. They were still done up in the pastel colors his mother had favored, the furnishings blending elegance and comfort. The suite contained a bedroom, a sitting room, a dressing area, an enormous closet that had stood empty for years now. He had spent a lot of time in these rooms when he was young. It had been the best place to go, when the world outside was too big or too hard or too confusing.

He idly rubbed the ring on its chain, feeling its shape beneath his shirt and remembering the days when his mother used to wear it. He could almost see her sitting in the big armchair, just there, and Elena would have come running in, probably indignant about something, while he sat on the floor next to his mother…

Ghosts. But pleasant ones.

Terrence shook himself back to the present moment. "I thought you'd like this part too," he said, crossing the sitting room to draw back the lavender curtains. They revealed a door, opening on a spiral stair leading down to a walled garden, shadowy now in the early dusk. It was much smaller than Rose's garden had been, but it was still flowers, grass, a bench. He had wanted to offer her this at least, and if it was less than the garden she'd had—well, no thorns encircled it either. A stone wall, but no thorns.

Rose joined him at the door, smiling as she looked down at the garden. A real smile, more real than the blank serenity she'd been wearing since the council meeting.

"I love it," she said, leaning her cheek against his shoulder as they stood in the doorway.

He liked feeling her there, warm and soft beside him, and her words echoed in his mind. They were so close to what he most wanted to hear—but they weren't it.

He almost said it himself. He almost told her that he loved her, almost took the wild chance on seeing what she'd say back. Because they were betrothed, but they hadn't said those words—and he did love her, had loved her, for what felt like so much longer than it had really been when he added the few days together.

The moment lingered—and passed, as Rose moved away to sit down on the couch, and he still hadn't said anything.

For a few seconds he watched her, Silvertips and Emerald Eyes vying for space in her lap. He wanted to sit down next to her, reach for her hand or draw her into his arms, kiss the soft skin of her neck. He took a breath, tried to get himself under rein again, because she had surely had enough of people for one day. "I should go. Let you rest. Send someone with food."

She could tell him to stay. He hoped she'd tell him to stay. But she kept her eyes on the kittens she was petting, and just said, "Yes, that's fine. I'm sure you have people to see, now that you're home."

"I expect Elena will be wanting all sorts of explanations," he agreed. He had glimpsed her in the throne room, and the gleam in her eyes confirmed she was alight with curiosity, as he'd expected. "I'll…introduce you to her tomorrow." It was probably kinder not to subject Rose to Elena's inevitable initial flurry of questions tonight.

Rose nodded. "I'll see you tomorrow then."

Of course. Surely she would have, even if they didn't have the specific purpose of meeting Elena, and surely she knew that… He should go. That sentence had been a dismissal, he had already said he was going, he should go.

He still couldn't stop himself from saying, "It is all right, isn't it? You and me, I mean?" He rubbed the back of his neck, almost sure he was blushing again, very sure that he wasn't making any sense. "That is—I thought we understood each other, this morning, when I said—and you asked about marrying me, but—and a betrothal, that's so official, and suddenly I was telling my father and the entire council, and I wasn't sure that we had exactly—"

"Terrence," she interrupted, sliding the kittens off her lap and walking up to him, putting her hands on his shoulders. "I meant exactly what you thought I meant this morning." A pause. "Unless you didn't think I meant a betrothal, in which case—"

But by then he was pulling her against him and kissing her. She gave one little, delightful squeak of surprise and then her hands were in his hair and she was kissing him back, and they seemed to understand each other much better in that than in words.

Maybe he could have said the rest now, but he let this moment pass too. Because asking her to love him was much harder than asking her to marry him. The two ideas had rarely been paired in his experience, and marriage had always been far more business-like than love. Love was much rarer, much more vulnerable.

Even Elena, though she tried to cover it under bluster and scoldings, sometimes revealed a surprising fragility when she looked at her husband Henry. Terrence sometimes wondered if he would have resented Henry's intrusion if she hadn't. As it was, it was hard to remember they'd been married less than a year. And they were the best example he had of something he'd never quite dared to want and certainly never expected to possess.

And now—well, Rose liked him, he was sure of that much. And maybe that was enough for now, better than pushing for more. He wanted her to feel comfortable, to feel safe, and his father and Gregory weren't going to make that goal any easier.

So it was better to wait, to accept that this was enough. At least for now.

Chapter Fourteen: Rose

The door shut behind Terrence, and Rose drifted slowly back to sit on the couch. Her kittens leaped into her lap again, and she absently stroked them, glancing back at the door. She wished he'd stayed. She wished she'd asked him to stay.

She liked having Terrence with her. He was steadying in this strange new-and-old world, but she also just—liked him, liked being with him. The council meeting had made her realize in a new way how lucky she was that that was true. She loved that Terrence had offered her the choice, had said that she didn't have to marry him, hadn't wanted to force her into anything. But would there *really* have been a choice, once they came back here, once they were in front of the king and his council? It was unsettling to realize that the answer was very likely no.

But it was all right, because she *had* chosen Terrence, and that was the right choice. It was the right choice to not ask him to stay this evening too. If she had asked him to stay he would have felt obligated, and he surely had other things he'd rather do. It had been easy in the garden, when it was just the two of them in the whole world. But she wasn't in the garden anymore. He probably had business to attend to, or at least wanted to change his clothes, to see his friends.

Rose reached up and pulled the red peony from the girl on the boulevard out of her hair, twirled it between her fingers. She set it on the low table in front of the couch, then plucked at the skirt of her dress. She'd like to change clothes too, for that matter. Maybe she could ask whoever brought up supper to send some. Terrence probably wouldn't think of it.

He'd be busy talking to Elena anyway.

"She's his cousin," she reminded Silvertips and Emerald Eyes and herself. "Practically like a sister." Would Elena be nice? Would Elena like her? What on earth was Rose going to do if she didn't?

She got up from the couch, prowled around the room. She wished there were more clues in it to the previous occupant, but the closet was empty, the small bookshelves below one window bare. She liked the décor, but that didn't tell her very much about Terrence's mother.

She wondered if the rooms would ever feel like *hers*. Maybe once she had spent more time in them, had established herself here with her own belongings. She felt a sudden, sharp longing for all the things lost when her garden vanished—her favorite books, her statue of Mariqwe, the little silver hand mirror. The books she might be able to find in the library, and she could surely get a new mirror. The statue was probably unique; she'd never seen another like it, no other example of Mariqwe as a woman warrior.

This line of thought was not helping. She needed to do something different, was just about to venture down into the garden despite how tired she was, how chill the evening air, when she heard a tap at the door.

She stared at the closed door for a moment, heart racing, then took a deep breath. She had already faced crowds lining the streets, the full throne room, the room filled with the king's council. She could handle whoever was out in the hall. And at least the neat little tap was less foreboding than, say, a pounding fist.

Gregory probably pounded on doors.

Rose opened her door, felt an immediate twinge of disappointment that it wasn't Terrence coming back, and tried to damp that down. Instead she found a woman dressed like a servant. She was going to have to learn the different uniforms of the different parts of the staff; it had changed in the last century.

There was *so much* she was going to need to learn.

"Your Highness," the woman said, bobbing into a curtsy and not quite meeting Rose's eyes when she came up again. She was balancing a tray with a silver dome over it, and had a bag hanging from one shoulder. "Prince Terrence came to the kitchens to say you'd be wanting supper."

"Yes, thank you," Rose said, and gestured toward the table at one end of the sitting room. "You can set it there."

"Yes, Your Highness," the woman said. Once the tray was in place, she slid the bag off her shoulder as well. "The head chef, she thought you might be wanting this too, nightclothes and a few other—" She jumped suddenly as Emerald Eyes came over to sniff her skirts. "Oh—go away, you."

"He's just being friendly," Rose said, taking the bag.

"Oh—oh, I'm so sorry, Your Highness!" The servant's eyes had gone wide, and she bobbed into another curtsy. "I didn't mean to be rude to your cat—"

"It's quite all right," Rose said. It wasn't entirely, but she did not have the energy for this right now. And anyway, the maid was reacting as though she was going to be fired for the offense, and it definitely wasn't *that* bad.

"If there is anything else I can do…" the maid said, gaze on the ground.

"No, thank you, I'm fine." She had mostly only wanted a change of clothes, which she had now, and she didn't want anything else from this clearly uncomfortable woman. When the servant didn't move, Rose racked her brain for what she was missing here. Oh, etiquette and formality— "You may go now," she said, and hoped the forms were still the same as they had been in the Before Time.

Apparently it was close enough. "Yes, Your Highness. Thank you, Your Highness." Another curtsy, and then Rose was alone again.

She rubbed her forehead, and looked into the bag. As promised, there was a nightgown, a hairbrush and comb, a bar of soap. Mariqwe bless the head chef, this really was just what she needed. Now if only someone had thought… She lifted the dome on the tray, revealing bread, cheese, slices of beef, an array of roasted vegetables and, yes, a plate of fish for the kittens.

"We might do all right for one evening at least," she remarked to the kittens. "And beyond that…"

For a hundred years, the garden had taken care of everything she needed, and the thorns had kept everyone away. Now she was going to have to deal with people again, rely on people again. People she didn't know, and some she already knew she didn't trust.

She jumped instinctively at the sudden sound of a bell in the distance. It rang three times, then stopped, but it wasn't until the new sound of doors opening and footfalls out in the corridors beyond that a memory swam out of the Before Time. They had always rung a bell to give notice before supper in the banquet hall began. Apparently *some* things hadn't changed.

It was a small comfort, but there was still too much new to deal with tonight. She had food, clothes, a place to sleep. If she thought too much about the future…she shook her head. "Beyond tonight, we'll see," she concluded. "But right now, we eat. And sleep. And we'll deal with the rest in the morning."

Rose was exhausted when she finally fell into bed, and she slept well that night, too deeply to remember any dreams. She awoke nose to nose with Silvertips, with Emerald Eyes curled up against the small of her back, and that was comfortingly familiar when awakening in a strange world.

She rolled onto her back, Emerald Eyes stretching against her side, and looked up at the hanging drapery of the four-poster bed. Very different from the blue sky through branches of her bower.

The garden seemed a world away already. How could it be possible she had woken up there only the day before? More had happened in a day than had happened in a year, maybe a decade, in the garden.

And now she was back in her father's castle, back where she had grown up.

She shivered, digging her fingernails into her palms.

Then she took a deep breath. This *wasn't* the Before Time. She wouldn't let it be the same. She had insisted on attending the council meeting yesterday. All she had to do was—keep on. She hadn't had any say in her life before, but that was a long, long time ago. It wouldn't be the same now, because *she* wasn't the same anymore.

She slid out of bed, because getting up was obviously the first step in facing whatever the day had to bring. She smoothed her hands over the long white nightgown. Was the same servant going to be back with breakfast and a dress for the day? She suspected a number of clothes fittings were in her immediate future, if she could judge by the Before Time.

A noise in the sitting room, just beyond the bedroom, brought her head sharply around to look in that direction. She was sure she had locked the door last night—but how many people had keys in this castle?

Gregory's glare from across the council room loomed up in her mind. His eyes weren't cold like his father's; they burned with rage and malice, dark things lurking in their depths that she never wanted to see clearly. What keys was the crown prince trusted with?

Silvertips gamboled happily out towards the sitting room, out the doorway before Rose could snatch her back. She bit her lip, took a step after the kitten, hesitated. She glanced around the room, but no one had helpfully left a dagger lying anywhere. Not that she knew how to use one anyway.

In the next room, a female voice said, "Oh! Hello, kitten," and Rose breathed a little easier. Whoever it was, at least it wasn't Gregory.

She plucked up her courage and stepped into the sitting room to see a new servant bending down to pet Silvertips. A breakfast tray was resting on the table by the window, and a pale pink dress was laid across the back of the couch.

"Her name's Silvertips," Rose offered.

The maid jumped, looked up at Rose, and hastily curtsied. "Your Highness—good morning. I didn't mean to wake you."

"That's all right." Rose studied this new woman. She looked a few years older than the one who had brought supper, and though her eyes were wide, she was looking directly at Rose. That felt better than the previous servant's refusal to meet her gaze.

"The kitchen gave me breakfast for you," the maid volunteered. "And I can help you dress, if you like. I think they're still working out who your ladies in waiting will be?"

That was a Before Time memory she hadn't thought of in a long time. Once she had aged out of having a nurse, various ladies of the court had been assigned to her. It had been all right sitting with them for embroidery or walking about the lawns, though they had been a quiet group—but she had never liked the production of five women helping her dress in the morning. And then doing it all again for supper.

She'd quite like to do away with help at all. She had never needed it in the garden, where her clothes had been so much simpler.

She eyed the full skirts of the gown lying on the couch, and felt a moment's regret for those dresses of the garden. She liked beautiful clothing, but she didn't like the loss of freedom that came with a dress so complicated she couldn't get in or out of it herself. Then she eyed the maid, who was still watching her. One woman might be better than an entire crowd. And she had been petting Silvertips.

"What's your name?" she asked.

The maid looked surprised. "Gabrielle, Your Highness," she answered, bobbing another curtsy.

"It's nice to meet you," Rose said with a smile. "Let's see if we can figure out that dress."

Fashions had changed somewhat in the past century—the neckline was higher, there was an extra layer of underskirt—but it was as complicated as the dresses Rose remembered. They managed though, and soon enough Gabrielle was off to her other duties while Rose sat down to breakfast. It was a large table, with enough space and chairs for six. She had been too tired the previous night to want much company, but now it seemed uncomfortably empty. She hadn't felt lonely in the garden, but now she wished she might have invited Gabrielle to join her. At least she was a friendly face. But Rose remembered enough of the Before Time to know that never would have done. No maid would have dared accept such an invitation, if she herself had dared to make it.

So she sat at one end of the table, nibbled on a muffin and fed bits of sausage to the kittens. She wondered how she could get in touch with Terrence, and how soon would be…well, *not* too soon to try.

She had to get used to being on her own, without Terrence. Even though part of her still wanted to clutch onto him and keep him next to her forever. It was only six days ago that they had met, even less time since she had realized how much she cared for him, and already he had become indispensable to her. But measuring time by emotions and events, she had lived longer since the day Terrence entered her world than she had in the hundred years before.

"Well," she said, rumpling Silvertips' fur, "Terrence isn't the *only* one I can rely on." The only one who could talk, but not the only one at all.

Rose was still sitting at the table, done with eating and wondering what to do with herself now, when a knock sounded at the door.

She hesitated. With only one person in the castle she wanted to see, and a great many she probably didn't, that didn't make for good odds. And yet, though she was still deciding who she was going to be now, she knew she didn't want to be a coward.

Picking up Silvertips, she went to open the door.

Two strangers stood on the other side, a man and a woman. Both were dressed in the silks and elegance of the court aristocracy, the woman a few years older than Rose, the man a bit older still.

"Good morning!" the woman said to Rose, then said over her shoulder, "You see, I told you she'd be awake." To Rose again, she continued, "Forgive the intrusion, we wanted to catch you before the court swallowed you up. I'm Lady Elena."

Rose blinked. "Terrence's Elena?" she said without thinking—and then, with a thought, winced. "That is, I meant…"

But Lady Elena merely said, "Oh good, he's mentioned me. Knowing Terrence, he probably hasn't told you very much that's useful, but at least that's something. This is my husband Henry, knight of the realm, etc. We have longer titles and can lay out court precedent if you really want to hear it all, but it takes such a long time. May we come in?"

Terrence hadn't mentioned that Elena was married. Between assimilating that information, and realizing how truly awkward her first remark had been, Rose was in no frame of mind to graciously refuse them entrance—and might not have been anyway. There was something so brisk and firm about Lady Elena that she made even a question seem like a declaration. "Do please come in," Rose managed, stepping out of the doorway. She had wanted to meet her, after all. She was Terrence's cousin, practically his sister. That meant she was simultaneously a good chance of an ally, and terrifying—because what if Lady Elena didn't like her?

They both stepped inside, crossing the room to the breakfast table. Rose closed the door slowly behind them. Even in the mere act of crossing a room it was evident Lady Elena was filled with energy. Her husband was tall, with the build one would expect of a knight, and walked more slowly, favoring one leg in a slight limp.

Rose followed them back to the table and sat down, Silvertips springing up into her lap. "I really didn't mean *Terrence's…*"

"It's all right," Sir Henry said, voice quiet, and smiled at her. His face was young despite the gray at his temples, but his eyes looked old. "It's not entirely inaccurate, in a way. Just not in the way you didn't mean it."

"Don't confuse her, Henry." Lady Elena had sat across from Rose. She folded her hands in her lap and looked straight into Rose's eyes. Her eyes were blue, not at all like Terrence's dark brown ones. "You likely realize that practically everyone in this castle will be trying to figure out if you're a suitable kind of princess, suitable to sit on the throne and suitable to bear the legend. We're not like that. *We* want to know if you're suitable for Terrence."

"I see," Rose said carefully, trying to return an expression as serious as Lady Elena's, though her lips wanted to twitch into a smile. The woman's gaze was as searching as the king's had been, but not nearly as uncomfortable. And what was it *like*, to be that…forthright?

"It's all happened very suddenly, you know," Lady Elena continued. "And we don't know anything about you. There are the stories, of course, but they're not very…"

"What do the stories say about me?" Rose asked, on a sudden daring impulse. Just what *were* all these people expecting from her? It was going to be hard enough trying to find out who she was now, without the distorted ghost of her own past self haunting her. It might be better to know what that ghost looked like, and it might be best to hear it from this woman, who evidently believed in speaking her mind. And who cared about Terrence.

"Well, they all said you were very beautiful, of course," Lady Elena said, and then hesitated, her fingers drumming on the table. "And quiet. A very…proper princess. Mild and obedient and…"

"And dull and stupid and silent, I should think," Rose said crisply. That would be about the sort of opinion the people she had known, the people who could have told those stories, likely would have had of her.

Lady Elena's mouth curved into a smile. "But a princess who actually was dull and stupid and silent wouldn't say that."

"I don't think you ought to put much credence in stories about me," Rose said. "No one who could have told them knew much about who I am."

"And who are you?" Lady Elena asked. "What *are* you like?"

Rose considered the other woman's open and honest gaze, and answered in kind. "I don't entirely know. I hope I'll be able to find out."

Lady Elena took this in with a brief nod. "We were worried about Terrence, the way he set off on this absurd adventure and disappeared for days. The whole thing was very like him, idealistic, romantic, completely mad—"

"Centered around something he read in a book," Sir Henry interjected.

"Yes, that too, very Terrence, that detail. And then he turns up with you, and suddenly he's defying his father and opposing his brother in council—"

"They were very mild defiances," Rose pointed out.

"Not in principle. Honestly, it's about time he did something like this, but if he's going to do all this over you…"

"You want to be sure I'm worth it," Rose said quietly, not insulted. It must be nice, to have friends who wanted to look out for you.

Lady Elena's lips pursed and she didn't quite agree—or disagree. "We want to be sure that this entire mad venture isn't, in fact, entirely mad."

"It can't be completely," Sir Henry said. "He succeeded, didn't he?"

Lady Elena pounced on this new conversational thread. "Yes, and about that. Why do *you* think he succeeded?" she asked Rose. "The legend always said that you could only be rescued by, you know…" She waved a hand through the air. "The strongest, bravest, most powerful of champions. Terrence has many, many good points, but that description doesn't exactly…"

"I think the spell changed," Rose said slowly. "The legend, that's describing the husband my father wanted for me. That was who was supposed to break the spell. But the magic changed, and maybe it changed because of me." That was what Terrence had kept saying, and based on the way the spell had finally ended—maybe he had been right, strange as it seemed. "I was in the middle of it all, and I didn't want that sort of husband. I think…I think I wanted the kindest one to succeed." She frowned, brow furrowing. "I didn't *know* that exactly. But perhaps the magic did, because Terrence is, isn't he? And he's what I want."

Both Lady Elena and Sir Henry were staring at her, and Rose awkwardly dropped her gaze, suddenly feeling she had said too much, ventured into areas that were too personal. She had only had cats to talk to for a hundred years. She had grown used to thinking aloud.

After a long moment, Lady Elena exhaled audibly and said in satisfied tones, "You may be all right for Terrence after all, Your Highness. If you can appreciate that about him."

"Cats like her," Sir Henry said, and when his wife turned her stare on him, he just shrugged. "Dogs like everyone. Cats are discerning."

Rose noticed suddenly that Emerald Eyes had wandered over and was sprawled on top of Sir Henry's feet. It seemed like a good sign.

"Please call me Rose," she said impulsively. "*Your Highness* is so formal and—it's a title, not *me*."

"I'd be glad to—Rose," Elena said with a smile. "Now how much *did* Terrence tell you about the court? Or his family?"

"Not very much?" Should she be discussing this with Elena? But it was obvious she and Terrence were close. The thought gave her a pang of envy. Elena probably knew all the stories about him. She must know how he'd gotten that scar by his eyebrow, remembered seeing him with his mother, a hundred other details. She wasn't certain if she should ask though. For the moment, they had been talking about the rest of the family. "He told me that his father is a—hard man."

"That's one word for it," Elena muttered. "I suppose you saw something for yourself yesterday, although he was being polite. Mostly."

Elena and Henry must have been in the throne room with the rest of the court. "Does he always talk about Terrence that way? Sort of...saying things without saying them?"

Elena rolled her eyes. "No. Sometimes he just *says* them. You shouldn't listen to anything the king says about Terrence, all right? His father has never appreciated him, but some of us do." She regarded Rose with her chin in one hand. "He's very special, our Terrence. The cook would have adopted him, I think, if she could. He's the favorite of most of the servants, he's so much, oh, nicer and politer than the rest. Even outside the castle, he knows people all over the capital. If you're going to marry him—you ought to know, just because his father can't see it—"

Rose reached out and pressed her hand over Elena's on the table. "I value him. I do. And I think he's very lucky, to have such friends."

Elena smiled at her. "Do you know, you're not at all what I expected. I'm glad."

"Thank you?" Rose hazarded, because she thought that had probably been a compliment.

Elena nodded once, brisk again. "Now let me tell you more about the court. There's all kinds of things about people at court that it would help you to know that Terrence would never think about mentioning. He probably knows most of it, but it's not what he dwells on."

Before they got far into that discussion, another knock came at the door. When Rose called permission to enter, the door opened to admit Terrence, who strode cheerfully in, saying, "Good morning, I was hoping you'd be awake by…oh." His gaze landed on Elena and Henry, and his expression grew more rueful. "I might have guessed." He very deliberately approached Rose, bending to lightly kiss the top of her head, then said, "I apologize for my friends, Rose. Are they being dreadful to you?"

She smiled up at him. "No, they're being very nice."

"Sounds suspicious," Terrence said, dropping into the empty chair next to her and letting Emerald Eyes jump onto his lap.

"I was about to be really vicious about all the people in the court she ought to avoid," Elena offered.

"Oh, that's always fun," Terrence said with a roll of his eyes. "Elena has a terrible opinion of most people."

"I have a discerning opinion," she corrected. "Terrence always wants to think the best of people."

"That's not a bad thing," Terrence protested. "If you give people a chance to live up to expectations—"

"Half the time they won't do it," Elena said.

"Yes, sure, but the other half they *will*."

Rose sipped her tea, and petted Silvertips, and felt a surprising amount of happiness, watching Terrence banter with his cousin. It was nice, to find out it wouldn't be *all* glowering kings and high walls here. And surely—it was a good quality, to think the best of people. She liked that about Terrence. And if somewhere underneath that she had a little bit of unease, a sense that it wasn't always the safest thing to believe the best of everyone…with tea and laughter, it was easy enough to push that feeling down. For now, anyway.

Chapter Fifteen: Terrence

Terrence was frankly relieved that Elena had taken to Rose, and vice versa. If they hadn't—he didn't have the slightest idea how he would have negotiated that conflict. But he wasn't sitting at the breakfast table long before it became obvious he wouldn't need to worry about that particular crisis.

He ate through a couple of muffins while Elena carried on a lively accounting of the principle personalities at court. It wasn't that vicious, and he even agreed with most of it. It was true that he tried to see the best in people, but that didn't mean he believed no one had a darker side. People were complicated, people at the royal court maybe especially so. Henry was quiet, as he usually was, but Rose talked more than he would have expected. Though Elena did have a talent for drawing people out, when she chose to. He liked seeing them laugh together.

They were out of muffins by the time Elena took charge of planning the day. "We'll have to sort out your wardrobe, of course," she said briskly, "that's the most urgent thing."

"Clothes are urgent?" Terrence said with a smile, amused by her serious tone.

"Clothes affect how a person is seen," Elena said, giving him her most superior look. "Rose can't venture into the incredibly complex web of Princess Penelope and her ladies-in-waiting without a suitable wardrobe. There are factions and hierarchies and the entire group runs on opinions, and clothes affect all of that. *Men* never understand that sort of thing," she concluded, with a commiserating glance at Rose.

Rose smiled, then asked, "Who's Princess Penelope?"

"The cr—ah, Prince Gregory's wife," Elena said. She had unquestionably almost said 'the crown princess,' but was Penelope still the crown princess, now that Rose was back? "I should have mentioned her—but people don't, mostly. She's very…quiet and mild."

"I see," Rose said, and there was something in her eyes Terrence wished he understood.

He knew he didn't understand much about Penelope. It was obvious how Gregory felt about Rose's arrival, but he didn't know his brother's wife well enough to guess how she might feel about all this. He had never managed to feel acquainted with her, for all that he'd tried.

"So, let's get on with picking out some fabrics from the court dressmakers, and we'll see about having a fitting for you," Elena said, rising to her feet, ready to begin at once.

Terrence stood up automatically when Elena did, and so did Henry. Rose stood too—and then her glance slipped over to Terrence, before sliding away again almost at once.

Elena apparently caught that glance, and interpreted it while Terrence was still wondering if it meant anything. "Why don't you come with us? Help me show Rose around."

He was amused by how entirely Elena had taken charge of Rose, if he'd been relegating to helping—and he was warmed by the thought that, maybe, that was what Rose had been wanting when she looked at him. If Elena had read it right. Rose was looking at him now, maybe hopefully?

It all made him regret having to say, "I can't, actually. I have to be at a meeting; I just wanted to drop by here first."

"I'll come along to the dressmakers," Henry offered.

"Don't be silly," Elena said, too quickly. "You'd be bored."

"You invited Terrence," Henry pointed out.

"Terrence has surprisingly good taste in fabric," Elena said.

"Only because you dragged me over to that part of the market all the time when we were growing up," Terrence said with a grin, and added for Rose, "I'm sure you can imagine how useful a skill it was for impressing people at court."

"And anyway," Elena continued to Henry, "don't they need you on the practice grounds today? There's those new soldiers and—"

"They don't need me," Henry said, and Terrence could hear how his voice had grown suddenly cooler.

If he heard it, Elena must have too, but she persisted, "I'm sure they do, the armsmaster said—"

"They *don't*," Henry said sharply.

Terrence had told Elena she should stop pushing about this, but she never listened. He'd never seen Henry get truly angry about anything, but he'd been touchy about everything relating to the military ever since the Battle of Red Valley, where he'd been wounded in the recent war with Melidan. He suddenly wondered if he had mentioned the war to Rose. He probably hadn't. After a hundred years there was a lot of history to catch up on, but this wasn't the moment for that piece of it.

"We should all be going, shouldn't we?" Terrence said as heartily as he could, trying to brush past the awkwardness that had sprung up in the room. "You wouldn't want to keep the dressmakers waiting, and I shouldn't keep my father waiting."

From the way everyone turned at once to look at him, this had not been the right thing to say to ease the tension.

"You're meeting with the king?" Rose said, gathering Silvertips up. The kitten rubbed her head against Rose's chin in a way that almost distracted Terrence from the sudden worry in her eyes.

"Just informally," Terrence said, shoving his hands into his pockets. "Not a council meeting or anything, he just said he wanted to see me this morning. You know. Business to discuss."

He didn't want her to worry about this, to worry about his father. Maybe he shouldn't have told her quite so much that was critical of his father—but he'd had to explain his own actions, going to find her. It had gone all right yesterday. Granted, he hadn't had a private conversation with his father yet, not since he came home with the Princess Behind Thorns, but... He knew there were valid reasons for worrying, but that didn't mean he wanted Rose to do it.

They hadn't entirely shed the awkwardness as they left Rose's room. Or maybe it was a new awkwardness, because if they were going different directions he wanted to kiss Rose, yet he didn't feel altogether comfortable about it in front of Elena and Henry. He'd seen *them* kiss—but it was all too new, too uncertain for an audience.

So he settled for kissing Rose on the cheek and wished her a good day, and they went their separate ways.

The garden had had some definite advantages to it. No inconvenient witnesses at private moments, no claims on their time except each other.

Well, and trying to break a spell threatening to consume them, of course.

It was funny how, a short while later, standing at his father's door felt surprisingly similar to standing in front of a wall of thorns. He tried to laugh at himself, at his own unease. What did he think was going to happen?

The possible answers to that weren't reassuring. Nothing for it but to knock on the door, and push it open at the command to enter.

This room, not coincidentally, looked a lot like the council chamber; Terrence had never been overfond of it either. His father was sitting where he usually was, behind his heavy wooden desk, papers spread across its surface.

Terrence had been through this enough to not need directions. He advanced into the room, bowed as a prince did to his king, and sat in the chair opposite the desk. That chair, a low one, always made him feel as though he was suddenly a few years younger.

His father didn't look up from the paper he was reading, and so Terrence waited.

It felt like a long time before his father finally set the paper down to regard him—though he hadn't fidgeted, so he counted that as a victory.

"So," his father said, voice low and heavy. "The Princess Behind Thorns."

It wasn't exactly a question, but Terrence nodded and said, "Yes, sir," anyway.

"I suppose it struck you as a very clever, very heroic thing to do, rescuing the enchanted princess. The odds were good you could have died instead. Did you know the legend records dozens, if not hundreds, of men died in those thorns, trying to rescue that girl?"

Had Rose had to listen to all of them die? But surely that wasn't why his father was bringing it up—was he concerned, that Terrence had gone on such a risky venture? It hadn't seemed that risky at the time. If there'd been no apparent way through the thorns, he had planned to walk away; it would have been foolish and risky to start hacking at the thing with his sword, but how dangerous could it be to go and look at it? The dangers, as it turned out, were inside, in the threatening shadows—but they had escaped those too.

His father didn't seem to expect a response. "But instead, you rescued the princess. And brought her back here."

"Yes, sir," Terrence said again, more pride in his voice. After all—no one else in a century had done it.

"I suppose that seemed clever too." His father rose abruptly to his feet, palms flat against the desk, his voice rising too. "Clever, to bring back a princess who is now completely disrupting the succession that's been planned since long before *you* were even born!"

Terrence knew not to stand up, though that would be etiquette everywhere else. Not in this room. Not when his father didn't approve, after all, of something he had done. His stomach sank with disappointment, just as though he hadn't mostly expected this reaction, and he had to fight his instinct to hunch smaller in the chair. Neither his father nor his own pride liked quailing.

"Do you even grasp the magnitude of this?" his father demanded. "To suddenly introduce a new heir—this is the kind of thing that destabilizes a monarchy, destabilizes an entire country. Did you think about that?"

He had—but he had thought it was a risk worth taking, because they were already on the wrong path, and if they stayed on it, if they continued as they were and Gregory someday became king, things were never going to get better. At least this way there was a chance. Besides, he wasn't really introducing a new heir; he had only brought back one who had always been heir. And changed his own place in the succession in the process.

When the pause lengthened, he realized his father actually expected a response this time. There were many things he could say, about his intentions, about how everything had developed beyond his expectations. But there was only one thing he could say that his father might respect, even appreciate. Fortunately, it was the truth too. "I wanted to be king," he said, as firmly as he could.

And his father stared at him for a long moment, then sat down again, tone more moderate as he said, "How unexpectedly ambitious. I didn't think you had that in you."

He had always been ambitious, though perhaps he'd been quieter about it than his brothers. He had always strived to do the best that he could at the goals in front of him—but he had usually fallen short of his father's standards, so how much could he expect his father to have seen the effort?

His father drummed his fingers on the top of the desk. "Never mind that Gregory has been slated to inherit the throne his entire life—did you think about *that*?"

"Of course," Terrence said, because he had. But there'd been no way around it. He knew the kind of king Gregory would be. A king who broke promises, who had no head for administration, who didn't pay attention to what his people needed. He had talents that were good in a war, maybe, but he wouldn't be very good in peace.

Their mother had always believed Gregory could be better than that, had more than that in him, but he hadn't been living up to it that Terrence could see.

"Although," his father said with a shrug, changing direction, "if he can't hold onto an inheritance, maybe it's right that he loses it. In any case, we are here now. The Princess Behind Thorns' claim as heir suddenly becomes meaningful. And you suddenly have a claim to a closer position in the succession. It could be worse—at least our family brought the girl back. It could have been a stranger. I suppose you ended up there at the right time. After all these years, the spell was probably ready to break."

Terrence wanted to deny that, to insist that he hadn't been merely lucky, that he'd done something to deserve Rose and the throne both. But…was he entirely sure that he *hadn't* simply been there at the right time? The spell had been disintegrating, that was clear enough. "Something like that," he said finally.

His father only nodded. "And now you've made a claim on the Princess Behind Thorns. How well have you secured that claim?"

Terrence wasn't certain what that meant. "We're betrothed—we announced it to the council yesterday—"

"No, not that," his father said with an impatient gesture. "Have you bedded the girl yet?"

Terrence felt his spine stiffen. "No," he said, and hated that he could feel his cheeks turning hot.

His father's expression remained neutral, and he only nodded again as he said, "I might have expected that from you."

It didn't sound like a compliment. But his father didn't understand what he was asking, what it would have meant. He didn't know Rose, didn't know how afraid she had been, how unwilling she'd been at first even to be kissed.

"I did what seemed best," Terrence said at last.

"And landed us with a terrific tangle to sort out," his father concluded, leaned back in his chair and picked up a paper from his desk. "As if we didn't have enough to handle, with the aftermath of the war with Melidan. I expect you to be at every council meeting from now on, while we're sorting this out."

"Yes, sir." He never missed council meetings anyway.

He knew he had been effectively dismissed when his father resumed reading his paper. But he still waited, while his father finished one page and started another, until he finally said, "All right, you may leave."

"Thank you, sir," Terrence said, rose to his feet, bowed again and walked out.

It could have been worse. His father wasn't reversing on the decision made the previous day at the council meeting; he wasn't disavowing Rose's claim to the throne or forbidding him from marrying her after all.

It could have been better—he might have been impressed. Terrence had been trying his whole life to impress his father, and every time he thought he'd done something that would finally achieve that, he'd always turned out to be wrong. He ought to be used to it by now.

Terrence didn't have long to think about it. Only a handful of paces down the hall from where he stood, his brothers were waiting for him.

Gregory, Tyler and Edward had always moved in a pack, one that he had never been able to catch up to all through his childhood. He was six years younger than Edward, the next oldest, so it had made a kind of sense that they'd grouped together in a way he couldn't entirely join in. It seemed like the age difference shouldn't matter so much by now, that the difference between twenty and twenty-six couldn't be that large anymore, but old habits were hard to change.

It was clear the pattern wasn't going to change today either. They were standing very definitely together, even if their expressions were individual. Edward wore his usual impassive look, Tyler's grin was part sneer, and Gregory was frankly glowering.

"Good morning," Terrence said, because they were all staring at him and he had to say something.

"Maybe for some people," Gregory growled. He had always been able to twist the most innocuous of comments. "You think you're very clever, don't you? And so much better than the rest of us, now that you've found a way to shove right past us all in the succession."

Terrence took a breath. He had known this reckoning would come. He'd seen Gregory angry often enough before. He tried to make his tone moderate, to not match his brother's heat. "Of course I don't think—"

"Should we all start bowing to you now?" Gregory spat.

"It's not like that," Terrence said, keeping his back straight and not looking away. "I didn't do any of this because I wanted to hurt you—"

"But you're taking *my* throne!" Gregory paced closer, jabbed one finger into Terrence's chest. He had learned long ago not to step back. "What makes you think you deserve it?"

"I don't think I *deserve* it," Terrence said quietly. It wasn't about deserving. It was that he thought he could do something better with it. *Saying* that, though… "I just—rescued the Princess Behind Thorns. You all knew the legend too; you know the law."

"So any of us might have gone off and brought her back?" Tyler said, and elbowed Edward. "Too bad we didn't think of it first."

Edward offered a faint smile. "She seems to like Terrence very well now."

"Maybe I should see if I can get her to like me," Tyler said, grin going entirely into a sneer now.

Terrence stiffened. Rose didn't need his brothers harassing her. He didn't think they'd hurt her, but—what they'd consider too far and what *she'd* consider too far were very likely different things. "Leave Rose alone," he said, hearing a new edge enter his voice. "You're angry with me, fine, but none of this is her fault."

Tyler laughed. "I don't think little brother likes us talking about his girl."

"Maybe we could make her like *you* less," Gregory said, voice still low and tight with anger. "How'd she feel about it if I scarred you up some? That one scar I put on your face doesn't seem to be enough."

Terrence's jaw clenched. Why did it always have to be a fight with Gregory? Yes, he had reasons to be angry, but why couldn't they talk through anything? Other families didn't have to come to blows over everything. "I don't want to fight you, but if it would make you feel better to name the time and weapons—"

"Will you *stop* playing the wounded saint?" Gregory shouted. "You always have to be so calm, so *understanding*, never meaning to hurt anyone! It's infuriating."

Most of the time, for most people, staying calm helped defuse a situation. It didn't usually work on Gregory, and there were times Terrence wanted to—if it wasn't for the memory of how sad it made their mother, when they used to fight— "What do you *want* me to do?" Terrence asked, voice rising in spite of himself.

Gregory jabbed a finger at his chest again, looming still closer, trying to force him to take that step back. "Why don't you just admit what this was all about, that you wanted to be king?"

He had already said it to their father. Why deny it now? Terrence spread his hands, looked Gregory in the eye, refused to back up. "Fine. Yes. I wanted to be king."

Gregory's face was dark with fury. "Because you think you'll be a better king than me."

Exactly, but if he said that out loud—Gregory would just hit him for sure then, and what good would that do anyone? "A different kind of king."

Gregory took a swing at him anyway. Terrence had had plenty of practice at avoiding Gregory's fists, and now he dodged out of the way, came up again with his own fists raised and heart pounding. It might be good after all to have a fight, maybe they could get this out and clear the air and maybe some dark part of him *wanted* to hit back at Gregory anyway—

But Edward was already pulling Gregory away, saying, "This isn't the way to do this, brawling right outside our father's door. You know he wouldn't like it."

Their father had never objected to their brawling, even approved of that, but not if it disturbed his work. Gregory subsided, though his hands were still in fists, his shoulders tight with tension.

"Besides," Edward continued, "let's be fair to Terrence. It was a clever gambit, a crazy risk that paid off. One of us *should* have thought of it, but since he's the one who did…" He turned to Terrence, though he kept one restraining hand on Gregory's arm. "Congratulations on the new bride and the new inheritance. I'm sure we'll all be very interested to see where we fit in this new situation."

It was the most open-minded response he could have hoped for. Terrence let his fists drop, took a deep breath and reached for diplomacy. He even tried to summon up a smile. "I never really expected all of this, you know."

"Of course," Edward said with a nod, then gave Gregory a mock punch to the shoulder. "Come on, let's go hit something in the practice yards. You'll feel better."

"I doubt it," Gregory muttered, but turned with Edward and Tyler to go.

Terrence knew he wasn't invited. He watched them walk away together, and told himself that really it was better that way. Anything could happen, if he and Gregory were around each other and a lot of weapons right now, and even if a part of him wanted that—he didn't *like* that part, didn't think that was the part he ought to be listening to. So this was safer.

He watched until they had turned a corner in the corridor, then took a deep breath. He had set himself on this path, set himself against Gregory, when he went to look for the Princess Behind Thorns. This was probably only the first of many conflicts to come, so he'd better accept that.

He couldn't do anything else about that now, so he made his way towards the castle dressmakers instead. It was a long enough walk, to another portion of the castle, that he felt calmer by the time he got there. The distraction was still welcome though.

The castle employed an entire staff to clothe the royal family, and they worked in a large, sunny room on the ground floor of the castle. Terrence had mostly found himself here when he needed a rip mended in some piece of clothing he still wanted to keep. He might have sent the clothes with a servant, but he'd always liked Maude, the head seamstress, who invariably chided him for being rough on his clothes and remarked how much he kept growing. She kept saying it even though he was sure he'd stopped getting taller a while back; he was an inch taller than Edward, still a couple inches shorter than Gregory and Tyler.

He paused today in the doorway, watching the happy chaos inside. A dozen women sat sewing, while rolls of cloth filled a wall of shelves. Rose and Elena stood with Maude in the center of a swirl of half-unrolled bolts of cloth. Every seamstress was openly watching, while Henry was standing by one of the windows, apparently bored already.

Rose was holding a length of blue cloth up against herself, while Maude displayed a purple one, apparently for comparison. Terrence made a private bet with himself that Rose would choose the blue, then strolled inside.

"How goes the very important wardrobe creation?" he asked, and was pleased to see Rose's face brighten into a smile as she looked up at him.

"Prince Terrence, good of you to drop by," Maude said cheerfully, while curtsies bobbed all around the room. "We need an opinion—doesn't that blue set off Her Highness' eyes?"

Rose lifted the cloth a couple inches higher until it was just below her chin. It did, in fact, make her eyes look impossibly blue. "It's—nice," Terrence said, trying to catch the breath he'd suddenly lost. "But Rose should get whichever one she likes best."

"Or she could just have a dress made in each color," Elena said practically, hands on her hips as she looked between the two bolts of cloth.

"I like the blue," Rose said, and Terrence mentally congratulated himself on that guess. She had worn blue in the garden, after all. Although, come to think of it, where had her clothes in the garden come from? Magic was mysterious.

At that moment Silvertips and Emerald Eyes emerged from behind a stack of cloth and dived into the half-unrolled bolts piled everywhere.

"Don't let them get their claws in my silks!" Maude exclaimed, and soon half the room was chasing kittens.

Elena chose that moment of confusion to step up to Terrence and ask without preamble, "How was it with your father?"

He had half-thought she might be too distracted by clothing questions, or possibly running kittens, to think of that, but he should have known better. Elena could keep a half-dozen ideas in her head all at once without apparent effort. "It was—fine," he said after a moment. Really, what else was there to say? And what would be the point of mentioning his brothers either?

She looked at him with narrowed eyes but didn't ask questions.

"It was *fine*," he repeated anyway, even though he knew she didn't believe him that time either.

"Later," Elena said, "we should talk more."

She turned away to help chase kittens and Terrence rolled his eyes, but somewhere deep down he was glad. He probably wouldn't like whatever questions she wanted to ask, but he'd miss Elena a great deal, if she wasn't around to ask them.

It occurred to him that he should talk to Rose about all this too. But how much could he tell her without frightening her? He had already promised himself to be careful about that. Yet another tricky line to walk. As if he didn't have enough of those in his family already.

Chapter Sixteen: Rose

A messenger arrived at Rose's door mid-afternoon with an invitation to a small family supper with the king that evening. She sat on the divan in her bedroom, smoothing the calligraphed note in her hand, and seriously considered pleading a headache.

"Maybe they sent a note to your rooms too," she suggested to Elena, who was ransacking the wardrobe.

"It said *small* family supper, right? Henry and I are invited to the family suppers, but the small ones mean just the king, his sons and their wives." She looked critically at a red dress—the dressmakers had sent a dozen dresses up while they were out, from among the ones they had on hand—then put it back again.

Rose shook her head. "That's an official designation?"

"It may as well be. It's all etiquette and code around here. You know—wasn't it that way before your enchantment? Intimate family parties include me and a few other cousins, select gatherings are the king's favorite political supporters, and so on, and so on."

"I see," Rose murmured. Had she known things like that in the Before Time? The memories were still coming clearer all the time, and while she didn't remember exactly what the designations might have been then, the *idea* felt familiar. All the etiquette and the hidden meanings and watching people to hear what they said and know what they really meant...yes, she had a feeling there had been a lot of that in the Before Time.

The memories that were still coming back weren't as bad as the ones she had remembered in the garden, not as bad as the terrifying days right before the enchantment or the sound of the champions dying in the thorns. They weren't good memories either though. She could remember enough to know why the stories said she had been quiet and meek. In the Before Time she had watched and listened, while saying and doing very little. She didn't like that. She hadn't liked it then.

Elena studied the array of dresses and shook her head. "The dressmakers really did do their best selecting these, but a dress that isn't made especially for you is never going to look as well as a tailored one. This is going to get easier once Maude finishes a few dresses for you, and once they assign you your own ladies-in-waiting."

Rose wasn't convinced that second part *would* make life easier, but it was neither here nor there with the challenge of tonight. "I could say I'm still tired," she offered, but it was half-hearted. She'd have to face this eventually. And despite understanding Elena's focus on clothes, she didn't truly believe a new dress was going to make supper with Terrence's family significantly easier.

"You could say that," Elena said, perching on the edge of the bed. "I'm sure they'd understand." Nothing in her voice rang with conviction.

Rose summoned a smile. "Aren't you going to tell me your family are lovely people and I shouldn't be intimidated? Isn't that what people say in this situation?"

Elena tipped her head slightly. "In some families, I expect. And Terrence would probably say something like that, if you asked him."

The echo of what hadn't been said, of Elena's lack of agreement on that point, was loud. If she had meant to offer Terrence's opinion as a reassurance, it was the opposite. Rose told herself that, after all, Terrence *ought* to know his own family, and perhaps Elena was the one with an unreasonable assessment. Except her own brief impressions did not add up to anything very reassuring, and the idea that Terrence *didn't* see the troubling undertones was…troubling.

Rose didn't know what to say about that though, not certain she wanted to say anything at all, and after another moment Elena resumed, "You'll be fine. If you go. Of course you will be. Just…don't expect them to all be like Terrence."

She didn't expect that. That was exactly the problem. She'd already seen enough, heard enough, to not expect that. And there was something in Elena's eyes that made her suspect that 'not like Terrence' was the most neutral thing she could say. That maybe she would have said more, if there weren't things smart people didn't say about their king. Even if you were related to him. Maybe especially then.

"Oh well," she said after a moment. "It can't be worse than having magical walls of thorns try to consume me."

"I did imagine Terrence downplayed that part when he told me the story," Elena remarked. "It would be like him."

So Terrence had told Elena about the garden and the thorns and…how much else? Rose thought of kissing Terrence as the shadows surrounded them and wondered just how many details Elena knew. The mere fact of a kiss wouldn't surprise anyone, but the details of one desperate, urgent kiss as the world was ending—*that* felt intimate, speaking to feelings deep inside of her that were new and private. But surely Terrence was…discreet. And it wasn't as though Elena was just anyone to him. She'd been in the castle barely a day and she had already worked out that Elena was Terrence's closest confidante.

"I'd love to hear your version of things," Elena was continuing, "if it wasn't absolutely imperative that we have your hair done right now. If you *are* going to the small family supper?"

"Yes," Rose said carefully. "I think I am." Because she didn't want to hide away while the whole castle was talking about her, and she *did* have to do this sooner or later. To refuse a first invitation was only going to make her look weak and scared. She didn't want to be weak, and she didn't want them to know it if she was scared.

She didn't want to still be the quiet, meek girl who had only ever watched and listened. She felt a pang for her lost Mariqwe statue from the garden, of the warrior woman with her lioness beside her. Rose had no fighting skills and doubted she'd ever be able to learn, but she still wanted to be more like that than the girl she had been. This was how *she* entered battle. Facing Terrence's family, and facing her own future.

Elena and Gabrielle, the serving woman who had brought breakfast, helped Rose with her hair and into a lavender dress that they both assured her was simply lovely. This was some comfort, and it was a bigger comfort when Terrence arrived at her door to escort her to supper.

"You look beautiful," Terrence said as they walked through the halls, her hand on his arm. "That's a nice dress."

Rose suspected this was a less informed opinion than Elena's, but she appreciated that he was trying. "Thank you." She touched her full skirts with her free hand. "It's very different from the garden. But I guess everything is."

A worried crease appeared between his eyebrows. "Is this too much tonight? Maybe it's too soon—"

"I'll be fine," Rose said quickly. She had decided it was right to come, and she didn't want Terrence worrying about her. "It'll be good, to have a better chance to meet your family." It would be useful, at least. Not necessarily enjoyable.

"Sure," Terrence said, but he didn't look less worried. After a long pause, he said, "You know, my brothers may be...unpleasant, especially Gregory. But it's not about you, they're upset with me, because of—anyway, I'll be there if you need me and it will...be all right."

None of this was very reassuring, nor was it surprising. Though at least Terrence wasn't completely unaware of difficulties among his family. That was worth something.

By now a footman was opening the door onto the King's Private Dining Room. A distant memory told her that's what they had called the room in her day, and its function seemed to still be the same.

The footman did not formally announce them, but the murmur of voices halted within seconds as they stepped through the doorway. Rose kept her head up and smiled as though it was the respectful kind of silence, and not the silence that meant you had interrupted people who were talking about you.

The room had not changed too greatly since she had last been in it, as far as she could trust her memories. Lit by numerous candles in silver candelabras, the thick curtains, cushioned seating in the parlor portion of the room, and even the gleaming wooden table at the opposite end, created a cozy enough setting. It was the people making her nervous.

She couldn't match most faces to names yet, but a brief glance still told her they were the last arrivals. There was the king, and three younger men who looked like him, including Prince Gregory. The two women must be Princess Penelope and Prince Tyler's wife, whose name Rose couldn't just now remember.

She tightened her grip on Terrence's arm instinctively, and wished she had brought her kittens, left behind in the Queen's Rooms. Terrence at least was steadying in the face of all these strangers.

The blond woman in the scarlet dress was the first to approach, smiling widely. "Princess Rose, such a pleasure to meet you! I learned all about you as a child when my governess was teaching me history. Terribly dull subject, but your story was one of the more interesting bits, with that nasty curse and all those brave champions going off to perish. Mostly everyone assumed you were dead too, of course. I suppose being asleep for a hundred years isn't that different, is it? I'm Princess Lenora, I should have started with that—Prince Tyler's wife, you know." She waved back towards the others in the room, apparently indicating Tyler. Since the gesture encompassed every man in the room except Terrence, it didn't tell Rose anything.

"I'm pleased to meet you," Rose said carefully, the polite phrase that the moment obviously called for, and tried to ignore at least half of what Lenora had just said.

"You must come and settle a question for Penelope and me—you will let me borrow Rose, won't you, Terrence?" Lenora said, flashing him a quite brilliant smile.

"If you wish," Terrence said, his gaze on Rose, and she could feel the question was really for her.

She offered him a small smile just before Lenora whisked her away without waiting for further assent. Within moments she was seated on a long, low couch with Lenora on one side and a pale, dark-haired woman on the other—Princess Penelope, clearly.

"It's nice to meet you," Penelope murmured, barely looking up from her hands, folded neatly in her lap.

"And you," Rose said, as warmly as she could. "I've been wanting to make your acquaintance." She was curious about this woman, about the crown princess her return was displacing. Penelope was—or had been—the highest-ranking woman in court. She ought to know a great deal and her opinion ought to count for even more.

Although Rose knew first-hand how a high-ranking position might not count for very much in any meaningful way. And Elena's description of Penelope had suggested something of that.

Still, if she could get on anything like a friendly footing with Penelope, it could help. If the woman set herself up as an enemy—that would mean a lot too, and none of it good. "It must have been a great surprise to everyone, my returning to court," she ventured, thinking that was the most direct way she dared to get onto the most vital topic.

But all Penelope said was a faint, "Yes." And then without lifting her eyes, her gaze cut sideways across the room.

Rose followed the direction of her attention, and found Prince Gregory looking back at them, expression dark. It was only a moment before he turned away, returning to his conversation with his father, but Rose shivered. Instinctively she looked for Terrence, found him joining his other two brothers. Rose drew in a breath. She tried not to be rattled by her prickling awareness of Gregory radiating hostility from across the room, tried to focus back on the two women in front of her.

Penelope's gaze dropped down to her lap, fingers twisting, and Rose noticed for the first time that Penelope was wearing a small gold ring with an oval on it. She couldn't see the details, but she was almost sure it was a signet ring. She touched her own ring, on the smallest finger of her right hand. Two rings, two crown princesses. This was going to be complicated.

"Anyway," Lenora broke in, "I was just telling Penelope that she absolutely must try doing her hair up in that new style the wife of the ambassador from Glyster was wearing. Apparently it's quite the new fashion, but Penelope isn't sure she has the face for it. What do you think, Rose?"

Clothes and hair and opinions. She could see already what Elena meant about the women's side of the court running on these things. But it was never *really* about clothes and hair, was it?

More memories came back to her, not with the force or the pain of the ones that had emerged in the garden. This was more like pushing aside a veil, to see clearly what had been murky and ignored for years. She remembered the ladies of the court, not so much names and personalities but the group of them all together and the way the world had worked within their circle. What clothes you wore, how you did your hair—it was all a sign of status and privilege and sometimes even loyalties, and it all reflected on the chief men in your life as well…

She had no idea what any fashion choice meant now. She was going to have to learn it all again, and in this moment she had to trust that Elena really had been looking out for her by suggesting this dress, or when she styled her hair.

She pushed back through the memories and the concerns to Lenora's original question. The new hairstyle, would it look good on Penelope? A ridiculous question to ask her, when she couldn't possibly know what the style looked like, but either Lenora was very silly, or she knew that perfectly well…

Rose smiled sweetly, lips curving into a particular smile that felt familiar even though she didn't think she'd worn it in a long, long time. "Penelope, your hairstyle looks lovely just as it is. I never believed in following a fashion just because it *was* the fashion. But tell me, what did the ambassador from Glyster's wife's hairstyle look like? I don't think I've had the chance to see it."

There. A perfectly innocuous response on the surface with a multitude of layers to it. Calling Penelope by her first name indicated they were of at least equal rank, and was evidently still the social norm among princesses, since Lenora had called Rose by name. Complimenting Penelope's hair signaled friendly intentions and a possible alliance. Stating her disapproval of trends indicated she wasn't weak-minded and easily influenced. And directly pointing out her own unawareness of the hairstyle under discussion drew a firm line against being made a fool of with ridiculous questions, while not being overtly hostile towards Lenora.

She had forgotten how exhausting conversation with the court ladies could be. But it was…sort of an interesting puzzle too. She hadn't played this game much in the Before Time, but she thought possibly she had wanted to, if she'd only dared.

There was the tiniest beat of a pause before Lenora's response, as though Rose's hadn't been what she had expected—or perhaps she was just deciphering it all. Then she gave a little tinkling laugh. "Oh, of course, how silly of me, naturally you wouldn't have seen it—although she was in the throne room when you and Terrence came in yesterday, but I suppose you wouldn't have noticed…"

Self-deprecation, that was conceding a point, but was that a small if unreasonable jab at Rose's powers of observation? Layers and layers.

Lenora went on talking, Penelope contributed very little, and Rose found it wasn't hard to fall back into habits she hadn't thought of in years—a certain way of nodding and murmuring neutral phrases and letting the world go on around her while she contemplated her own private thoughts.

Was Penelope always this quiet? Probably. Elena had said something along those lines. Rose had to hope it was the norm, or else she could only interpret Penelope's quietness as unfriendliness. Considering the way her husband was glaring at Rose from across the room, that was a very real possibility.

Was Lenora always this talkative, and was she reading all the layers Rose did, or was she really thinking only of hairstyles? Was she as genuinely friendly as she seemed to be on the surface, or was the shiver of unease Rose had felt when Lenora had so insensitively mentioned her history a truer guide?

After Elena, these were only the second and third women of the court she had met. She was going to have a lot of work to do, learning new names and faces and personalities, factions and loyalties and so on. It was slightly comforting that at least she had met three of the most important women. Many of the others were surely taking their cues from the princesses, perhaps from the king's niece too.

Were they going to start looking to her for cues? She was almost certain they hadn't, in the Before Time. But things didn't need to be the same. She didn't want things to be the same.

Lenora had not yet exhausted the topic of hairstyles when they were all summoned to the table for supper. Terrence came to Rose's rescue before she could start worrying about the complicated business of who sat where. He arrived at her side, took her arm, and led her towards the table.

"Enjoying the evening so far?" he asked, smiling, but his eyes looked worried.

"Of course," she said lightly, squeezed his arm. It wasn't entirely untrue.

The table looked uneven, with one larger chair at the head—for the king, obviously—and four seats down the left side, three down the right. Terrence had just started to reach for the farthest seat on the left when his father said shortly, "What are you doing at that seat? Sit here." He indicated the chair to his immediate left as he sat down himself.

For just a second Terrence looked blank, then recovered enough to lead Rose to that end of the table. Layers. It was plain enough that Terrence's usual seat was at the end, farther away from his father, a less important position. Moving up at the table, that was an advancing of rank—although, Rose noted, Gregory was still in the right hand seat, which was likely higher still. From the dark stare he was giving Terrence as it was, it was perhaps best that King Elgin hadn't pushed him out of his seat. But he *should* have, if he was really recognizing Terrence in the new position of crown prince.

Rose had just sat down next to Terrence, opposite Penelope, when she felt a pawing at her feet. A moment later, Silvertips hopped up into her lap. Emerald Eyes peered out from beneath the long tablecloth.

"How did that animal get in here?" King Elgin said, voice cold as he stared at the kitten in Rose's lap.

"Cats always go where they will," Rose said automatically, because it was true and how she had always explained their presence in her garden. She didn't know how they had got here any more than she had known how they got to the garden. She reviewed the words after they were said, and decided they were all right. If he was offended by the cats' presence, she had disclaimed responsibility. But she also hadn't apologized or offered to send them back to her room.

The king kept his gaze on her a moment longer, then looked away. Perhaps he thought it was beneath his dignity to order the removal of kittens.

One of the other princes sat down on Rose's right, and when Lenora sat down next to him Rose concluded he must be Tyler. That meant the one who sat down next to Penelope was the unmarried Edward. It was a relief to have everyone sorted. All four princes resembled their father, with dark hair and eyes, but it wouldn't be hard to keep them straight. Gregory was the tallest but Tyler was the broadest. Edward had the slightest build and narrowest face, and Terrence was, of course, Terrence. She'd need to understand this group, and names were a start.

The king said the Invocation Before Meals, repeating the words and naming the gods with no particular indication of either piety or irreverence. It was just what one said, and Rose was comforted to find that the words hadn't changed in the past century.

The first course served was soup. There were three spoons at each place setting; Rose knew which one would have been correct in the Before Time, but was it still the same? She watched out of the corner of her eye to see which spoon Terrence picked up—not the one she would have guessed. No one was dipping their spoons though, and she suspected an old etiquette rule still held—confirmed when everyone started eating a beat after the king did.

Maybe she'd sit down with Elena tomorrow and start a full interrogation on etiquette, court rules, current styles… Distracted, she wasn't prepared for the piquant flavor of the soup in her first taste. She coughed, reached for her drink.

"Are you all right?" Terrence asked instantly, that worried line appearing between his eyebrows again.

"Fine," she said, waving her free hand. "It was just spicier than I expected."

"I don't imagine dzonkhang peppers were common before your enchantment," Edward remarked. "Aren't they a more recent import?"

"I've had them, actually," Rose said, dipping her spoon into the soup again. "My father opened diplomatic relations with Querendell when I was sixteen, and their cuisine was introduced at court when I was eighteen. It was rather popular shortly before my enchantment."

"Fascinating," Edward said, and she wasn't certain how to read his smile. Had she misstepped there, correcting his impression?

"Has anyone thought of having Rose talk to the court historians?" Terrence asked. "There must be a lot of information you could tell them, if you'd like to."

"That sounds nice," Rose said. She would have said it even if it wasn't true, because it was Terrence suggesting the idea, but it really *did* sound nice. It would probably be restful to talk to people who wanted to hear stories about the past, not jockey for current political advantage.

"Oh, that sounds perfect," Gregory said savagely, thunking his cup down on the table. "Go bury yourself with the historians. Pity you weren't buried in history, behind those wretched thorns."

The clinking of spoons around the table suddenly ceased and Rose could see Terrence tense beside her. She reached out without thinking, put a hand on his knee. She smiled her very sweetest smile at Gregory. "I was only buried for a hundred years. And I do feel so *very* lucky to be back and to assume my proper place in court again." Her proper place that outranked *him*. He was likely going to hate her no matter what she said or did, so she'd rather show him that she wasn't frightened of him.

And if that appearance was completely untrue, well, if she pretended long enough not to fear Gregory, maybe it would become true.

Before Gregory could respond, Edward spoke up again. "I'm quite curious about the end of the enchantment, in fact. Do you imagine a hundred years was simply the intended span of the spell? It was ready to break, in a sense?"

His tone was one of academic curiosity, but wasn't there an implied insult to Terrence in the question? Did Edward see that, or not? Either way, there was only one response to make . "No, I don't think that's why the spell broke. I think it took a hundred years for the right champion to finally come along."

She felt Terrence's hand cover hers, his fingers curl around hers. She smiled at him, and didn't care if everyone saw it. If they were wondering where her loyalties were—they could stop wondering.

"History is boring," Tyler announced, "and nobody understands enchantments but enchanters. Why worry about it when you can enjoy a good bottle of wine instead?" He gestured and a servant hastened forward to refill his glass.

As the soup bowls were being cleared away, Rose realized that King Elgin had not commented on any of the discussion. She glanced his way without turning her head, saw that he was watching with an inscrutable expression. Watching and thinking and studying them all, probably weighing strengths and weaknesses and alliances and conflicts. It was what she was doing too, but it still made her uncomfortable, the silent, judging king.

Supper wound its way through four more courses. Penelope was silent throughout while Lenora chattered in any quiet spot. The king kept watching, and Gregory—Rose tried not to look at Gregory, and the smoldering fury behind his eyes. After the final course they all sat a while longer until the king finally dismissed them.

Terrence took Rose's arm again when they were standing, asked quietly, "May I see you back to your room?"

She smiled, nodded, and it was a relief when they were alone again in the hall –comparatively. There were the kittens, trailing along behind, and people were always passing, even this late in the evening. But they were out from under the eyes of his family.

"I'm glad you came to supper tonight," Terrence said, and possibly he seemed a little more relaxed than he had been. "I hope it wasn't—too hard."

"Not *too* hard, no," she said in considering tones. It had been challenging, yes. But interesting too. Like suddenly attempting a game she used to know well but hadn't played in years. She wasn't certain she had actually *played* it in the Before Time, only watched.

"I'm sorry they're not friendlier, and I know Gregory is—making everything uncomfortable," Terrence said, expression concerned again. "It should get better. There's just—some adjusting to do."

Rose thought back to Gregory's barely contained rage, and Terrence's reassurance wasn't enough to take the threat out of it. "Yes. There's adjusting for me too."

He hesitated when they got to her door, glancing around. There were two servants down the hall one direction, a couple of men who were probably aristocracy the other way, more people passing in the farther distance. Another of her father's rules swam out of her memory—it was not proper, not dignified, for royalty to show affection in public. Had that rule survived down through the generations too?

"Good night, Terrence," she said softly.

"Good night…" Then he came to an apparent decision, leaned in and kissed her. His lips were soft and his hand curled around her cheek and it was sweet even if it didn't last very long. He hadn't kissed her all day, and she admitted to herself that she would have been terribly disappointed if he hadn't now either. Those servants, probably others too, would surely see and spread the story—but it was worth it.

Terrence turned to go with a new lightness in his step that made Rose smile. She pushed open her door, then looked after him. "Terrence?" He stopped to look back. "I'm glad it was you, who came to break the spell."

He smiled at her. "So am I. Good night, Rose."

She stepped into her room, kittens frisking past her feet, and closed the door behind her. She leaned back against it, letting out a breath. It hadn't been a terrible evening, but it was a relief to have it done, to be back in her own room—

"Your Highness?"

Rose jumped, and Gabrielle, rising from the couch, turned pink. "I'm sorry—I shouldn't have presumed—but you'll need someone to help you out of that dress, and I thought…"

Rose tried to martial her thoughts again. "No, that's all right. I just didn't think." She hadn't thought about it, that she couldn't reach all the buttons of this dress herself. She'd have to start considering that sort of thing. "Thank you, that was very thoughtful of you."

Her mind kept working as Gabrielle helped her out of the dress. She'd need a Lady of the Wardrobe; one should have been assigned by now, and should she read anything into it that no one had been? Well, she'd look into it tomorrow, see who Elena recommended. She'd have to rely on Elena until she could make her own observations of the court ladies. She could ask Terrence, but were the genders as separated now as they had been in her own day? She'd need to select a staff, discuss styles with Maude and the other dressmakers. She didn't want to need three people to dress and undress her every day, and maybe that was a fight worth having. If she was going to take a stand on something, to prove that she could, maybe insisting on clothing she could manage herself was a reasonable battle to choose. There had to be a way to design beautiful dresses that weren't so complicated.

At last the business of preparing for bed was done, Gabrielle departed, and she could climb into bed with her kittens. Distantly she could hear the castle bells ringing for the hour, and counted off to eleven. Late, time to sleep, and she tried to put thoughts of politics and etiquette and the rest out of her head. She'd much rather think about that good night kiss from Terrence.

But it was hard not to let her mind drift back to the supper before it, to the family around the table.

This was to be her home now, these the people she was going to live with. Though her memories of the Before Time kept growing clearer, it was hard to say for certain if her family, if the people around her then, had been better or worse. In some ways, she didn't think it was all that different—a powerful king, a court surrounding him with complex loyalties and hidden intentions.

But now there was Terrence. And Elena. And herself. Who was *she* going to be now?

Living outside of the garden was clearly going to be an entirely different challenge than merely escaping from it.

Chapter Seventeen: Terrence

Terrence made his way back to his own rooms, after seeing Rose to hers. He was thinking about her smile, about kissing her. He needed to find more opportunities to kiss her. All that time alone in the garden, and now, when they could really make the most of some time alone…he could find it in himself to wish the spell hadn't broken quite so quickly.

He let himself into his rooms, still thinking things that put a smile on his face, and found Elena sitting on his couch, reading a book.

This was normal enough that he merely greeted her with, "Good evening," and sat down in the armchair opposite the couch.

She'd been dropping into his rooms for as long as he could remember. The first time she did it after she was married, he had asked if Henry knew where she was. She had given him such a lecture on the subject (of course Henry did, how dare Terrence imply otherwise, furthermore there was nothing in the least wrong with her being there, and besides which, why did he think she needed Henry's permission?) that he'd never asked that again.

"So," Elena said, closing her book, "how was the small family supper?"

"Fine. You know." He rubbed the back of his neck, fingertips brushing the chain for his mother's ring. "Nothing particularly unusual." It was mostly true. It was true on a surface level, though under that he'd felt more tense than usual, wondering what people might say, whether Gregory was going to be horrible, whether his father was going to start in on lecturing, whether it would all go wrong somehow. It wasn't that unusual to think all that around his family, but Rose's presence, worrying about how she was feeling, added so much more weight to it.

"Hmm," Elena said, arching an eyebrow. "So Gregory glowered, Tyler drank too much, Edward was diplomatic, Lenora talked incessantly, and Penelope was quiet?"

"You're always trying to sum people up," Terrence protested. "They're more complicated than that."

"But?" Elena prompted.

"But…yes, that's pretty much how it went."

"How bad was Gregory?" she asked, toying with the edge of her book.

Angry, rude, openly hostile. If he told Elena that, she'd probably go on for the next hour about how terrible Gregory was, and that wouldn't help. She had always taken the bleakest view of Gregory; even Terrence's mother hadn't been able to argue her out of it, when she was alive. "He wasn't that bad. I mean, he's not happy, but you can't blame him for that. He didn't throw a table knife at me or anything." He meant it as a joke, obviously.

Elena didn't laugh. "That's something. How was your father?"

"He was good," Terrence said, maybe too heartily. His father had been the one missing from her earlier list, hadn't he? "He was pleasant. In a good mood." Quiet, mostly, which was a better mood than when he decided to lecture everyone on their failings. He was trying to make them better, of course, but it always made for an uncomfortable evening.

She nodded as though she was filing this information away. "And how was Rose?"

He felt his cheeks warm, remembering kissing Rose good-night. This was ridiculous, he couldn't start blushing every time her name came up! "Fine. She's fine." He looked up at the ceiling, willing his cheeks to cool, hoping Elena wasn't noticing.

Of course she was noticing. Out of the corner of his eye he could see her mouth curve into a smile. "Speaking of Rose…"

"Were we? I thought we were talking about the supper—"

"Speaking of *Rose*," she repeated, "you were holding out on me yesterday."

He spread his hands. "I don't know what you're talking about." A flat lie.

She leaned forward, jabbed a finger at his chest. “I asked you how you felt about marrying her, and you said you thought it would be fine. And I asked how you felt about *her* and you said she was nice and I’d like her.”

“And that was true!” Terrence protested.

She snorted, an unladylike snort he knew she’d never do in front of most people. “You were being formal yesterday in the throne room in front of your father, but it only took two minutes this morning to see that you like this woman. I mean, you *really* like her.”

“I told you she was likeable—”

“No, no, you like lots of people, but this is not the same thing. Come on, this is *me*, Terrence. You really like her.”

He ducked his head, face burning again. He probably should have told Elena the whole thing yesterday but it had been too new, too sudden. It wasn’t like he’d expected to hide anything from her for long though. “She’s…something special.”

Elena leaned back on the couch again, expression smug. “Special. Mm-hmm. Go on.”

The words spilled out in a sudden rush. “She’s…kind, and brave, and smart—and beautiful, obviously, and she has this *laugh*—and I want to protect her from everything and find out what she thinks about everything and—when she smiles, it’s so…” He shook his head. “I don’t know, she’s just—I’ve never met anyone like her.”

Elena was looking at him with a new softness in her eyes and a half-smile on her face. “Oh, Terrence. You don’t just like her, do you?”

He looked away, for all that could hide. He should have known Elena would be able to see this. “I don’t—I don’t know.” But of course he did.

That didn’t fool Elena either. Her smile grew, and she reached out to squeeze his hand. “I’m glad for you, Terrence. Really. You should have something like this. I know when I met Henry…” Her gaze drifted away, her smile taking on a different meaning. She shook her head after a moment. “Anyway. I’m really glad.”

There wasn’t much point denying it after that. One other thing though— “Don’t say anything to Rose, all right?”

Elena frowned, brow furrowing. "Wait—Rose *knows*, doesn't she? You have told her?"

"Things have been—happening very fast, and it's been a lot in the last few days, and I wouldn't want her to feel—pressured or overwhelmed or..." He sighed. This all sounded very noble and considerate and it was only half the truth. "And I don't know how she feels."

"Oh, Terrence, don't be an idiot," Elena said, straightening up on the couch. "That woman lit up when you walked into the room this morning. And again later at the dressmakers."

He wanted to believe her. But Elena was bound to be biased in his favor. "She's in a strange place and I'm the only familiar face."

"That is not what was happening," Elena said, shaking her head. "It's not like she said it in words, but it was all over her face. And remember she agreed to a betrothal too."

"You're grasping at straws with that one. We both know a betrothal doesn't prove anything." Maybe for most people it did, but not with royalty.

Elena hesitated, then shrugged. "All right, I'll grant you that one. But that doesn't change the main point here. You're smitten with Rose and she feels the same way and you ought to talk to her about it."

Terrence frowned down at his feet. "But..." There was no one else in the world he would say this to—but this was Elena. "But why would she be?" How could he assume that she felt the same things for him that he felt for her? How could he imagine he deserved a gift like that?

"Oh, Terrence," Elena said again, voice effused with exasperated affection. She stood up and leaned down to drop a light kiss on his forehead. "You're an idiot but you're a very lovable one. Now I need to get home, and you need to figure out what you're going to tell Rose."

Maybe. He watched Elena walk towards his door. Before she got there, he said, "Hey, Elena? What do you think of Rose?"

She glanced back. "I like her. And I'm curious about her. I think she's been underestimated for a long time, and that...could prove interesting. Get some sleep, Terrence. And talk to Rose tomorrow."

He didn't talk to Rose tomorrow, not about the things Elena thought he should. He did see her though. He went to her rooms early, caught her alone eating breakfast, wrapped in a blue dressing gown that was very distracting in the way it clung to her shape. The result was a much better kiss than the fleeting one in the hallway, and when she invited him to join her for breakfast, he seriously considered whether it was appropriate to make a declaration of love over muffins.

Before he could get…really anywhere, a serving woman arrived to help Rose dress.

"Good morning, Gabrielle," Rose said with a smile, rising from the table. "I think the red dress today. We'll have to see later how Maude is getting on with the new ones. I want to talk to her about some of the styles."

"Very good, Your Highness," Gabrielle said, bobbing a curtsy and retreating to the bedroom, presumably to get out the dress in question. Both kittens tumbled out from under the table and chased after her.

Rose tapped her fingers against the edge of the table, evidently thinking. "I'll have to talk to someone today about selecting a Lady of the Wardrobe. I assume Penelope and Lenora each have one. Do you know who's in charge of that sort of thing?"

This was not an area of court politics he was intimately familiar with, but he'd picked up some ideas here and there. He at least was aware of the concept, of a sort of chief lady in waiting assigned to each princess and put in charge of dresses and other personal matters. "I think the crown princess arranges—oh." Was that still Penelope, or Rose herself?

Rose half-smiled. "It does make things a bit awkward, doesn't it? I suppose I'll have to talk to Penelope—and I want to ask Elena if she'd recommend anyone. Unless you have an idea which court lady might be suitable?"

He knew most of them by name, had a passing acquaintance with a good number from various social functions, but had never thought about them in this context. "Um…Lady Sylvia and Lady Maeron are friendly."

"I'll keep that in mind," she said, and he only realized he was staring at her when she asked, "And what are you thinking about, when you look at me so intently?"

"Oh—just that I didn't know you were so interested in all…this." That wasn't it exactly, but it was the best he could manage to explain it. It was that he was suddenly seeing a new side he hadn't known she had. It wasn't a bad thing, maybe even a good thing—but a new thing.

She tipped her head slightly, looking at him. "I like pretty dresses as well as anyone. But also, dresses and ladies in waiting and the right hairstyles, they're all about status. If I'm going to have status in this court, I have to claim it, and this is one way women do it. What do men do? Hit each other with swords?"

"Something like that," he admitted, thoughts of his last fight with Gregory coming to mind. If he had won that fight, would he ever have charged off to look for the Princess Behind Thorns? "Rescuing cursed princesses is a good way too," he said with a smile.

Her answering smile was arch. "That doesn't mean you ought to go rescue another one."

"Would you dislike that?" he asked, looking down into her blue eyes.

"Exceedingly," she said, voice soft.

They had drifted close together somehow, and she was still wearing that blue dressing gown, and if he didn't know Gabrielle was in the next room…

Terrence took a reluctant step back. "I should go, let you get dressed. There's a council meeting in an hour anyway, so—"

"There's a council meeting this morning?" Rose said, gaze suddenly intent in a different way.

"Oh—yes, there always is one this day of the week." It belatedly occurred to him what he should have realized sooner. "Do you want to come?"

"Yes," Rose said, a newly determined set to her mouth. "I do."

By the time he was letting himself out, having promised to come meet her before the meeting, he was sure Elena was right. People had been underestimating Rose. Maybe he had been too. Although at least he had been certain, right from the beginning, that there was much more to her than the stories said. He didn't know just what those depths were going to reveal—but he was looking forward to finding out. And to watching the rest of the court find out too.

Chapter Eighteen: Rose

Rose at least expected Gregory's glare and his demand of, "What is *she* doing here again?" when she came in the door for her second council meeting. It wasn't pleasant, but the predictability gave her a small sense of being more in control than before.

And she was ready to hide her shiver of unease, smile sweetly and respond just as though he'd asked the question in the spirit of polite inquiry rather than it being obviously rude and rhetorical. "I'm here because I want to learn about my country and my government now that I've returned." Let him notice that repetition of *my* if he liked. She looked around for the nearest servant, spying a footman. "Please fetch another chair. You can place it there." She pointed to a gap between chairs at the table. It was not a larger gap than any other, but that wasn't the point. It was the space next to the chair at the king's left. She had no intention of letting herself and Terrence remain at the far end of the table any longer.

The footman obeyed the order and Gregory glowered, but the king didn't countermand the directions. By the time the council meeting began, the chairs had been adjusted and Rose was installed in her new seat, with the kittens curled up under her chair and Terrence taking the place between herself and the king. She didn't altogether want to be that close to the king, but the status of it was obvious. Whether an advantageous seating position was going to lead to any power remained to be seen. But it counted for something.

She folded her hands on the table, gold signet ring glinting in the light, and prepared herself to learn what she could from the meeting ahead.

The next three hours proved to be long and difficult to follow, and her confidence flagged as they went on about issues she couldn't entirely keep track of. Taxes and land claims and plans to renovate the big tournament arena behind the castle and a new guard post that was being built in some port somewhere and wrinkles in the trade alliance with Thaydan and on and on and on. A hundred years was a lot of missing context, and this was not a situation where she could ask for clarification. And it wasn't just the matter of a hundred years; she'd never been in council meetings in the Before Time anyway.

So she did her best to study personalities and to make mental notes of questions to ask Terrence and Elena later.

Gregory was still in his seat to the right of the king—she hadn't dared to try to oust him from there, and besides, Terrence probably ought to do it. And to say something about Gregory's silver signet ring too. She suspected Terrence would have an explanation about not moving too quickly if she mentioned it. The oldest prince didn't speak much, but people fell respectfully silent when he did, which seemed more a function of rank than the value of his words.

Tyler was not at this meeting, maybe because of the amount of wine he'd drunk the night before. Edward had a seat halfway down the table, and spent the meeting making notes. People didn't give him the kind of attention they gave Gregory, yet she saw him turn the direction of a discussion at least twice. Edward was smart, but how many other people in the room realized it?

Rupin, the Chief Librarian, seemed to be the nicest one on the council. There were four other lords she decided she didn't like. The most vocal was the one who had objected to changing the succession during her first council meeting. All four leaped to agree with the king, no matter what was under discussion.

The Chief Priest of the Temple of Mariqwe, the Chief Priest of Arthian the God of Wisdom, and the head of the Court Enchanters all sat on the council, which she didn't think had been the case in her father's day. All three were competing to appear otherworldly.

The gray-haired man at the foot of the table, who she remembered as General Graybourne from the last meeting, commanded more respect than most in the room. Like Gregory, people listened when he talked, but it seemed to Rose that what he actually *said* mattered more.

The remaining three councilmembers were nobility, and would require more time for an assessment. She'd like to know what Terrence thought of all of them. And what Elena thought, because the impressions could be different.

Terrence frowned more often than he spoke, and when he did say something, it didn't seem to Rose that enough attention was paid. And maybe she was biased, but she thought he had good things to say—thoughtful, well-reasoned, well-put. And usually coming in on the side of moderation, or pointing out something or someone who had been forgotten in the discussion.

And the king—King Elgin sat at the head of the table, a commanding presence of mercurial moods. He often let people talk while he watched, then without warning would suddenly cut in with a biting comment, a flat decision, or an abrupt redirection of the discussion. As she had thought, he was someone who knew well how to observe and learn, but no one would ever accuse him of being quiet and meek. He showed deference to no one, but was slightly more polite to General Graybourne and to two of the lords who supported him. He interrupted Terrence twice, which irritated Rose both times.

Her mind felt positively crowded by the time the meeting closed, and yet much of what it was crowded with were questions, seeking still more information.

"Care to see the royal gardens?" Terrence asked her as they left the councilroom, kittens trotting beside them.

That was perfect. She'd been trying to think how she could get him alone to ask some of her questions. "I'd love to."

Outside, it was a beautiful sunny day, the kind of day it had almost always been while she was enchanted but that, she remembered, was not the case in the rest of the world. The air was cooler than it had been then too, but not uncomfortable.

"It's not as big as your garden, somehow," Terrence said, a trace of apology in his voice as they reached the edge of a rose garden that she was certain had not been there in the Before Time. "But this part is nice."

"Are there benches? We could sit," Rose suggested, and so they did.

The roses, in contrast to the riot of blooms in her garden, were just starting to bud. She was curious about that, about what varieties there were and when they had been planted, and it was a nice day for a walk—but she had too many questions!

She leaned towards Terrence on the bench, while the kittens ran about between the glossy green bushes. “So they kept talking about the war. And I couldn’t ask them *what war*, but—what war?”

Terrence took a deep breath. “Ah. Right. You were away for a hundred years. That was recent, though, against Melidan in the west. It ended over a year ago, but we’re still dealing with the clean-up.”

There had been a long history of skirmishes with Melidan in the Before Time, so this wasn’t entirely shocking. The mountain range between the two countries had had the border through it redrawn repeatedly. “How did it start?”

Terrence shook his head. “How do these things ever start? There was a dispute about the existing treaties and trade agreements, things got more acrimonious, honor got involved—they think we started it, we say they did, the whole thing was a diplomatic mess. I was only starting to join the council meetings near the end, when fighting was pretty much inevitable. The war went on for over two years, mostly in the mountains so nothing moved very fast because mountains are a terrible place for rapid advancement. Gregory married Penelope a couple years ago, when it looked like we were going to be bogged down forever; she’s from Relnyra, and part of the marriage negotiations secured new resources we needed to throw at the war. We managed to take a key pass about 18 months ago, and that was pretty much the end. We came out of it with new mining access and control of a new trade route, so my father calls it a victory.”

“You don’t think so?” Rose asked quietly.

“I don’t know. Yes, on balance, but it had a high cost, is all. I wasn’t on the front line, but…I heard all the stories, and we’re still dealing with the aftermath.”

“Like the land and education plan,” Rose prompted, and watched him frown again. “Do you know you got exactly that expression when it came up in the meeting?”

He sighed, face smoothing again. “No, but it doesn’t surprise me. The land and education plan was a promise made near the beginning of the war. The government promised land for the soldiers, and education for their children, which would really mean establishing schools in under-served areas and educating all the children. Since the war ended…nothing's happened. They put Gregory in charge of it, but he doesn't have a head for administration and just keeps reporting all the obstacles whenever it comes up, which isn't often anymore."

Rose studied Terrence's face. There'd been a number of things he didn't like in the council meeting, but there had been something *more* about this particular topic. She thought possibly he'd mentioned something about promises to soldiers, back in the garden, when he explained why he had come to find her. It was a good thing if he wanted to keep promises to soldiers, to educate children, but she wasn't certain that was the whole story here. "Why did it bother you *so* much?"

Terrence ran a hand through his hair, looked off into the distance. "Because I worked out a plan. I started doing research, I looked at the decrees and the records of enlistment and the current schools in the country—*and* the tax records that show the revenue changes of the principle lords and the crown since we opened the new trading route as a result of the war. I presented it all at a council meeting earlier this month. Based on place of residence, I estimated at least half of the soldiers or their widows wouldn't actually want land—they didn't have that kind of profession—and would prefer the monetary equivalent. For those who would, a lot of them were already renting land that could be granted to them, and I found some options for where we could deed land over to the rest. It was going to cost each lord something, of course, but it was mostly balanced by increases in revenue anyway. They were also likely to see a tax increase within a few years, because all that money going out was going to circle through the cities, and the people who had new ownership of their land were likely to produce more; it tends to happen that way. I thought the crown could lead the way, making our own contribution and possibly supplementing some of the lords who'd be giving the most. The schools were the comparatively easy part, costing some money but not actually that much." He waved a hand. "Anyway, you don't want all the details…"

"I might," Rose said.

Terrence's smile had a grim edge to it she hadn't seen before. "No one else did. No one was interested. They said it would cost too much and be too complicated and they'd defer it for later and that was all."

"That's terrible," Rose said, genuinely offended on his behalf, and also bothered by what it suggested about the council itself.

Terrence shrugged. "People love a good rallying speech about going to war. No one gets excited about a fifty-page plan for peace time."

"They should. It's more valuable."

"Maybe." Terrence was silent a moment, then sighed again. "So. If you want the *whole* story…"

"Of course I do."

"Well—after the meeting Gregory got angry with me about it, that it was none of my business since it was his project. There were…words. He asked me what I thought I knew about war anyway, it somehow ended up in a swordfight in the practice yard with most of the court watching, and…I lost. I always lose when I fight Gregory. And then the next day I went to find the Princess Behind Thorns."

"Ah," Rose said, a few pieces suddenly fitting together more clearly. "You wanted to be heir so that they would listen to you." When he had said that back in the garden, he hadn't meant it as broadly as she had imagined. Or rather, he probably had, but he had meant it very specifically too.

"Something like that. But of course that's going to take time," he said quickly, as though he could read her thoughts—that the council was still treating Gregory to much more attention. "Anyway," he said, running his hand through his hair again, "here I'm supposed to be the clever one, and I'm sitting in a garden with a beautiful woman telling her an embarrassing story. Very clever, that."

"I'm the one who asked. But I have other questions if you'd rather not talk about…" She caught up suddenly to the deeper implied meaning in his statement. "Talking about governing isn't what you had in mind when you suggested walking in the garden, is it?"

He smiled. "Not exactly."

"I'm sorry—there's just so much I'm trying to catch up on, so much to try to understand. And I *want* to understand, I want to know what's happening and to try to do something about it. I never had the chance before the enchantment and maybe I won't get the chance now, but I want to try. I'm not even sure who I am now, but I think that's who I want to be, someone who knows what's going on in the important conversations and the important decisions and who can actually do something that matters…and I'm still talking too much," she wound up, ducking her head. When had Terrence become so easy to talk to?

"I like it when you talk," Terrence said softly. "I find you fascinating."

"That might be the nicest thing anyone's ever said to me," Rose said honestly. It was nicer than being told she was beautiful, which was what usually came up and didn't mean half as much.

"If that's true, I should be complimenting you more."

They were leaning close together on the bench by now, and it was the most natural thing in the world to lean a little further in and kiss him. Rose slid her hands over his shoulders, touching the back of his neck, running her fingers through his hair. He wrapped his arms around her, palms pressing against her back. With the rustle of the breeze among leaves and the warmth of the sunshine, it was like stepping back to a simpler time in the past—but there had been nothing as magical as kissing Terrence then.

"You could do this more often too," Rose said at length.

"I'll keep that in mind," he said with a smile, before pulling her closer again and following the suggestion.

The idyll in the garden gave way to more practical matters—luncheon, and then a trip to the dressmakers where Maude and the other women seemed initially confused by Rose's request for dresses she could manage herself, but then increasingly enthusiastic on the idea. By the time she left, they were full of designs for side buttons, strategically placed lacings, looser sleeves, and the like.

She was back in her bedroom, making notes of what she remembered from the council meeting and marking questions she still wanted to ask, when Elena came knocking at the door.

"Oh good," Rose said, greeting her, "I have so much I want to talk to you about!"

"Really?" Elena said, raising an eyebrow as she came in. "I hear you've been busy with the royal dressmakers. Going to introduce some new fashions to the court?"

She'd have to keep in mind how fast news traveled in the castle. Probably everyone knew that she'd been kissing Terrence in the garden too. No one had seemed to be in sight, but that didn't mean they hadn't been glimpsed by someone. "I guess you could call it new fashion," Rose said, sitting down on her low couch and gesturing to Elena to do the same. "I just want clothes I don't need five people to help me with. What do *you* do?"

Elena shrugged, and stroked Emerald Eyes, who had leaped into her lap. "I don't attempt the elaborate costumes Penelope wears, and Henry is actually very good with buttons."

That was a thought, that someday Terrence would be able to—suddenly the thought of Terrence helping her undress turned into thoughts she didn't really want to have in front of his cousin and almost-sister. She coughed. "Well, I'll—keep that in mind. But speaking of clothes, I wanted to ask your advice about selecting a Lady of the Wardrobe."

Elena's eyes narrowed. "They still haven't appointed someone?"

"Not so anyone has told me." She had thought of asking Elena to take the role, but wasn't certain it was appropriate for the king's niece. Elena would surely volunteer if she wanted the job, and perhaps it would be better anyway to use it as an opportunity to gain an additional ally.

"It would be Penelope's role to do appoint someone, which means Gregory is the one really in control, so…" Elena shook her head. "Actually, it's probably for the best if you make your own choice."

"I agree," Rose said firmly. She hadn't quite put those pieces together, but she definitely did not want anyone Gregory chose to be involved in something so intimate as selecting her clothing. "I can say it's part of my role as crown princess, so therefore I *should* make my own selection." And ignore the insulting aspect of no one else having done it. Gregory had probably meant it to be insulting; it was lucky he wasn't craftier, and used the opportunity to do more damage.

"That's not untrue and would be the best way to put it," Elena agreed.

"The trouble is," Rose continued, "I don't actually know who to select. I asked Terrence, and he suggested Lady Sylvia and Lady Maeron…"

Elena was already shaking her head. "No, definitely not good choices. Exactly who he *would* say, but no."

"He only said they were friendly."

Elena laughed. "Of course he did. And of course they *were*. They're both in the right rank and position to see an unmarried younger prince as an advantageous match."

That put a different color on things. "Oh. I see."

"There wasn't actually anything between them," Elena said hurriedly, suddenly looking concerned. "Terrence is friendly to everyone. They just had ideas, you know, but there hasn't been anyone special to Terrence."

Rose studied the folds of her skirt. "It wouldn't really be any of my business, would it? What happened in the past, I mean." Which was perfectly reasonable and perfectly diplomatic and had nothing at all to do with her ridiculous relief in hearing that there hadn't been any romance between Terrence and either of these two unknown women. They were probably beautiful and clever and knew exactly how to manage the complicated currents of the court and how to take advantage of handsome princes and lovely rose gardens—but Terrence *hadn't* chosen them, so that was all right. She had felt something similar, she realized, when he had first explained that the wonderful

Elena was his cousin. Only, she felt it more now. She felt everything about Terrence more now, didn't she?

"He's not that oblivious either," Elena went on, apparently oblivious herself to Rose's internal muddle. "I mean, he *does* tend to think the best of people, but even Terrence would see why they wouldn't be a good choice for your Lady of the Wardrobe, if there'd been something between them. And they may *not* be a bad choice, it just…seems better not to chance it."

Because she very possibly had additional enemies at court, just by being here and being betrothed to Terrence. Besides the ones she'd made by being the Princess Behind Thorns, heir to the throne. "Who would you suggest?" Rose asked, trying to pull the conversation back to point.

Elena frowned down at Emerald Eyes, a thoughtful frown, and rumpled the black cat's fur. "You need someone who isn't threatened by you, who has good sense and enough time for the job. Maybe…you might want to ask General Graybourne's wife. She has very good sense, and would probably run your wardrobe like a military campaign, which is a good thing. She's been a little at loose ends since the war ended, so she'd probably be glad of a new project. And she'd be a very helpful ally too."

The wife of the general everyone listened to—yes, she sounded very helpful. And a little intimidating too. Rose would have to get over being intimidated by people, if she was going to make the position of crown princess count for anything. She outranked nearly everyone. She'd have to start acting like it. "You think she'd agree to the idea?"

"Most likely," Elena said. "It's too close to supper now, but let's go see her tomorrow morning. She's an early riser."

"Good. So am I." And she was slightly relieved that Elena had offered to come along on this interview. She'd have to do things for herself, but it was nice to have help along the way.

Elena smoothed her skirt over her lap. "We have *some* time before supper—you had other questions?"

Rose smiled, and reached for her papers. "So many questions."

Chapter Nineteen: Terrence

Terrence felt some trepidation approaching the practice yard of the castle. Usually he was there most days, for weapons training or just to see what everyone else was doing. It was the central gathering place for the young men of the castle, whether princes, lords or guards. With one thing or another though, he hadn't had a chance to go by in the four days since he brought Rose back to the castle. It was hard to know what kind of reception he was going to get now.

The armsmaster was standing just inside the main entrance, inspecting a rack of practice swords. Terrence offered a friendly nod and said, "Good morning, Graham."

The man barely glanced up, gave the smallest of nods and more grunted than said, "Your Highness."

Terrence's walking pace faltered. That was…not usual. Graham had never exactly been emotive, but he was at least *friendly*.

Graham had also always liked Gregory. It made some sense—Gregory was here more than Terrence and probably more than either of their brothers. Terrence had never taken the armsmaster's preferences personally, but it had never really mattered before this.

He'd be within his rights to confront him on such a surly greeting, but—what would be the point? He just nodded again and kept walking. Good thing he didn't have to explain to the armsmaster about losing his sword.

The practice yard was roughly circular, weapons and other equipment stored along the back walls. A lower, half-wall encircled the open, dirt-packed central area, with gaps at intervals to allow access. Men were scattered across the yard, engaged in exercises or practice fights, while others stood by the half-wall and watched. There was a much larger arena out behind the castle, used for tournaments, but the practice yard was the daily gathering place. Terrence walked along the outer edge, greeting people as he passed them. Some were friendly. Some were not. Some looked at him like they didn't know who he was anymore, like he was some new figure of legend. In some ways, those were the most disconcerting.

He stopped finally at a convenient point along the wall, where a group was watching a swordfight between two of the guards. The group seemed friendly enough, so he settled leaning against the wall, watching too.

The two guards, Commander Gerrand and Guardsman Barret, were both capable, and well-matched in ability. The fight went on long enough to attract more spectators, and looked like it might come to a draw, until Barret managed what might have been a merely lucky move to disarm Gerrand.

There were general applause and congratulations, the two men shook hands, and the atmosphere was so congenial that Terrence found himself relaxing a little more. And when Barret offered to fight anyone else who was interested, Terrence volunteered.

He would have found some way to back out of it if Barret had looked hostile or awestruck—but the man gave him the same grin he always had. So Terrence turned to get a practice sword off the wall, and found three offered to him before he could get there. They all looked about the same so he took the one from the friendliest person and stepped out onto the practice yard proper to face Barret.

"Good luck, Your Highness," Commander Gerrand said as they passed.

Terrence nodded, already studying Barret as they each lifted their swords. He had been watching the man fight, of course, which gave him some idea of his capability. They were about the same height, with the same reach. People said they resembled each other, actually, though Terrence had never really seen it—Barret was a distant cousin on his father's side, too distant to have an aristocratic title, but maybe there was still some family resemblance there. More relevantly, he was quick with a sword but Terrence thought he might be just a little faster himself.

Their swords met and the fight was on. Neither moved too fast at first, testing each other out, circling for position. The pace picked up gradually, until Terrence felt himself falling into the familiar rhythm of move and countermove, a strange kind of dance in its own way. He'd never describe swordfighting as his favorite activity, the way many of the men around here probably would, but some days it was good to do something that was more physical than mental.

The fight didn't go as long as the previous one. After possibly several minutes, though he was never a good judge of time while fighting, Terrence saw an opening and took it. Barret was a little too slow responding, and Terrence leveled his sword at the other man's throat.

Barret held up his hands, grinning. "Well done, Your Highness."

"You didn't make it easy," Terrence said, grinning back.

"What happened, little brother," Gregory's voice came from the edge of the yard, "pick up some new skills fighting thorn bushes?"

Terrence hadn't noticed Gregory approach, but he could see him now among the onlookers by the half-wall. Everyone else had backed off a respectful foot from Gregory, so that he stood alone within the crowd. They didn't usually do that with Terrence, and how he interpreted it depended on his mood. Sometimes it felt like acceptance. Sometimes it felt like disregard.

Terrence lowered his sword, nodded to his brother. "Gregory. Good to see you," he said, because he didn't see much point in responding to what Gregory had actually said. It wasn't the time to explain that getting through the wall of thorns had not involved a sword at all, and he knew perfectly well that Gregory wasn't looking for that kind of information anyway.

Gregory ignored his words, continuing right along as though he hadn't spoken. "Or maybe," he said, voice pitching louder, "stealing a throne finally gives you some confidence."

Terrence gritted his teeth. If they had to have this out, did it have to be with an audience? "Just for a change, could we try being civil to each other?"

"Or *maybe*," Gregory continued, "stealing a princess is making you more confident."

He knew Gregory, and he knew they were one sentence away from a far more inappropriate remark. "Leave Rose out of this," he said in a low voice, taking two steps closer to Gregory. "I told you already, none of this is her fault. You can be angry with me, but—"

"I don't need your permission," Gregory sneered.

"I didn't mean it like—"

"And your *Rose* has everything to do with this. If she wasn't here—"

"It's *not her fault*, so you can stop talking about her, stop making nasty remarks whenever you see her—"

"Are you going to stop me?" Gregory asked, eyes glinting, and Terrence suddenly realized how loud their voices had become, how close they were standing to each other.

His grip tightened on the sword he was still holding. "Would you like to find a sword?"

Gregory shrugged, grinned. "You'll only lose again."

"Shall we find out?" Possibly this was a terrible idea. Possibly he would lose, and possibly it could go very badly even if he didn't, because in calmer moments he didn't really think the way to solve the current enmity with his oldest brother involved swords. But this wasn't a calmer moment, and maybe it would solve *something*, prove something…

But Gregory shook his head, still grinning. "Some other time, little brother, when you can't claim you lost because you were tired from already fighting."

And with that he turned on his heel and strolled away, people parting to let him pass.

Somehow, it never looked like backing down, if Gregory was the one doing it.

Terrence slowly let out his breath, slowly relaxed his grip on his sword.

"Too bad," Barret said. Terrence had complete forgotten he was still there. The other man smiled, even if it was a little grim around the edges. "You would have beaten him."

It was more than Terrence could be sure of. He could beat Tyler, and he hadn't fought Edward in years but he had won against him at least once, but he'd never beaten Gregory. "Next time."

Barret lifted his sword again. "Care to go another round?"

For a space there, this place had felt comfortable. It didn't anymore. "No—maybe another day." Right now, he just wanted to leave this place that was still more his brother's than his own. He could only hope that wasn't backing down either.

Chapter Twenty: Rose

Rose poked a needle at her embroidery and shifted her position in her spindly, gilded chair, listening to the chatter of the court ladies around her. Silvertips and Emerald Eyes were asleep in a pile by her feet. When Rose wasn't in council meetings, or discussing wardrobe ideas with Lady Graybourne, or when she couldn't steal time with Terrence, she had mostly been in the company of the ladies of the court over the past three weeks since her return.

She had been pushing them—carefully, politely—to sit outside more often. The weather was warming as the year turned towards spring, more leaves on the trees and more flowers appearing in the garden. Today they were in a circle of chairs looking out on the long lawn stretching behind the castle. Rose took a deep breath, glad to be out under the sky. Some days, the castle's walls felt more confining than walls of thorns.

She had a tentative grasp of everyone's names and brief histories by now, and a glimmer of who was loyal to whom. She still listened more than she spoke when the court ladies were in conversation. As complicated as the politics of the royal council were, the web of gossip and relationships and intrigue among the women of the court was even more tangled.

Just now, Lenora was complaining about the wife of the ambassador from Thaydan, who apparently was far too independent and not sufficiently attuned to the courtesies due a princess of Avala. Three women including Elena were very politely disagreeing—there was always a surface politeness, no matter how acrimonious the topic—while four other women agreed with Lenora. That didn't seem to satisfy her, however, as she was pressuring Penelope to weigh in, while Penelope was keeping her eyes on the handkerchief she was embroidering and declining to comment.

Rose was half-listening, paying some attention to her own embroidery, and also getting distracted by the rose bushes lining a nearby walkway. They were starting to shoot out new springtime growth, but they needed pruning and guidance to be at their healthiest.

"What do *you* think, Rose?" Lenora appealed suddenly. "The ambassador's wife's curtsy was far too shallow, wasn't it?"

"I didn't see her curtsy," Rose said mildly, "so I really couldn't say." She didn't have strong feelings about this particular question, but it was a good policy to refuse to go along with Lenora's ideas regularly. It kept the other woman remembering that she had her own mind. "Perhaps the standards of curtsies are different in Thaydan. Have you ever been there?"

"No," Lenora admitted, "but that's hardly the point—"

"For all we know, a deeper curtsy is insulting there," Rose persisted. "So I really wouldn't like to pass judgment on her motives." She found it unlikely that a deeper curtsy was an insult anywhere, but that wasn't the point. The point was that she wasn't going to let Lenora browbeat her into an opinion, and she'd like the rest of the group to know it.

Perhaps some of them picked up the idea. There was more murmuring amongst themselves, Lenora turned pointedly to continue conversing with Lady Gertrude, who had agreed with her, and Penelope glanced at Rose across the circle. Their gazes met for just a moment, Penelope smiling very slightly, before she looked back to her embroidery.

It wasn't often that Penelope made eye contact with Rose, even rarer that she actually said anything. Rose had learned little more about her since their first meeting. To all appearances she was as quiet and meek as Elena had said. Rose was relieved that Penelope hadn't set herself up as an adversary, but disappointed not to make a friend.

They were still existing in an uncertain state, no one exactly sure about their relative ranking. The ceremony to recognize Terrence as heir, to officially acknowledge Rose's return, was still long weeks away. Rose was trying not to pin too many hopes on this one event—as if suddenly her position would feel more secure, as if people would actually start listening to Terrence or even to her.

In the meantime, a long meantime, Rose and Penelope were both still wearing signet rings, both still being referred to as the crown princess, as though both could somehow be next in line for the throne. Or married to a man who was.

She added another stitch to her embroidery, then glanced around the circle again. The conversation had moved on to a gossipy discussion of people she didn't know. She glanced at Elena, who was participating with apparent ease, while working at an indeterminate bit of knitting.

Rose's attention strayed back to the distant flowers. If it was up to her, she'd put in a trellis and encourage the roses to grow in an archway over the path. That variety did better with more height.

Since she was looking at the pathway, she was the first in the group to notice the woman walking down it, coming their direction.

Here was a distraction far more significant than roses. The woman was wearing a long red cloak of some light material that fluttered and swirled as she walked. Her stride was assured and confident, her head held high. Neither the cloak nor her black gown beneath hid her arms, shockingly bare from shoulders to wrist.

The woman had reached the end of the rows of flowers before Rose realized the conversation had dropped off around her, that more of the court ladies were also looking at this new arrival.

"Who is that?" Rose asked the group at large, but glanced at Elena, who seemed to always have a complete understanding of every detail about everyone.

"She's an enchantress," Elena answered. "Not one of the court enchanters, not officially, but she visits sometimes." Her voice dropped. "She did some work for the king during the war."

What was that life like? Beholden to no one, powerful enough to make a difference in a war, not needing to pick your battles because you could probably just rout everyone any time you liked. "She looks…interesting," Rose said after a moment.

"*I* think it's quite unnatural," Lenora said with a sharp tone in her voice. "She lives all alone in some castle in the mountains, and who knows what she did to gain all that magical power?"

"People are born with magical abilities," Rose said absently. They were gifts from the gods; no one earned them or chose to have them. Sometimes they were hereditary, sometimes they turned up unexpectedly.

Down at the end of the path, the enchantress had paused and was looking up at the sky with one hand touching her opposite wrist.

"Yes, but what did she do to learn how to *use* her magic?" Lenora countered, and stabbed a needle into the handkerchief she was embroidering as though this was decisive.

"You could ask her if you like," Rose said, keeping her voice serene despite the bubble of mischief she felt. "She's coming this way."

Any heads that hadn't already been facing towards the enchantress whipped that direction, then most turned just as quickly back to their sewing.

The enchantress strode right into the midst of their circle. "Good afternoon," she said, voice low and throaty, and looked directly at Rose. "You must be Princess Rose Amelia." She inclined her head slightly, and Rose suspected that this woman curtsied to no one. "I've been wanting to meet you."

"I am Princess Rose," she said, rising to her feet. She remembered a heartbeat too late that standing meant all the other women would rise too, in a rustle of skirts and shuffle of sewing projects, and quickly gestured for them to remain seated. That only created more shuffling and awkwardness as they tried to change direction again. Rose tried to ignore all that, and fell back on court etiquette. "Who do I have the pleasure of greeting?"

The enchantress looked at her through thick lashes, eyes a deep blue, and said simply, "I am Xevrix."

It was an enchanter's name, and the starkness of the single name with no title, no family house, was striking in this place where most people prided themselves on the lengths of their introductions.

Up close, Xevrix formed a sharp contrast to the court ladies around her, all carefully coiffed and attired. The enchantress' hair tumbled loose over her shoulders, streaked golden blond and raven black, a coloring Rose had never seen before. She was tall, six inches taller than Rose; the dark dress below her cloak hid little of her figure, and her bare arms were covered in tattoos. All seemed to be symbols and none that Rose could recognize, save for the fox symbol on her left shoulder, the emblem of the Veiled God.

As Rose looked at her face, she had the strangest shiver of recognition. It wasn't tied to any memory, she couldn't place it in any context and yet it was there. But how could she possibly have met Xevrix before? She had been under a spell for a hundred years. Besides, she certainly wouldn't have forgotten seeing someone as unusual as this. It had to only be another echo, a resemblance to someone she had once known.

"I think you remind me of someone," Rose said carefully. "Is your family from Avala?"

Xevrix's lips curved into a smile. "I have no family. Nor do I offer allegiance to any king. But I am still pleased to see you returned safely from your long enchantment. Perhaps some other day we could discuss what such an enchantment looked like from the inside."

"Perhaps," Rose said, a noncommittal response to this vague invitation. Xevrix might have insights that would be valuable, that would help her understand what had happened to her. But did she want to discuss something so private with this woman she didn't know?

Few people had asked about her time behind the thorns. It was enough for most to know that she had been behind them. The more considerate seemed reluctant to pry. The less considerate wanted to know about all those champions who had died, a line of inquiry Rose shut down absolutely. She suspected at least half the court still believed that she had been asleep behind the thorns, that Terrence had woken her up with a kiss. So far, she hadn't seen a reason to disabuse them of the notion—not one that outweighed her own reluctance to talk about the experience.

Any awkwardness in this moment vanished as Xevrix passed smoothly on to another topic, and Rose wondered if the enchantress was ever ill at ease. "I have a gift for you, Princess Rose." She reached into her cloak, and extended her hand with a small object wrapped in cloth.

Rose accepted it, fingers never quite touching the enchantress. Unwrapping the bundle, she found a silver mirror as big as her hand, decorated on its back with engraved roses. It was identical to the one she had had with her in the garden, to the one that had sat in her bedroom in the Before Time. But of course it couldn't be the same one; that had vanished with the garden.

"It dates from before your enchantment," Xevrix said. "I thought you might value it."

"Thank you," Rose said, studying the roses curling around the mirror. It was astonishingly similar. "I had one like it, once." Could it have existed both in the garden and outside of it, somehow falling into Xevrix's hands? The thought was disconcerting, and besides, how could Xevrix have gotten her mirror? More likely it had been made by the same craftsman, working from the same design.

"I am pleased," Xevrix said, then glanced skyward. "I believe my ride is here. Good day to you, Your Highness. Ladies." The last word recalled the court ladies to Rose's mind again, and she glanced around even as Xevrix did the same. Most of the women didn't meet the enchantress' eyes, while Elena gave a slight nod. The enchantress herself merely turned away and strode toward the long lawn.

No evidence of a horse or carriage was in sight. Rose looked upwards as Xevrix had done, and felt her breath catch.

A red dragon was spiraling down from above, still shrunken by distance but growing larger all the time.

Dragons were rare. Tame ones, almost unheard of.

Rose half-expected the court ladies to shriek and run for cover, but though all eyes fastened on the dragon, some of them gone wide, no one moved.

"She's always showing off with that pet dragon," Lenora muttered, though she watched as closely as all the others.

The dragon landed as neatly and lightly as a bird, if birds ever grew to twenty feet in length, a mere yard from Xevrix. It was wearing a harness and saddle, and she swung up onto its back in a practiced gesture. In another moment they were in the air, soaring swiftly into the distance.

Rose let out a breath. What must that be like? To fly through the air that way? To be that *free*?

"I wouldn't trust her, if I were you," a new voice in the circle said, and Rose almost didn't recognize Penelope's. She'd never heard the woman sound so firm, and she'd never before seen her hold her own gaze so steadily. After a moment, Penelope gave one acknowledging nod, then returned her attention to her embroidery.

Chapter Twenty-One: Terrence

Terrence sat at Rose's table, ate a leftover pastry, and waited for her to finish dressing. In the past two months they had fallen into habits, including that he came to see her every morning. He thought it would be much nicer, as he brushed crumbs off his hands, if he didn't have to walk to her rooms, if he didn't have to wait to see her, if instead they could wake up together…

Eventually. It would happen eventually.

Maybe he'd get to wake her up with a kiss someday yet.

The kittens burst out of the bedroom first, Silvertips chasing Emerald Eyes until they tumbled together in a playful bout of wrestling. Rose was behind them, wearing a blue dress; he had never paid so much attention to a woman's clothes before, couldn't have said what colors Elena favored, but that shade of blue always brought out Rose's eyes…

"Good morning," she said with a smile, and it was her real smile, not the one she used when she was being polite—or when she wanted to *seem* polite but was actually saying something stinging. He enjoyed that smile, but he didn't want it turned on him.

He rose to meet her and she kissed him, fleetingly. It was always good and never enough and if it wasn't for Rose's maid, who was politely turning away but also smiling… Oh well, he liked Gabrielle, it wasn't her fault, but he wished he could get Rose alone more often.

It would happen eventually.

This might not have been the morning for more anyway. Rose was always distracted when there was a council meeting, and their morning greetings and conversation were somewhat perfunctory. Soon he was taking Rose's hand and they were leaving to walk to the meeting, kittens trailing along with them. He glanced back to check for them, another habit he'd picked up. Rose never seemed to give much thought to whether the kittens were in line or not. But maybe she knew something he didn't; they were always where they should be, whenever he looked. However unlikely that seemed. The kittens stuck close by today, as though they recognized that the halls were crowded; were kittens that smart?

Conversation was always necessarily impersonal whenever they walked through the halls, with so many people around to overhear. If Terrence was still noticing the curve of Rose's cheek, or the way her hair caught the light—well, there wasn't much he could do about it right now.

He always tried not to stare at her too much. So many other people stared. It always happened, was happening now, gazes snagging as they went past. At first he had thought it was only because Rose was new, or because she was beautiful, but by now he'd seen something in the stares that said it was more. Not among the aristocracy; they tended to stare, and then pretend they hadn't been staring, and then talk somewhat pointedly amongst themselves. But with the servants, there was a kind of awe in people's expressions, and it wasn't going away as time passed. He glanced at Rose again, and couldn't tell if she was observing it too, the wide eyes of the servants they were passing; he thought she didn't like being stared at, but also that she was resigned to it, accepted it as unavoidable.

Terrence hadn't fully realized how big the legend of the Princess Behind Thorns was until he became a part of it. He had heard it told and retold throughout his life, mostly by servants or shopkeepers in the market. But he hadn't realized the level of attachment people had, to the mythical princess trapped behind walls of thorns.

They were nearly to the council chamber when they turned a corner and almost bumped into a serving girl balancing a precarious stack of folded cloth. She jumped when she saw them, stumbled back two steps, and the cloths began to slither out of her grasp. Her frantic efforts to grab the sliding fabric only led to more slipping down until there was a snowy mound all about her feet.

"Oh—oh, I'm so sorry," she gabbled, "I didn't mean—I shouldn't—"

"Not at all," Terrence said, "we walked into you." He bent down to help pick up the tumbled cloth. Looked like sheets, possibly.

The serving girl turned red. "Oh no, you shouldn't—Your Highness, it isn't right!"

He came up again with an armful of sheets and offered them to her. They'd still need to be refolded, mostly, but at least they were off the ground and wouldn't be stepped on. "It's no trouble."

She just stared at him, eyes enormous. He didn't recognize her, so she was probably new. He knew almost everyone, but he couldn't always keep up with the newest arrivals. Maybe she wasn't used to seeing royalty, and that was why she was staring at him.

Or it was the new thing, the rescuing-the-princess thing. As much as he'd noticed people staring at Rose, he found it even more disconcerting when people looked at *him* with some of the same awe, as though he had suddenly become a figure of legend and hero of ballads. It didn't last with most people. The ones he knew well got over it within a few days, though some seemed to be keeping up an extra degree of pride in him; the cook kept pushing extra servings on him, a few of the friendliest guardsmen extra claps on the back and offers to find him better practice weapons. He didn't mind all that. He minded more the ones who still sided with Gregory, who met him with a frosty politeness or hostile glances. And usually at least once a day he still encountered someone like this, who looked half awestruck and half afraid. Those ones made him feel like he didn't know exactly who he was anymore.

He couldn't stand here forever with a pile of sheets in his arms, so he gently pushed them at the maid. "Here you are. Better get those delivered."

"Oh!" She jumped again, but took the sheets. "Yes, Your Highness. Thank you, Your Highness."

He took Rose's hand again, and they resumed walking.

"That was nice of you," she murmured after they were a little distance away.

"I don't know," Terrence said, and snuck a glance over his shoulder. The maid was still staring this direction. "I think I terrified the poor girl."

"Maybe," Rose allowed, "but you didn't *mean* to."

Most people didn't. But...some did, he couldn't deny that.

Terrence pushed open the door of the council chamber, and they found half the council already gathered. They made for their seats to the left of the king's chair.

Rose was just settling her skirts when Gregory strode in, and Terrence tensed. Maybe it would finally be different this time.

"Aren't you tired of playing at this, Princess?" Gregory said loudly, sneer in his voice and on his face. "Don't you have embroidery to do or something?"

Every meeting. *Every* meeting he had to say something, no matter how many times Terrence had told him to stop. "She has the right to be here," Terrence said tightly. He believed that, and if Rose wanted to be here she should be—even though sometimes he wondered if it was actually good for her, to be here and to face Gregory.

Though she usually held her own well enough. Today she smiled, her not actually polite smile, and said, "I never quit playing a game until I'm very good at it. And no one's perishing for the lack of my embroidery."

The king came in then and Gregory subsided and the room grew busy as the rest of the council arrived. Terrence reached for Rose's hand under the table, wrapped his fingers around hers. She smiled at him, her nicer smile, but he still worried about her. About what that other smile was masking, when she looked at Gregory.

Their mother had always wanted him to be patient with his oldest brother, to not take too seriously anything nasty that he said, but that was getting harder every day.

The council meeting began, running through the usual business. Tax updates and reports from various ambassadors and the renovation of the large tournament arena was on schedule and the city guard in the capital was still understaffed and the bandits in Slate Province were stirring again. He had been attending council meetings for four years now, and though in many ways it was the same as it had always been, it felt different with Rose there.

He really did believe she had every right to be there, but he felt sort of...embarrassed, sometimes, knowing she was listening to the council discussions, to his family's discussions. Everyone else had been part of the conversation for years, but Rose was new, and thinking of her, he sometimes worried what impression she was getting.

Not that he hadn't *known* there were problems in the council, in his family. Of course he'd known that. That was why he had gone to rescue the Princess Behind Thorns to begin with, to give himself the legal standing to someday make things different.

Or maybe, to try to make something different *now*, as his attention came to a newly sharp focus when the question of the land and education promise came up once again.

"We never have any news there," Lord Bellham said languidly. "I think we can move on to the next item on the agenda."

If that next item was started, it would be too late. This was his moment. "On the subject of the land and education promise," Terrence spoke up, "we still haven't discussed the plan I proposed." Out of the corner of his eye, he saw Rose shift—she at least knew this was important to him. But probably everyone at the table did.

"That project is not your responsibility," Gregory snapped. "You don't know anything about it."

Terrence didn't often argue with Gregory in front of the council, but sometimes he'd had enough. And Rose was watching. "I have a fifty-page report showing I *do*. So maybe it should be my responsibility. As crown prince."

If the council, or his family, wanted to display just a tiny bit of the awe the rest of the castle was regarding him with—he might not object to that. Not if it meant he could finally get something *done*.

Gregory stiffened and someone at the table coughed. But how long were they supposed to go on like this? One public heir and one legal heir? Two crown princesses?

Before Gregory could speak, the king's voice cut through the room. "We all understood there would be a period of transition. So as to not destabilize the country." His gaze was heavy on Terrence, who instinctively wanted to drop his own gaze—but he fought the impulse. "And to give everyone time to adjust. Gregory, after all, has been trained for this role. You, Terrence, have not."

Terrence took a deep breath. "I'm prepared to accept the responsibility—"

"And there is nothing to be gained by moving too quickly," his father continued, as though he hadn't spoken at all. Definitely no awe from that quarter. The king's gaze flicked away, went farther down the table. "But perhaps now is an opportune moment to discuss the planned ceremony for publicly recognizing our new heir to the throne, and welcoming back the Princess Rose Amelia."

It was a clear attempt to change the subject, to distract from the land and education promise they had been talking about. Terrence drew in a breath, about to try to bring the conversation back—but he glanced at Rose, who was watching the king intently, and though maybe it would be good to talk about *this* too. Maybe if they finally got somewhere on this, they could more easily get somewhere on other issues.

This ceremony had been discussed at intervals, but it had been hard to tell if any great advancement in plans was being made. A date had been set, four months out, and Terrence had been trying not to feel that this was unreasonably far away. He'd been waiting in some way for this all his life. Surely he could be patient for a few months.

His and Rose's wedding was set for six months after that—and that sometimes seemed even harder to be patient for. Like every time he had to say good-night at her door.

"Xervon, what is your report on the planned entertainments?" King Elgin asked the head of the court enchanters.

Xervon spread his hands, looking around without meeting anyone's eyes. He never did, and made it look mysterious rather than subservient. There was nothing the least bit subservient about the head of the court enchanters—or any enchanters Terrence had ever met. "We have discussed the matter at length, and the conclusion is that we simply do not have the available time or attention to properly attend to a bit of light entertainment for the masses. We will perform the necessary functions within the ceremony itself, but the entertainment for the crowd…" He let the words trail away, as though the unimportance of this particular task should be self-evident. "We are consumed with more vital affairs. Perhaps we might call in another enchanter. That woman who did some service in the war. We spoke with her recently about other work, and she should be capable of handling this."

"Very well," King Elgin said as though it was no great matter. "Send a message to Xevrix. Have her report to the capital again to discuss these new plans."

Terrence remembered Xevrix, though he had never exchanged any actual words with her. She was…striking.

The conversation went on, discussing matters of protocol for the planned ceremony, then moving on to other subjects. Terrence tried to feel that this was enough, that at least they were moving forward in the transition his father kept talking about, and that maybe that meant they could move other goals forward too.

He tried to keep his gaze off the signet ring still glinting silver on Gregory's hand across the table.

Chapter Twenty-Two: Rose

More weeks ticked by, and Rose began to feel that, after everything changing all at once when she first left the garden, now things had almost entirely stopped changing. She was surprised when she realized it had been three months since she had come to the royal court; it seemed like both more and less time. More because she was so entirely immersed in this world now—and because how could she possibly have known Terrence for only three months? Less because surely there ought to be more progress—she ought to have more power, Gregory ought to be backing down. The ceremony to formally recognize her as heir was still another three months away.

Council meetings in particular were beginning to feel decidedly rote, nothing important really moving forward. Just talking around and around. She sat through yet another one, wishing she knew how to really *change* things.

Rose and Terrence generally left council meetings together, but as they rose to go today, his father summoned him into a private conversation at the head of the table.

Rose lingered at the door, reluctant to either interrupt or leave. After a few moments, she was greeted by a prince—but Edward, not Terrence.

After a moment of perfectly unobjectionable pleasantries, Edward said, smiling, "I understand I'm living in your old rooms, up in the north tower. I appreciate that you haven't demanded them back. I've been meaning to ask if you'd like to visit them."

She hesitated, trying to parse this. She had mentioned her old rooms to the historians, on one of a few conversations she'd had with them. Edward must have heard the information from one of them. As to what to do about the suggestion—if it had been any other prince, she would have known exactly what to do. An unbrooking, unyielding *no* for Gregory or Tyler, though her fears with each might have been slightly different. With Terrence—she'd go anywhere he cared to suggest.

But Edward was a puzzle. Up until now, he had been neither friendly nor unfriendly, greeting her courteously when the moment called for it but making no overtures beyond what etiquette demanded. Was it dangerous to agree to his invitation, or could this be an opportunity, to learn more or even make a new ally? Rose glanced back towards the council chamber, but Terrence was still speaking with his father. Maybe it would be better to be cautious. She let her eyes drop, and murmured, "I wouldn't want to impose on you."

Edward's smile only grew. "It wouldn't be an imposition at all. I only feel badly I didn't invite you sooner. I knew you'd be interested to see the place." He took her arm—but politely, unthreateningly—and steered her down the corridor. "It's right this way. Well, you know that, of course."

She still could have said no. She could have yanked her arm away, and she thought she would have, if he had gripped it any tighter. But it was a polite, even courtly hold, and she wasn't entirely certain she *didn't* want to see her old bedroom. She didn't want to live there, but she didn't want to turn it into some kind of ghostly chamber she had to always avoid. And maybe she'd finally make more sense of Edward, if she spent a few minutes with him away from the council and his father. This conversation was already more words than they'd ever exchanged at one time before.

She would have made a screaming scene in the hall before going off alone with Gregory. She was always careful to ensure he couldn't corner her alone, at the end of a council meeting or while everyone was casually talking before supper. She put a lot of thought into that, considering he'd never actually tried to do it, and she didn't know what would happen if he ever did—but she didn't want to find out. She thought Terrence might be thinking about it too, though he'd never said anything. He always said that Gregory would calm down in time—but he also seemed to stay between Rose and Gregory whenever they were all in the same room.

"I quite like the tower," Edward remarked as they walked. "So quiet, so removed. Gives me plenty of space for thinking, you know."

Sometimes she had liked the quiet. Sometimes she had wondered why so many stories put princesses away in a tower, all by themselves, and why her own life had to conform to that particular story.

The spiral stone stair seemed largely unchanged from the century that had elapsed since she had last climbed it. Maybe the worn places in the center of the steps were a little smoother. Most of the wall-hangings were different but she recognized some, more faded, more ragged on the edges. Some had been bright and new in her day, others old even then.

She shivered partway up, just as they passed a tapestry of a knight slaying a red dragon.

"It's a somewhat drafty place," Edward said, in concerned tones. "Are you all right?"

"Yes," she said. She wasn't cold, but she wasn't all right either. She had climbed these steps hundreds, thousands of times in the Before Time, and she had climbed them on the last day, the day she was enchanted. She had started pleading with her father not to go through with it just as they passed that tapestry with the dragon.

Her father's role as king had always been more important to him than his role as father. That seemed plainly to be true of King Elgin too. She wouldn't have gone off alone with him either. He was outwardly polite most of the time, but could snap out with a bitingly cruel comment at any moment—and his eyes, no matter how pleasant he might be, never changed. She had known from almost the beginning that she couldn't trust his smiles, and nothing gave her the least reason to change that opinion.

As they continued up the stairs, she suddenly missed her kittens. She often brought them to council meetings, but today the weather had been so beautiful she'd left them behind to play in the Queen's Garden. She wished that she was with them there, instead of in this dim tower, or that they were here with her, furry and playful and comforting.

Edward pushed open the wooden door at the top of the stairs, and she took a deep breath before she stepped inside.

"I suppose it looks completely different," Edward said.

"Not completely," Rose answered, stepping past him into the room.

There stood the big old fireplace, the two windows with distant views of the mountains in the west and the much closer ocean in the east. Edward had his bed in the same place hers had been, though his was a heavy affair in dark wood, not like the curtained one she'd had. The morning light must still hit the head of the bed early every morning, and she wondered if he minded that. Probably not. He could likely have his bed moved, if he wanted it somewhere else.

"It must be very strange for you," Edward said, "coming back after all these years. Back to this room, back to this castle. So many things different. So much change."

"And a surprising amount the same," Rose said, almost absently, glancing past his wardrobe and desk, looking for familiar things still remaining.

"It was never supposed to be this long, was it? You were supposed to be back here in, what, a few weeks?"

"I suppose," Rose said. The enchantment had happened here too, when all the enchanters had gathered around her, stealing her away from the life she had known, placing her down in an unexpected haven. She still didn't know why or how that had happened, but who was there to ask now? Maybe Xevrix, but she still wasn't certain she wanted to have that conversation, even if it gave her answers.

"It would have all been different, wouldn't it?" Edward continued, conversationally. "If someone had got in to rescue you back when they were supposed to."

It certainly would have been different for all the men who died among the thorns, died trying to claim her. 'Claim' seemed so much more accurate than 'rescue.' At least, until Terrence. But she didn't want to think of all those other champions. "Did you know," she said abruptly, "there's a loose stone there, in the center of the room?"

"There's—what?"

She didn't think Edward was a man who was frequently confused; she had seen enough of him to realize that already. But she didn't care if this topic change was not what he had expected; she didn't want to talk about his topic.

"Just there," she said, toeing ineffectively at a rug covering the place she meant. He probably didn't know either that there was a hollow under the stone, a perfect place for hiding things. After a moment she knelt down, to roll the rug back. She reached for the stone she remembered, prodded and found that it still rocked, just a little. Perhaps more easily than it had decades ago.

She had learned the trick of lifting it out in her childhood, and her fingers remembered even after all this time. In moments she had lifted the stone up, set it to the side, revealed the dark hollow beneath—and was that something lying there in the shadows?

"Well, aren't you full of surprises," Edward said, voice dropping into a lower tone.

She looked up, one hand already reaching into the hollow, to find that he had stepped closer to her. Suddenly she wished she hadn't knelt down, because he loomed so tall above her now. He was standing between her and the door. Almost without thinking, she set her free hand back on the loose stone, fingers gripping its rough edges.

"You certainly surprised everyone, just by arriving here," Edward continued, "just by still being alive."

Her hand within the hollow touched cloth; automatically her fingers grasped the bundle, drew it out even as she rose to her feet, stone clutched in her other hand.

"I should really be going," Rose said, heart beating hard, trying to keep her voice steady.

"Without even looking at your find?" Edward said, and smiled again. He held out his hand, palm up, open. "Let me unwrap it for you."

Something in his smile looked a little like Terrence's, and she cautiously handed the bundle over. She held onto the stone though.

He peeled back dusty cloth, layers falling away to land in a heap by his feet.

What they revealed surprised her so much that she actually moved closer to him, to better see what he was holding.

"It's my statue," she said without thinking, staring down at the woman with the lioness beside her. The god Mariqwe as a woman warrior, something she had still never seen depicted anywhere else.

She had found this statue in this same hollow before, hidden away by someone else, perhaps generations earlier. She had kept it hidden here, knowing it wouldn't be well-received by her parents. And then it had been there in her garden, another part of the magic she had never been able to explain, and it had vanished with everything else when the spell had broken. Unlike the silver mirror, there was no way to explain this as a duplicate; she recognized every detail of the hand-carved statue. Had it returned here after the spell ended? Or had it, somehow, been here all along—and in her garden too?

Sometimes magic made her head hurt.

"A woman warrior," Edward said, with a slight laugh. "What an unusual notion."

"It's Mariqwe," Rose said. "You see, the lioness with her—"

His hand closed on her wrist, on the hand she had been using to point to the statue, and she looked up into his face, suddenly realizing she had come closer to him than she had intended.

"I don't think that would be a very popular idea," he said, voice soft and even friendly, while his fingers were still tight around her wrist. "It might make some people uncomfortable. Rather like a princess who disrupts a line of succession."

She still had the stone in her other hand, if she had to she could—

He released her arm as suddenly as he'd taken it, offered her the statue. "Just a friendly warning. Be careful who you show this to. Not everyone is as...open-minded as you and I."

She stared at him for a moment more.

Then she snatched the statue out of his hand, backed away towards the door, heartbeat loud in her ears. "Thank you for the tour, I think I'd best be going," she said in one breath, just in case, just so he wouldn't think she was entirely mad if she had read this all wrong.

She was out the door and onto the stairs before he could respond, hurried down two or three turns of the spiral before she took in a full breath and remembered she was still holding the stone that belonged in his floor.

She looked up. No sign of him coming behind her, but she wasn't about to go back up to return it. She set the stone down on the step, to the side so it wouldn't trip anyone, and continued down, statue clutched in one hand.

She rubbed at her wrist. Had he known he was holding it too tightly? Had he really intended a friendly warning, or was the warning not friendly at all?

She didn't have an answer to that. But she knew she would be putting Edward in the same category as Gregory and Tyler and the king after all, at least in that she wouldn't be going off alone with him again. Just in case.

Chapter Twenty-Three: Terrence

Terrence managed to see Rose nearly every day, but it was never for long enough. So when he found himself with extra time and happened to be near the solarium, he thought he might drop in, knowing the castle ladies often sat there. The possibility of facing a dozen or more court ladies was unnerving, but it would be worth it if he could pull Rose out of the group.

He entered the sunny room and found there was no crowd, and there *was* a princess—but it was the wrong one. "Hello, Penelope," he said, and offered a smile, because the least he could do was be friendly, even if she wasn't Rose.

"Good afternoon, Terrence," she said softly, inclining her head slightly and barely looking up from whatever she was embroidering. Maybe a handkerchief. "Were you looking for Rose?"

Apparently he was very transparent on this subject. He had known that though. "I was. Any idea where she might be?"

"I believe the ladies are gathering here shortly," Penelope murmured. "She may be coming soon."

Terrence hesitated. He could go try to find Rose, while if he waited here, a crowd of other women could easily show up before Rose did. But on the other hand, it wasn't often he saw Penelope alone. She had been married to his brother for a couple years now, and he was still trying to get to know her, without feeling that he had ever made much progress. And the situation had only turned more uncomfortable recently.

"Are you…um…" How could he say this? "I hope it hasn't caused too much…disruption for you, my bringing Rose to court."

She looked up, eyes wide. It always surprised him how blue her eyes were, on the rare times when she looked directly at him. "What do you mean?" she asked, voice faint.

"Well—having another crown princess, and—all the protocol and everything, it must be—awkward?" He was fumbling this badly, but something in her face was unsettling him. He really didn't know her, because he couldn't read why she was looking the way she was, why this question seemed to be stirring up more than he had intended.

And then she blinked, and the expression was gone, as she went back to the remote, distant look he was used to from her. "Oh yes," she said, returning to her embroidery. "That's no great matter. I was never especially fond of court ceremony anyway."

"Ah. Well. Good," Terrence said lamely. He was usually *good* at talking to people, from noblemen on down to the guards at the city gates. But Penelope always had a wall up that he didn't know how to get past. Unlike the wall of thorns, she didn't seem inclined to open a passage for him. The best he could think of now was to just charge forward anyway. Because there really had been something on her face, when she'd looked at him— "Are you happy here, Penelope? Do you…miss where you grew up?"

A long pause stretched out, as Penelope continued with her embroidery, and he thought she wasn't even going to answer. But at last she said, "The castle in Relnyra was close enough to the shore to hear the waves, especially at night. I miss that sound."

The ocean was visible from some windows of the castle here, but more than a mile in the distance, across a wide stretch of the city. It must be very different from where she had grown up. This hint of her past was a more personal remark than he'd ever had from her before—but it didn't answer his first question. "That sounds nice. It must be hard, to be in such a different place," he said carefully, not certain they were actually talking about waves. "Do you—"

"Why, Terrence! What brings you here?" This new voice was louder than he'd ever heard Penelope be, and he turned without surprise to see that Lenora had entered the room. She sauntered up to him and poked his arm. "You were looking for Rose, weren't you?"

Somehow, what had been a simple statement from Penelope sounded vaguely scandalous when Lenora said it. Terrence took a breath. "Yes. But she's not here, so—"

"You're very fond of her, aren't you?" Lenora said with a smirk.

Yes, of course, and it wasn't at all a secret, but as much as he'd tried to be friendly to Tyler's wife, he had realized swiftly that if you said anything the slightest bit personal to Lenora, the entire castle would know about it within hours, probably with added distortions. "Rose and I are betrothed."

"But that doesn't signify anything about whether you're *fond* of her," Lenora said with a laugh. "I mean, I like Tyler, but it's hardly a guarantee, is it?"

He'd always had the impression that Lenora and Tyler liked each other well enough, even if neither one was sentimental about it. He hadn't hoped for much more than that for himself, until he met Rose. What neutral thing could he possibly say now? "Well, ah…"

"What about you and Gregory?" Lenora asked, nudging Penelope. "Are you *fond* of each other?"

"Gregory is my husband," Penelope said composedly, which didn't even come close to answering the question.

Terrence had never known how to read the relationship between Gregory and Penelope. He rarely saw them interact, even when they were in the same room, but any number of marriages at court were like that. Both parties carried on their lives mostly separate from each other, and seemed content about it.

"Ooh, are we discussing husbands?" a new voice said in evident excitement, as another court lady—he searched his memory—Sophia, that was her name—came in the room. She plopped down on the low sofa next to Penelope. "My favorite subject! Are you here to give us the man's perspective, Prince Terrence?" she asked, and batted her eyes at him.

This was exactly the sort of thing he hadn't wanted to deal with when contemplating facing a dozen court ladies. At some point they had learned that he blushed, and now they all too often tried to provoke it. In the past, his consistent avoidance of romantic entanglements had also meant that any number of unattached women had tried to inveigle him into one, and he wasn't positive his betrothal to Rose was much protection.

"No, I was just leaving," he said quickly. "I wouldn't want to intrude."

"You really wouldn't be!" Lenora called after him, but he was already beating a retreat to the door.

He ducked out past two more court ladies and attained the relative safety of the hall outside. He would have liked to talk to Penelope more, but no confidences would be shared under these circumstances. He'd have to try again some other time.

In the meantime…still no sign of Rose. If he waited here he was going to be accosted by every woman going in, so—better to try her rooms. He might miss her in passing, but it was possible she hadn't left yet.

He lengthened his stride, walking as quickly as was reasonable in the busy halls. He didn't encounter her on the way, and when he knocked on her door Rose opened it to him. He was so pleased to see her that it seemed the most natural thing in the world to take her into his arms and kiss her. At length.

They were still doing that when the door opened and Elena strolled in, announcing, "Rose, Maude says they finally got that silk you and Lady Graybourne wanted—oh, hello, Terrence."

"Hello," Terrence muttered, disentangling from Rose. And now he was definitely blushing. At least there weren't a host of court ladies to observe it. He glanced at the door, just to make sure—no, Elena was alone. And grinning at him.

"Was that the…lilac silk?" Rose said, smoothing her hair, and Terrence was gratified that at least it took her a moment to reorient.

"That's the one," Elena said, sitting on the couch and waving a handkerchief-sized bit of vaguely purple cloth. "I brought a sample, to see if it's the shade you wanted."

Rose sat down next to Elena, and Terrence found himself suddenly superfluous. Well—he wasn't going to just leave, after all his trouble finding Rose to begin with. He could wait. How long could it take to discuss a shade of purple?

He wandered off towards the low bookshelves near the window, which Rose had begun stocking with books from the library. He looked at the titles briefly, different ones than his mother used to have here, then glanced around the room. It hadn't changed that much, although— He frowned, attention arrested by a small statue on an end table. That hadn't been here before.

He went closer, confirmed what he had thought from across the room, and dared to interrupt the important discussion of shades of lilac. "Hey, Rose? Isn't this your statue from behind the thorns?"

"It seems to be," Rose said, looking up from the scrap of cloth. "I found it under Edward's floor."

Terrence ran that sentence through his head twice. No, it still didn't make sense. "What?"

"You know Edward has my old bedroom, up in the north tower? Yesterday he asked me if I'd like to see it. And while I was there I checked under the loose stone in the floor where my statue used to be hidden, and…somehow it was there." She shrugged. "I don't understand magic."

Neither did Terrence, but he was also trying to chase down the reason for the vague unease the story gave him. Maybe…well…Rose hadn't been to *his* bedroom yet, and he didn't love the idea of her going off with Edward—not that he thought there was anything wrong in it, he just—Tyler, now, he would have had entirely different concerns, but Edward was…fine. It was fine. "Oh. That is…strange, yes."

"The statue is unusual too," Elena said, studying it. "It must be, what, 200 years old? That's the last time there was any popularity for worship of Mariqwe as a female warrior."

"I didn't know there was a specific time," Rose remarked.

Elena waved a hand. "Oh sure, during the reign of Queen Adelora. No one here talks about her much, but I read some records in Glyster's library. After she died in a battle, and her brother took the throne, things changed. Anyway. That was…friendly of Edward," she said, tone changing as the topic changed. She was suddenly more serious, more questioning.

"Yes…" Rose said slowly, "I guess it was."

Terrence didn't have a great burning desire to talk about Edward just now. Obviously it was all fine, but—still. "So was that silk what you wanted?" he asked abruptly.

"Oh—yes, I think it's perfect," Rose said, handing it back to Elena. Then she looked at Terrence apologetically. "I'm really supposed to be meeting Lenora and the others…"

Elena patted her arm. "I'll give them your excuses. I promise to be very, very diplomatic."

Terrence had always been fond of Elena.

Chapter Twenty-Four: Rose

Rose had not minded the prospect of an afternoon sewing with the court ladies, but it was nicer to go to the royal library with Terrence instead. She had left the kittens at home, because it was better for them to roam in the Queen's Garden then get into the piles of books and papers habitually scattered around the library. When she bid Terrence good-bye and came home, she found that the kittens had come inside and got into mischief in her belongings instead.

Emerald Eyes had somehow got his claws hopelessly ensnared in one of Rose's lightest, filmiest scarves, and she was engaged in trying to untangle him when there was a knock at her door. It was a little early for Gabrielle to be coming to help her dress for supper, but not remarkably so. "Come in," Rose called without looking up from her squirming kitten, trying to unhook another tiny claw.

So she was completely unprepared when she glanced up a moment later and found, not Gabrielle, but Gregory, standing at the end of the couch and smiling at her. It was a terrible smile. Her heart jumped into her throat and she instinctively pressed back against the padded arm of the couch.

"Hello, Princess," he said in a low voice, and though he was smiling, the fire was still there in his eyes, the smoldering fury he always looked at her with.

Rose swallowed, gaze darting to the door—of course he'd closed it behind him. She took a breath, straightened her spine. She spoke fiercely enough to him in council meetings; she was not going to sit here silently now. "Prince Gregory, I was not expecting you. I am not currently disposed for visitors."

Emerald Eyes gave a yank with his paw, finally pulling his last claw free. He scrambled out of her lap to run to the bedroom, abandoning her.

"I've been thinking you and I ought to have a little talk," Gregory said, just as though she hadn't said anything, and sat down at the opposite end of the couch. "You avoid me, don't you? After council meetings. At family suppers."

Of course she did, deliberately and with dedication. "I have never had the impression you wished to be friends," she said carefully, a diplomatic and vast understatement. He had never treated her with anything but rage and contempt. She could feel it there still, under this surface of polite conversation, and the combination of a kind of twisted charm and simmering hatred was even more frightening than open hostility had been.

"I don't know if *friends* is just what I had in mind," Gregory said, sliding closer to her on the couch.

She was in the corner of the couch and if he moved any farther there'd be nowhere for her to go—she stood up abruptly, took several steps, turning so she could keep her gaze on him. "I do not understand why you are here. Unless you have business to discuss—"

"I hear you went off with Edward to his bedroom," Gregory drawled, leaning back on the couch and stretching his arms to either side. "Thought maybe you'd like to come back to my bedroom some time."

Her face burned. How dare he suggest— "No," she said coldly, with all the outraged dignity she could gather while her hands wanted to shake and she was all too aware he was still between her and the door. "I would *not* like that. Nor do I expect your wife would like it."

He looked blank for a second, as though he genuinely had to think who she meant and why this was relevant. "What, Penelope? She wouldn't care. She doesn't care about anything. She's silent all the time because she's got nothing to say."

"I very much doubt that." Rose did wonder at times what Penelope was thinking—but she thought she *was* thinking something.

"She's weak, boring. Not like you."

He was up from the couch with a suddenness that caught her unawares despite her attention on him, crossed the space between them in just a few strides. She backed up, bumped into her breakfast table, and then he was in front of her, hands on the table on either side, trapping her.

"I'd like to get you alone in my bedroom," he said in that low voice that sent chills up her spine.

She shoved against his chest but it was like pushing a wall. "Get away from me!" Her heart was pounding in her ears and he was *so close* and she couldn't—

"You'd fight me, wouldn't you? I'd like to see how long it would take, to drive that out of you." He leaned in even closer, lips pressing against her neck.

She threw all her weight to the side, jarred his arm enough to break his hold on the table so she could stumble away. There was a writing desk in the corner—she backed towards it, keeping her gaze on Gregory, reached and felt blindly through the things scattered across its surface until she came up with the knife she used to open letters. It was small but it was sharp, and it was better than nothing. "Don't come near me," she said, breathing hard, heart still racing.

Emerald Eyes and Silvertips erupted out of the bedroom, darted over to crouch between her and Gregory, backs arched, spitting defiance. They were brave and tiny and she wished desperately that they'd run away and stay safe.

"Two little kittens and one little princess," Gregory said, and laughed. "You would be fun, wouldn't you? I'd like to see how you'd try to defy me." The rage sparked brighter in his eyes. "And then I'd like to punish you for it."

"If you ever touch me, I'll—"

"You'll do what? Tell the king? Do you think my father would care? I might not even bother denying it. Or will you tell Terrence?" he asked, a new interest in his voice.

"Terrence would care," she whispered. He always thought the best of his family, of Gregory—but this would be too much to ignore.

"And wouldn't that be interesting?" His smile grew. "See if that finally provoked him into having some spine. And who could blame *me* if my little brother got hurt in a fight that he started? That wouldn't be my fault, would it?"

"You wouldn't dare." But he might. He really might, if he was fighting Terrence—could Terrence defend himself against Gregory? She didn't know. She'd never seen them fight, only knew their reputations. Terrence had said he was the scholar in the family, the one who couldn't beat Gregory in a swordfight. And Gregory had fought in the war, was taller and broader—

He paced closer, slowly and deliberately. "I don't think you ought to count on the things I *wouldn't* do. You can imagine it, can't you, the things I'd like to do right now? Do you really think that a couple of kittens and a tiny little knife are going to stop me?"

They wouldn't. They obviously wouldn't, but she gripped the knife tighter, lifted it higher, tried to think where she ought to aim for, and he was striding towards her faster now, in another moment—

There was a new knock at the door.

"Come in!" Rose called instantly, because anyone, literally anyone, was welcome right now.

Gregory's face twisted in a new fury, but now the door was opening and—Gabrielle, it was only Gabrielle, coming in to help her dress for supper. Rose's stomach dropped, disappointed of her momentary hope.

Gregory's face smoothed again as he looked back at the maid, standing near the door, and he said shortly, "Go away. The princess doesn't need you right now."

Gabrielle's eyes were large as she looked between Gregory and Rose. It had to be obvious what was happening. "Your Highness?" she said uncertainly, gaze on Rose.

"I *said*, you can go," Gregory snapped.

If Gabrielle helped her, could the two of them overpower Gregory, a man who had led armies, who knew how to fight? Probably not. And if he thought he could harm a crown princess with impunity, nothing would stop him when it came to a serving woman. If they tried to fight him, he'd hurt Gabrielle, he'd hurt her kittens, he'd hurt her…

"You can go," Rose said, voice hollow in her ears, but at least she could protect *someone*. "It's all right." Could Gabrielle go and get help? Could she bring anyone back before—Gregory would stop wasting time and—

"Yes, Your Highness," Gabrielle murmured, but didn't move. "Did you remember that Lady Graybourne will be here any moment, to discuss your new summer dresses?"

Something changed on Gregory's face, in his stance, when Lady Graybourne was mentioned, and Rose seized on what Gabrielle was offering. "Yes, of course. I had quite forgotten," she said, sounding ridiculous and false to herself but would Gregory have any idea? "She *is* due now, isn't she? To discuss my—my dresses."

Gregory's lip curled into something more like a sneer than a smile. "Beginning to have quite a crowd, aren't we? Well, then. Another time, Princess," he said, and it sounded like a threat.

He inclined his head in some parody of courtesy and stalked out of the room, every inch of his bearing suggesting that this was nothing like a retreat.

Rose didn't lower her knife until the door had closed behind him, and then she said, "Lock the door," to Gabrielle, who was already moving to do exactly that.

"Are you all right, Your Highness?" Gabrielle asked, standing with her back against the door.

"Yes, I—yes." Rose set down the knife, pressed a hand to her forehead. Her legs suddenly felt as though they weren't going to support her and her hands were shaking… "Thank you," she said softly, meeting Gabrielle's gaze. "*Thank you.*"

The other woman offered a very small smile. "Of course, Your Highness." A pause. "Everyone knows Prince Gregory doesn't like Lady Graybourne. And he doesn't like to anger General Graybourne, who is very fond of his wife."

"I see," Rose murmured. "She isn't actually coming, is she?" She could remember no such plans, though the way her head was spinning, perhaps that didn't mean very much.

"No, Your Highness. I don't believe so."

Rose nodded, clenched her hands into fists to try to stop their shaking. "I think—I think I would like to rest. Before I dress for supper."

"Of course, Your Highness. If there is anything I can do?"

"No, just—feel free to sit down. And—no, that's all."

She fled to the bedroom, closed the door behind herself and the kittens. She stumbled across the room, fell across her bed, dragged a pillow closer to bury her face in and try to muffle the sobs escaping her throat. She clutched the pillow and cried, shoulders shaking and body shuddering, as her kittens scrambled up and huddled against her.

He had looked at her just like the champions had, all those years ago. Like an *object* he could use however he wanted. Like he could hurt her and not even care—no, worse, like he'd enjoy doing it.

She had been careful around Gregory, and yet some part of her had still believed that she was safe at least from that, that being engaged to Terrence meant no one else would touch her.

She rolled at last onto her back, sobs abating and tears slowed to a trickle, stared up at her ceiling and tried to think. Could she tell Terrence? She *wanted* to tell Terrence—she wanted him right now, this moment, to fold her into his arms and hold her tightly and tell her it was all going to be all right. She wanted his touch to banish the feeling of Gregory's lips on her neck, wanted the safety and reassurance of Terrence's kindness. She wanted the way *he* looked at her, like he saw her.

But *should* she tell Terrence? She remembered Gregory's words about fighting him and shivered. What if—what if that was even the point of all this? If she accused Gregory of threatening her, he could deny it, and then look blameless in whatever happened if Terrence fought him anyway. Gregory didn't want him taking his place as crown prince, and if he could get rid of Terrence…

Her stomach rolled and she pressed her hands over her face. All those champions in the thorns, screaming and dying, trying to claim her hand. She could not, *could not* cause Terrence's death, could not live with the memory of him bleeding and dying for her. All those other champions, but not this one. Never this one.

Emerald Eyes scrambled up onto her, rubbed his head beneath her chin, and she brought her hands down to stroke him. She took a deep breath and it steadied her. "We have to protect Terrence, don't we?" she whispered to her kittens. "So we can't tell him. We can't tell anyone."

Gregory could scare her, and he might be able to hurt her, but that didn't mean he could use her in this complicated game. She wouldn't do it, wouldn't play into his plan.

Of course, if he was really clever, he wouldn't have said that about fighting Terrence at all, wouldn't have given that away—maybe it had even been a misdirection. But no, she didn't think Gregory *was* that clever, that subtle.

"I'll keep avoiding him," she said, rubbing Emerald Eyes' fur. "I'll be more careful about locking my door, and about who I open it for. And maybe—maybe it will be better, once Terrence and I are married."

This in-between state couldn't go on forever. There were plans to recognize her as heir, to recognize Terrence's claim through her, plans for their marriage. It was all still a long way away, but maybe when it was official, maybe that would give her more power, and maybe Gregory would have to come to terms with it.

It sounded good. Hopeful.

She even almost believed it.

Chapter Twenty-Five: Terrence

Terrence had always worried some about Rose, about how she was feeling and how she was adjusting to this new life he had brought her to. He started worrying more in the days after that visit she took to her old bedroom with Edward. He didn't think that was necessarily the cause; it was just the only way he could date her new preoccupation, the sense that *she* was worrying about something she wasn't telling him. He asked, but she denied anything was wrong, and there were, troublingly, too many possibilities for him to easily guess; it could be anything from an issue with her dress fitting to the latest argument in the council meetings to the way Gregory still kept glaring at them. Or maybe it was something in the complicated tangle of relationships with the court ladies.

The only solution he could come up with was to take her away from all of it, seizing on an unusually free day to plan a trip to the market, out in the capital city. This required a more elaborate proceeding now than it used to in years past, with Elena and Henry each on their own horse as chaperones, Rose riding with Terrence on Barley, and their half-dozen guards following behind.

Terrence had promised Rose he'd teach her to ride eventually, but for the moment he liked having her ride in front of him, his arm around her waist, her hair brushing his chin as she turned her head to look around them.

"Does it look different?" he asked as they rode down the main boulevard leading from the castle and into the city proper. "From how you remember before your enchantment?"

"I don't know," she said. "No? But I don't remember it well. I didn't see it often. Even from my bedroom, I didn't have a good view of the city, and I didn't come out of the castle much."

"This section shouldn't be too different," Terrence offered. The castle was at the very top of the hill. Just below it was the Skysun District, with the city homes of the aristocracy, mostly hidden behind high walls and lines of trees. They had just entered the third tier, the Temple District. "Most of these temples date from your time, I think."

"Yes…" Rose said, and though he couldn't see her face, he could tell her head was tipped in her thoughtful pose.

Each principal god had a temple complex along this road. They had already passed the blue stone temple of Laekces the Sea God, with its dome roof and front pillars covered in fish-themed mosaics. It was followed by the elegant marble temple of Eltaor, the God of Art.

"Oh—I remember that statue," Rose said, with a sudden shiver.

They were passing the temple of the Veiled God now, with its twenty-foot tall statue of a cloaked figure in front. It was impossible to distinguish the figure's gender, and a carved veil covered its face, only the slightest hint of facial features beneath. The head was thrown back, one arm reaching up towards the sky. It had always given him a deep-down uneasiness, but it was probably supposed to.

"When I was small, I used to be sure it was going to come creeping out of the shadows at night," Terrence remarked. "Even though it's too big to sneak anywhere."

Rose giggled. "Me too."

It was better to move beyond the Veiled God's temple, past the temples devoted to Arthian, the God of Wisdom; Ravarra, the God of the Hearth; and Sylmare, the Traveler God. The last one before the market district was Mariqwe's temple, the God of Passion.

As he always did when he passed, Terrence gave a deep nod of his head in respect. Usually he also touched the lioness tattoo on his inner forearm, but the maneuver was impossible with Rose in front of him and Barley's reins to manage. He just turned his arm slightly to glance at the tattoo, and trusted the god would understand.

He only realized Rose was noticing when she touched his arm—next to the tattoo, not on it. "Was it a difficult decision, when you chose to follow Mariqwe?"

It had been almost too easy, the obvious choice, and sometimes he thought that meant he should have done more reflection. But he *had* thought, and it had felt right. "No. The royal family has followed Mariqwe for generations."

Rose nodded. "My father did too. The male aspect, though."

He wasn't surprised, seeing as his father and brothers were the same. He shrugged. "I don't know. A lioness felt more right." He didn't mention the awkwardness involved in his family when it became apparent that he preferred worshipping Mariqwe in female aspect. His father still didn't understand that, and it would have been simpler to add a mane when he was getting his tattoo, to get the male version of the traditional symbol. But you have to worship the gods the way you're called to.

"The market square is just beyond that arch, past the city guard post," Terrence said, moving on before this conversation went uncomfortable directions. He liked talking to Rose, even or especially about complicated things—but today was supposed to be for enjoyment, for escaping the troubling parts of their lives.

They stabled the horses, leaving one guard behind, and ventured on foot into the market. They attracted more than the usual number of stares, undoubtedly because of Rose. Most people here were used to Terrence and Elena, and Henry stood out even less. But the Princess Behind Thorns attracted attention. Terrence stuck next to her, the guards glared if anyone pushed too close, and mostly people only looked and didn't try to do anything else, except possibly whisper to their neighbors. It was similar in the castle, just—more, here.

He wasn't certain if Rose even noticed. She was wide-eyed and interested in everything they showed her and every shopkeep they introduced her to, happy to touch everything and try anything. It had to be a lot to take in, after a century alone in a garden.

It was good to see her smile like that, to see some of the tension that had been in her eyes lately fade away.

Silvertips, who had ridden down from the castle asleep in Rose's bag, woke up while they were still exploring stalls and wanted down.

"You shouldn't let her loose," Elena said, as Rose lifted Silvertips out of the bag.

"She'll be fine," Rose said, setting the kitten down and returning to her study of a display of small statues of the gods, the kind people would have on private altars. They were similar in size to Rose's Mariqwe statue but there were no female warriors among this collection.

"But cats run off," Elena protested.

Silvertips, oblivious to the conversation, darted over to sniff Elena's shoes, then trotted back to Rose again.

"Yes," Rose said, sounding thoughtful. "I know that. But…she won't." She shook her head. "I don't know, I just think she knows where she's supposed to be."

Terrence and Elena exchanged a glance, and he shrugged. It was true that he'd never yet seen one of Rose's cats get lost, no matter where she took them in the castle. He knew on some level that it was strange, but he'd mostly stopped questioning it. Maybe being born in a magic garden made a difference for a kitten's degree of sense.

"Come down this way," Terrence suggested, nodding to a quieter side street. "You have to try the best cookies in the city. Just don't tell the castle baker I said so."

The baker and his wife were both in their small shop when the group stepped inside, bringing the kitten and leaving the guards at the door.

"Ah, Prince Terrence, it's like you always know when I've just made my frosted cherry drop cookies," Foster said with a wide grin.

"Did you just make some?" Terrence seized Rose's hand, drew her forward. "Rose, you have to try these cookies. They're amazing."

The baker's wife, Edaline, paused in the middle of plating the soft round cookies. "Is this Princess Rose? The Princess Behind Thorns?"

Suddenly she was dipping into a curtsy, while her husband tried for a bow while maneuvering trays of sweets.

"Oh, please don't," Rose protested with a smile. "I'd love to try a cookie, though."

"Do you have any of your peanut butter cinnamon cookies?" Elena asked, perhaps also trying to diffuse the sudden attempts at formality.

It was a more flurried trip to the bakeshop than usual, but they did end up with the normal assortment of Foster's specialties. Terrence was eating his fourth, a honey almond cookie, when Edaline said, "Now is it true, the stories we've been hearing? They say the line of succession is changing."

Terrence swallowed cookie fragments. He should have expected the rumors would be flying. They were in this strange, middle state, where nothing was official but nothing was secret either. No formal ceremony, but no injunction of silence. Which meant stories had likely been rampant all over the country for weeks. "There's still a lot of arrangements involved, but yes, the succession is changing."

Edaline's eyes grew big again. "And it's true then—*you're* going to be the next king!"

"Well…" Terrence looked at Rose. "That is the idea, yes."

"Imagine that," Edaline said, elbowing her husband. "Our Prince Terrence, going to be king. Who would have guessed that, the first time he wandered in here and asked about your cookies?"

This set off a series of reminiscences that were touching if slightly embarrassing. Eventually, they went through their traditional dance, as Foster insisted they must accept the cookies for free, Terrence insisted on paying, and they finally wound up by paying for what they'd eaten and taking a few away as gifts for later. That much felt comfortingly normal.

It wasn't so normal when they stepped out of the shop, and found the guards they'd left outside in a standoff with a crowd of several dozen people. It was a peaceful standoff, but still.

"I'm sorry, Your Highness," Commander Morgan, the highest ranking of the guards, said over his shoulder, sounding irritated. "They heard the princess was inside and refused to leave without seeing her. I didn't want to create an incident, but if you want us to see them off…"

Terrence glanced at Rose, automatically stepping closer to her and taking her arm, the one that wasn't cradling a kitten. "I think they're just curious," he said to her, "but if you're uncomfortable…"

It was a varied crowd, men, women and children, all united in expressions of hopeful interest.

"It's all right," Rose said, putting on a smile. It wasn't the smile she wore when they were alone, but it wasn't the smile she wore in council meetings either; he'd already learned that one meant she was entirely on her guard. "I don't mind greeting them."

"Are you really her?" a woman's voice called from the crowd. "The Princess Behind Thorns?"

More voices picked it up. "Are you? Are you really the princess?"

Rose lifted her head higher. "I am Princess Rose Amelia. The Princess Behind Thorns."

The crowd murmured and pressed closer, eyes shining.

"All right, you've seen her," Commander Morgan said, and gestured to his men. "Now make way—make way, there!"

The guards worked to open a corridor, and the crowd fell agreeably back. It was growing though, more people gathering at the edges. Terrence could see several of the city guard too, in their brown uniforms, apparently drawn from their nearby post to see what was going on.

"We should probably get the horses and go back to the castle," Terrence said into Rose's ear as they started to walk behind the guards. "We're never going to shake the crowd now."

"That's all right," Rose said, and smiled up at him. "At least we got the cookies already."

She was wonderful, and he wanted to tell her so and probably kiss her, but this was no time for it. Not only because someone in the crowd shouted his name just then. "Prince Terrence! Is it true? Are you going to be our king?"

He squared his shoulders. "Yes. I am." It felt strange, declaring it publicly that way. But it was true—if not as immediate as the question made it sound. "Someday," he amended.

The crowd didn't seem to care about that minor prevarication. "A cheer for Prince Terrence!" a new voice called. "And for the Princess Behind Thorns!"

Cheers followed them through the market, only left behind once they reached the stable and the horses. It had been a friendly crowd, but Terrence still felt easier when he and Rose were seated on Barley again, Silvertips curled up in her bag, riding with Elena and Henry on either side and the guards around them. He had never felt that royalty ought to stay away from their people, but he worried about Rose.

"Are you all right?" he asked as they began the trek back up to the castle.

"Yes," she said, and she sounded sincere but also thoughtful. He wished he could see her face, but it wasn't a good angle. "Why did they all look at me like that?"

"Who wouldn't want to look at a beautiful woman?" Terrence said swiftly.

He could just see the edge of her smile, but it apparently wasn't enough of an answer all the same. "No, that wasn't it. This was something else. They all looked…hopeful? Expectant?"

"You're part of a legend," Elena contributed. "A legend that's important to people."

Rose shook her head. "But why? Why should the legend matter to people? And they weren't just hopeful about seeing me, it was…I don't know, it was *something else*."

"It's the other part of the legend," Henry spoke up, surprising Terrence, since he was usually so quiet. "Neither of you have told her that? No one's explained this?"

Terrence was almost sure he knew what Henry was talking about. It hadn't seemed like something that was going to help Rose feel comfortable, help her adjust into this new life. She didn't need even more expectations put on her. "It's not that important—"

"It's important to a lot of people," Henry said steadily. "It's important to all those people back there."

"*What* is?" Rose asked, sounding nettled now. "I missed a century. Someone please explain what you're talking about!"

"A lot of people think the country started to go wrong during that century you missed," Elena said, frowning. "That it started, actually, when you went under the enchantment. That that was when we began to go the wrong direction."

"What do you mean?" Rose asked. "Things seem…all right?"

"At the castle, they are," Henry said. "And even in the capital, it's not that bad."

"It's not that bad anywhere," Terrence said, and when both Elena and Henry cast him expressive looks he amended, "Yes, I know there are problems. But don't make it out worse than it is. It's not like there's been mass starvation and a descent into barbarism."

"How many people in the country could read, when you went behind those thorns?" Elena asked Rose. "Roughly?"

"I don't know…" Rose shrugged. "Most people. Less in the rural areas, but it wasn't as necessary there. Maybe eighty percent?"

"The last census puts it at forty-three percent," Elena said quietly. "Education numbers are dropping, land is owned by fewer and fewer people, and taxes keep rising. We haven't had an open court since the war with Melidan, and you've heard all about the land and education promise we aren't keeping. There are other issues, but you get the idea. Life keeps getting harder for more and more of the country."

"Governing is complicated," Terrence said, feeling an instinctive need to defend his family. "There are a lot of factors, and…all right, it's bad. Why do you think I wanted to become king anyway?"

"What does any of this have to do with me?" Rose asked.

"You tell her, Terrence," Henry prompted. "You're the one who brought her back."

Terrence sighed. "Part of the legend is—I mean, if someone believes that it all went wrong because you were enchanted—it's supposed to turn around again if you return. That you were the rightful heir all along, that the problem is with who's sitting on the throne, and if the Princess Behind Thorns is woken up from her enchantment and returns to be the next queen, the gods will be pleased and balance will be restored or…something, and the country will prosper."

"But I'm just *me*," Rose said faintly. "I can't—I don't know how to change everything."

Exactly why he hadn't wanted to throw all of this at her. She had enough to be thinking about. "It's just a story. We *will* try to change things. But you don't have to turn a whole country around tomorrow. No one expects that."

"They expect something," Rose said dubiously.

Terrence tightened his arm around her, put a smile into his voice. "Then isn't it a good thing I have a fifty-page plan about land and education?"

Despite his best efforts, the atmosphere was subdued on the ride back, even though it had been a mostly pleasant day. At least they were going home with extra cookies, and they hadn't lost Rose's kitten in the crowds.

If the tension in their group never quite dissipated, it still became suddenly dwarfed by the tension in the castle when they arrived. Everyone they passed as they brought the horses to the stables was talking in hurried, hushed tones to each other, no one seemed to want to meet Terrence's eye, and he could practically hear an ongoing buzz of conversation from everywhere else in the castle too.

Finally, just as they were about to enter the main part of the castle, Terrence spotted a guard he'd known for years, a reliable source of information. "Sam, what's going on?" he asked. "We've been out all day, and the place is in some kind of uproar…"

Sam looked over their group, glanced around as though checking for spies, then leaned in closer to ask Terrence, "You haven't heard about Princess Penelope?"

Terrence's thoughts flew to accidents, assassinations, suddenly discovered illnesses. Everything about the tone in the castle suggested this wasn't going to be good news, not something pleasant like an expected baby. He had never been close to Penelope, but he still felt a sickening drop in his stomach from the sense that something terrible was about to be announced.

"What about Penelope?" Elena demanded.

Sam looked wretched. He shifted from foot to foot, tugged on the edge of his red coat. "It's—His Majesty, and Prince Gregory. They made the announcement, just an hour ago—they're sending her away. In disgrace."

That…was not something Terrence had imagined.

"*Penelope*?" Elena said, voice rising to a sharp note. "Why? What for?"

"Because…" Sam's gaze darted between Elena and Rose. "They're saying…I mean…because…"

It didn't take any great leaps to deduce the reason a princess would be sent away in disgrace, a reason a guard wouldn't feel comfortable saying in front of court ladies.

"Thank you for the information," Terrence said, and tried to steer everyone inside. He had still been looking for another chance to talk to Penelope. Apparently that wasn't going to happen. Would she have said anything that would have made more sense of this news?

"They're not accusing her of *unfaithfulness*, are they?" Elena demanded before they got past Sam, who turned as red as his coat—a clear confirmation. "But that's ridiculous!"

"Let's go, Elena," Henry said, the firm note that commanded troops entering his voice.

"But it's absurd," Elena protested as they continued inside. "You know Penelope! She's the last person in the world who would—it's just ridiculous."

Terrence never would have suspected Penelope as someone who would have a passionate extramarital affair. But then, he'd never gotten to know her well. She had seemed so quiet, so meek, barely ever making eye contact. To do something like this seemed entirely out of character…what little he knew of her character. "There must be some reason Gregory believes she did it," he said aloud, wondering how his brother had taken the news. He had been angry and on edge ever since Rose came to court. This must have sent him to a new height of rage.

Elena stopped in her tracks, everyone else halting a step later. "Are you saying you actually believe this?"

Did he believe it? He wasn't sure. What *would* Penelope have said, if he'd ever really talked to her? "I'm only saying Gregory must believe it—"

"Does he?" Elena hissed. "Do you think he really does?"

"Do you *want* to be arrested for treason?" Henry said under his breath, sounding no less furious for the low volume.

"I *want* to know if Terrence actually thinks that—"

"I think," Terrence said over her, "that there is a lot we don't know, and we should stop talking about it in the middle of the hall!"

Elena subsided at that, and as they continued silently on, Terrence looked at Rose for the first time since the news had broken—and felt guilty that he hadn't sooner. She had gone pale, staring straight ahead.

"Rose?" He squeezed her hand. "Are you all right? Were you fond of Penelope?" He couldn't remember her ever saying anything significant about the castle's other crown princess.

"I think she was afraid," Rose said, voice distant. Slowly her gaze met Terrence's, and he didn't like the fear he could see in her blue eyes. "I think Penelope was afraid, all the time. I mostly thought she was just quiet or timid or shy. But now I think she must have been very, very afraid."

Part Three

Spring, Year 512

Chapter Twenty-Six: Rose

Rose felt afraid from the moment she heard the news about Penelope. She told herself she didn't know why, which might have done more to quell the fear if she had actually believed it. She also told herself that Gregory's problems with his wife had nothing to do with her, that it was rank arrogance to assume they did, and that there was no connection at all to the way Gregory had looked at her, that day he had invaded her rooms.

She didn't really believe any of that either. She kept repeating the ideas to herself anyway, because it was too terrifying to think about what she really did believe, about why a former-crown prince might dismiss his wife just after a new heir to the throne arrived. That was too hideous to contemplate.

She was betrothed to Terrence. She was going to marry Terrence. It was legal, official, publicly recognized. Gregory might be able to come into her room, to stand too close to her, to make vague threats, but—surely that was all. Terrence was the one who had come through the thorns, who had brought her out again. That *counted* for something.

Not thinking about the worst possibilities—trying not to think about them—didn't dismiss the fear either. It was all the worse because it was so damnably familiar. It felt like the old fear, the fear that her life was hurtling her towards something horrible, unwanted, and outside of her control.

It had already been bad enough to find out that large portions of the country were expecting her to be some sort of savior. She wanted to help people, but to find out that a century-long legend had led people to *expect* her to change the world…that was a lot to get her mind around, a lot of people to worry about disappointing. And then it was like a sudden slap to be immediately reminded that she had so little control after all.

She had been playing at having power. She had been pretending that all her little efforts and decisions mattered, that insisting on a seat at the council table, choosing her own clothes, successfully navigating conversations with the court ladies, all meant something. She had been pretending to be someone like Xevrix, the enchantress - someone who had real power.

But the truth was, she had what power the king allowed her to have. Because what made her different from Penelope? She thought she had some understanding of court politics, some skill at deciphering motives and meanings—but maybe Penelope had understood just as much, had been quietly thinking all the while, and it had done her no good.

Rose had her own claim to the throne, wore her gold signet ring because of who she was, not because of who she was married to. But did that matter? Being heir hadn't kept her from being enchanted and hidden away behind thorns for a hundred years. Her own father had done that to her. Who knew what this king would be willing to do?

She had Terrence. And that mattered. That mattered to *her* very much. Not having Terrence—her mind leapt away from that thought, as instinctive as snatching her hand back from a fire.

The nightmares came back the same night she learned about Penelope. She dreamed a confused jumble of shadows and walls and thorns, of champions staring at her, laughing at her, screaming at her as they died. She dreamed of her father, sternly shaking his head, giving orders that she be handed over to a parade of bloodied, furious champions, some with thorns still wrapped around them, some staring at her through dead eyes. And there, at the end of the line, grinning while his eyes burned with hatred, stood Gregory. In her dream she screamed and pleaded and no one, no one could hear her.

She finally awoke tangled in her blankets, heart pounding, drenched in sweat. The kittens had fled. She lay on her back on the bed, fingers clutching the blanket beneath her, trying to breathe, trying to assure herself that it was a dream, only a dream, and nothing to fear. Her breathing did not slow, her body did not relax, and at last with a moan she rolled over, wrapped her arms around the nearest pillow, and sobbed into it.

Eventually her sobs subsided. Eventually the kittens came cautiously back. Eventually she fell asleep again, and did not dream. But she woke knowing that fear had followed her from the Before Time, had followed her out of the garden, and was still lodged deep, deep inside of her.

She lay in bed for a long time in the early dawn, staring at the ceiling. When she finally got up, she went out to the sitting room and picked up her statue of Mariqwe. She brought it back, and set it on top of the small table beside her bed.

Rose stared at that defiant warrior woman. Surely *she* was never afraid. But then, she was a god.

Maybe it would help, having the statue where she could see it at night. Maybe it would help her feel a little braver.

The first step, the next step, was to get dressed for the day.

She only had two black dresses in her wardrobe, and she was drearily contemplating one of them when there was a knock at the door.

Her heartrate sped up. This was *ridiculous*. She had been jumping every time someone knocked on the door, ever since Gregory—that brisk tap didn't even sound like him, though she couldn't really remember what his knock *had* sounded like, she'd been paying so little attention and then the events after had so overwhelmed her memory… She hurried into the outer room, stopped a few feet from the door.

"Who is it?" she called, her days of carelessly inviting anyone to come in probably forever in the past.

"Lady Graybourne, of course, who else would it be?"

Rose let out a relieved breath, and went to unlock the door. Even that slightly irritated reply didn't signify anything to worry about; she knew Lady Graybourne well enough by now to know that.

The older woman swept in with a rustle of gray silk and a brisk, "Good morning." She looked at Rose's face and her eyes narrowed, but she didn't comment on whatever she saw. "And what are we wearing today?"

"I thought maybe my black silk," Rose said, drifting back towards her bedroom with Lady Graybourne in her wake.

"Oh my dear, absolutely not!" Lady Graybourne said sternly, without even glancing at the dress. "You already look entirely too pale this morning. Black is going to make you look dreadful, and you'll appear to be in mourning besides."

She felt like being in mourning. For herself, mostly, maybe for Penelope too. She didn't know how much she should worry about Penelope. No one seemed to know what had happened to her, only that she had been sent away.

She probably should have been worrying about Penelope long before this. She *had* wondered, after Gregory came into her room, what it was like for Penelope, married to that man. To a man who could look at her, Rose, with so much hatred, with so much horrible meaning in his eyes. She had wanted to believe it was different for Penelope, that perhaps he wasn't like that with her. He had no reason to hate Penelope.

That had probably been a naïve and self-indulgent belief.

She had meant to try to talk more to Penelope, to find out…something. And then it had been too late, before she'd ever found the right chance.

"I feel like wearing black," she murmured, even as she reached to rifle through her other dresses hanging in the wardrobe. If Penelope had died the whole court would be in mourning, but no one donned black for princesses sent away in disgrace.

"And that is exactly why you shouldn't wear it today." Lady Graybourne's voice was firm but not unkind, and when Rose looked up she found the other woman looking at her intently. "Never let them see you flinch," she said quietly. "True in battles, true in politics. Wear your brightest and your best today, and if recent events trouble you, don't let anyone see it."

Rose felt obscurely encouraged. At least—at least Lady Graybourne understood. "Maybe the light blue, then," she said, lifting the long sleeve.

"Excellent choice," Lady Graybourne said with a firm nod. "That shade does good things for your complexion."

"Do you think Penelope did it?" Rose asked abruptly, because she might not have the nerve if she waited for an appropriate opening.

She pulled the dress out of the wardrobe, held it gathered in her arms as though the soft folds could be a comfort.

Lady Graybourne did not appear surprised by the question. "I would not presume to state," she said, voice careful. "My husband was at the meeting where she was accused. She confessed to everything."

"Really," Rose said, and knew the skepticism was heavy in her voice.

"My lord the General did find the confession somewhat... irregular." Her face was perfectly impassive. "The king and Prince Gregory were satisfied regarding her guilt." The underlying message was clear—to say anything in contradiction was unwise, perhaps treasonous.

"Do you think Penelope's all right?" Rose asked in a small voice, fingers tightening on the dress she was holding.

"I hope so."

That was undoubtedly the most reassurance she could give. Rose nodded, took a deep breath, and said, "Perhaps we should discuss my new summer dresses."

Lady Graybourne nodded, eyes still serious. "Perhaps. The question, of course, is the impression you wish to convey to the rest of the court."

Gabrielle arrived to help Rose dress in her blue silk, Rose and Lady Graybourne discussed summer dresses over breakfast, the kittens romped about the room and got generally underfoot, and on the surface all was serene and normal and as it should be.

Under the surface, Lady Graybourne seemed more stiff and solemn than usual, and Rose was still afraid.

Lady Graybourne was probably never afraid. She surely never had nightmares. Rose kind of longed to be her when she grew up.

When everything was finally settled regarding her dresses, and Gabrielle and Lady Graybourne both betook themselves elsewhere, Rose took refuge in the Queen's Garden with her kittens. There was no real work to do there, no weeding or pruning of dead blossoms, but she explored more carefully than she had taken time for so far, gathered enough flowers for three bouquets, and spent time sitting under a tree, watching the kittens play.

She told herself that she wasn't hiding. She was just—gathering strength.

The castle bells were ringing for ten o'clock when Elena came to join her, answering a message Rose had sent with Gabrielle to ask her to come by.

"There's a bench over there if you want to sit," Rose said, starting to rise from her own place on the grass.

"No, that's all right," Elena said, dropping down and tucking her skirts around her legs. "Lucky I'm wearing green, right? Grass stains won't even show." She laughed as Silvertips came tumbling over to scramble into her lap. "I don't know how you keep cat hair off of your clothes, Rose."

Rose merely shrugged. Despite whatever peace the garden might offer, she couldn't join in with Elena's light-hearted tone. "I needed to talk to you—I need to know more about the court."

She had thought this through, in the early hours this morning. She had thought about asking Terrence, and she probably would—but instinct told her there was more Elena could tell her. Terrence thought well of more people, and that wasn't the perspective she needed right now. She was glad, in a way, that he did see the world like that, but it wasn't what she needed.

Elena nodded slowly, stroking Silvertips. "What do you want to know?"

"No, that's not going to work. I don't *know* what I need to know, so I don't know what questions to ask. I just…" Rose laced her fingers together in her lap, stared down at them. "What have you not told me? About the royal family, and the council, and loyalties, and—I don't know what it means, Penelope being sent away. I don't know what the king is thinking. I don't…there's just so much that I *don't know*!" And too much that she was afraid she did know.

Elena leaned back on her hands, looking at Rose with a thoughtful expression. "You probably know more than you think. I've seen you observing everyone. You may have a better read on some things than all of us who have been here forever. Like Penelope—she was so quiet, right from the start, I didn't ask enough *why* she was quiet. I should have, knowing Gregory, but…" She shook her head.

"All right. You want to know how things work here. I haven't been able to find out yet why they sent Penelope away, but I can tell you more about how the court works."

"Thank you," Rose whispered, feeling as though a significant decision had been made in her favor.

"King Elgin is the center of everything, of course, because he's the king. He likes to pretend he's absolutely powerful, but it isn't true. The council has limited legal power; their official job is to advise the king, nothing more. In practice, they have a great deal of actual power. The king doesn't *have* to abide by majority opinion, but in most cases he'd be a fool not to. The eight nobles on the council have more combined wealth and land than the crown, and they each have a standing guard besides. Each one functionally represents an entire province, so that means a great deal of influence. High priests, naturally, have enormous influence on the populace, and the power of the Head Enchanter should be obvious."

"And General Graybourne?" Rose prompted, pinpointing the one councilmember not yet included in the list.

Elena half-smiled. "General Graybourne was high commander during the war. He's a lord too, a relatively minor one, but it's the military title that counts most with him. The soldiers all swear an oath to king and country, but General Graybourne leads them. No one's exactly sure where loyalties would end up if they had to choose between the general and the king, and King Elgin doesn't want to test it. Did you know some of this?"

"Some of it." She had guessed at parts, seen evidence of other aspects. "What about the succession?"

"The key question, isn't it?" Elena rumpled Silvertips' fur, frowning as though she was choosing her words carefully. "I think…first, a little history you might not know—no first-born son of a king has inherited in the past century."

Rose drew in a breath. "That's…that can't be good for a country." It seemed to imply a level of instability and uncertainty that could only breed chaos.

"No. And it means that Terrence's great-grandfather was ruthless enough to seize the throne out of near-anarchy, and everyone who's sat on it since has been the most ruthless of their generation. They've managed to keep it in the same line, but Elgin is a second son, and his father was a third son. They both had brothers who died unexpectedly or went mad. The kind of madness you might get from poison, incidentally."

Rose's heart was pounding. She had suspected that level of brutality, but it was frightening to hear it confirmed. "Did either of them have sisters?"

"Yes, and three of them had husbands who made attempts at the throne, but none managed to take it. Elgin's sister was never officially implicated in the plot that led to her husband's execution, but rumors abounded; eventually the king essentially exiled her, although he said she was sent away from court for her health. Anyway, what it all means for the present is that, even though Gregory was officially the heir, people have always tended to look at every prince as a potential king."

"And what does that picture look like?"

"Gregory is the king's choice. Loyalty to the king is loyalty to Gregory and vice versa. In theory Gregory could pit himself against his father, but I haven't seen signs of it. I think it suited him being crown prince. Lots of power, less responsibility. Everyone agrees Tyler is useless. He doesn't appear to particularly want the throne himself, and no one has thought seriously about installing him as a puppet. He doesn't give or take orders well. Edward is uncertain. He's quiet, smarter than most people realize, and seems to be loyal to his father, but I'm never sure what he's thinking."

So far, this aligned with Rose's own impressions. "And Terrence?"

Elena smiled. "And Terrence. Well, now. Terrence has always been *my* choice. And not just me. Did you notice, when we were in the bakery, Edaline called him 'our Prince Terrence'?"

Rose had noticed that. It had seemed sweet. She nodded now.

"It's actually fairly common. Many people, the people outside the court, the common people, think of him that way. Nothing's universal, but people who have met Terrence, people who hear stories from the ones who do—a lot of people think Terrence would be the one who'd make things better for *them*. He's the youngest son, his father wrote him off because he was busy with the older three, and Terrence got to go his own way a lot more. It made a difference."

Rose thought back over the times she had seen Terrence interact with people—the trip between the garden and the capital, the visit to the marketplace, times around the castle. "Everyone's always glad to see him, and he always knows everyone's name."

"Exactly," Elena said with a nod. "Don't think it would be that way with any of his brothers."

She wouldn't have. "But does that matter? Which prince the people like?"

"I think so," Elena said frankly. "The king pretends it doesn't, but anyone can do the numbers. Each person might not have much power, but if you get enough of them together…there was a popular uprising in Thaydan twenty years ago, and the nearby royalty have been a little spooked ever since. Just as important, there's a reasonable number at court and on the council who'd like to see Terrence inherit. Lords Bellham, Chapman, Ratliff and Gastrell are pretty solidly behind the king. Rupin—Lord Quintrell, properly—and Lords Dawson and Camden believe Terrence would be a better choice. The high priests have generally supported the king but they both recognize it would be hard to shift public opinion on Terrence, so they could easily change position. The Head Enchanter has done well himself with Elgin, but the group of royal enchanters has its own splits and factions, and there's a decent amount of pressure there that could go Terrence's way. Lord Elffire is an opportunist—he'll throw in with whoever has more support than everyone else. And that brings us back to General Graybourne, who believes his loyalty is to the country and the law. He'll support whoever the legal heir is, and I think he's glad that it's going to be Terrence now—he has a lot of respect for him because of Terrence's efforts to get benefits for the soldiers. He also respects his wife's opinions and she likes you, so that helps too."

Rose's head was spinning. This was a lot of information—and the fact that Elena had it, and could lay it out so easily… "You've been plotting a revolution."

"I don't know if I'd go that far," Elena said, looking modest. "It's more like I've been hoping for one, and finding out who else is too. We hadn't been able to work out how to actually get Terrence on the throne, or at least next in line."

"You seem to have worked out a lot."

"Well, maybe. I'd think I might have a magical talent for politics, except I'm not sure that's an actual affinity, and I've been tested and don't have magic anyway."

"And while you were plotting all this, all the while there was me," Rose said slowly, toying with her gold signet ring on her finger. "Is that—did you suggest it to Terrence, going to find me?"

"No, that one was all him. None of the rest of us thought it was a realistic idea. We told you about the legend, about people thinking you'd somehow wake up, come back and change everything, but it's a *legend.* Most people didn't take it that seriously. There were no clear details. Some stories say you were cursed, some say it was your father's plan, everyone said you were asleep and even that wasn't true. There was a strong competing story, especially at court, that you were actually dead behind the thorns—or, most likely, that you were never there to begin with, and the wall of thorns was just some kind of ruse. Probably an attempt to make it appear there was still an heir after you'd died here at the castle. So while I've spent years weighing out loyalties and incremental advancements, Terrence cut right through it all, rescued you, and gained the legal claim to inherit."

"Does he know all of this, though? That for years you've wanted to depose his father and put him on the throne?" Rose felt daring, saying it that way, half sure that Elena was going to contradict her, tell her she wasn't aiming for anything so extreme.

No contradiction came, not of that idea. Elena just laughed and said, "Of course Terrence doesn't know. You must have realized by now, any rebellion in Terrence stops short of opposing his father. He wants to be heir, he wants to have more influence, and he wants to be king *someday.* I don't think he recognizes how popular he is, either. He knows people like him, but he's too aware of how much he doesn't impress his father, and doesn't really believe he can impress anyone else very much. But I do recognize it, I see bigger problems in the country than he does, and I'm not convinced we can keep waiting. But even though we're closer than we ever were, I'm not sure we have a viable way to move any further forward. Rupin is researching it, but the law is complicated and the records concerning you are hard to even find. A few years of anarchy followed by a revisionist king will do that."

Rose let out a slow breath. "No wonder it upset people when Terrence brought me back." She had known she was bringing new instability. She hadn't realized how unstable the world already was.

"Hey, some of us are glad about it," Elena said, reaching out to squeeze Rose's hand. "And not just because of how you fit into the line of succession."

"Thank you," Rose said softly. But the warm feeling of Elena's words didn't dispel the larger worries. "Gregory isn't glad. And now they're sending Penelope away…" And that brought them back to the original question.

"They're planning something," Elena said. "I don't know exactly what, but…it won't be anything good."

That much, at least, Rose felt sure of too. Unfortunately.

Chapter Twenty-Seven: Terrence

Terrence spent the morning after Penelope's exile trying to work out what exactly had happened. He was worried about her, and he was worried about Rose, and he thought maybe finding something out was going to help somehow.

He didn't ask his father, on the grounds that he didn't want to bother him, and he didn't ask Gregory, because he was the probably the last person in the world Gregory wanted to see right now.

And maybe, part of him didn't want to know how either of them would describe the situation, how they'd talk about Penelope now.

So he hunted up Penelope's Lady of the Wardrobe, found a few different lords who usually knew everything that happened at court, talked to the stableboys and to the cook, even cautiously sounded Lenora for information. The picture that emerged suggested events had moved at a shockingly fast pace, but reassuring notes were in there too.

Then he went in search of Rose, finding her in the Queen's Garden with her kittens. The kittens were chasing each other around the space while Rose sat on the grass, and it looked very much like a scene from those first few days after he'd met her, like they could have been back in the enchanted garden. Except Rose's eyes looked different. She looked more uneasy here, in his family's castle, than she had behind walls of thorns. He hated that.

He dropped down to sit on the grass next to her, leaned in to kiss her cheek and received a smile in response, which was something at least. "So," he said without further preamble, pitching his voice as hearty and reassuring as he could, "I found out more about Penelope."

The smile vanished, Rose's eyes going wary, so apparently his tone of voice hadn't done any good at all. "Oh?"

"It's not bad," he said hastily. "I mean—I don't think it is. But apparently my father and Gregory and a few of the council members met with her yesterday morning to discuss the evidence they had about—unfaithfulness." He thought he stumbled on it less than the guard had, but it was true, it was not a topic generally considered polite for discussion with princesses or court ladies. At least, not by princes—he'd gleaned from Elena that it came up often enough amongst themselves.

"That sounds terrifying," Rose murmured, smoothing her skirt over her lap and not looking at him. Was she worried about how Penelope had faced that? Or—was she imagining herself in that position? But of course Rose wouldn't ever—

"She confessed," he said, interrupting his own thought. "She signed a written confession."

"And don't you have to wonder why?" Rose said.

Yes, more than he wanted to. "She might have done it," he offered doubtfully. "I mean, none of us knew her very well..."

"Who was it with?" she asked, still looking at her hands in her lap.

"No one you'd recognize." He'd barely recognized the three names himself. He wasn't positive he wanted to mention there were three. It seemed—more scandalous and also less reasonable. "Minor aristocracy."

"So what happened to her?" Rose asked in a small voice. "Infidelity to a king or prince is high treason."

Right, yes, this was the reassuring part—he should have led with this. "Apparently they've sent her to a community of Ravarra in the southwest, near Ansindale. The God of the Hearth takes in refugees and—people who need somewhere to go. So that's good news. I mean, it's not bad. It's a nice place."

Rose frowned slightly. "How do you know?"

Communities of Ravarra had a good reputation as a rule, but he could give a better answer than that. "I've actually visited there a few times. My Aunt Jacinda lives there. She retired from court for her health when I was child." He hadn't seen her for years after that, but a few years ago other business had taken him that direction and he'd gone to visit. He'd returned a couple of times since. She hadn't seemed particularly ill, for a woman who'd retired for her health, but she'd always said there was no need to talk about that. Not all illnesses were obvious.

Rose's eyes narrowed. "Your Aunt Jacinda. Is that your father's sister?"

He wasn't sure why that mattered, but he nodded. "Yes—all my mother's family lives in Glyster, except Elena."

Rose nodded slowly, as though this told her something. Maybe it was reassuring, that the community was nice enough for the king's sister. "That is good news, if Penelope's all right. I hope she is."

Not much of the worry had faded from her face. She looked pale, too. Women didn't like to be told they looked tired—at least, Elena didn't, and told him other people didn't either—so he groped for a different question. "Are you…feeling all right?"

She looked down at her lap again. "I'm fine. I'm just—I didn't sleep very well."

His thoughts flew back to the enchanted garden again, to Rose screaming in the night, and his stomach clenched. He really, really hated that they had to sleep at opposite ends of this castle, that she was so far away every night when he wanted to be there, with her… "It'll be all right," he said softly, lightly touched her hair.

Her smile was wan, but she leaned against him, her head on his shoulder as he wrapped his arm around her. "I know," she said, and he couldn't tell if she meant it.

He hoped, with everything in him, that he could make it true.

A week after the news broke about Penelope, Gregory announced at a family supper that he was formally seeking official dissolution of their marriage. This, compared to historical example, was also very rapid. It was also not surprising to anyone. Terrence watched Rose turn a shade paler, and she seemed to be very deliberately not looking at Gregory.

He had been concerned about her all week, with the conviction that this whole situation was upsetting her out of proportion to the relationship she'd had with Penelope. She wouldn't talk about it with him, though she did admit she was having nightmares.

So it also wasn't surprising when he came to meet her before the next morning's council meeting and found her sitting at the breakfast table, leaning her head on her hand with a listless air and an exhausted look in her eyes.

"You had nightmares again," he observed, heart heavy, as she rose from the table. He wanted to *fix* this, but he didn't even know what enemy he should be fighting.

She sighed. "Yes."

He reached out and wrapped his arms around her, drawing her to him. She sighed again, putting her arms around his waist, resting her head against his shoulder. He wished it was enough, wished he could hold her and keep all the rest of the world at bay.

He pressed his cheek to the top of her head. "I wish you'd send for me, when you have a bad dream."

It was not the first time he'd raised the thought in the past few days, but her answer was always the same. "You know you can't come to my bedroom in the middle of the night."

"We're *betrothed*." His voice sounded firm enough, but he could feel that his cheeks had warmed. He wasn't even suggesting—he just didn't want her to be afraid and alone.

"All the more reason," Rose said. "We're not behind a wall of thorns anymore, and the court would be scandalized."

"I know," he muttered. And it wouldn't be his reputation that suffered, it would be hers. So he couldn't really do anything but abide by her wishes in this. "But I don't like it. I don't like you being afraid."

"I'm all right," she said, and he didn't believe her. She took a step away, smiled up at him. It wasn't the smile she wore among strangers, but it wasn't the smile she usually had for him. This one looked like it took too much effort. But all she said was, "Let's not give Gregory something to be nasty about by being late to the council meeting."

Terrence grimaced, and muttered, "Sure, all right," because he'd apologized for Gregory's glares so many times that it didn't mean anything anymore.

They were on time to the council meeting, which was fortunate since no one bothered very much with preliminaries at this particular meeting. He and Rose had only just taken their seats and Terrence had felt a brief hope because Gregory was smiling, when the king made his announcement.

"After extensive discussion with my most trusted advisors," King Elgin announced, "I have grave concerns about my youngest son's betrothal."

Terrence's stomach dropped. No, they couldn't—they wouldn't—he had had fears about this when he first brought Rose back to court, but everything had gone so smoothly, so easily then, and that had been weeks ago now…

He was staring at his father, trying to read something on his impassive face, but out of the corner of his eye he saw Rose turning to look at him. He reached automatically for her hand, clasped her fingers tightly. Her hand was cold.

"We all know," the king continued, "the legend of the Princess Behind Thorns, and it is long established that the princess' hand in marriage and a right to the throne would be claimed by whatever champion successfully overcame the challenges to rescue her. The concern has been raised that we have no actual proof that Prince Terrence overcame the challenges in question."

"I'm *here*," Rose said tightly, into the fraction of a pause before King Elgin could continue. "Terrence came through the thorns and brought me back here. What other proof could you need?"

His father smiled but Terrence couldn't find anything reassuring in that. "But we have no witnesses. No evidence. I understand in the past champions generally went to the thorns with an entire retinue, with members of the council as witnesses. As things stand now, we have no way to prove just exactly what did happen."

"We *told* you what happened," Terrence protested. "Surely that should be enough." It had to be enough, because he couldn't lose Rose.

And the country. His claim to the throne was through her, but that seemed vague and abstract compared to the reality of Rose herself.

King Elgin spread his hands. "And I see no reason to believe you would be capable of inventing such a clever and complex story. I am sure it happened as you say. But we are discussing a claim to the throne. It must be ironclad if we do not wish to leave the door open to chaos and disorder. What would stop any adventurer from coming in here tomorrow and claiming he rescued the princess before you arrived?"

Terrence shook his head. "But that's not…"

"Fortunately," the king continued as though he had not spoken, "we have devised a solution. We will hold a public challenge in three days' time, with crowds to witness it. Re-enchanting the princess would be most appealing, but a great deal of trouble too. We can arrange some suitable obstacles, however. If, as you say, you rescued the princess once, surely you can do it again. It will be a mere formality, of course. But then none will be able to dispute your claim."

That was—better than if his father had announced they weren't going to validate his and Rose's betrothal after all. And yet, even if this was a kind of solution to what seemed like a completely manufactured problem, it didn't *feel* like a solution. And it didn't explain why this supposed problem was suddenly coming up, why anyone thought they needed to do anything at all—

"Terrence?" Rose said faintly, as her hand slipped out of his.

He turned towards her just in time to see her eyes slide shut, to see her start to slump to one side. He reached out, catching her before she could fall, wrapping his arms around her as her head came to rest against his chest.

"Rose?" he said over the sound of his heart hammering. "Are you all right?" A ridiculous thing to say, she was obviously unconscious, but he wanted so badly to hear her say that she was fine, that it was a moment's dizziness, nothing more.

No response from Rose.

When he had thought about losing her, he hadn't meant—but no, it couldn't be *that* serious.

From the head of the table, his father sighed loudly. "This is why we do not normally permit women at these meetings. They are entirely too unstable. Someone get a footman to carry the princess back to her rooms and we'll continue our discussion."

Terrence lifted his head to stare at his father, his grasp on Rose tightening. He didn't know what expression was on his face, but for just this one moment he didn't care. He did not often let himself get angry—but the idea that he should hand Rose over to whatever servant happened to be nearby, carry on with the meeting as though she didn't matter— "I'll take Rose to her rooms," he said tightly.

His father's eyes narrowed, usually a warning signal that Terrence had long ago learned to heed, to take as a sign that it was time to retreat and make apologies. He didn't look away now.

"Very well," his father said at last, tone sounding bored. "If you really believe you're the only person who can handle this obviously vital situation. I should think you'd want to be in the discussion regarding the upcoming challenge, but…" He gestured as though he was surrendering Terrence to his own decisions.

"Someone can fill me in later," Terrence said, and sought out Rupin's gaze. The other man gave a small but definite nod, and Terrence dismissed the meeting from his mind for the moment. It was important, yes, but less than this sudden, more immediate crisis.

He gathered Rose up, lifting her in his arms. A wide-eyed guard opened the door to the council room as he approached. He recognized Sam, the same guard who had told them about Penelope—a good man, but also known for dropping things, and definitely not someone he was going to just hand Rose to.

"Find Lady Elena," Terrence directed Sam. "Tell her I need her in the princess' rooms."

He nodded and hurried away down the hall. Terrence started in the opposite direction, Rose cradled against his chest, not so quickly.

He hoped he actually *could* carry her to her room. It would be humiliating if he couldn't, after that display in the council room. But she was a small woman, and even though he preferred books, he'd spent a lot of time training with heavy swords and the like. And her room was on this level, so no stairs to negotiate. Lucky she wasn't in that tower bedroom anymore.

He was so distracted with maneuvering Rose—and worrying that she still hadn't opened her eyes—that he was halfway to her rooms before he noticed that Silvertips was trotting briskly along beside him. The kitten looked up every so often, but didn't seem unduly distressed. This was obscurely comforting. Somehow, he thought Silvertips would be more upset if anything was really wrong with Rose.

Terrence got her inside her rooms, laid her down on the long couch, and knelt next to her to study her still face. She was so pale. His heart was still pounding and it wasn't all from exertion. "Rose?" he tried again, touching her cheek. What did he *do* now? Should he get her water, put a blanket over her?

Silvertips seemed more confident, leaping up onto the couch and settling down across Rose's stomach. A moment later Emerald Eyes emerged from the bedroom and scrambled up onto Rose's skirts. Fine, that was fine, but she still wasn't awake…

He had the sudden, absurd idea that maybe he should kiss her. This was, more or less, what he had expected when he had first plunged into that thorny tunnel. A sleeping princess, waiting to be awoken.

Before he could decide if this was a good idea or just madness, the door burst open and Elena rushed in. "Terrence? What's going on? What's wrong with Rose?"

"I don't *know*," Terrence said, dragging a hand through his hair. "She just fainted in the council meeting."

Elena's brisk efficiency had never been so welcome as she brushed past him to lay a hand on Rose's forehead. "She doesn't feel too warm—do you know if she ate breakfast?"

"I don't—um, she was sitting at the breakfast table when I came in, so—probably?" He couldn't remember what had been on the table, and it had been cleared since then.

"All right, did they say something to upset her?"

Terrence stared at Rose's face. "Yes."

"And it only just happened?"

It felt like hours—but yes, it was really only a few minutes, so he nodded.

"Is it possible she's expecting a baby?"

This question was asked in the same tone as the others, but Terrence's head still jerked up to stare at Elena. Distantly he noticed that Henry was standing by the closed door—must have come in with Elena. "No! Why does everyone want to know if we—I mean—*no*." He ducked his head, cheeks hot.

Out of the corner of his eye he could see Elena give him her curious look. "Who else asked?"

His father, Tyler, other people making less direct remarks… "*Never mind*, shouldn't we get the court physician, or an enchanter who knows healing or—"

"I think she's stirring," Elena interrupted.

Terrence's gaze snapped back to Rose, whose eyelids had begun to flutter.

"But then," Elena added, "you definitely have to tell us what happened at this meeting."

Chapter Twenty-Eight: Rose

Rose might have got through the meeting if Gregory hadn't been sitting directly across from her. She had gone into it already unsettled, already on edge, exhausted from nightmares that left her more tired in the morning than she had been when she lay down.

And then the king had made his announcement. It wasn't really unexpected—not the details, necessarily, but the mere fact that there was *something* like this. If it was unexpected, she wouldn't have been having nightmares for the past week. Yet hearing it laid out, so definitively and officially, made her breath catch in her throat, her heart pound louder, because it was really *happening*, not a vague fear but the king actually moving to steal this fragile control she had felt over her life.

But she still might have got through the meeting, if Gregory hadn't been there, across the table. Or if he hadn't smiled at her. It was the smile he had worn the day he came into her room, and it sent chills up her spine.

Everything was there in that smile, all that he wanted to do to her, and she was cold with the sickening horror of a man who could smile at her while hate burned in his eyes.

It was all so clear, how Gregory and the king intended this to end up. Somehow, some way, they were going to hand her over to Gregory. They were going to force her into a marriage she didn't want, a life she didn't want, with a man she didn't want to share a room with, let alone a bed.

It was the same fear that had haunted her a hundred years ago, grown only more monstrous. At least those long ago champions had been vague in their very numbers, no single terror to center her nightmares around. Gregory was specific and real and terrible.

She had felt light-headed as Gregory smiled, as the king spoke and brought her world crashing down. That was her larger world, her metaphorical world, but the world just around her had begun to spin too. She'd tried to breathe, to think, to approach this strategically, but fear had locked around her throat, fear was crushing her lungs, because it was all going wrong. It was all falling apart and she could do nothing, she had no say, they were turning her back into a chess piece and she was going to be swallowed up by this terrible game all over again. The room had shrunk around her and shadows were filling her vision and it was like the spell, she needed Terrence to help her push back the shadows…

She'd just barely managed to gasp his name before everything went black.

Later, she would think that her body, or some instinctive part of her mind, had been trying to help her. Because when she woke up, her head felt clearer. The fear was still there, but it was coiled in the pit of her stomach, contained for now, and she could think again.

Her eyes opened to see the ceiling of her own sitting room, and she knew she was lying on the long couch. It was barely an instant before Terrence's worried face moved into her view, close enough to see every shade of brown in his eyes, to see the little scar by his eyebrow. "Rose? How do you feel?"

"I'm all right," she said, surprised herself by how true it was. Well, comparatively, at least. Only then did she notice that he was holding her hand, his fingers warm and reassuring laced through hers. She pushed against the couch cushions to sit up, automatically shifting kittens as she did.

"Don't rush," Terrence said, frankly hovering.

"I *am* all right," she repeated, straightening her skirt and settling against the back of the couch. "I don't think I've ever fainted before. It was just—I feel better now."

She really did, possibly better than she had for the past week. It was as though part of her mind had gone on working without her while she was in a faint, assimilating the king's news and assessing what to do with it. The initial shock was past, and now that she knew what they were dealing with—Terrence was right that it was better to deal with one known thing than the endless possible fears she'd been carrying since Penelope's exile.

She took a deep breath, looked around the room to see that Elena and Henry were sitting nearby. Elena looked concerned, and perhaps Henry did too, though his face never showed emotions as clearly. Terrence had sat down next to her on the couch, and the worry was most apparent on his face.

"I'm *all right*," she said a third time. "Stop looking at me like I might break. We have to decide what we're going to do about this challenge business."

"What challenge business?" Elena asked immediately. "What's going on?"

Terrence exhaled, and didn't look reassured. "Are you sure you want to talk about—"

"I think we have to," Rose said, squeezing his hand. It would be nicer to go out to the Queen's Garden, to ignore what was happening, to talk about literally anything else. But then she would be accepting that she was a pawn in the game. Maybe if they talked about it…maybe the talking would matter somehow.

"Someone please tell me what's happening," Elena said in plaintive tones.

"All right," Terrence said, though he was still watching Rose closely. "I'll explain it."

He sketched over the council meeting, the king's announcement, the proposal of a challenge. He kept holding Rose's hand and she was glad, though she didn't feel any renewed faintness as he told the story, repeated what they were up against. But she was glad of his hand, and of Silvertips and Emerald Eyes purring quietly on the couch on her other side.

"It's completely ridiculous, isn't it?" Elena said when Terrence was done, her hands clasped in her lap. "That's obvious, right? It must be some sort of trick."

"He said it was just a formality," Terrence said, but even he didn't sound convinced. When everyone stared at him, he lifted his free hand defensively. "I'm not saying I think it's entirely true, I just—I'm not sure what this is all about. And I'm not sure what plan we can make. We'll find out what we can about the challenge, we'll see what Rupin can tell us after the meeting. Then I'll try it and—"

"No," Rose said instantly, shaking her head. Apparently her fear wasn't as contained as she had thought, as it reared up and threatened to swamp her again. "No, no, no, that's exactly what you *can't* do." She drew in a breath, because hysteria wasn't going to help. "That's what they're telling you to do, so that has to be playing into their hands."

"It would be very easy," Henry said quietly, "for a man to die in a challenge that was supposedly a formality, and have it all look like an unfortunate accident. Or the will of the gods. Things can always be blamed on the gods."

It chilled Rose to hear the words put so bluntly, and yet it was obscurely comforting too. Henry understood what was frightening her about the challenge, and had said it aloud when she probably wouldn't have been able to form the sentences.

Another champion dying for the Princess Behind Thorns. Her grip tightened on Terrence's hand. No, not this one. Not Terrence. He couldn't. She couldn't face that.

Terrence looked around at the group, as though he was looking for someone to contradict Henry's assertion. No one did. "That can't be—he's my *father*. He wouldn't do that."

"Or maybe the plan is only to ensure that you fail," Rose offered, even though she didn't believe that cold-eyed king wouldn't do whatever he thought was to his advantage. It would do no good to bog down arguing the point though. "Success must be impossible, or they wouldn't bother with all this. Why do it if it would put us back where we already were?"

Terrence took a deep breath. "All right, so maybe it's all a way to stop me from marrying Rose and inheriting the throne. But they didn't need to do something this elaborate. My father could have forbidden the betrothal from the beginning."

"People wouldn't like that," Elena said dryly. "Too many people saw you ride into the capital with Rose. They have to somehow convince everyone that you *shouldn't* marry Rose, despite what the legend says. They've probably been making plans right from the start—if they can hold this ridiculous contest in three days, they *must* have been making plans for weeks at least. That's why they agreed so easily to a betrothal, then spent so long delaying any formal ceremonies. Maybe now they've finally worked out the details of the challenge, they think they can counteract the legend. I'm not sure how much that helps them, but…"

"They want me to marry Gregory." Rose's voice sounded clear in the suddenly silent circle. The timing added up, the conclusion was obvious. And Gregory had been smiling at her. "They want to give me and the throne to Gregory."

"Oh. Penelope," Elena murmured. "Of course. That's what they were waiting for. I should have put that together."

"Gregory was heir," Rose continued, trying not to look at Terrence's face. Maybe, somehow, it wouldn't sound as bad out loud as it did echoing in her head. Maybe someone would convince her she was wrong, that her nightmares of the past week were only that, nightmares, irrational and insubstantial. "Gregory and the king want him to still be heir. But they can't ignore the legend of the Princess Behind Thorns. If I had come to the castle quietly, they probably would have tried to sweep it all away, but like Elena said, too many people know. They're not worried that someone will dispute Terrence's claim. They don't want anyone to dispute Gregory's claim as a replacement."

It only sounded more real out loud, more definite.

"No, that's not…" Terrence shook his head. "Gregory wouldn't—they all know we…"

If even Terrence, who tried so hard to believe the best of his family, could only come up with half an objection, a vague murmur of doubt, she had to be right.

"It would be a reasonable strategy," Henry said, nodding slowly. "They stage a challenge with a crowd of witnesses. They arrange it so Terrence fails, and they can call it Fate or magic or something—it's enough to counter the popular story that he was meant to rescue and marry Rose. Then maybe they bring out other champions, maybe not, but eventually Gregory tries the challenge and they ensure he wins. Now they have an alternate story, with a different prince rescuing the princess, and this one has witnesses. They'll probably find a way to make the part about Penelope sound…" He grimaced. "…romantic. New love after betrayal, that sort of thing."

Elena groaned. "I can imagine the ballad already. They probably have some bard writing it now."

Rose was imagining other things. She was remembering Gregory in her room, the way he had looked at her. The way he always looked at her. Hungry, angry, never seeing *her* but only what she represented, looking on her only as something to be owned and used as he liked. How different it would be from Terrence, if it was Gregory who the world felt had the right to kiss her, to touch her…

Her hand tightened almost convulsively on Terrence's, as she leaned in to feel the warmth of his shoulder against hers. He turned his head, dropped a kiss on her hair, but it felt absent-minded. She looked up at him, and his gaze was distant. "What are you thinking?" she asked softly.

His brow furrowed. "I'm trying to convince myself you're all being paranoid and my father and brother wouldn't do that kind of thing. Except…" His brow smoothed and he just looked weary. "Except I don't seem to be succeeding. Maybe if they believe it was best for the country…"

Rose didn't believe for an instant that *that* was what the king was thinking about. But if that was what Terrence needed to tell himself, it wasn't worth arguing right now. Still, she glanced across the circle at Elena, and something in the other woman's eyes told her that she too had a very different idea than Terrence about the king's priorities.

"So," Elena said, "at least we're all agreed about what we're dealing with." Or agreed enough.

Terrence turned towards Rose, looking into her face. "You still don't have to do this. Just refuse outright. I'll support you. All of us will."

She loved that he said it, that he made the offer, that he truly believed her refusal might make a difference. "It won't work. At most we might buy some time, but that's not enough."

She had refused before too. She had protested and pleaded and tried to change the mind of another king, and had still ended up under a spell, behind the thorns, waiting for a rescuer she hadn't expected to want. If she couldn't change things with her own father, she had no hope a refusal would work now.

"Buying time could give us a chance to rally support though," Elena said, tapping her fingertips together. "Not everyone will back this. That has to be why they sprang the news with only a few days' notice, even though they must have been laying plans for months. I've thought for years that we need someone to oppose the current line of succession, and this could be the moment to do it."

Henry sighed, and glanced at Rose. "I hope you realize it means you've been fully accepted, if she's discussing revolutions in front of you. She reserves that for people she really likes."

"People I *trust*," Elena countered, and though Rose knew Henry had been half-joking, she did feel touched. "And anyway," Elena continued, "isn't that what Terrence was trying to *do*? Changing the succession, that *is* a revolution in a way."

"I wouldn't call it that," Terrence objected. "I mean, Rose was already the heir, and it's not a…violent overthrow, or something."

"But marrying Rose changes the succession. That's what it means, that's what the king sees it as."

"That's not *all* it is," Terrence said, voice tight.

Elena waved a hand. "Of course, but politically speaking…"

They kept talking, and eventually Rupin came in to report on the council meeting. "It went about how you would expect," he said, shrugging as he claimed a place on the couch. "There was some argument about whether all this was worthwhile, but the plan is still going forward. The lords split the way you'd think, some against and some for, and exactly the ones you'd guess on each side."

"The head enchanter?" Elena asked, gaze intent on Rupin.

"Obviously not surprised by any of this."

"What about General Graybourne?" she persisted.

Rupin shook his head. "Harder to say. He didn't look happy about it, but he didn't argue that hard against it either."

"At least he didn't like it," Elena said, tapping her fingers against her leg. "That's something."

"Did they say what the challenge actually *is*?" Rose asked. What was the king asking men to do in her name?

"King Elgin avoided that completely," Rupin said. "The evasion was masterful." His tone sounded as impressed it was regretful. "He managed to deflect every question that might have said what this was or made clearer who was involved—though I think we can guess—or how long they've been planning this."

And so the discussion went on and around with the same meager points, about buying time or building support or pushing the king in a different direction or who might be able to change the king's mind. Rose had thought she was getting a fuller picture of Elena's impressions of the court when they had discussed the subject in the Queen's Garden, but she saw now that they had only covered the outlines. She still hadn't fully anticipated how knowledgeably the other woman would be able to speak about loyalties and potential factions and complex court intrigue. Rose talked at first but grew gradually quieter, listening to the theories and the strategies that went on being proposed. Her kittens fell asleep in a bundle at one end of the couch, and the conversation still went on.

The longer they talked the clearer it was that none of them, not one of them, really understood how impossible this all was. Terrence refused to believe the worst of his father, Elena believed anything could be done if she could find the right piece of information, Rupin seemed to view it all through a lens of interesting historical detail and legal technicalities, and Henry—well, there was a shadow in his eyes that said maybe he did understand, a little more than the others, but he was as quiet as Rose.

They didn't seem to understand how hard it was to defy a king. They had no idea how solid their ground had to be in order to have even a chance of success. None of them had had their life torn apart once already by a king with ideas.

Maybe it would be better to run away, to flee and leave all this behind. Would Terrence be willing to run away with her? Could she go without him if he wasn't? Elena would probably help her. She had no idea where she could go, but anything was better than ending up married to Gregory.

But she didn't like the idea of running either. It was refusing to be used in the king's game, but it was also giving up the game entirely.

She didn't want to let him win, or to disappoint all those people who believed the Princess Behind Thorns could save them.

She didn't know, though, if she could even save herself. If she wasn't going to run, she could see just one other path, one possibility that might give them a whisper of a chance.

"There's a simpler, better solution than all of this," she interrupted the ongoing musing on strategy. The bells had already rung indicating midday—if they were going to pursue her solution, there was no more time to waste. It was frightening to propose it, but much less frightening than the alternative. She took a breath and looked up at Terrence. "Will you marry me?"

The corners of his eyes crinkled, faintly confused. "Of course, we already—"

"I don't mean some time in the future," she hurried on, wanting to get this all out and clear before she lost her nerve, "when we've found some way to convince your father to agree. I mean get married *now*, today." She managed a tentative smile. She wasn't afraid to marry Terrence, but she was afraid that he was about to say no—and that fear wasn't only because she couldn't see another plan. "They can't force me to marry someone else if I'm already married."

A moment's considering silence filled the room.

"Oh, that's good," Henry said. "I like this woman. Straightforward, direct, cuts right to the heart of the whole business."

"They'll try to invalidate the marriage, of course," Elena pointed out, tapping one fingertip against her chin.

"But I can make sure we're legally sound," Rupin offered.

"The king will bluster and rage, but it might work." Elena grinned suddenly. "And I'd love to see his face when he finds out."

Terrence still hadn't said anything. She didn't know how to read the troubled look in his eyes, and that meant she couldn't relax yet. If only he'd give some sign of what he was thinking! Rose tugged on his hand, wrapped around hers. "Terrence?"

"We need to talk about this," he said abruptly, rising to his feet and pulling her after him. "Excuse us for a minute."

Terrence led her where she had expected, out to the Queen's Garden, out to a little nook with a shaded bench. She had no such clear expectations about what he was going to say. Did it bother him, her suggesting a hurried marriage? Did he still not believe what his father was doing? Or, even worse, did he not want to marry her after all? At least, not enough to defy his father to do it?

She sat down on the bench, smoothing her skirts. She wished either of the kittens had come, for the sake of the distraction. Terrence remained standing, fidgeting, not looking at her. She watched his face, trying to read his expression, but all she could tell was that he wasn't happy. He was looking away from her, head turned so she could see that scar by his eyebrow. She still hadn't asked about that. She wondered suddenly if she was going to have the chance or if, one way or another, things were going to go so badly that—well, that she wouldn't be asking Terrence personal questions in the future.

If she was married to Gregory, he'd probably make sure she was never alone with Terrence ever again.

"What did you want to say?" she prompted, because she couldn't stand that thought, or the silence any longer. It had to be better to know than to deal with all the possibilities she was imagining.

He looked at her finally, his brow still furrowed. "You don't have to do this. We can find another way."

When he didn't elaborate further, she said, "This is the best plan. It gives us the most solid footing to defy your father." And was that the problem, that he wasn't willing to do this against his father's wishes?

He groaned, and at last sat down next to her, taking both her hands in his, grasp tight. "But I don't want us to get married that way." He looked into her eyes, a searching look. "I don't want you to marry me because you feel forced into it by another powerful king. I don't want to be the least bad of a range of very bad options."

The warmth from his hands spread through her. It was going to be all right after all, at least this part of it, if that was the only thing bothering him. "You were never a bad option, Terrence," she said, squeezing his hands tighter. "This isn't accepting something in a bad situation. This is me, choosing. I'm choosing you. I *chose* you, when I thought the world was ending and the shadows were going to consume us and I was angrier that I never got to really kiss you than I was about dying."

And at that he kissed her, lips hard and urgent against hers, and she leaned into him, leaned into the kiss. It felt like kissing him as the spell ended, only better. They knew each other so much better, knew how their mouths and bodies fit together. She clenched her fingers in his hair and he pulled her half onto his lap, holding her close. Rose clung to him and thought that she would, very much, like to marry Terrence right now.

She almost told him that she loved him. She had, of course, for a long time. Maybe since she had watched him playing with her kittens, long ago on the lawn of the enchanted garden; at least since that moment when they broke the spell together. But somehow there had never seemed to be the right moment to *say* it, and he hadn't either, and now so much time had gone by that she felt shy about putting it into words—at least, the simplest, most direct words. She had said it a dozen different ways, using other words. But it was still easier to ask him to marry her than to say straight-out that she loved him, to find out what he'd say in response. And she didn't want him to say it back just because she was scared and he was trying to be kind.

"You know," she said at last, when she was free to speak again, "you keep on telling me that I don't have to marry you. I could almost start to think you don't want…" She trailed off. She had started this line of thought somewhat as a joke, somewhat as a way to sweep aside her last lingering uncertainty, but somehow it had stopped being funny halfway through. Even though of course it was nonsense. That kiss had said it was nonsense, the way he was trailing kisses along her neck right now said it was nonsense. But he hadn't ever said that he loved her either.

"Of course I want to marry you," he murmured into her hair. "I came to rescue you, didn't I?"

That was not the right thing to say. Rose pushed him back a few inches. "You came to rescue me when you decided to marry the idea of me. But everyone wanted to marry the *idea* of me." Surely she hadn't got this wrong, she couldn't have misunderstood him all this time. "The stories about me—they're not who I am, and I can't be what you expected, and—"

"Rose," he said softly, "I want to marry *you.* I never paid that much attention to the stories, and I knew they were wrong anyway the first time you ordered me not to follow you in the garden. And I knew I wanted to marry you ever since…" He frowned, expression considering. "Since the night in the garden when I heard you screaming. When you told me your story, how afraid you had been. I wanted to be the one who made sure you were never that afraid again. And I wanted to marry a woman who would cry over people who had made her that afraid."

Chapter Twenty-Nine: Terrence

Terrence told himself that Rose choosing him, choosing to marry him, was as good as saying she loved him. It meant the same thing, didn't it?

He could have said it himself—but he didn't want to rush it, didn't want her to think he was only saying it to reassure her in a frightening moment, didn't want her to feel she had to say something in response. Which were perfectly good, perfectly altruistic reasons, with nothing cowardly about them. So he told himself. At least twice.

They went back inside, some things decided, other things left still unsaid, and rejoined the others before anyone became anxious enough to go look for them.

Henry and Rupin probably wouldn't have asked questions when they re-entered the room. Elena, predictably, asked immediately, "Is everything all right?" with her gaze first on Terrence, and then traveling down to their joined hands. Though they'd been holding hands when they left, so he didn't know what she thought that was telling her.

"Everything's fine," Terrence said, as they sat down again on the couch. "If we can work out how to plan a wedding in the next few hours."

Elena beamed at them. "Perfect. We've been discussing details while you were out. Rupin knows all the legal requirements to make sure it's a valid ceremony."

"I'll go find the decree with the precise law later, but I've been reviewing protocol for royal weddings recently in anticipation of your planned one anyway," Rupin volunteered. "It's fairly straight-forward. The usual forms and vows of a wedding that anyone does—"

"Has it changed in the last century?" Rose asked.

There was a moment's considering pause, and Terrence at least was trying to think what he knew about the history of weddings. "I don't think so?" he said doubtfully.

"Did brides wear green a century ago?" Elena asked.

Rose smiled. "My mother and my grandmother wore green at their weddings. It's not that new an idea."

"Then I don't think anything significant is different," Elena said with a shrug. "Royal weddings have special requirements…"

"Including at least one member of the council as witness," Rupin resumed. "Which I can be. There also has to be a relative of the groom present. Not the bride, interestingly."

"Says something about our society," Elena remarked. "But since I'm related to Terrence, we're all right there. With our two legally required witnesses, all we need is an authorized representative of a god worshipped by either one of the couple to preside."

"And with devotional ink on your arm," Rupin said with a nod at Terrence, "it would be difficult to make a legal claim for any temple but Mariqwe's. Also the traditional choice for the royal family, of course."

"It was supposed to be the high priest," Rose remarked, though she was frowning. They had got that far with plans, before everything went wrong.

Terrence wasn't convinced that they weren't all exaggerating how terrible the situation was—but he could still see that this part of the plan wasn't going to work in the present circumstance. "The high priest would refuse to do it and go straight to my father." Luckily, it wasn't hard to think of an alternative. "We can ask Priestess Armina, from that little chapel in the market. I've known her for years."

"You know everyone," Elena said with a smile. "And that's why this might actually work."

"So we get married," Terrence continued, "we tell my father, and he calls off the challenge."

He wasn't expecting the renewed tension in the room when he said that. Elena rolled her eyes. "Oh, Terrence, don't be an idiot."

She said it often, but not usually in front of Rose, and he found himself more aggravated by it than usual. "What?" he demanded. "What did I say?"

"If you tell your father privately, he can have the marriage invalidated at once and nothing will be changed," Elena said in her patient tone that had frequently annoyed him in childhood. And sometimes still did.

"They're dissolving Gregory's marriage," Rupin pointed out. "And it's harder to undo a marriage of two years than of a day. There are forms and laws, of course, but it's all possible."

Terrence threw up his hands. "All right, so we *don't* tell my father. And what does a marriage he doesn't know about accomplish?" Well—it accomplished *some* things. But not ones relevant to the discussion they were having.

"We have to tell him in the right way," Rose said. "It's like the legend about the Princess Behind Thorns. A secret marriage can be dissolved more easily than one people know about and support."

"We'll have to spread the word somehow," Elena said, tapping one fingertip against her lower lip as she thought. "I know exactly who to tell—but it'll take time. If we can stall, somehow delay the challenge…"

"Why not use the challenge?" Terrence asked. If they really believed the point of the challenge was to gather a big enough crowd to counter the original legend of the Princess Behind Thorns, then why not use that? "Announce it in front of the crowd gathered for the challenge."

Elena beamed at him. "You see, I knew you weren't really an idiot."

"Thank you?"

"That could work," she continued. "It'll already be easier for us to get popular support, because we're building on the existing legend instead of trying to overturn it. And everyone likes Terrence, so that helps."

"Not everyone," Terrence muttered, not because there was anyone specific he was thinking of who didn't, but because it was uncomfortable, being held up as universally liked. Elena had always projected her own feelings about him onto everyone else.

"Lords Dawson and Camden will back us up in the council," Rose said, and he was surprised how knowledgably she said it. She was probably right, but—she had really been paying attention all these weeks. "General Graybourne could be swayed on legal grounds; he cares about the law, and the king cares about the opinion of the man who leads his armies. And if the high priests don't want to pit themselves against the public sentiment…"

"The whole crazy idea might work," Henry summed up.

There was a moment of companionable silence, everyone apparently feeling satisfied with their own planning. Terrence was thinking he would, in fact, quite like to marry Rose today. The timeline of the council had always seemed painfully long.

"There's just—one other problem we haven't considered," Rose said, and her voice had taken on a shade of fear again.

He turned to look at her, and didn't like the tightness around her eyes. She smiled when she met his gaze, but it vanished quickly. "What is it?" he asked.

She reached out, picked up Emerald Eyes, who stretched sleepily then curled up in her lap, and bent her head over the kitten as she spoke. "There's another way to make me marriageable again. If they can't dissolve a marriage. They could make me a widow."

The idea seemed so strange, he actually had to parse that—she would be a widow if—he died. He reached past the kitten to put his hand over hers. "Hey, that's not going to happen. My father wouldn't do that." He looked over to the others. "Come on, tell her that wouldn't happen."

No one said anything immediately, and when Elena spoke it was to say, "We should think about which of the guards we can trust. There's Cole and Madlan—oh, and definitely Barret."

"Barret's away," Henry said. "Sent to Thaydan with a message."

"Too bad. We can still come up with a good half-dozen though."

Terrence shook his head. "Nothing is going to happen." If he said it enough, maybe it would be true. And besides, this was ridiculous. He knew his family could be ruthless, he knew Gregory was angry with him, but to kill each other? Surely they had to be better than *that*.

"It can't hurt to be careful. And we're still better off with the crowd's support than without it," Elena said. "It's harder to get away with killing popular princes too."

"Fine, if it'll make you all feel better." Terrence let go of Rose's hand to slide a finger under her chin, lift her face to look at him. "Hey—it's going to be all right. It will be."

And she smiled, something close to her real smile, even though he didn't really think she believed him. But maybe it was enough that she smiled anyway.

The group dispersed after that. Rupin went to collect the necessary forms and copies of the relevant laws. Elena carried Rose away to find a green dress. Terrence and Henry found a couple of trustworthy guards, then left the castle for the market. No one tried to stop them. Maybe no one found anything unusual about it. Maybe no one anticipated they could be planning anything. Or maybe, if Rose and Elena and the rest were right, Terrence mused, his father would find it convenient if he rode away today and didn't come back until after the challenge.

At the little chapel to Mariqwe in the market, they left the guards at the door and went in search of Priestess Armina. They found her in the main sanctuary, with its twin statues of the god—a woman with one hand over her heart, a man in armor with sword drawn, each resting their free hands on the lioness standing between them. Terrence automatically nodded to the statues, touching one hand to his lioness tattoo, before turning to greet the priestess, who was lighting candles at the feet of the statues.

"Prince Terrence, how lovely to see you," Priestess Armina said, beaming and extending both hands. "And what brings you to the market today?"

"More to the chapel, actually," Terrence said, taking her hands in a brief clasp then letting go again. "I have a kind of—request." It was tempting to call it a favor, but he didn't want to sound as though what he was asking for was that unreasonable. Even though it probably was.

"I'll take a look around while you talk," Henry volunteered, one hand on the sword he always wore, though Terrence hadn't seen him draw it in months. What threats did he think he was going to find here?

"Do sit, Your Highness," Priestess Armina urged, moving to the front row of seats. Terrence followed while Henry began a prowl around. "Our evening worship service isn't for a few hours, so we shouldn't be disturbed. What do we need to speak about?"

Terrence had already noted the emptiness of the chapel, or else he would have asked to move into a more private area. But now how to explain this? "I suppose you've heard that I'm betrothed to Princess Rose."

Priestess Armina beamed again. "What a wonderful thing. I couldn't have been prouder when I heard you had brought her back from that enchantment. That's our Prince Terrence, I told everyone, who always comes by for a prayer when he visits the market. Although then you *didn't* come when you were here last week!"

He hadn't actually given that a thought. Too bad, it might have made this conversation easier. "I'm sorry—we were attracting a lot of attention, and had to leave rather quickly. I *would* have, but…"

"Oh, nonsense, there's no call for apologies. I just would have liked to meet your lady."

He was somehow glad the priestess hadn't called Rose the Princess Behind Thorns. It was nicer to think of someone wanting to meet his betrothed, rather than to meet the object of the legend. He took a reckless stab towards the heart of the matter. "Would you like to meet her today?"

Priestess Armina blinked, looking faintly surprised. "Of course. Does this connect to the request you mentioned?"

"It does." Another deep breath. "My father…has been supporting our betrothal. But we're afraid that may change. So Rose and I want to get married. Today. In a couple hours."

Priestess Armina was silent for a moment, evidently thinking. "The news has been going through the streets that there's going to be a kind of—exhibition in a few days, bringing the legend to life or some such thing. You're not certain how that's going to go." For all her smiles and air of warm friendliness to everyone, the priestess was shrewd too.

"Something like that," Terrence admitted.

"It's not a small thing, you know, to perform a wedding against the wishes of a king."

That was putting it bluntly—and accurately. "I know. And I wouldn't ask it, but…" He could give all sorts of complicated reasons, involving politics and advantages and strategic positioning, about wanting to secure a claim to the throne and manage public support. But was any of that the heart of the matter, at its deepest core? "I love her," he said simply. "And I don't want to lose her. And I don't want her to…end up in a life she doesn't want."

Priestess Armina was studying him, and he tried not to shift under her gaze. "I'll want to talk to the princess. I have very firm feelings about coerced marriages—not that I think it of you, but…"

"No, I understand," he said, because this sounded like she was coming closer to agreeing. "I'm sure you could talk to Rose, before the ceremony. And she is willing—I mean, *she* asked *me* to marry her today."

Priestess Armina smiled. "I think I will enjoy meeting her. And as to your request—well, the priestly class has always professed independence from any kings or queens, after all. And I wouldn't be a very good follower of Mariqwe if I wasn't willing to fight on the side of love."

Terrence let out a breath. "Thank you. That—means a lot." He had suggested asking the priestess, but he hadn't been certain she'd agree. And then the whole plan would have fallen apart.

After that it was just details. The priestess bustled off to gather her prayer book and ceremonial candles and the other things necessary.

Henry didn't turn up any threats, but took a position near the back door, still looking ready to deal with any. Terrence found himself sitting in the front row alone, with nothing to do but think. Well, and pray. That was the thing to do in a chapel, wasn't it?

Terrence studied the faces of the god, mind drifting. This was going to happen. By the end of the day, he was going to be married to Rose. Was he ready for this?

He was sure about Rose, had been for what felt like much longer than it had actually been. He didn't have any doubts about whether he was marrying the right woman. He fished his mother's ring out of his shirt, toyed with it between two fingers. His mother would have liked Rose. He wished she could be here, for his wedding. Just—to have her here, but also because she had always seen the best in him, and it had been easier to see it himself then too.

As sure as he was of Rose, he was less sure about himself. The council's timeline had felt long, but it had also given him time to…become better, somehow. He had had some hazy notion that he had time still to—get closer to the person he wanted to be, to be more sure that he could be the husband Rose needed.

Not to mention to tell her how he felt about her, find out what she'd say in return.

Then there was the matter of his father. This was far more directly in defiance of his father than going off to rescue the Princess Behind Thorns had ever been. Granted, his father was still officially supporting their betrothal, had never told him *not* to marry Rose—but princes were not supposed to go off and get married in secret. The laws governing royal weddings seemed designed to prevent exactly that. A family member present, a member of the council present. The reason why was obvious.

And if Elena and the rest were right about his father's plans for the challenge—no, there was no way to pretend this wasn't openly and absolutely defying his father's wishes. And that was a difficult thought.

He had never managed to live up to his father's expectations for him. Elena could bluster all she wanted and say it didn't matter and his father's expectations were ridiculous, but that had never weighed much against the sinking feeling in his stomach when his father looked at him with disapproval, or the ache when Gregory was granted the praise he never managed to gain himself. This could be the moment, the decision that put that kind of approval out of reach for good.

He knew that six months ago, he never would have risked it. Nothing would have seemed important enough. But now there was Rose, and the fear lurking in her eyes that morning, as they talked about his father and the challenge and their plans. It wasn't a new fear—it had been there ever since Penelope was exiled, for all that he'd tried in the past few days to laugh or reassure or kiss it away.

If marrying Rose was the way to take the fear out of her eyes, then it was worth it. Whatever the consequences.

And if marrying Rose was the only way to not lose her, just as he'd told the priestess…he knew, in his deepest heart, that he'd do anything for that. No matter what his father said or did about it.

He looked at the two statues, at the warrior and the lover, and thought that Priestess Armina had been right—he would be a poor follower of Mariqwe, God of Passion, if he wasn't willing to fight for love.

Chapter Thirty: Rose

Rose studied herself in the mirror. She wasn't sure she looked like a bride. She and Elena had ransacked her wardrobe, but she only had two green dresses. One was intended for a colder season and the weather had grown too warm for it. The other was a dark green shading towards blue, with a low neck and a full skirt. It was elegant, suitable for a formal dinner perhaps, if not a grand ball.

"I think it looks lovely on you," Elena volunteered, standing a few feet away and looking the dress over critically.

"It's complicated."

"Trust me, selecting a wedding dress always is. Even when you have enough time to have one specially made. Maybe it's even more complicated then, with so many more options to think about."

Rose half-smiled. "No, I meant—the *dress* is complicated." Lady Graybourne, while enthusiastic about her idea of having simpler dresses, had argued for keeping some dresses with more elaborate styling, including this one. "It's not one of the ones I got the dressmakers to design that's easier to manage. It has all these buttons up the back. I wouldn't be able to get out of it myself."

Elena's expression was mischievous, which should have warned Rose. "Were you planning to get out of it alone?"

"I like Gabrielle, but I don't think I want her to realize anything special is—"

"I didn't mean *Gabrielle*."

"Oh. *Oh*," Rose said, as she caught up to what Elena did mean. She blushed. "Yes. Well. I guess the dress is…all right, then."

"It's perfect, and Terrence will love it." Her expression softened. "You know, he's—really happy, when he's with you. I haven't seen him like that in a long time." She hesitated, and then in an oddly diffident tone for such a direct woman, asked, "I know it's not any of my business, but…do you love him?"

Rose dropped her gaze, smoothed her skirts. She could prevaricate or dodge the question or refuse to answer. But this didn't seem like the day for pretending. "Yes," she said softly. So very much.

Elena let out an audible breath. "I thought so. He doesn't know it, does he?"

"I don't know. Maybe?" She'd said it in every way but the most direct. She hadn't quite found the courage for that yet.

Elena's expression turned mischievous again. "You should probably think about mentioning it. You know. Some time. But right now, we have to do something with your hair."

"Just a braid," Rose said, relieved to move to a less charged topic. "I just want to put it in a braid." The way she'd worn it in the garden.

"Really?" Elena said with a frown. "But that's so simple."

"I know. That's why."

While Rose braided her hair, fingers remembering from all those days and years in the garden, Elena reached into her bag and drew out a flat square box. "I thought—well, if you'd like to, you can borrow this."

Rose tied off her hair, then turned to accept the box from Elena. When she lifted the lid, she found a circlet inside, a circling branch with jade leaves and gold flowers. It was the tradition for brides to wear crowns, from elaborate gold and diamond affairs to simple rings of real flowers, because every bride was a queen.

"I'm sure you have other crowns," Elena said, with an unusual self-consciousness in her voice, "but I wore that at my wedding. It was a gift from my uncle in Glyster, and I thought you might…"

"It's perfect," Rose said, and impulsively stepped forward to hug the other woman.

And when she put it on and looked at herself in the mirror, in her green dress with her hair in a braid down her back, both kittens wandering up to sit next to her, she still wasn't entirely sure she looked like a bride—but she looked like *herself.*

"It's not what you would have worn if you did the full court wedding," Elena said.

"No," Rose agreed. She probably would have had a train yards long, attached to a dress requiring six servants to get her into, that she may or may not have been able to breathe in and that she certainly wouldn't have had much say over. Likely they would have piled her hair up in a style that made her head ache, and given her an enormous heavy crown. "It's much better, isn't it?"

Rose and Elena were able to slip out of the castle without incident, taking two trustworthy guards and an enclosed carriage. Only Elena looked out the window when they went through the gate of the castle, and as far as anyone knew, Princess Rose was resting after feeling faint and did not leave home that day.

It wasn't as nice a ride as it had been sitting in front of Terrence on his horse, but they reached the market and the little chapel and that was all that counted. They entered by a side entrance and were greeted at the door by Priestess Armina, who sent Elena off to the sanctuary and whisked Rose away to her office.

"It really is such a pleasure to meet you," Priestess Armina said, beaming at her. "I've known Prince Terrence since he was a child. Now, do you feel quite ready? Do you have any questions?"

Rose wasn't entirely sure. "Should I? I mean, how much do I need to know for the ceremony?" Any weddings she had attended had been in the Before Time, and while she had a vague idea of the general outline, she didn't know what she might be forgetting.

"Not much," Priestess Armina said with a comfortable laugh. "I do most of the talking, you answer a few questions in the affirmative, and there's not much more you need to do."

"Then—I think I'm all right."

The priestess' face grew more serious, looking at Rose in a searching way that was intent but not unfriendly. "That is all assuming that you *want* to answer in the affirmative. That you want to get married today."

Rose was surprised. "Of course, that's why we're here."

"What I mean to say is, I don't preside at ceremonies where either party feels compelled—"

"Do you think Terrence would? Try to compel anyone?" Rose was genuinely curious what the priestess would answer.

She smiled. "No, I don't. But it's not the sort of thing I like to take a chance on. Also I know something of his family and…" The words trailed away. Perhaps they would have been treasonous if they had continued. "I merely want to be sure that *you* are sure."

"I am," Rose said firmly. Surer than she was of almost anything else.

Priestess Armina clapped her hands together, smile broadening. "Good! Then let's have a wedding."

Terrence's face when Rose came into the chapel was everything she could have hoped for, and so much more than she had ever expected. He was looking at her like—like she was everything *he* could have hoped for. Her eyes felt unexpectedly wet as she walked towards him. Long ago, in the Before Time, when the enchantment was being planned, she had thought she would cry someday at her wedding. She had not expected it to be good tears.

"You look beautiful," Terrence said as he took her hand, brushing a kiss onto her cheek.

She squeezed his fingers, not quite trusting her voice just then.

The ceremony, even the official version for royal weddings, was simple. There would have been a good deal more flourishes if it had been a full court wedding—thousands in the audience, a few dozen attendants, lots of music and special speeches added in at strategic points. But none of that was required—it was only etiquette and custom and show. So instead they only had the heart of it.

Priestess Armina did have most of the talking, pronouncing a benediction and asking them each for their vowed commitment to each other. The service for royal weddings did not put any special emphasis on love. It was mentioned, as were the chief virtues of each of the gods, but it was given no more attention than loyalty, creativity or wisdom. The actual vows they were asked to assent to were about valuing each other, about loyalty and fidelity. Rose had wondered, long ago, how she'd ever be able to answer an honest yes at that moment, but this—this was easy.

In just a few minutes it was done, and when, at the close of the ceremony, Terrence took her in his arms and kissed her—that was better than she ever could have hoped for.

After that it was hugging everyone, and signing paperwork that Rupin helpfully produced.

"Who knew it was so easy to get married?" Rose said, setting down her pen after the last page.

"Was it, though?" Terrence asked quietly, arm around her waist.

She smiled up at him. "Yes. It really was."

He smiled too, then sighed. "There ought to be a big banquet and a grand party that goes on for hours now."

"It doesn't matter," Rose said, and didn't regret it. "You know what I'd rather do? Let's go get some of those cookies again."

Returning to the castle was easier than leaving it. For most people, the guards asked more questions coming into the castle than going out, but for royalty it was the opposite. They timed their return during supper, when everyone was off eating or wishing they were. The guards barely paid attention as they entered, and there was no one in the halls to observe when Rose went with Terrence to his room, instead of her own. Should anyone noticed she hadn't been in her room, Elena was prepared to affirm that she had stayed in the extra bedroom in hers and Henry's suite. Feeling delicate after her faint that morning, of course.

She wasn't feeling delicate. Or worrying about the morning.

She hadn't been to Terrence's rooms before. They were simpler than her own, a smaller sitting room, a bedroom. The details—she wasn't paying much attention to the details.

"Remember the night you let me sleep in your bower in the garden?" Terrence murmured, kissing her just below her ear, lips soft against her skin.

"Yes," she whispered, hands exploring the planes of his back. "On the other side of the room."

"Mm-hmm," he said, and she could hear the smile in his voice when he asked, "Do you want me to sleep on the other side of the room tonight?"

She knew he was joking but she also knew he really would respect whatever she said, and her answer was what it was in part because of that. "No," she said, fingers sliding around to unfasten the buttons of his shirt. Her stomach was fluttering and it was part nerves—but it was more excitement. "I don't."

Terrence helped her with all the complicated layers of her own outfit, and it was better and more blush-inducing than her best imaginings. By the time he drew her down to the bed, her skin was tingling, burning from the feel of his hands on her. She lay on his bed and he kissed her everywhere, touched and caressed until her body ached with a desire she'd never known before.

When at last they came together, what had seemed in theory to be awkward at best and terrifying at worst was beautiful instead—so beautiful that she cried out as desire gave way to ecstasy, clutching him to her as he sighed against her neck.

After, when he tried to roll off of her, the air felt cold and she wasn't ready to let go. With a half-articulated protest, she rolled with him, curling against his side. His arms wrapped around her and she rested her head on his chest, bare except for his mother's ring on its chain that she remembered from back in the garden.

"Are you all right?" he whispered, breath tickling her ear, but something in his voice made her think he already knew the answer, that he just wanted to hear her say it.

So she did. "I'm wonderful."

She felt as much as heard the low chuckle deep in his throat, his arms tightening around her.

Rose stayed curled up in his embrace as his breathing gave way to a quiet snore, and she thought that, whatever happened now, at least they had had this. At least *this* had been theirs, hers, her choice. No one could undo that, whatever else they might be able to do. And just for tonight, she wasn't going to think about that. Tomorrow, she'd have to—but not tonight.

She turned her head far enough to kiss his chest, just below the gold ring. Then she closed her eyes, sinking into the feeling of his body against hers. At least they had tonight.

She stayed awake for a long time, listening to Terrence breathe, not wanting to lose any of these hours. When she did finally drift away, it was into a dreamless sleep without nightmares.

Chapter Thirty-One: Terrence

Terrence woke up an hour before dawn, moonlight pouring in through his window, painting the room in silver. The spring night had taken on a chill, but Rose was still warm against him, nestled with her cheek on his shoulder, her breath whispering across his skin. He carefully lifted one strand of her hair, smiling at how golden it looked even in moonlight.

Probably he should let her sleep. He wanted to wake her up, to see how her eyes would look reflecting moonshine, to talk to her and kiss her and maybe even—after all, if they only had this one night…

He tried to push that fear down and away. Surely they had many other nights, a lifetime of nights ahead of them. Gregory might throw a punch at him, yes, or his father might rage and disapprove, but they'd get through it. Elena had always been a pessimist, and yes, he recognized that his family could be ruthless, both in the present and through history—but they were his *family*. He'd spent his entire life trying to find the best in them, trying to believe that best was there.

His mother had always believed the best of all her sons, had always believed they could be better than they sometimes seemed. He couldn't let go of that.

He wasn't letting go of Rose either, which meant there were about to be difficult days ahead, but they'd find their way. His father respected boldness and decisive action, and a secret marriage had certainly been that. Maybe that would even count for something.

He didn't believe it, but it sounded good.

So he should let Rose sleep. Or—he could kiss her to wake her up. He never had gotten the chance to try that. He was shifting position, trying to decide if it was a good idea, or if it was even something he could manage at this angle with her tucked against him like this, when Rose stirred and lifted her head.

"Sorry, I didn't mean to wake you," he said automatically. Not by merely changing position, anyway.

She gave him a sleepy smile that made his heart jump. "That's all right. And I thought you *did* mean to wake me, remember? All the way back in the garden?"

He smiled too. "Yes, but that was going to be with a kiss."

Her smile widened. "Something to try some other night, then. What time is it?"

"Early—not dawn yet."

"Good." She rolled away onto her back, reached her arms above her head to stretch, something cat-like in the movement.

Never mind some possible future night—he couldn't resist leaning over and kissing her now. She gave one surprised squeak, and then she was kissing him back, one hand tangling in his hair. He broke it off only because he wanted to look at her again, at her face all soft and shadowed in the night.

She smiled up at him, fingers twining through his hair, then drifting over to touch his face. She ran one fingertip over his eyebrow, stopped on the small scar near the temple. "How did you get this? I've kept meaning to ask."

"In a fight with Gregory," he said lightly. "Years ago." He didn't want to talk about his brother, so he propped himself on one elbow, freed his other hand to catch hers, drew her fingers down to be kissed.

She smiled, then slipped her hand away to stroke across the scar on the back of his hand. "And this one?"

"Weapons training," he said without looking at his hand. "I don't even remember when exactly. Lots of cuts happen training with swords. Most don't scar."

She nodded, trailed her fingers down past his wrist to lightly touch the tattoo on his forearm. "When did you get this?"

"Almost two years ago. Princes usually get a tattoo for whichever god they follow when they're eighteen." He might have told her about trying to decide between a lioness or the expected male lion, about how Elena had backed his choice and his father had disapproved. But he didn't want to talk about his father either.

And her hand was already drifting on to the scar on his upper arm, three thin lines in parallel, darker and newer than his other scars. "What made this?"

He hesitated before answering. "Thorns." Almost every scratch from the thorns had healed and faded, but this one, from the slash he'd had after he was already inside the walls, had left marks.

Her eyes went shadowed in a way that wasn't about the moonlight. "Oh. I'm sorry."

"Hey, no..." He caught her hand again, squeezed her fingers. "It's not your fault. And it was a small price to pay anyway."

"I don't know..." She ducked her head, hiding her face against his chest. "Lots of prices come with me. I must be a much more—complicated choice than you expected."

He shifted onto his back, pulling her with him and wrapping his arms around her tightly, searching for the words to take away the sadness in her voice. "You're so much more, so much *better* than I ever expected. I always thought—before I ever thought about going after the Princess Behind Thorns, I mean—that I'd end up marrying whoever my father and the council picked out. Princes do, you know, and I thought that could be all right, maybe. I never expected to be able to choose, so I just hoped... My father always made my mother sad, and I didn't want to do that. So I just hoped I'd marry someone who—I hoped we could be kind to each other. I looked at your portrait, and I thought the Princess Behind Thorns was as good a chance as whoever my father would choose. And then I met you, and you were so much *more* than I ever hoped for. I never hoped to marry someone I loved."

The words were out before he thought, he didn't entirely realize that he had half-said something he hadn't meant to say right now, until he felt her draw in a long breath.

He swallowed, could feel his cheeks turning hot. Of all the moments when he could have said something, now he'd slipped. This hadn't been the plan—he didn't *have* a plan—but he couldn't just leave it there now, could he? Not half-said like that. He touched the fall of her hair, looked at the ceiling. "But I did. I do. I mean..." He swallowed again, and the words still came out hoarse. "I love you, Rose. Did you know that?"

She raised her head to look into his face, one corner of her mouth curving up into a smile. “Kind of. I wondered when you’d say it.”

“Oh,” he managed, and looked at the ceiling again, tried to be all right with it if she didn’t feel the same way, because liking him and choosing to marry him and wanting to be with him, that ought to be enough.

Then she was raising herself up, leaning over him so her face was just above his, her hair falling like a curtain enclosing them both, and in a soft breath she said, “I love you too. Didn’t you know that?”

Obviously there was nothing he could do but pull her down against him and kiss her, her mouth warm and soft against his. He rolled her onto her back in a tangle of hair and entwined limbs and kissed her and kissed her, until their breaths were coming quickly and her fingers were digging into his shoulders, and then he brought his lips to her ear and murmured, “Say it again.”

“I love you, my Terrence,” she whispered, and it was so much more than he had ever dreamed of.

Chapter Thirty-Two: Rose

Rose hated leaving Terrence's rooms in the morning. But she had to return to her own rooms, carry on the illusion that everything was normal and nothing important had happened, nothing that would disrupt the king's plans and inspire him to new action.

So she spent the day before the challenge waiting. Waiting for the challenge, waiting for the crowds to gather, waiting for the moment when there would be enough people, enough witnesses, enough opportunity to sway public support to make it safe to announce their marriage. Waiting for the moment when she and Terrence could stop being a secret, when she could take control of her life in front of everyone.

Everything around her, everything inside her, seemed to be holding its breath. In some hours she could feel the calm she'd possessed in the quiet moonlight of the long night. In some moments she remembered Terrence's voice, saying he loved her, and a smile would creep unbidden across her face. In other hours she was afraid, of what was coming next, of the memory of Gregory's smile. Of how it all might go wrong, and how this fragile opportunity to seize hold of her life might still slip out of her fingers, losing everything in the process.

And often, she felt everything all at once.

Life had been much simpler, in the garden.

On a normal day she spent much of her time with the court ladies, so she did that today as well. She convinced them to take their sewing projects out to the lawn, because the walls of the castle felt especially smothering.

It only helped slightly, sitting out under the blue sky, able to breathe in the open air. Her nerves still jangled and she couldn't concentrate on the conversation around her, but at least she could force herself for a little while to sit quietly and sew, presenting an outward appearance of calm and decorum. If she had been inside, she thought she would have screamed by mid-morning just to break the tension.

As it was, she still felt increasingly on edge as the morning hours wore away, rebelling against sitting here, embroidering without giving it much thought, doing *nothing* useful while huge events swirled all around them and the court ladies talked on and on. They weren't even saying anything useful, avoiding the topic of the challenge and any rumors around it so completely that it had to be deliberate.

"I think I'm going to take a walk," she said abruptly, when she felt she couldn't stand it anymore.

The conversation broke off, everyone looking at her. "I suppose," Lady Sylvia said doubtfully, "we could all…"

"No, that's all right," Rose interrupted, because wandering about with the entire crowd of court ladies was not going to help. "You just—carry on here, and I'll—only be a few moments."

She surged up to her feet, desperate to get away for a moment of quiet to collect herself again. She glanced Elena's direction as she moved away from her chair, found the other woman looking at her intently.

"Be careful," Elena said softly, and Rose nodded.

She wasn't very worried for herself. The king would want her for his challenge tomorrow. It was Terrence who might be—no, she couldn't think about that, or she wouldn't be able to keep up any kind of composure today.

She made her escape, walking away from the circle of women to the nearby path cutting between rose bushes. She followed it until it made a bend around high hedges, hiding her from sight, and then she let out a slow breath. Better. She had been alone for so many years, and maybe if she could be alone for a few minutes now…

A small, furry gray face popped out from beneath a bush, swiftly followed by the rest of Silvertips. Emerald Eyes was right behind her. The two kittens trotted happily over to her, twining amongst her skirts and looking very pleased with themselves. Rose laughed, bending down to pat them.

All right, not quite alone, but she hadn't meant *them*.

Rose and the kittens walked along the winding path through flowerbeds and hedges. She was thinking of going to a nook she remembered, tucked among some trees with a couple of benches. It was a good secluded space to think.

Or to kiss someone, but that probably wasn't going to be an option today.

Seclusion was apparently not an option either, as she came around a bend and found someone already sitting on the bench she had in mind.

Xevrix the enchantress rose in a rustle of flowing red skirts, regarding her with a cool gaze as she inclined her head slightly. "Good morning, Princess Rose. How pleasant to see you again."

"Xevrix," Rose said, the name feeling strange with no title attached. "I was not aware you were at court." The words came from honest surprise, and the slightly disconcerting experience of meeting this so unusual woman when she had expected to be alone. After the words were out she regretted them, as a kind of admission that she wasn't aware of all that went on. Most days she would have thought first, to consider the subtler meanings.

Xevrix's mouth curved into a small, unreadable smile. "I arrived at court yesterday. King Elgin had requested my services in a certain…project that is coming to culmination." She looked away, expression growing more serious. "It is not the most palatable enterprise, but kings do not appreciate having their requests refused."

Rose tried to parse that. The king surely had one primary project right now, and apparently Xevrix was involved—but she wasn't happy about it? Could Rose learn something useful from her? Assuming they really *were* talking about the challenge… In a sudden decision, she sat down on the opposite bench and said, "You're working on tomorrow's challenge, aren't you?" Somehow, of everyone at court, she thought Xevrix might appreciate directness.

Xevrix smiled that smile again, and sat down on her own bench. "Yes, I am."

So it was a magical challenge, then. That shouldn't have been shocking, but Rose felt a new tightening in her stomach. Magic was so much more uncertain, so much more unknowable than common threats.

But it would be all right. Terrence wouldn't be fighting in the challenge. No one would be.

Still, it might feel better to know what it was, even if that was probably hoping for too much. "And I suppose kings don't appreciate having their plans shared widely either?"

The enchantress' smile grew. "Not even a little bit. But you may find it…familiar."

Thorns. She had to mean thorns. What else would be familiar? Gods help her, there were going to be thorns.

Rose drew in a slow breath. Terrence *wasn't* going to fight whatever it was. They would make their announcement, and everything would be fine.

She was still trying to work out a careful way to ask for more information, just in case, when Xevrix remarked casually, "I expect they wanted me involved because I have some experience with this kind of enchantment."

Rose frowned. What could that mean? Maybe it wasn't thorns after all? "I always understood the enchantment on me to be unique."

"Exactly," Xevrix said, still smiling. "I was quite young at the time, of course."

Rose stared at her. She couldn't mean what she seemed to mean—and yet, the first time she'd seen Xevrix, hadn't there been that tickle of recognition? She could feel it now, looking at the enchantress' face. "But…that was a hundred years ago."

"Enchantresses can live a very long time," Xevrix said. "If we choose."

Rose's stomach clenched. She had thought—everyone was gone, there was no one left to be angry with, no one left to blame for what had happened. But here this smiling woman was, freely admitting that she had been one of the enchanters standing around her, chanting their spells, taking her away from her life—

"It was a terrible thing, wasn't it?" Xevrix said softly. "As I said, I was quite young—a mere apprentice, in fact. I empathized with you very much. Neither of us had any real say in what was happening. But I am sorry, for my role in it all."

Rose let her breath out. She had thought…there was no one left to apologize either. "Thank you. That's…I appreciate that." Hearing it meant more than she could have guessed. Her eyes felt hot, and only the imagined humiliation of crying in front of Xevrix kept her from actually doing it. She reached down to pick up Silvertips, to cuddle the purring kitten on her lap, to collect herself.

"I was hoping to have the opportunity to speak with you about your enchantment," Xevrix continued, unaware of Rose's turmoil of emotions or, more likely, too polite to comment on it. "To offer my apologies, of course, but I am also very curious as to your experience. Rumors suggest the spell turned out quite differently than intended."

"I wasn't asleep, if that's what you mean." Maybe Xevrix had some answers about that. Maybe she could finally understand more of what had happened to her. Was Terrence right, that her wishes had changed the spell? Or was it something else? Had it been Xevrix herself, one sympathetic enchanter in the group whose influence had changed how the spell turned out?

Maybe—that would make a difference tomorrow too. She felt a sudden twinge of guilt as she realized how thoroughly she had become distracted. The enchantment was the past. She should be focused on tomorrow, on the challenge, on what she and Terrence might be facing –

"It *is* curious that the sleeping spell was so ineffective," Xevrix remarked. "Though so many things can influence the results of an enchantment of course."

"I suppose many things will influence tomorrow's challenge as well," Rose said, looking Xevrix directly in the eye, all but daring her to reveal more.

Xevrix smiled, that mysterious smile Rose had already seen more than once, that made her think the enchantress was thinking a great deal she wasn't sharing. "Oh yes. Many things."

Rose was just trying to formulate a more direct question when a rustling of leaves and footsteps along the path announced new arrivals. A moment later Lady Sylvia and two other court ladies appeared around the bend.

"You were right, Your Highness," Lady Sylvia announced, face bright, "it's a really lovely day for walking—" She came to a comically abrupt halt as she caught sight of Rose's companion.

The other ladies crowded behind her, while Elena approached from a few steps behind them. She met Rose's gaze with a shrug and a mouthed apology.

Before Rose could say anything, Xevrix rose to her feet. "Perhaps I will leave you to your walking. Good day, Princess Rose. I hope to see you again soon."

So much for solitude *or* answers.

Xevrix glided along the path, the court ladies hurriedly moving out of her way. Rose sighed, and stood up too. Maybe if they walked, she could still *think* at least.

So they walked, and she tried to think. Had she learned anything useful?

Not nearly as much as she would have liked, as she might have done if she had had longer with the enchantress. She had learned the challenge would have a magical component. And possibly the enchantress managing the challenge had some sympathy for her, for Terrence. Maybe that would make a difference, if it came down to Terrence fighting in the challenge.

But if it came down to that, something would already have gone horribly wrong.

Chapter Thirty-Three: Terrence

After the events of the previous day, the previous night, Terrence found it hard to focus on anything else. But there was still the challenge to think about, that could still be a problem. Maybe. The whole plan, of course, was for no one to actually compete in the challenge, to simply announce their marriage in front of the crowd. But he'd still like to know what the challenge was, to make sure there would be an opportunity for an announcement.

And maybe, deep down, part him liked the idea of actually fighting through something, finally proving something. He wasn't going to *do* it, it was too likely to be a trap, but maybe that little part still wanted to know what the challenge would be, just…to think about it.

So maybe he should spend the day trying to learn something about the challenge. Maybe from his brothers. Gregory at least probably knew something. With that idea in mind, Terrence went to the practice yard, because that was the most likely place to find them, especially during the morning. The much larger combat ground, where tournaments were held, was still closed off.

Sure enough, when he arrived, Gregory, Tyler and Edward were already in the practice yard, shooting arrows at targets, evidently midway through some kind of competition with each other. They wouldn't want to be interrupted, so Terrence just greeted the knights and guards and servants who were also hanging around the area. Then he settled leaning against the wall bordering the yard, watching his brothers shoot.

He had only been there a few minutes before Henry walked in and took up a position next to him, said an entirely too casual, "Good morning," as he folded his arms on the wall.

"Good morning," Terrence returned. Henry didn't come here anymore. He suspected that the other man was keeping up some kind of private training, but he didn't come here. That fact, along with the timing, pointed in one clear direction. "Did Elena tell you to keep an eye on me today?" Because she was probably worrying about what might happen to him, in this castle he'd lived in his entire life, with people he'd known his entire life.

"Elena doesn't give me orders," Henry countered, entirely evading the point.

Terrence shrugged. "She gives them to *me*." He chose whether to follow them, but she definitely gave them.

A chuckle escaped Henry at that, and Terrence smiled. It was pleasant and companionable and it was hard to believe in conspiracies and threats on a sunny morning when he was feeling especially good about life.

It made arguing seem impossible too, so he went ahead and pressed the point. "Seriously, did Elena tell you to keep an eye on me? Because nothing's going to happen."

There was a pause before Henry said carefully, "She and I discussed the idea. I know *you* don't believe there's danger, but we're playing with very big stakes here. People would do a lot for a throne."

"We're not talking about abstract people. We're talking about my family—"

"And you trust them? Your father? Your brothers?"

Terrence had rarely put the question to himself so directly. It wasn't a comfortable question. "Do you trust your father?" he parried, trying to buy himself a moment. Because—he wouldn't trust them with *everything*, he wouldn't tell them the same things he might tell Elena or Rose, he hadn't told them about his plans before he'd gone in search of the Princess Behind Thorns, he knew they'd laugh at some of the ideas that were important to him—but surely he trusted them not to *kill* him. That was a low bar of trust.

Henry exhaled in a huff. "My father isn't the king. And I have watched *your* father send men to their deaths before."

"It was a war," Terrence said, trying not to pitch his voice in a tone that would turn this into an argument after all. "It's not the same."

"It's about the same things, though," Henry said quietly, eyes on the practice yard as Gregory's arrow narrowly missed a bull's-eye. "Power, and who gets to keep it."

"It's going to be fine." Terrence seemed to be saying that a lot lately.

Henry sighed, and some tension relaxed out of his shoulders. "Oh well, it would make Elena sad if you ever stopped being so damned hopeful about people."

"I just don't believe anyone wants to kill me," Terrence said. "I'm not being unreasonably hopeful; the rest of you are being too suspicious."

The debate ended abruptly at that point, because Terrence's brothers had concluded their shooting and were heading this way. Terrence did a quick survey of faces and concluded Gregory must have won. He wouldn't be smiling if he hadn't.

"So little brother decided to come to the practice yard today," Gregory called as the three approached. "What grants us the honor?" He made an exaggerated bow, clearly mockery, not respect.

The bow didn't help the nettled feeling Terrence was already getting from being addressed as 'little brother.' When he was very small, he had believed it was meant affectionately, but he'd gotten over that idea years ago. He took a breath, and decided to ignore the question. "Nice shooting out there," he offered, because usually that sort of remark pleased Gregory.

Gregory's grin broadened, though there was a glint in his eye too. "Care to try your hand? Or maybe we should mix it up and get a couple of swords instead."

He still had never beaten Gregory in a swordfight. He'd been told more than once, by people who knew fighting, that he should be able to, that he had won against other opponents who were as good or better. But Gregory somehow always got the best of him in the end with swords. Though they hadn't fought in the past few months, since Rose came to court.

He was tempted to agree to a fight. He was never going to get any better if he never accepted a challenge. But before he could say anything, for or against, Henry kicked him, out of sight behind the wall.

Terrence glanced at Henry, who looked quite impassive and didn't make eye contact, but he got the message anyway. "Maybe not today."

Gregory's grin didn't change, but did the glint in his eyes turn sharper? "Sure you don't want to get a little practice in? No telling what you might need for that challenge."

Terrence had intended to bring that subject up himself. It figured it would be on his brother's mind too. "It's an interesting question. I was sorry to miss the rest of the meeting discussing the idea." He let a pause hang, and when it wasn't filled with additional information or any of the obvious questions, he added, "Rose is fine, by the way."

"That would rather spoil your plans, wouldn't it?" Gregory drawled. "If something happened to your princess now."

Terrence didn't like Gregory's tone, or the way Tyler smirked and nudged Edward. "Fortunately," he said evenly, voice growing tighter, "Rose is perfectly well. And nothing is going to happen to her." He wished it sounded more like a threat and less like a hope.

"What a relief," Gregory said, exchanging a glance with Tyler beside him. "So now you can heroically rescue her tomorrow and heroically claim the throne. Do you suppose that will be the thing that finally makes Father approve of you?"

Terrence took a breath. All right, so Gregory was in a mood and trying to needle him. It wasn't like he couldn't recognize what was happening.

While he was searching for something neutral to say, Gregory continued, "I'm looking forward to that challenge. Who knows what you'll have to do? Scale a tower, fight a dragon. Is the throne worth that much?"

Did he know something about what it would be, or not? Both of those proposed possibilities seemed more elaborate than anyone was likely to set up. He told himself it didn't really matter. They just needed to get in front of the crowd gathered for the challenge, announce their marriage with such a big audience that no one could keep it quiet, and that would be that. All he said to Gregory was, "Yes, I think it's worth it. And I know she is."

Gregory's laugh was loud and harsh. "You always were a *romantic*." He made it sound like a very bad thing. "Haven't you learned yet that no woman is worth that kind of effort? They're all too much the same. Or was she really that good, when you had her behind those thorns?"

Of course Terrence knew his brothers said things like that. He never liked it, but he could usually get past it. This time—this felt different.

Something very dark and very cold uncoiled in his stomach and spread through his veins. He was surprised that his voice sounded even when he said, "Let's try that sword fight after all."

"*Terrence*," Henry said in a low voice, one hand closing on his arm.

"Any time you're ready, little brother," Gregory said, arms spread and grin even broader still.

Terrence shook Henry's hand off and hoisted himself over the wall, landing on the packed dirt of the yard with a satisfying thump. He accepted the sword Edward offered him, weighing it in his hand. Good weight, good balance.

He waited until Gregory had his own sword raised, but didn't wait for his brother to make the first attack. He lunged forward, a rapid thrust that Gregory parried, their swords crashing together.

"Taking the offensive, little brother?" Gregory said, moving back a pace. "How unusual for you."

Gregory liked to cover his attacks with taunts, a strategy that might work to distract an opponent who had fought him less often. Terrence knew it was his tell, and was ready for Gregory's counter-strike.

They circled around the practice yard, swords meeting and disengaging, sometimes one of them on the defensive, sometimes the other. Gregory was two inches taller with a longer reach, but Terrence was better at reading his opponent.

They were both sweating by the time they locked close together, swords crossed almost at the hilt.

"Do you really think you deserve the throne," Gregory hissed, face inches away, "when you can't even beat me in a swordfight?"

"I haven't lost yet."

Answering back was the wrong thing to do. He knew better, knew it was a mistake the instant he felt Gregory's foot hooking around his ankle. By then it was too late, the crucial half-second of distraction already having done its work, and before he could do anything he was off-balance and falling. He landed hard on his back on the packed earth, air slamming out of his lungs, sword slipping from his grasp and skittering away. He reached for it but it was an inch out of range, and before he could move Gregory's sword point was pressed against the hollow of his throat.

"Do you yield?" Gregory asked, and it was some comfort that at least he was breathing hard.

"Yes," Terrence said, letting himself sag backwards. The word was faint, forced out from his burning, air-starved lungs.

For a second he thought Gregory hadn't heard him, because the sword didn't move. He looked up into his brother's face, and something in Gregory's eyes made his spine crawl. There was—a fire there, as Gregory stared down at him.

The sword pressed harder against his skin, Gregory's gaze still locked with his.

"I yield," Terrence pushed out, past the constriction in his chest, past the sword against his throat.

And Gregory smiled.

There was nothing, nothing at all, reassuring about that smile.

But then Gregory said, "You know, it's far more fun in the long-run if you stay alive, little brother."

Then he lifted the sword, turned away, walked out of Terrence's view.

Terrence didn't get up immediately. But he pushed himself far enough to reach his sword, to wrap his fingers around its hilt. For all the good it was likely to do him now.

His grip tightened on the weapon when he heard footsteps approaching, but Henry came into view before he could do anything more than that.

"It is one thing to be hopeful," Henry informed him, voice tight with anger, "but *that* was stupid."

"Yes, I got that," Terrence managed, still trying to drag air back into his lungs. He accepted Henry's hand stretched out to haul him back to his feet. "Don't tell Rose about this, all right?" She'd worry. "Or Elena."

"I *should* tell Elena. She'd have your head."

"I know," Terrence said, and rubbed his throat. The spot Gregory's sword had touched still felt cold.

Had Gregory seriously considered killing him? Had he only been joking? And what was he planning, that he thought would be more fun with Terrence around?

"You know," Henry said, tone moderating into something more conversational, "I haven't seen you fight in a while. You're better than you tell people you are."

"I lost, didn't I?" He was all right with a sword, but he couldn't beat Gregory.

"Yes, but you should have won. There were at least two times when you could have had him if you'd pressed an advantage. And he only won because you let him get in your head."

Terrence shrugged. "Maybe." Another person telling him he should do better than he did against Gregory. But it never seemed to count for very much, considering he never actually *won*. "Maybe next time."

Assuming he fought Gregory again. A chill went down his spine, because for the first time he had serious doubts about what that next time might look like. Practice bouts in the yard were one thing, but this, for at least a moment, had felt far too real.

There had been a look in Gregory's eyes, staring down at him across the length of his sword, that Terrence never wanted to see again. And that he was never going to forget.

Chapter Thirty-Four: Rose

Rose wasn't able to talk to Terrence for the rest of the day. Usually they found some time together, but today circumstances kept interfering; she didn't believe it was chance. Whatever the king was planning, keeping them apart today was likely not even a difficult achievement for him.

She told Elena what little she'd learned about the challenge from Xevrix, for whatever good it might do.

The evening was taken up by a large banquet, celebrating the visiting delegations of three nearby countries. They were here to witness the challenge the next day—and since they must have been traveling for days, this was further proof that plans had been in motion since long before the king had announced it to his council.

The banquet was the only time she even saw Terrence, sitting most of a table and twenty people away. She saw him try to move her direction three times, but people kept catching him in urgent conversation; certainly not a coincidence. So they could only exchange glances across the loud, crowded room, and even that was enough to make her feel warm all over.

Maybe it was better they were separated after all. How well would they be able to hide their new secret, if they were together? What would the king do, if he suspected?

But Rose missed Terrence, with a fierce ache she had never felt for anyone or anything before. She was sure that in all those long years in the garden, she had never missed anyone from the Before Time the way she missed Terrence now, after only a dozen hours apart.

She wished she could slip into his bedroom tonight, spend another night wrapped in his arms—but it was too big a risk. She might have chanced it, if only she wasn't afraid that revealing the truth to King Elgin too soon would lead to Terrence's swift and silent execution. That was too dangerous a chance, far too high a cost.

She spent the night in her own rooms and slept badly. What she had learned from Xevrix was too vague and left her endless scope for imagining. It shouldn't matter. No one should be attempting the challenge, but that seemed to weigh little in the dark hours, so different from the gentle shadows of the previous night.

In the morning, maids appeared with a breakfast she had no appetite for, and surrounded her to dress her for the challenge. Gabrielle wasn't among them, and neither was Lady Graybourne, though by all protocol both should have been. Elena didn't appear either, though she had said she would.

Rose dug her fingernails into her palms and told herself it didn't matter. She forced herself to breathe through the tightness in her chest, told herself that she had half-expected this. Of course the king wouldn't want any potential ally around her this morning, of course he'd take steps to prevent it. She wondered what he thought they might do, if she and Elena were together.

She glanced across the bedroom at her statue of Mariqwe, standing bravely by the bed, and wished she felt half as confident as the statue looked.

It was fine. It was all fine. Their plan didn't depend on anything happening *now*, it was later that counted. They planned to act at the challenge itself, not now.

Rose left her kittens asleep on her bed and submitted without protest to the maids' work; it wasn't as though protesting would do any good. They pinned and primped and twisted her hair up into a design as complicated as the one for her long-ago portrait, and slipped her into a white dress with simple lines that hung heavy with beading in the long, trailing skirt. At the last they put a thin gold circlet on her head.

Rose looked at herself in the mirror and thought, dispassionately, that she looked like exactly what she was meant to be. A sacrifice. Her cheeks were pale, her eyes overbright, the white dress clung to her form even as its ornate beads weighed her down. The gold crown felt even heavier on her forehead.

How different from how she'd looked two days ago, dressed in green and a bridal crown.

"You look so beautiful, Your Highness," one of the maidservants murmured, and Rose made herself smile, because it wasn't the poor woman's fault.

There was a knock at the door and Rose's heart gave a throb. She took a breath, told herself very firmly that it wasn't Terrence. There was no reason it would be Terrence, and the king would surely prevent it, and so it wasn't—but her heart beat harder and she wished so desperately that it could be, that just maybe, somehow—if she could finally see Terrence this morning, even for a moment, none of this would feel as bad. They had a plan, a good plan, and one confirming glance, a confirming nod, would steady her.

Or just to see him at all, that would be enough.

One of the maids opened the door, King Elgin strode boldly in, and Rose's heart throbbed again in an entirely different way, the way a deer must feel at the sudden appearance of the hunter. The maids hastily dropped into deep curtsies, and Rose dipped too, enough to be polite and enough to hide her face until she could control her expression again.

It could have been worse. It could have been Gregory.

Would that be worse? Maybe.

"Good morning, Princess Rose," King Elgin said, his gaze heavier on her than the dress, heavier than the crown. "I've come to escort you to the challenge. It should be an…interesting day."

He extended his arm, and she made herself put her hand on it, let him lead her away. She had rarely been this close to him, and it was strange looking up at his face. She could see the traces of Terrence there, and yet the eyes were so cold.

All her fears intensified, as she looked at those eyes. Terror uncoiled from the pit of her stomach, reached tendrils all through her body, and she clutched her skirts with her free hand in a desperate grip to keep it from shaking.

The hallway outside was filled with people, an entire escort—guards with their gleaming swords, councilmembers with their straight backs and lifted chins. At the very back, somehow with the crowd and yet not appearing to be a part of them, Xevrix was standing. Her gaze was on Rose, and when their eyes met she gave the same nod she had given before, an acknowledgment so aloof, so unbowed—and yet it was still the friendliest gesture of anyone in the crowd.

Rose didn't expect to see Terrence. But she also didn't see Rupin among the councilmembers, still didn't see Elena or Henry, and she had to bite her lip to keep from shrieking.

She wondered what this crowd of people would do, if she *did* suddenly shriek that she wouldn't do this, that they couldn't force her to, that it was all, all wrong.

Probably tidy her away into her room long enough to put her to sleep with a spell, and then carry on just the same with an unconscious princess. That would line up better with the legend anyway.

Surely Xevrix's enchantments extended far enough to taming a rebellious princess, if she could tame a dragon. Would Xevrix agree to do it? Maybe not, but Rose had far too much doubt about that to risk it. She couldn't announce a secret marriage, couldn't affirm any announcement from Terrence, if she was under a sleeping spell.

Rose let the king lead her to the head of the crowd, lead the way through the castle with the escort around them, out to the large combat ground behind the castle. She hadn't seen it since the Before Time; it had been "in renovations" and now suddenly she understood why. They must have been preparing it all along for this challenge. Usually the site of tournaments and exhibitions, the area held a wide circular arena, with enough tiers of seats to hold thousands. She could hear the voice of the crowd long before they reached it.

They entered at one end of the arena, through the Royal Entrance. First a shadowed tunnel, and then she was blinking in the glare of the sunlight, trying not to shrink back before the stares of thousands, the renewed roar of the people. They were cheering as they saw her, the Princess Behind Thorns, the object of the legend. She was a story to them, a symbol, a perfect portrait of a perfect princess.

The small crowd in the marketplace, the ones who had looked at her with so much hope and had felt like almost too much to face—that seemed laughably small in scale now, compared to this.

If she could sway the crowd to the story she wanted, that would give her a kind of power—but *could* she do that? Could she and Terrence win the crowd to the version of the legend they wanted?

She kept her head up, her hand on the king's arm steady, and walked beside him as her heart pounded and fear tightened her throat.

Where was Terrence? She was here, the crowd was here, now was the time to step forward with their announcement and end this. To see just how much power they had.

They continued walking forward and her vision was growing less dazzled by the light, her ears dismissing the crowd's roar into the background. She looked at the arena, and saw what had been prepared for the challenge.

The ground sloped slightly downward toward the center, giving her at the edge a vantage point to see the entire space. First, a circle of guards, at least fifty of them, a third of the full castle guard. Inside that outer ring, they had set up a circle of thorny brambles.

So she was to be the Princess Behind Thorns again in truth, just as Xevrix had implied. Something inside her instinctively recoiled, and yet—for anyone who had seen the true thorns, the enchanted thorns she had lived behind for so many years, the hedge of thorns arranged here, perhaps five feet tall and half that in width, was an almost laughable barrier. Today's danger was as real, but it wasn't from thorns today.

Inside the thorns was a dry moat, perhaps ten feet deep, and at the very center, a small circular plateau. Presumably that was her destination.

But they weren't going to do this. She and Terrence had a *plan*.

She tried to look for him in the crowd, but there were too many people, too many faces, a mass of shifting color, and the king was still leading her forward, away from the tiers of onlookers. Could she say something alone? Would anyone listen?

The guards parted as Rose and King Elgin passed within their circle. A narrow gap had been left in the thorn hedge. The king halted before it, and stepped away from her.

He looked down at her face, and in a low voice she could only just hear over the crowd, he said, "You know what to do, Princess Behind Thorns. Be the stupid, obedient girl all the stories say you are, or I will personally ensure you regret it afterwards. Deeply, and for a long time."

Her heart was already hammering, her throat already tight, and it was almost easier, having the king's pleasant mask slip. She had always felt that this lurked beneath. But even in this moment, her gaze darted out towards the crowd again. *Where was Terrence*? What was he still waiting for?

The king gave one imperious gesture to urge her through the bramble hedge, and reluctantly she walked forward alone. She passed through, not stopping even when thorns caught at the hem of her dress, when the crowd's roar grew deafening, to see her behind thorns again.

She walked over the bare ground beyond the brambles, over the planks arranged as a bridge across the dry moat, and stood alone at the center of the arena. Even the crowd couldn't drown out the sound of her own heartbeat.

Guards hurried forward to remove the planks, trapping her within the moat, then retreated themselves towards the thorns.

There was another barrier she hadn't seen from a distance. Looking down into the moat, she could see two golden lions, sprawled in the sunshine, seeming far calmer than she herself felt.

Movement out of the corner of her eye drew her attention away from the lions, back to the hedge of thorns, and her breath caught. The hedge was *growing*. The guards had retreated, and now it was filling in the opening where she had walked through. The branches writhed and twisted and continued expanding, growing in height and breadth until it was no longer a low, inconsequential hedge but a towering wall eight or ten feet high of thickly interlaced branches, spiked with thorns.

Her throat tightened. Of course, if Xevrix was involved, of course it was magical thorns. But seeing them, seeing those branches twist and shift, triggered a deep-seated horror she couldn't reason away.

She dug her nails into her palms, hiding her fists among the folds of her skirt. Terrence wasn't here, they were about to start the challenge, she was just *standing* here but what could she do—would announcing their marriage hold any weight at all without Terrence there too?

King Elgin was ascending the steps to the royal pavilion at one end of the arena, and more guards were quieting the crowd for the king to speak. She tried to make out figures in the crowded pavilion. Most blurred together, a crowd of minor nobility. Xevrix, in her vivid red cloak, was the easiest to spot. After the enchantress, she distinguished three men standing beside the king. Three, not four, and despite the distance, despite the resemblance among the princes, she was almost certain none of them were Terrence.

The king's voice rang out, amplified by magic. "My people, I welcome you today. This is a very special moment in our country's history. Today, we will see the end of the long legend. We will see the rescue of the Princess Behind Thorns."

More roars from the crowd went on and on, quieting again only when the king gestured for silence.

"We will begin with the man who brought the Princess Rose back to our midst. None of us can say with certainty what happened in the countryside where the princess lay under a spell. But we can affirm that my youngest son, Terrence, Prince of Avala, has earned the right to be the first champion for the princess' hand."

Now. It had to be *now*.

Rose waited, holding her breath, scanning the crowd.

Nothing. Nothing at all. Only silence, until the crowd began murmuring its uncertainty and confusion.

"It would seem," King Elgin continued, after letting the crowd's doubt grow, "that Prince Terrence is not here. That he has, in fact, chosen not to make a claim for the princess' hand." The crowd muttered uneasily at this, and the king played another, obviously planned card. "We cannot speak to the ways of magic or the intentions of the gods, but evidently the legend was not meant to end with Prince Terrence after all. Today you will all be witnesses to see the champion whom the gods have selected to rescue the Princess Behind Thorns."

The crowd liked this better, judging by the roar of approval that went up. They might like Terrence, but they liked a spectacle too.

Rose wanted to sink down and cover her face with her hands and sob. And she wanted to fly at the king, demand answers, somehow force him to admit every detail of his plot.

What had they done to Terrence?

He wouldn't *choose* not to come, wouldn't decide that she was too much trouble after all. She could almost still feel his lips against hers, his chest warm beneath her cheek as he told her that he loved her. He would be here, if he could be, so King Elgin must have prevented it.

Or had the king made a more permanent arrangement? Was Terrence already dead?

She stayed standing, gaze fixed on the distance, terror and fury warring within her, turning her stomach and making her chest tight. She breathed shallowly, fought to keep the shadows at the edges of her vision from consuming her. There was no Terrence to catch her now.

There might be no Terrence, ever again.

She couldn't think of that, not now. And she didn't know that it was true. Not yet.

She had to think of now, of what she could possibly do now.

But she was trapped, trapped behind thorns again, powerless, with so many eyes staring and yet no one, *no one* seeing her. No one would believe her claim that she and Terrence were married, not after the king's speech, not after he had told everyone that Terrence hadn't bothered to come. She had dared to think she could be someone different, live a different life, but it was only for one night, because now—now—

A small furry form twined between her ankles, and she blinked and looked down. Silvertips. The kitten could not possibly have got here on her own and yet—either Rose had gone truly mad or her kitten had come to join her in the center of the king's trap.

Cats went where they wanted to go. They always had. If they could get into the garden, past the other thorns, why not here?

Rose bent down, lifted up the tiny gray cat, held Silvertips against her chest and breathed a little more easily. Her breathing steadied and her head cleared and she seized hold of a new resolve. She still didn't know what she could do, could see no way to stop this—but she would wait and watch and find some opportunity. She would do *something*. Even a pawn could move one space.

Around her, the challenge was beginning. Champions were apparently ready and waiting, dispelling any doubts that everything was proceeding exactly as the king had planned. At this distance, in the bright sun, she had only a vague impression of large men with swords, striding forward, ready to fight to possess the Princess Behind Thorns.

Some sort of order was worked out and the first champion stepped up to try the challenge. The whole business was a pageant, of course. Fifty guards could stop any single man with a sword; no one outside of legends was that good. But the guards must have had orders, as they held to their places in the circle, no more than three or four engaging the champions.

That was still difficult odds. The first champion surrendered the challenge and walked away with little apparent damage on either side. The second did the same.

The third had to be carried away, cursing, a wound in his leg bleeding heavily.

Rose clutched Silvertips tighter, the cat squeaking in protest. Another man bleeding for her. Another man cursing the Princess Behind Thorns.

They still echoed in her ears, the screams of the champions before, their shrieks and moans and curses as they died in the thorns.

And Terrence was missing, had Terrence…

Surely the guards would be more merciful than the thorns that had surrounded her garden. Surely they weren't aiming to kill anyone, in the king's theatrical challenge. The lions were unlikely to be that considerate, though, and the wall of thorns—how dangerous were these enchanted thorns?

She found out when the fifth champion fought his way past three guards, to approach the brambles. The guards held back, watching, while the crowd roared with approval. The fifth champion lifted his sword high, hacked at the thorny hedge—and immediately branches slashed out, whipping towards him. He jumped back a pace, tried to parry with his sword, but another branch snaked its way towards him, then more and more, great reaching boughs spiked with thorns.

The champion gave up quickly, shaking his head and retreating. Only when he was several paces away did the wall of thorns go quiet again, and only then did Rose feel she could breathe. Was another champion going to die among thorns today? Was she going to listen to another man screaming as he died?

She breathed in, out, told herself that surely Xevrix was controlling the thorns, that surely she wouldn't let it go that far. Why even have the lions, if the brambles were going to kill everyone who approached them?

Rose kept an eye on the lions below her, as more champions tried and failed, and she began to think something was wrong with the big cats. A male and a female lion, they sprawled at the bottom of the moat, occasionally stretching limbs or flicking an ear. They were too calm. She knew cats, and no cat would have been this calm through all this noise. Even Silvertips was squirmy and unhappy. And the lions ought to be able to smell the blood too, as another champion and then another retired with wounds from the guards.

Xevrix probably had the lions under a spell. Maybe they were sleepy, maybe they were enspelled to keep them calm. They probably weren't enchanted to let only the right person past—that would be meticulous magic—but something had been done to the lions.

The morning wore on and the sun approached the top of the sky. Silvertips settled down draped on Rose's shoulder, and her furry weight was Rose's only comfort as she stood in the hot sun and watched men fight and bleed in her name.

She forced herself to keep count of the champions, even as they blurred together, even as her mind tried to skitter away to worry about Terrence. She had no idea how many champions had died in the thorns around her garden, but she could at least keep track of these. And it gave her something to focus on, when her mind kept screaming about what would happen when one of them (Gregory, surely it would be Gregory) finally got through. And about Terrence.

Her feet, clad in ridiculous silver slippers, ached before the sixth champion was done. The glare from the sun was making her head hurt by the eighth. By the twelfth, the crowd was growing restless. Sword-fighting was all well and good, but they wanted to see a rescue.

No doubt King Elgin had waited for just that moment.

Because that was when Prince Gregory stepped forward.

Chapter Thirty-Five: Terrence

Terrence hit his fist against the wooden door and cursed himself for being ten kinds of a fool.

He should have arranged for guards outside his rooms. He should have spent the night in Elena and Henry's suite. He should have spent the night in Rose's rooms, court gossip and his father's suspicions be damned. He should have done something, *anything*, rather than stroll blithely out of his bedroom this morning and straight into an ambush.

He should have reacted faster, he should have noticed that none of the castle guards facing him in the hall were ones he was friendly with, he should have been clever enough to realize that *of course* they'd have at least one guard ready to come up behind him and hit him over the head.

But he hadn't done any of the things he should have done, and so he had woken up here, locked in the south tower. With a splitting headache.

Although the thing he really should have done, the one thing that would have made up for all the others, would be if he had moved just a little faster when Gregory came to pay him a call.

He had barely woken up, was still trying to get his head around why he was lying on the ground in the midst of a clutter of boxes and trunks, weapons missing and only an empty scabbard at his side, when the heavy wooden door opened and Gregory stepped in.

For an instant, Terrence had believed that Gregory would help him. He was as furious with himself now for that thought as much as for anything else.

The idea had dissipated as soon as Gregory had said, "I do like how you look sprawled on the ground, little brother." And his eyes had burned as if there was a drawn sword between them.

"What the hell do you think this will accomplish, Gregory?" Terrence demanded, sitting up and bracing himself on his hands.

"*This*, getting you out of the way, will get my throne back," Gregory said, voice low and hard. "You thought you could take what was mine, but I'm proving you couldn't hold onto a throne even if you had one."

"You're proving you'd be a terrible king," Terrence threw back, too angry to bother with the care and diplomacy that usually came so automatically around his family.

Gregory only grinned at him. "I don't think Father will see it that way, do you? Now sit there and relax. I couldn't resist coming to see you, but I have a challenge to get to. I have to go rescue the Princess Behind Thorns." Then his grin had turned coarse. "I'm looking forward to finding out how good your princess really is."

Terrence had already launched himself towards Gregory. One hand closed on his brother's shirt while he threw a punch with the other. Gregory jerked back and only a glancing blow hit his jaw but it was something. Terrence was off-balance, unsteady on his feet, but he hung onto Gregory's shirt and pulled him down with him when he fell.

They hadn't brawled seriously in years. Every recent fight had been swords or other weapons, a test of skill against each other. This was different. This was bare-handed and haphazard, fueled by rage instead of thought. They rolled across the small tower room, crashing into boxes. Terrence was barely aware of Gregory's fists hitting him, intent on making his own blows land.

For a moment, Gregory held the better position, pinning him down, lifting one fist to strike. He was taller and heavier, but for once, he wasn't angrier. Terrence got one foot into position to sweep Gregory's knee out from under him, shoving up at the same time. Gregory fell sideways, cursing, and Terrence followed the advantage to land on top of him, knees pinning his chest. Gregory was trying to hit his face but Terrence had his hands around his throat and in just—another—moment –

Hands grabbed him, hauled him backwards, and he found himself held between two guards. Gregory's guards, the guards who had come with him, the guards he had forgotten about in his own stupid, unthinking rage—

Gregory got to his feet, brushing himself off. "Well, little brother," he said, breathing heavy, "about time you dropped the saint act."

Terrence strained against the guards' hold, if he could just—he had been so close—

Gregory hit him, snapping his head to the side, and while he was still dizzy from the blow the guards tossed him into the back corner, crashing into a pile of boxes. He struggled out, flung himself towards the door, but it had already slammed shut behind Gregory and the guards, leaving him nothing to hit but the wooden panel.

"Are you too afraid to fight me?" he shouted after Gregory, because maybe, if he could make his brother angry enough…

"No, but I have a princess to go claim," Gregory said, and laughed. "Don't worry, I might let you have her sometimes. When I'm feeling bored with her."

The laughter had trailed Gregory all the way out, and Terrence had been left pressed against the wooden door, pounding his fists against the unyielding wood until his hands ached.

Half the morning had passed since then. It felt like an eternity, and also like it was rushing by too quickly—because he was *still here*, he had accomplished nothing, and all too soon it would be too late. He had tried and failed to break down the door, the window was far too small to climb out of, the door's hinges were on the far side so he couldn't do anything with that, giving orders and offering bribes to the guards both proved equally ineffective…*nothing was working*.

If he had only moved a little faster, if the guards hadn't stepped in so quickly—what? He was—mostly sure he wouldn't have killed Gregory. He shouldn't have even bothered with trying to prove he could beat Gregory in a fight—although, he *had* been winning—he should have concentrated on getting past him and out the door. But he hadn't and he was here and he *couldn't get out.*

He could hear the cheers from the crowd, a distant roar. It was an agonizing, useless piece of information, his breath catching every time they reached to a new height, because *something* was happening—

but what? When would it be over, and any chance of fixing this missed?

He didn't bother demanding answers from the two guards outside the door. They wouldn't be able to answer the questions he cared about.

He had tried hunting through the boxes cluttering up the tower. This wasn't supposed to be a prison cell, it was a gods-damned storage room, which in some way made the whole business even more humiliating and infuriating. And frustrating, because every box might be useful, and yet none of them were. No one was storing swords or lockpicks up here. It was mostly blankets and old clothes, which might have helped if he needed a makeshift rope, if the window had been big enough to climb out of, but as he had already determined, it wasn't. That didn't stop him from testing it again, but it still wasn't.

He searched and he paced and he cursed Gregory and he cursed himself.

What was happening in the challenge? What was happening to Rose?

What was she thinking, that he wasn't there?

He hadn't told her enough that no price was too high for her, that he would do anything for her.

Which sounded nice, but when it came down to it, he couldn't even get out of a locked room.

He sank down onto one of the larger trunks, held his head in his hands. It still ached, along with a lot of new aches from fighting Gregory, but those were far down his priority list of problems.

Rose pretty well occupied the entire list, in fact.

He was failing her. He had promised her she wouldn't end up married to a cruel man who would hurt her. He could remember how she had shivered when she had said she feared that, and before that how she had looked at him when he first came into the garden, eyes wide and frightened. And now her worst fear was on the brink of happening.

Would it even matter that she was already his wife? If Gregory succeeded at the challenge in front of thousands of witnesses... Yesterday he would have told himself that obviously the council would uphold their marriage, wouldn't force Rose into a life she didn't want.

After today's betrayals, he felt all too sure that the council, and his father, would give Rose to Gregory.

And Gregory would hurt her, in ways Terrence couldn't even imagine.

And some he could, which was enough to turn his stomach and send him to pacing again, back and forth in a space too small for more than a few strides, his anger and his fears only increasing with every turn.

Breathing as hard as though he'd been running, he pushed up the sleeve of his shirt, pressed his palm over his lioness tattoo. He had no words; he could only *feel* a prayer that was one desperate throb of pain and need, filling his whole being.

He squeezed his eyes shut, fell back onto the trunk, hand locked around his own arm. If Mariqwe responded to passion, he was feeling it, in every shade.

The response, if it was one, was small and quiet, a rustling sound from one corner of the room. Terrence's eyes snapped open, his gaze went that way—just in time to see a furry black face with brilliant green eyes pop up over the boxes.

Terrence gaped at the kitten. "You can't—that's not possible…" He surged to his feet, went to look behind the boxes. A small drain was set in the floor, leading down into the rest of the castle. Something of an explanation, but for the cat to have found his way here was still…

Emerald Eyes trotted over to him, rubbed his head against Terrence's leg. "It's nice to see you too," he said numbly. But what good did it do, really? A kitten wasn't an answer he had expected, wasn't an answer that solved anything. If he could even claim the cat's presence as divine intervention.

Emerald Eyes emitted a muffled meow, then spat out something he'd been holding in his mouth, something that landed on the stone floor with a clink.

It was a key.

Terrence looked from the kitten to his tattoo and then back to the key.

"Oh, you clever cat," he breathed. It was, in fact, far too clever for any cat he'd ever known or even heard of. Either Mariqwe was giving him a miracle, or the niggling feeling he'd had that there was something odd about Rose's kittens was correct. Or both.

It didn't matter right now. He snatched up the key, advanced to the door. And then he paused, stooped to pick up a board from a box he'd kicked apart earlier. It wasn't much of a weapon, but it was the best one he could formulate. It was about the length of a sword, heavy and solid. That would have to be enough for the guards outside. They'd be better armed, but they couldn't possibly care as much.

"Stay back for now," he warned the kitten, then wondered if he could actually understand. Not the time for that either.

He slid the key into the lock, unsurprised that it fit, then turned it slowly, trying to make this as silent as possible. Through the tiny window in the door he could see that the guards were still facing away, standing with stances relaxed.

A tiny click as the lock gave way—no reaction from the guards. He dropped the key into a pocket, lifted his makeshift weapon, then shoved the door open as hard as he could.

The swinging door connected solidly with one guard's back, sending him stumbling forward with a curse. Before the man could find his balance again, Terrence got a swing in with his board, striking his head and shoulder and sending him crashing to the ground.

It only took seconds but it still gave the other guard enough time to back away, drawing his sword and turning to face him. Terrence got the board up barely in time to block the guard's first strike. They circled in the small space, and he knew if this went on for long he didn't have a chance—a sword was a much more dangerous weapon, and though he could block blows, splinters were already flying. The board wouldn't last for long.

"Hey!" the guard yelled towards the stairs. "We need help up here!"

He had even less time if reinforcements were coming. The next block brought them into a tighter clinch and Terrence saw his moment, hooking his foot around the guard's ankle in the same move Gregory had used on him the day before. The guard went down hard and Terrence raised his board—but the guard's eyes were already rolling back, head having struck the stone floor.

Terrence dropped the board, snatching up the guard's sword even as footsteps sounded on the stairs. He turned that way. At least he was better armed, but if they outnumbered him too badly—

He blinked as the owner of the footsteps came into view. "Henry?"

The other man looked relieved and smug at once. "I knew there had to be a reason guards were stationed at the bottom of this tower."

"Good to see you too," Terrence said, and then he was running for the stairs. Out of the corner of his eye he saw the black kitten dart along beside him. "What's happening in the challenge?" he threw over his shoulder as he passed Henry.

"I don't know," Henry said from a step behind him, "I've been looking for you all morning. I took care of the two guards at the bottom, in case you were wondering. You're welcome."

"Thank you," Terrence said, and took the stairs two at a time.

Maybe he wouldn't completely fail Rose after all.

Chapter Thirty-Six: Rose

Rose's hands started to shake as soon as she saw Gregory, as soon as she heard his voice. She had *expected* him, and yet...and yet... She didn't take in everything he said to the crowd, something about the good of the country and his broken heart and past betrayals and his duty. Some back corner of her mind noted that Henry had been right, that they were already prepared to spin the story of the not-quite-unmarried-yet prince rescuing the princess.

Mostly, she could only think that she wanted Terrence, she wanted Terrence so badly, and that she did not want to belong to this horrible man whose last wife had always been afraid. And Terrence wasn't here, so she had to find some way out of this.

They put on a good show, when Gregory fought the guards. He defended against two, then three, then four at once. Two guards fell to the ground over the course of the fight and Rose couldn't tell if that was only an act. Gregory broke past the last two, and they retreated back to their original places in the circle to let him continue. Of course. He was always intended to continue.

For one wild moment as he approached the thorn hedge, she thought perhaps this would stop him. The wall of thorns around her garden had protected her for a hundred years, had never let any of those terrifying men from before come through to claim her.

But these weren't the same thorns, and if it had ever mattered to the other ones what she had felt, she had no reason to think this spell was the same. No reason to think Xevrix would so directly defy the king, to stop the clearly chosen champion from advancing.

Gregory charged straight for the brambles, sword raised, slashed at the branches. The hedge shuddered—but didn't fight back. He slashed and cut and hacked his way through, the branches moving just enough to remind everyone they were enchanted, but not enough to harm him or prevent him from continuing.

Rose looked for Xevrix in the king's pavilion, but she was much too far away to read the enchantress' face. Probably everyone was too far away to read her own expression, to see any sign of the way her heart was pounding, the way her mind was skittering around for some escape.

Gregory was past the hedge now, the branches reweaving to fill the gap he had cut, and the crowd went wild as he strode onward. *This* was what they had all come to see, and it didn't seem to matter that it was the wrong prince. Maybe it did to some, but it didn't matter enough to enough of the crowd to make any difference. They were too caught up in the drama and the excitement of the moment, in the story the king was so carefully orchestrating.

Only the lions as a barrier now, and Rose had no real hope that they would achieve more than the other obstacles had. Gregory half-jumped, half-slid down into the moat, sword raised.

Something was definitely wrong with the lions, as the lioness didn't even rise and the male lion strolled toward Gregory with only a lazy curiosity. It probably looked well enough from a distance—a man with a sword approaches lions, what difference did the details make? From Rose's view, it was a painfully one-sided fight.

Gregory waved his sword and circled the lion and made the thing look something like a contest. He jabbed and he stabbed and the lion took far more goading than he should have before he finally started tossing his head, started growling and raising his paws to fight back.

Before the lion even got half-started, before he shook himself into anything like a lion's normal fighting spirit, Gregory leapt forward and made an expert thrust deep into the lion's chest. Rose flinched in sympathy, stomach rolling with nausea. There was a spray of blood and one dying roar as the lion slumped over. Only then did the lioness finally stir, finally wander over to investigate what had happened to her mate.

Rose stared at the lions for a few seconds too long, suddenly realized she hadn't been watching Gregory—he was already climbing out of the moat, up onto the much too small space where she stood. There was blood on his hands and a grin on his face, and he looked at Rose with the same hungry, possessive leer she had seen on so many champions' faces before. With the same smile, the same fire in his eyes, from that day in her rooms. And now he was victorious and had come to claim her.

She backed away as he approached, heart racing, but she had nowhere to go, no space to retreat.

"Got you now, princess," Gregory said, words just reaching her through the cheers of the crowd. "You and the throne both. You were always too valuable for Terrence to own anyway."

"What did you do to him?" Rose asked, heart in her throat.

"Doesn't matter, because you belong to me now. All nice and official."

He seized her by the arms, smearing blood on her white dress, and dragged her towards him, Silvertips leaping away. She strained to pull away from him but it was no use, he was so much stronger. His face filled her vision, blotting out everything else, and—were those bruises on his neck? There was another by his eye, and they didn't seem like the kind of injury you'd get in a swordfight—then he was crushing her against him and kissing her, mouth hard and painful on hers. She squirmed and twisted, but his grip was too tight to escape, his heavy silver signet ring digging into her arm.

At last he let go, wrapped one arm around her to imprison her against his side, used the other to wave at the crowd for quiet.

"My people," he called, "I have defeated the challenge to claim the hand of the Princess Behind Thorns."

Cheers. The mob cheered.

But in another moment the cheers were going to stop, because they would want to hear what Prince Gregory had to say next, and for all her terror and horror, some quiet, strategic corner of her mind told Rose that this was her one, last chance. She waited until the cheers were dying away again, until she felt Gregory inhale for his next pronouncement, and spoke first.

"I cannot marry you, Prince Gregory," she called. Her voice rang out loud and true through the arena and there was sudden, complete silence. Maybe this wasn't worth anything without Terrence here to back her up, without Rupin and his forms and papers and legal understanding. But she had to do *something*.

"What do you think you're doing?" Gregory growled, grip tightening painfully on her arm.

He'd punish her for this later, if he could. She knew that with blinding, horrible clarity. But right now they were in front of thousands of people, so how much could he do to her? For just this moment she still had her chance. So she ignored him, ignored the throb in her arm, announced, "I cannot marry you, because I am already married to Prince Terrence."

She heard the gasps of the crowd, and it was the best thing she'd heard all day, because it meant she might win them after all. People loved a good twist in the story.

"That's impossible," Gregory snarled, face distorted in an expression of fury that only she was close enough to see.

"We were married two days ago," she continued. "I have the papers and witnesses who will confirm it." At least, she hoped she could get the papers, hoped she could find her witnesses.

Gregory's expression smoothed, eyes calculating. Then he backed away a step, spread his arms out as though inviting the crowd into the conversation. "You *say* you're married to my brother. But he didn't even show up today to claim you!"

"Because you locked me up this morning!" a shout came from the edge of the arena.

Rose's knees went suddenly weak and her eyes burned even before she turned to look for him—and there, there Terrence was *at last*, coming through the Royal Entrance with Henry behind him. She couldn't see from here if he was all right, she wanted to run and throw herself onto him, she was so, so happy to see him alive that she almost believed she could fly if she tried—

Gregory's hand closed on her arm with a bruising grip, yanking her around to face him. "This doesn't change anything. I defeated the challenge. You belong to *me*."

Rose glared at him, and put all of her fear and her fury into one word. "*Never*."

Something cracked in Gregory's expression. There was one fleeting instant of pain, and then it disappeared behind a towering rage that turned his face monstrous.

"You were supposed to already be dead," he spat, grabbing her other shoulder and shaking her hard. "You were never supposed to come back. *I* was the heir. You're ruining everything!"

Her teeth clacked together and her neck ached as he shook her and she could feel Silvertips trying to scramble up her dress with worried mews.

"You should have stayed dead," Gregory said, and shoved.

She stumbled back, lost her footing on the edge of the pit, stomach dropping in instinctive terror. She grabbed blindly and felt her fingers close on Gregory's shirt. It was only for a moment though, not enough to stop what was happening—fabric slipped between her fingers, her feet couldn't find purchase, and she fell backwards. And fell. And fell.

It all seemed to happen strangely slowly, though it couldn't have been more than a second or two. Yet she had time to realize, to understand that she had gone off the edge of the plateau, was falling into the moat, would probably be dead when she hit the ground. She had time to look up at Gregory standing above her, his face twisted into a hideous expression of fury and satisfaction. It was worse because he resembled Terrence so much, as if he had turned into some horrible, twisted version of the man she loved.

She had time to see the ground crumble as Gregory stood too close to the edge—had she pulled him forward, just a little, when she grabbed his shirt? She had time to see his expression turn into one of horror as he struggled to regain his footing.

Then she had fallen far enough that the angle had changed and all she could see was the blue sky overhead, and she was glad, glad, *glad* that Terrence was still alive, and she hoped that Elena would take care of him, and that he wouldn't ever regret rescuing the princess trapped behind the thorns.

And then she landed.

She landed on something soft and furry that gave beneath her, so that she landed hard enough to knock the breath from her lungs but not any harder than that.

Almost simultaneously, Silvertips scrambled onto her lap and she realized she had landed on the dead lion, on its outstretched side.

She was sure she'd have bruises, but at least she was still alive. She caught Silvertips with one hand and scrambled off of the lion, because this was no position for facing anything. She struggled to force air back into her burning lungs, a pain in one hip from how she had landed. Her feet had barely touched the dirt when she saw Gregory. He seemed to have slid down the side of the moat, ending up only a few feet away. His gaze locked with hers, his face still twisted with hatred.

Her heart was already pounding, breath still shallow, as she stumbled backwards, past the dead lion's paws, trying to put some distance between herself and Gregory. If she was going to fall into a pit, couldn't she at least get away from *him* in the process?

He shoved up to his feet, took a step towards her—and his face twisted in a new way as one leg buckled beneath him. For a moment she felt a surge of relief, because if he had hurt his leg, if he couldn't walk, surely she could evade him long enough for help to get here. *Was* help coming, though, or would the king's guards stop Terrence, stop anyone else—

Gregory grimaced, took another step, and this time he stayed upright and kept coming. Injured, but not badly enough, and she could try to run but she wasn't that steady on her feet herself, didn't know how much her sore hip would let her run, and he still had a sword—her mind spun and she wished she had a weapon, anything—

"It's over," she managed to gasp, with what little air she had. "You can't change anything now."

"I can still kill you," Gregory growled, advancing as she retreated.

If he got closer, maybe if she kicked his injured leg—and then she saw movement behind him.

The lioness. She had completely forgotten about the lioness, who was now emerging around the curve of the moat, padding silently up behind Gregory. The feline looked past him towards Rose, gazes meeting for just a moment, and then the big cat swung her attention towards Gregory again.

Rose opened her mouth to—was she going to warn him? Did she want to?

There wasn't time anyway, the lioness springing forward in one bound, paws outstretched. She landed on Gregory's back, bearing him down with a thud, claws in his shoulders. He only managed one muffled shout before the lioness' teeth closed on his neck.

Rose flinched, looked away. She dragged in a breath, looked back, saw a spreading puddle of blood. She hadn't seen the blood, for all those champions in the thorns, and those had all taken so much longer… She gritted her teeth, began to edge farther away, because was the lioness going to stop with Gregory or—

The big cat's head lifted, blood on her mouth, gaze fixing on Rose again.

She froze. Should she try to run? Should she stay still? The lioness was watching her already, she couldn't hide, but lions chased their prey, didn't they, so running might only make things worse…

She clutched Silvertips to her chest, backed up one careful step, then another. She bumped back against the outer side of the moat. If she could only get out of here—the side was high, but not perfectly vertical, but her dress was so *heavy*. Keeping her gaze still on the lioness, she pushed Silvertips up onto her shoulder and bent down to tear the skirt of her dress away. The beads were weighing the dress down but the fabric was light and thin, tearing easily, and she might, she just might—

The lioness moved away from Gregory, padded closer and closer, and Rose turned to press her back against the dirt side of the moat, as though she could somehow get out of the way. The lioness kept on advancing until her enormous face was mere inches away, until her wide whiskers nearly brushed Rose's cheeks. And she sniffed.

Rose knew cats. She knew how cats investigated something they weren't sure about. And that was exactly what this lioness was doing. She hadn't even hesitated with Gregory, but this—was different.

"Nice kitty," she breathed. "You don't want to hurt me. I've always been kind to cats. Always."

Silvertips popped her head out from behind Rose's neck, craned her tiny face up towards the lioness and meowed.

The lioness rumbled in what seemed to be a response—but was it the angry kind of rumble or not?

The crowd had gone on shouting all this while, but a different sound was emerging from the ongoing background roar.

It was her name. It was Terrence, shouting her name and getting closer.

Chapter Thirty-Seven: Terrence

Terrence thought his heart would stop when Rose plummeted over the edge of the moat—when Gregory *pushed* her over the edge. How deep was it, how hard would she land?

He had to get there—he had to reach her—he hadn't thought he could want anything more than he had wanted to get out of that tower, but if Rose was lying at the bottom of that moat, injured or—dead—

He had no space to feel anything at all when Gregory, too, slipped off the edge.

The crowd was fading from his awareness, all he could see was the path to Rose and the obstacles in the way. He had outpaced Henry and Emerald Eyes both, but he had no time to wait.

The guards were still circled and the nearest lifted their weapons as he ran towards them. He didn't have *time* for this! He raised the sword he had taken from the tower guard, blocked the first blow aimed at him, thrust and parried and dodged, fighting on pure instinct and muscle memory. Three guards at once tried to stop him, worse odds than in the tower but at least he had a sword now and *he had to get to Rose*—his sword locked with one of the guard's swords, bringing his face close to the other man's.

"*Get out of my way,*" Terrence growled, and shoved. The guard stumbled back and that gave him enough opening to push forward, past the guards, to run across the sand of the combat grounds.

If the guards were following, they were slow enough to ignore. More important was the hedge of thorns in front of him. It wasn't as impressive as the original one, but it still reached up above his head, the branches thick and the thorns long.

"All right," he said softly, sheathing his sword. He couldn't leave it behind this time, he didn't know what he had to deal with on the other side, so this had better be good enough. He spread his empty hands to either side. "Let me through."

He was going to collide straight into thorns at any second but he kept going forward. He had walked through more impressive thorns than these, and that had only been for the Princess Behind Thorns, not for Rose.

He held his breath, took one more step—at the last possible moment, the branches shivered, twisted. Creaking, groaning, they rearranged to form a narrow archway.

He ducked through, and now there was nothing between him and the moat. "Rose!" He ran, drawing his sword again as he went. Could she hear him? Could she answer him? If she was hurt, if she was unconscious—would it do any good at all if he kissed her? *"Rose*!"

He reached the brink of the moat and slid down the steep dirt side. He landed jarringly on his feet, even with knees bending to absorb the impact.

And there she was, only a few yards away, standing against the side of the moat. With a bloody lioness staring her in the face.

His breath hitched in his chest. Those claws, those teeth—and Rose seemed so small, so vulnerable in her torn, bloodied white dress. One lock of hair had fallen out of the complicated mass on her head, was lying golden and bright against her pale cheek.

He slowly lifted his sword. How could he fight a lioness who could bat Rose aside with one big paw? How could he…

"It's all right," Rose breathed, waving a hand at him, a clear gesture to stay where he was. The lioness lowered her head to sniff at Rose's skirt. "I…think it's all right. Cats like me."

Cats liked her? This was an enormous lioness, not a house cat, a lioness with *blood* on her mouth, and how was he supposed to just stand here and watch while she decided whether to eat his wife—the lioness gave a low, throaty rumble and Terrence lifted his sword higher because he *had* to do something—and then Silvertips (how had *Silvertips* gotten here?) meowed back at the lioness from her perch on Rose's shoulder.

The big cat turned away. She padded off to drop down next to the dead lion Terrence hadn't given a single glance to.

Rose stepped sideways, stumbled towards him, and he sheathed his sword in time to catch her. She was warm and alive and he pulled her against him, clutched her to him as her arms crept around him, her face pressed to his neck. Silvertips mewed reprovingly and jumped away, and Terrence kissed Rose's hair.

Whose blood was on her dress? Should he even be holding her this tightly—but she was holding onto him too, and he couldn't seem to let go, holding her so close that he could feel his mother's ring pressing into his chest. "Are you hurt? When you fell—or the lioness—"

"I'm all right, my Terrence," she whispered.

A long, shuddering breath escaped him and his eyes grew hot. "Oh gods, I thought she was going to kill you," he murmured, breath still coming hard. "I thought I was going to watch her kill you."

"I was afraid you were already dead," Rose said, her fingers clenching in the folds of his shirt. "When you weren't here for the challenge."

He groaned, somehow held her even tighter. "I'm sorry, love, I'm so sorry—Gregory's men jumped me this morning, I only just got out and Henry and I ran straight here…"

He hadn't thought about Gregory at all, but now he remembered—he looked past Rose, looked towards the two lions, the alive one and the dead one, and he saw Gregory lying beyond the dead lion. He took in the pool of blood and closed his eyes.

He had had his hands around Gregory's neck just hours earlier, but he hadn't—he hadn't really wanted—he had been so angry with him, was *still* so angry with him, but…

"We have to get out of here," Rose said after another moment, and pulled away from him. "We have to end all this."

Terrence had not thought beyond getting to Rose, holding Rose, and he still wanted to be doing that second one, but she was right, the lioness could change her mind. Plus the rest of the world was filtering back into his consciousness, the roar of the crowd, the guards finally appearing on the scene at another point around the moat. They were lowering planks down as a ramp.

"If I pretend to faint, can you carry me out of here?" Rose asked.

Despite everything, Terrence found himself grinning. "You're all right. I can do *anything* right now."

"The crowd's going to love this," she said, and slumped against him.

He lifted her up, held her against his chest, remembered when he had carried her out of the council room. This time, she wrapped her fingers around the fabric of his shirt, just above his heart.

"Come on, cat," he said to Silvertips, who obligingly followed along next to him.

He carried her up the ramp, out of the moat, and the crowd's noise rose to a deafening level. There were a half dozen openings in the thorn barrier now, the magic apparently having let the guards through now that the challenge was done. He carried Rose out through one of the gaps now, setting her back on her feet once they were beyond the bramble hedge. Emerald Eyes came scampering up to dart around their feet and Terrence didn't even question that at this point. He kept one arm around Rose's waist, kept his gaze on her as she looked out at the crowd, lifted one hand to wave.

He was still taken by surprise when she turned back towards him, caught him by the shoulders, and kissed him.

The cheering of the crowd rose to new levels, but Terrence was only distantly aware of that. Because her lips were warm and soft on his, and he had his arms around her again, and it didn't matter if she had kissed him to impress the crowd, what mattered was that she was his, and nothing and no one was going to change that.

He held her close, let his lips drift across her cheek, to her ear, and said, too softly for all the thousands of people watching to hear, "I love you so much."

And she whispered back, "I love you too," just for him.

Chapter Thirty-Eight: Rose

In the days that followed, the legend spread faster than enchanted thorns and the ballads practically wrote themselves. How the evil prince tried to steal, and then to kill, the Princess Behind Thorns. How the good prince, her true love, rushed to save her. Terrence had made a strong impression on the crowd, fighting the guards, passing through the thorns and jumping into the moat, calling Rose's name. In most of the ballads he slayed the lioness before carrying her to safety. There were many verses written about the love of the prince and princess; Rose kissing Terrence had also impressed people. The ballads ended with the prince and princess riding off together, blessed with True Love, to live happily ever after.

The truth, of course, was more complicated. For one thing, Rose still didn't know how to ride a horse.

Also, they had to confront the king first.

At first it seemed as though the cheering of the crowds would go on forever. Rose considered pretending to faint again, if that would give them an excuse to leave the arena. It wasn't that she didn't appreciate the people's support, or what it would mean for them—but the sun was so bright and she was so tired, she was starting to be conscious of all the places she ached from Gregory grabbing her, from falling into the moat, and she knew the work of the day wasn't over yet.

It was, in a way, Gregory who ended things. The guards who had gone into the moat came out again, carrying the prince's body. It was apparent enough to everyone, either from the way the body lay on the makeshift stretcher of planks, or the way no one was running for a healer, or perhaps from the blood, that he was dead. A hush replaced the former cheers.

In that hush, King Elgin spoke. He didn't leave his place in the royal pavilion, though his gaze seemed to be towards his son. Gregory, not Terrence. His voice rang out, "It would appear the Princess Behind Thorns has taken one final victim. And so the curse ends at last."

It was so…expected, so much so that Rose didn't even flinch. Of course they would blame her, and why not? Didn't she blame herself for all the other champions? It wasn't only her choices that had brought their deaths, Gregory's perhaps least of all. But it had all been about her somehow.

And there had been that moment, when she grabbed Gregory's shirt, maybe pulled him closer to the edge. Had that made any difference, mattered at all in what had happened next?

Terrence, one arm around her waist, stiffened beside her. She looked up and saw his mouth was set in a hard line, eyes narrowing.

She nudged him with her shoulder. "Don't argue with him," she said in a low voice. "Not here in front of everyone." Even as she said it, she recognized that something had changed for Terrence since yesterday, if she felt the need to say it.

They'd have a great deal to say to the king, very soon. But that wasn't a conversation to have in front of a roaring crowd. Insisting on their marriage, on their right to inherit, would only be made harder if they stole the king's pride in the process. And she didn't want to see what King Elgin would do if they cornered him like that.

Terrence let out a breath, shoulders dropping a little, and Rose felt reassured that he wasn't going to do anything rash. She frowned, though, as she looked at Terrence's face. She wanted to ask about the cut by his lip, the bruise forming by one eye –what had happened to him this morning?—but this wasn't the time for that either.

The moment passed, and the king turned to leave. The royal pavilion emptied behind him, Edward and Tyler and the other nobility of the court, the visiting dignitaries and the royal enchanters and all the rest following behind the king. Xevrix, in her vivid red cloak, was one of the last to go, and Rose could feel the enchantress' gaze on her for a long moment before the woman finally turned away. Terrence had come through that wall of thorns; had Xevrix done anything to help him? Where did the enchantress' loyalties ultimately lie?

Rose bent down to pick up Silvertips, who had been frisking by her feet, needing a kitten's comfortable furriness just then. She noticed

Emerald Eyes had plopped down sitting next to Terrence, looking extremely pleased with himself.

"If you would like to return to the castle, Your Highness?" One of the guards had approached, asked the words in a diffident enough tone, with a polite inclination of his head.

Rose *did* want to go back to the castle, very much, but she felt a chill of unease despite the sun when she looked around and realized that they were surrounded by guards. They were all at a polite distance, all looking very inoffensive, and yet… "Wait," she said in an undertone, fingers tightening on Terrence's arm, "they were all part of the challenge."

And what would happen to her and Terrence, if they went away from the eyes of the crowd in the company of the men the king had chosen for his spectacle? If they disappeared with men the king trusted.

Terrence's brow furrowed, so at least she didn't have to explain the problem to him. "If we…there must be…"

And then Rose saw that a half-dozen more guards were coming up at a rapid pace, but this group had Elena and Henry with them. The leader—Morgan, she remembered him from the trip to the market—shouldered past the one who had spoken.

"Go handle the crowd," Morgan ordered brusquely. "We'll take care of the prince and princess."

The first guard looked as though he wanted to argue, but there is such a thing as rank among the guards, and besides, the ones with Morgan had already streamed in to surround Rose and Terrence in a closer circle. Rose sought out Elena's gaze across the group, and received a tight nod in response.

"Thank you so much," Rose said quickly, "I *would* like to go in." Now to get out of here before the king's guards could rally a new plan together.

They escaped the arena, escaped the hot sun into the shaded tunnel of the exit, and the noise of the crowd cut noticeably too.

Elena pushed through the guards, to envelop first Terrence and then Rose in a hug, accompanied by a rapid flurry of words. "Are you both all right? I was so worried, I thought Henry would never find you—and Rose, when you went into that moat, I was so sure—I can't believe you're both walking away from this, it was just..."

"She's glad you're all right," Henry said, taking Elena's arm and steering her so they could resume walking.

"They're holding an emergency council meeting," Elena resumed. "I was in the royal pavilion; I heard the king say it as he was leaving."

Rose hadn't been able to see Elena in the pavilion, but she had been so far away, and focused on the king and those closest to him. The rest had blurred together.

Terrence dragged a hand over his face. "They're holding a meeting right now? They think *now* is the time?"

"Now is the best time," Rose said, surprised by how clearly her mind seemed to be working. It was easier to think now that she didn't have the crowd's roar in her ears. "He's probably hoping we won't come, but if we do, we're never going to be in a better position." The king was never going to be able to create a better story than the one they'd just shown to the crowd.

"Do you want to at least...change clothes?" Terrence asked doubtfully.

She glanced down at her torn white dress, the lion's blood still on her sleeves, and smiled. "No. Makes me look dangerous, don't you think?"

"Terrifying, love," he said, and kissed her cheek. It sounded like a compliment.

"Rupin is going to make an announcement," Elena volunteered. "You know he's been looking into the inheritance laws, and he found something last night..." She frowned, looking thoughtful. "No, maybe it's better if you don't know. Genuine surprise might play better."

"Don't you think you're overthinking this?" Terrence said, sounding exasperated. "Whatever it is."

Elena met Rose's gaze, and an expression of perfect understanding passed between them. You *couldn't* overthink court politics. "Just get General Graybourne on your side," Elena resumed, "and the rest should fall into place. And it will be good, it really will. And Terrence? Terrence, look at me."

He had been looking at Rose, but he turned towards Elena. "What is it?"

"Think about all the good things you want to do in the country, all right? Keep that in mind."

"You are being really ridiculously mysterious—"

"I'm sure she has her reasons," Rose interrupted, and squeezed Terrence's hand. "And who else can we trust?"

He smiled at that. "Point taken."

Elena beamed. "Just wait. And good luck!"

Chapter Thirty-Nine: Terrence

The council room had never been so tense before in Terrence's memory. All the council was already gathered when he and Rose arrived.

And the king. His father was there too.

For the first time, the council rose respectfully to their feet when Terrence and Rose entered, though some stood more quickly than others. Only the king remained seated, staring at the table in front of him.

The seating had changed too. The only two empty chairs were side by side at the far end of the table. It was the foot—or the head, depending on perspective. Terrence wondered who had orchestrated that. They sat down, and with a shuffling of chairs everyone else did too. Rose's two kittens scrambled up into her lap, and no one commented on them today.

Terrence studied the faces at the table. Lords Bellham, Chapman, Ratliff and Gastrell looked furious, Lord Elffire nervous. Lords Dawson and Camden, while solemn enough, seemed quietly pleased behind their eyes. The priests looked troubled, the head enchanter was frowning, and General Graybourne seemed thoughtful. No one was visibly grief-stricken about Gregory, something that seemed wrong and sad and yet…somewhere, deep down, Terrence knew it wasn't all that surprising to him either. He would have said that Gregory was popular—but it was a kind of impersonal popularity. Maybe that was why the idea of someday catching up to him had never seemed wholly impossible, if perhaps out of his own inadequate reach. If he could do the things Gregory did, achieve the position Gregory had, finally beat Gregory in a swordfight…Gregory's popularity was something of the mind, not the heart, and minds are comparatively changeable.

Apparently he was never going to beat Gregory in a swordfight now, and that seemed as wrong as anything else.

He knew perfectly well that all this searching of faces, all this philosophizing and reflection, was just to avoid looking at the face most directly in his line of vision, at the opposite end of the table. To avoid looking at his father.

Tyler was sitting on his father's right, Edward on his left, and Terrence felt every inch of the distance between himself and the rest of his family. His mother was gone, Gregory was gone, and it was hard to believe there could be much space left for him in the family that remained. Not after the last few days.

Not after the choices he had made, or the things that had happened.

His mother would have hated it, hated an irrevocable break in the family—but maybe she would have understand why there had been no other way.

He felt Rose's hand on his knee, reached down to cover it with his own, and took a breath. He couldn't have done anything differently. He knew, as painful as the knowledge was, that he wouldn't change it if he could. Whatever the consequences.

He finally—though really it had probably been less than a minute since they sat down—looked directly at his father. His father wasn't looking at him or at anyone, glaring down at the surface in front of him. And then, slowly, he raised his gaze to glare down the length of the table—at Rose.

"You killed my son," he said in a low voice, breaking the uneasy silence of the room.

Rose flinched, and Terrence tightened his grasp of her hand. "Gregory fell to the lioness," she said softly, even as Terrence said, "It wasn't Rose's fault."

The sore spot by his eye twinged, and it seemed impossible that Gregory could be dead, when his face still ached from his brother's fist. Other places felt stiff and painful too, starting to make themselves known now that he was finally holding still long enough to notice them. He tried to shove the awareness down, because he didn't have time for it right now.

His father's glare swung to him. "If it hadn't been for her—if *you* hadn't brought her back—none of this would have happened!"

Now Terrence flinched, because it was true, wasn't it? He wasn't sorry that he had gone in search of the Princess Behind Thorns, *couldn't* be sorry for that, and yet...none of this would have happened, if he hadn't started this chain of events. But he wasn't the only one who had made choices here. "Gregory pushed Rose," he said flatly. "He wouldn't be dead if he hadn't tried to kill Rose first."

His father brushed past that as though he hadn't even spoken. "Gregory was my heir," he spat, "my first born, and now he's *dead*."

"He was the future of this country," Lord Bellham spoke up in blustering tones, "and I for one feel—"

"Gregory was going to destroy this country and we all know it," Lord Dawson interrupted. "Yes, you do too, you just won't admit it because his reign would have been good for *you*. I'm sorry the man is dead, but I'm not sorry he'll never sit on the throne. I'm glad we got through that ridiculous challenge with Terrence as heir, and I don't mind admitting it."

"If I may say a word on that subject?" Rupin put in smoothly, and Terrence remembered for the first time in some minutes that Elena had promised something unexpected. Rupin, he now saw, seemed to have an air of suppressed excitement about him.

No one told him to proceed, but no one stopped him either. Rupin smiled, spreading papers on the table in front of him. Some were old and yellowed, glimpses of calligraphed script and ribboned seals visible.

"I have been researching the question of the Princess Behind Thorns and her impact on the succession since Princess Rose Amelia's return to court," Rupin continued, voice taking on the scholarly tone it often did when he was about to lecture on legal matters. "Most of the references on the subject are documents written over the past several decades, many of them making reference for their basis to earlier decrees. The records from the time of her enchantment are considerably confused, a predictable byproduct of the chaos of the time. Many documents have been lost or presumed lost, somewhere in the depths of the royal library. These are what I have been searching for—and have finally found."

"We all know she has a claim as heir to the throne," the king snapped irritably. "What is your point?"

Rupin raised a finger. "That it is not precisely accurate to say she has a claim to *the throne*. Later records do consistently state it in that manner, that the princess and her rescuer have the right to claim position as heirs and eventual rulers of Avala. She has been named in the coronation day ceremonies as heir for decades, but that is tradition only, not a legal statement. And I have found the original, first decree regarding the subject, which is a legal document still valid today. The wording does not say that the princess is heir to the *throne of Avala*, but rather heir to the throne of King Randolph II, the princess' father."

There was a shifting at the table—General Graybourne stopped drumming his fingers on the table, Lord Ratliff looked troubled, the high priests exchanged glances. Everyone else looked confused. Terrence himself was trying to parse the distinction. Heir to the throne or heir to a particular king's throne, the difference was…he inhaled suddenly, because he thought he saw where Rupin was going. But that couldn't be right.

"What is your *point*?" King Elgin growled again.

"King Randolph II is dead," Rupin said bluntly. "Has been for decades. And *his* heir is his daughter. We have been wrong to regard the princess and her husband as heirs and future rulers. They are, legally and by official decree, the rightful, *current* king and queen."

Dead silence at the table, and then gazes swung towards Terrence and Rose.

Rose's face was calm, but her grip on his hand beneath the table was tight, and he thought he could see thoughts racing behind her eyes. "How remarkable," she murmured.

For himself, he doubted he looked so calm. He didn't feel it. He felt—vaguely guilty, somehow. "I didn't—that is, I never…" The country. Elena had told him to think about all the plans he had for the country and *this* is what she had meant. She had known he'd be right here, in this spot, instinctively feeling he ought to decline the whole thing, because—taking his father's throne, he had never—but there *were* all those plans for the country. Land and education and diplomatic relations with their neighbors and he had some ideas about the tax system and they hadn't held an open court for petitions in two years and he wanted to start those again and…there were so many things. And if he was king now, if he and Rose ruled *now*, not ten, twenty, thirty years from now—they could do something. "…never expected to assume the throne so soon," he said carefully, "but obviously we can't deny Rose's inheritance rights."

"That decree was never intended for a situation like this!" Lord Bellham snapped. "King Randolph never intended—"

"I do not think," Rose said suddenly, "that you can presume to know my father's intentions." She smiled, and it was her sweet smile, the one she didn't mean. "I am, after all, the only person here who ever met him. And I know that he intended my rescuer to be king. He certainly would not want his decree disregarded. If we do not value the laws of our country, where does that leave us?"

"In chaos and anarchy," General Graybourne said bluntly, folding his hands before him on the table. "I don't see how this is a matter for debate. The law is the law."

And then Terrence believed this might actually happen. If the general said so, the one who the soldiers followed—because for all his ideals, Terrence knew perfectly well that the man who could command the most people with the most weapons had a great deal of influence—this might happen.

"You expect me to simply hand over my throne to these two?" King Elgin snarled, with a wild gesture towards Terrence and Rose.

"No, we are saying that it is not *your* throne to keep or to hand over," Rupin said serenely.

"They don't even know anything about governing," Lord Bellham protested, but it sounded feebler than before.

"I think we all know that Terrence knows more about it than Gregory ever did," Lord Dawson said, a triumphant gleam in his eyes.

"And it appears that we saw the will of the gods today in the youngest prince's successful defeat of the challenge and rescue of the princess," the high priest of Mariqwe said in pious tones.

The high priest of Arthian nodded gravely. “There has long been belief that the Princess Behind Thorns was the chosen of the gods to restore balance and prosperity to the country.”

Never once had Terrence heard the priest cite that particular belief before as something to take seriously. But the tide seemed to be turning.

The king appeared to see it too. “This is absurd,” he said, and his face was pale.

Terrence felt his stomach twist, fought an urge to back down, and kept his head up. It was too late for backing down now.

“Perhaps,” Edward spoke up, voice smooth and conciliatory, “we might consider the possibility of a period of transition. We would not want to throw the country into instability, of course, with a too swift change of government. After all, we have the death of the former crown prince to mourn, and a change of regime is always complicated. What if we give it a little time for a peaceful transfer of power? Our father continues to rule, Terrence and Rose can travel the country to meet more people and instill greater confidence, and then at a set date in the future, the throne passes.”

There was a considering silence around the table.

“Perhaps three months?” Rose said, and smiled sweetly again. “It has been a hundred years already.”

Edward regarded her with an expression Terrence couldn’t quite decipher. “I was going to suggest six months.”

“Nine months,” the king growled. “We’ll hold the coronation on the anniversary of the Princess Behind Thorns’ return to court, nine months from now. That ought to satisfy the crowd and their silly need for *stories*.”

There were nods around the table, some reluctant, some enthusiastic. “That settles the question, then,” General Graybourne said quietly, and the words seemed to make it irrevocable.

Terrence let out a slow breath. He might need at least nine months, just to process all of this and what it was going to mean. He looked at Rose, and wished they’d had some warning, some time to talk about this before…just before. But she looked back at him with a smile, a real smile, and he thought that one way or another, it was going to be all right.

He promised himself to do whatever he could, to make it all right for her. For her, and for everyone.

"I think we're done here," King Elgin said darkly, rising to his feet. "We can discuss the peaceful transition of power tomorrow." He turned to go, paused, and looked back to stare hard at Terrence, who narrowly managed to hold his gaze. "I suppose you'll want this."

He flung something down, something small that bounced and skittered down the length of the table to come to a halt just within arms-reach, to lie glinting in the light.

It was Gregory's silver signet ring. He had worn it for as long as Terrence could remember. It had cut Terrence's face once, years ago, and left the scar by his eyebrow. Gregory had been wearing the ring this morning, presumably had been wearing it when he died. Someone must have…taken it off.

Terrence stared at it, unmoving, until he heard the sound of the door close as his father left the room.

"Congratulations," Rupin said, picking up the signet ring and offering it to him as the rest of the council began to shift and stand and talk amongst themselves.

Terrence studied Rupin's face. The other man looked perfectly guileless, entirely innocent. Had he *really* found a decree at just this crucial moment? Had it really said what he claimed? Terrence knew he'd be a fool to ask the question—and Rupin would probably lie anyway—and yet… "There probably was some way around that decree," he said quietly.

"Maybe," Rupin acknowledged. "But they didn't want to find it, Terrence. King Randolph II didn't make this happen. He just gave us the excuse."

Slowly, Terrence reached out and accepted the signet ring. It felt heavy in his hand.

"Terrence?" Rose said softly, one hand on his arm. "I'm *very* tired. Perhaps we could…"

"Yes, of course," he said, hurriedly rising to his feet. He slid the ring onto his finger. It was loose, but he could do something about that later. He took Rose's hand, smiled at her. "Let's go home, love."

Chapter Forty: Rose

For a moment, Rose had really been afraid that Terrence's loyalty to his father was going to ruin everything. She had not expected Rupin's announcement. In the Before Time, there had been no meaningful distinction between the throne of the country and the throne of her father. If she had ever even heard the original decree, that wasn't the part she had paid attention to. But once she heard it now, she saw immediately what an advantage it was to them.

King Elgin had proved himself a threat and a danger, setting himself in opposition to herself and Terrence. Taking the throne from him took most of his power to harm them. Not all of it—deposed kings can still have influence and she didn't believe he would simply retire quietly. But maybe it would be enough, the checkmate that finally won the game she'd never had enough control in, during the Before Time or now. A queen had so much more power than a pawn.

And Terrence had apparently seen the advantage quickly enough himself, so that was all right.

She wasn't certain who Edward was trying to help with his compromise. Perhaps they would have succeeded if they had pushed through to try to take the throne immediately. Or perhaps they would have lost it all. So maybe it was better this way. King Elgin still had power for now, but they also gained time. Their legal standing would be more solid through this agreement, their marriage more established, and there would be time to let the legend of her rescue continue spreading and generate more support. The time and the traveling would give them opportunities to learn who they could count on to back them in any eventual struggle for power. They would have time to lay plans, to determine how to secure the throne they would one day take. The throne they'd hold *together*. It wouldn't be like her mother, or Terrence's mother. It would be different for her, for them.

And in the months ahead—they'd have time for each other too.

She wasn't quite as tired as she let on when she suggested leaving the council chamber. But she didn't want Terrence to have second thoughts and ask too many awkward questions. And she was tired enough to want to be done with this, all of this, for the rest of the day at least. To stop thinking about politics and principalities, to catch her breath from the terrors of the day, to let it sink in that they were alive and together and the future looked more promising than it had in far too long.

Gabrielle and three maids were waiting at the door of Terrence's rooms when they got there, to help Rose out of her bloodied sacrifice dress. Rose regretted their presence a bit—Terrence could have undone her buttons—but couldn't resist their tray of food or the hot water they had also brought for a bath. All the sweat and blood and dust on her seemed suddenly magnified in the face of that gently steaming water.

When she was finally clean, damp hair in a braid and maids sent on their way again, the kittens curled up asleep on the couch, she wandered into Terrence's bedroom wearing her blue dressing gown. She found him lying on the bed, changed out of his dirt-stained clothes from the challenge. He was twisting the silver signet ring and frowning.

"You'll have to have that resized," she commented, perching on the bed next to him. The way it was turning, it was plainly a size too large.

"Yes," he said, still frowning.

"Are you all right?" she asked, wanting to reach for his hand but not sure if she should. The bruise by his eye was darkening and she wondered if there were others out of sight—but that wasn't really what she was asking about.

"Yes," he said again, then shrugged. "Or I will be. Losing a brother and gaining a throne in one day is—a lot to think about. And there was so much…unfinished, with Gregory."

She should probably say she was sorry about Gregory, but she didn't think she was. She hadn't exactly wished him dead, but that didn't mean she was sorry. Not the regretful kind of sorry, or the guilty kind of sorry. Had she pulled him forward as she was falling? Would he have fallen, ending up in the reach of the lioness, if she hadn't? She truly didn't know. But she was not going to take on guilt for Gregory's death. The champions in the thorns, maybe. But for Gregory, it was clearly his choices, his attempt to kill *her*, that had led him to that point.

Silence lingered for a moment, then Terrence finally looked at her and smiled.

"Hey, I should ask how *you* are," he said, and reached out for her hand himself. "You went through more than I did today."

"Just different things," she said, lacing her fingers through his. "I'm all right. Sore from falling onto a lion but—not bad, considering." She had fingermarks on her arms from Gregory grabbing her, a bad bruise on her hip where she'd landed, but as long as she didn't move too quickly, nothing hurt too badly.

"I didn't mean just that," he said, and she appreciated that he recognized that. "I told you I'd be there, at the challenge, and I'm sorry—that I didn't—"

"It wasn't your fault," Rose said, squeezing his fingers. "And you got there when it counted."

"I love you, Rose," he said softly. "I thought I knew how much but I didn't, until… I thought I was going to lose you today. More than once."

She felt tears on her lashes when she blinked. "I love you too," she said, looking down at their interlaced hands.

He sat up suddenly, gently tugged his hand away, and reached for the thin chain around his neck. He drew it up out of his shirt and over his head, gold ring sliding on the chain.

"What are you doing?" She had never seen him take this chain off; it had seemed almost as permanent as the tattoo on his arm.

"I want to give you something," he said, fiddling with the clasp until it finally sprang loose. The chain slid like water through the ring, leaving it lying on his palm. "I want you to have this."

"I can't," she protested, as he reached for her hand again. She curled her fingers up. "It was your mother's."

"Yes," he agreed, half-smiling at her. "That's why I want you to have it. It used to belong to the most important woman in my life. I think it should again."

His words set off a warm glow deep inside her, a feeling she couldn't remember ever having before she met him. "If you're sure," she said, as he carefully slid the ring onto her finger.

"Of course I'm sure, love," he said, kissed her fingers, and drew her into his arms. "I've never been more sure about anyone."

Rose's eyes were wet as she held up her left hand to look at the ring, at its braid of gold strands. It was a good fit for her finger, and felt as natural as the gold signet ring she'd been wearing for the last century. "I was never that important to anyone before." She knew as she said it that on the surface it didn't make much sense. "I mean, not *me*. The Princess Behind Thorns was, but that's different. Although even then, if I'd thought about it in all that time, I would have assumed everyone had forgotten about me." She might have preferred to think that. "I didn't know there was a legend until I left the garden."

Terrence drew her head down onto his shoulder and she nestled closer against him. "Are you sorry I took you out of the garden?" he asked softly, breath warm on her cheek.

There hadn't seemed to be much choice. "The garden was being consumed by shadows anyway."

"Maybe that got worse because I was trying to get in. Or if there'd been a way to stop the shadows and stay…"

"No. I'm not sorry," she said slowly. "All the stories will probably say that you woke me up, and it will be true. Just not the way they think. Because in a very real way, I *was* asleep all those years. I started waking up when you came, and I've been getting more awake all the time. More than I was even in the Before Time, I think."

"I should think sleep would be better than some of what you've gone through since you got here."

"Maybe." Rose looked up into his eyes. "But some parts have been worth all the rest."

He kissed the tip of her nose, then rested his lips against her forehead. "I'm glad. But also, I sort of expected you to be less definite. And then I was going to…try to convince you."

Her mouth curved into a smile. "You could try anyway."

"I could do that," he agreed, tightening his arms around her.

He did. And even though Rose knew there would be harder days ahead, even though she knew nothing was really resolved—still, in that moment, it felt like living happily ever after.

The story continues in

The Princess Beyond the Thorns

Book Two of the Thorns Saga

Also by the Author

The Guardian of the Opera Series
A retelling of the Phantom of the Opera from Meg Giry's perspective, exploring love, betrayal, and the masks we all hide behind.

Nocturne
Accompaniment
Dawn Melody
Collected Pieces:
Overture, The Confessions of Christine Daaé, and *Entr'acte*

The Beyond the Tales Quartet
Revisit familiar fairy tales from new angles,
giving voice to the characters usually disregarded in the story.

The Wanderers
The Storyteller and Her Sisters
The People the Fairies Forget
The Lioness and the Spellspinners

Find out more on Cheryl's blog, Tales of the Marvelous.
http://marveloustales.com/NovelNews

Acknowledgements

This novel has been four years in the writing, with a pandemic and a new baby happening somewhere in between the first line and the final edit. It's been a strange few years for everyone, and I am grateful for the family and friends who helped see us through this time.

Thank you to Stonehenge Writers, for your ever helpful suggestions, encouragement and creative community.

Thank you especially to Karen, Ruth, Kelly, Dennis, and Meaghan, for your beta-reading and invaluable feedback.

Thank you to E.A. Deverell for your first line writing prompt, "The garden shrank at night." It's amazing (and ironic) how much grew from a short story exercise.

And thank you always to my husband Tim, for support, encouragement and reassurance, for listening to the entire novel out loud as a final review, and for always helping me prioritize my writing.

About the Author

Cheryl Mahoney lives in California and dreams of other worlds. She has been blogging since 2010 at Tales of the Marvelous (http://marveloustales.com), where she gives updates on her writing and reviews the books she's been reading. She has been a member of Stonehenge Writers since 2012, and has completed NaNoWriMo eight times.

Cheryl has looked for faeries in Kensington Gardens in London and for the Phantom at the Opera Garnier in Paris. She considers Tamora Pierce's Song of the Lioness Quartet to be life-changing and Terry Pratchett books to be the best cure for gloomy days.

www.ingramcontent.com/pod-product-compliance
Lightning Source LLC
LaVergne TN
LVHW010602100826
845148LV00014B/2812
* 9 7 8 1 6 8 0 1 2 6 4 9 5 *